B. Quick

B. Quick

C. S. Laurel

Five Star • Waterville, Maine

This novel is a work of fiction. Names, characters, places and incidents are either the product of the author's imagination, or, if real, used fictitiously.

First Edition
First Printing: November 2005

Published in 2005 in conjunction with Tekno Books and Ed Gorman.

Set in 11 pt. Plantin by Ramona Watson.

Printed in the United States on permanent paper.

Library of Congress Cataloging-in-Publication Data

Laurel, C. S.
B. Quick / by C.S. Laurel.—1st ed.
p. cm.
ISBN 1-59414-380-3 (hc : alk. paper)
1. College teachers—Fiction. 2. College students—Crimes against—Fiction. 3. Colorado—Fiction. 4. Gay men—Fiction. I. Title.
PS3612.A944226B17 2005
813′.6—dc22 2005019073

Dedication

To Rebecca Lickiss, for encouragement, criticism, brainstorming and a whole lot of laughter.

I

Ooh, Ooh, Ooh, What a Little Moonlight Can Do to You

Fall had been warm and rainy. The first snow of the year arrived in the Colorado Rockies late on Halloween night. To make up for its late arrival, it rushed in, eager and heavy, trying to make an unforgettable impression.

It caught me halfway between Cowpattie and Lythia Springs, driving my MG unsteadily along a rutted and narrow country road hemmed in by tall cliffs on either side.

One moment, all was clear under a moonlit sky and my only problem was the sign I'd just glimpsed, that warned *DANGER: rock slides next five miles.* The next minute, the moon had vanished, curtains of snow fell all around, and I had to worry about causing a rockslide by crashing against the roadside cliffs.

Everything a palm or so beyond my windshield disappeared beneath snow. And the bourbon I'd drunk at the Halloween party at Bad Boys kept blurring my focus and giving me a suggestion of pink elephants in tutus and high heels can-can dancing at the edge of my vision.

The curls of my black wig brushed against the stiff expanse of my Elizabethan collar.

Three months short of my thirtieth birthday, a staid college professor in a little Colorado town, I had no business being out in weather like this, wearing a Shakespeare costume and a bit more than half-drunk.

But I didn't have much choice. My hometown of Lythia Springs was three hours away from Bad Boys.

Well, an hour by highway or as the crow flew—three hours by backcountry roads as the closeted professor drove.

Bad Boys had thrown a Halloween party for its patrons. And the blond I was supposed to meet at Bad Boys had told me that I would look ravishing dressed as Shakespeare. My eyes—so I was told—burned with the same intensity and inspiration as in the portraits of the bard.

Then, predictably, I'd been stood up and left to get drunk on my own. You'd think I'd know my luck by now.

I crept along, under the storm, cursing my own stupidity. I should have stayed home, alone and warm and safe, getting drunk in decent privacy.

After a long time of tight-knuckled driving that left the shirt of my costume soaked with sweat, I noticed the snow easing up.

At first it was almost unnoticeable, but, little by little, though the pink elephants remained there, at the edge of my vision, the snow wound down to a mild white drizzle.

By the light of the moon that—just then—peeked out from beneath a cover of tattered clouds, sparse flakes hesitated before coyly dancing down onto a deserted, snow-covered road, and the deserted, snow-covered rocks and crags that hemmed it in.

Familiar rocks and crags.

I sighed with relief and felt my hands relax their maniacal grip on the wheel. I was less than half an hour away from Lythia Springs, less than half an hour from the safety and warmth of my condo.

On that thought, I crested the hill that commanded a view of most of Lythia.

Not a large town, it consisted almost exclusively of Bile College and its subsidiaries. Its population oscillated between two thousand in summer and seven thousand during the school year.

But it was large enough to look like a Christmas tree twinkling at me from the snow-covered distance.

Nearer at hand, the road went down sharply toward the rocky banks of Nugget Creek and narrowed to one lane across the picturesque stone bridge that led into the center of Lythia proper.

Another road, in worse upkeep, veered off this one just before the bridge, turned left, and followed the course of the Nugget, leading to backwoods wilds—abandoned miner shacks and flooded mine shafts.

As I started down the road toward the bridge, pumping my brakes, a VW Beetle entered the bridge from the other side and stopped halfway, taking up the entire space between the picturesque redstone parapets.

I pumped my brake pedal frantically.

Someone with long, light-colored hair got out of the bug, dragging a heavy bulk.

I jammed the MG into first gear and pumped the brake harder, but it barely slowed down. It had picked up too much speed on the way down. I couldn't stop before the bridge. I didn't want to crash into the bug. And if I turned my wheel too sharply, chances were I'd go into a fishtail skid and end up plunging into the frozen river, car and all.

Sweat beaded on my forehead and stung my eyes as I turned the wheel carefully and slowly. Very slowly and carefully, so that I turned to the road that followed the course of the river.

As the MG bumped along the rutted surface, I exhaled with relief.

I looked back to the bridge, to see what the lunatic was up to and if he was likely to move the car soon.

He being a matter of speaking, since at this distance both age and gender were a puzzle. The only reason I was fairly sure he was real was that there was nary a tutu or a pink elephant around him.

He hoisted a heavy, shapeless bundle onto the low parapet of the bridge, dropped it over and bent low, hands on knees. Suddenly, he straightened and scurried back to the VW.

I slowed almost to a stop and started to turn the car around, ready to go back.

Turning, I faced the bridge fully when the moon came out from behind clouds, shining a light almost as bright as day upon the landscape.

It shone full on the thing that the person had dropped.

The bundle unfolded and fell apart, revealing a blanket or rug, shapeless, amorphous refuse, and . . . a large human body.

I blinked and stomped the brake, bringing the MG to a full stop.

The body fell, solid and rock-like, starkly lit by the white moonlight, until it hit the dark silvery water below.

The bug backed out of the bridge, turned around on the other side, just past the bottleneck, and sped away.

I could have driven to the nearest phone booth and called the police. I should have called the police.

However, sleepy and still half-drunk, I put the car in park, pulled the parking brake and ran out, leaving engine and headlights on.

Before my brain caught up with my frantic, running body, I ran toward the river and jumped in.

Hitting the icy water woke me fully and I panicked.

The body. I must find the body. I swam away from the lights and up, trying to intercept it.

But what if there was no body? What if there had never been a body?

The water was cold, making my bones ache. And I started to doubt what had happened.

Not more than half an hour ago I'd seen pink elephants in tutus and high heels dancing across the road.

Lythia was so small, so peaceful. Who would be throwing a body in the river?

I'd hallucinated the whole thing.

I struggled to propel myself crosswise on the rushing current. No bodies. No pink elephants.

My arms hurt, my legs tingled with cold and my lungs felt as though they'd burst.

Small branches and trash washed down from city streets floated by on the clay-reddened water. I'd never find a body. If there had ever been a body.

Snow started falling harder. It clung to my wet wig like an icy cap.

While my heart and lungs struggled not to burst, a river of irrelevant thoughts and annoying questions ran through my brain like a laugh track through a tragedy. *Why did I jump in? I'm so cold. I'm going to get a frostbitten brain. I'm going to die from head freeze.*

I silenced the thoughts by an effort of will, and found the lights of my MG and started to swim toward them.

There was nothing in the Nugget worth rescuing, except a very wet middle-aged English professor fast becoming much too sober.

Something hit me mid-body. It clung to my legs, pushed against my face, tried to smother me, pull me under.

A giant octopus. I was being attacked by a giant octopus.

No. Idiot. Where would a giant octopus hide in the Nugget? Nine months out of the year, the river was a miserable little trickle dripping down a wide bed. It was only the floods that gave it illusions of grandeur.

Still, the image of a giant octopus kept returning, while the mass wrapped around me, clung to me. I should never have read Jules Verne as a kid.

I pushed a tentacle away, desperately. Another one wrapped around my ankles. Reaching down to liberate them, I found my chest in the coils of my giant foe, my hands and arms wrapped in its tentacles.

The blanket. That part of me that remained rational shouted and screamed about the blanket that I'd seen thrown from the bridge. Water-soaked and possessed of a life of its own, it would behave just this way. *It has to be the blanket.*

But the rational part of me, pinpoint small at the best of times, had shrunk down to almost nothing beneath a dark wave of panic.

I thrashed and went under, and swam up, and screamed, and swallowed water. The blanket still clung to me.

By sheer luck, I freed my ankles with my frantic kicking.

With my last bit of hysterical strength, I pushed the wet, unwieldy mass away from me.

Shoving my head above water, I took an aching breath.

My teeth chattered like the castanets of a flamenco dancer on speed.

I'd lost my wig to the water, but my tights remained and had shrunk till they cut my circulation.

I found the headlights of the MG again and started swimming toward them, hoping that my breath would hold and that I could remain conscious long enough.

It was one thing to be found dead in Elizabethan

clothing. Thus—presumably—had Shakespeare died. It was quite a different thing to die looking like an Elizabethan drowned rat.

You imagined the body, I told myself. *There was no body. No body at all. Just a blanket and some trash.* My teeth rattled to punctuate my attempt at words. *Probably leftovers from a Halloween party.*

Another impact knocked the air out of my lungs. A heavy, malleable bulk draped itself around me.

My brain, helpfully, went into full alert, giving me images of giant octopuses draping their tentacles around me and bright visions of immense, shapeless bodies dragging me down.

The moon hid behind a cloud; snow had started up again, full force, hiding even the nearest floating objects—a jagged tree trunk and what looked like a black trash bag.

I couldn't see the shape of the thing that hit me. It felt heavier than a blanket. I tried to pull away from it.

I pushed at it and punched its heavy bulk.

A human moan froze me mid-action. My reaching hand clutched something—four slim somethings and a thicker, shorter one.

Four fingers and a thumb. My breath caught in my throat. A hand. A human hand. I felt upwards, found a wrist.

The river pushed the person against me, tangled a pair of legs with mine. I couldn't move my legs. I couldn't swim. Helpless, I sank into darkness. Black water closed over my head. I'd always said I didn't want to die alone, but this was not what I'd meant.

My lungs hurt. I needed air. I fought my way to the surface. I fought free of the body. I got my mouth above water. I took a deep breath.

But the body—No. The man. I remembered the definitely masculine body falling under the moonlight. I remembered pushing against the bulk and hearing him moan.

I couldn't leave another human being here, to drown alone.

I had to get him.

But I couldn't dive down again. I would die.

But I had to.

Shaking with cold, shock and fear, I took another deep breath. I dove back down. I found the body. I grabbed it around the chest with my left arm, while keeping my right arm free for swimming.

As though one arm would be enough in this rushing water.

What am I doing? I thought. *What do I think I'm doing?*

Bits and pieces of the lifesaving course I'd taken in high school came back to me. I adjusted my hold on the body, forced myself to take deeper, slower breaths.

Swimming one-armed, towing the dead weight, I turned around and around in the water until I found my headlights again—a faint glow in a blindness of white. Cold stung my hands and feet, my legs and arms. The current pulled on me, but, somehow, I managed to swim across it.

My lungs burned from the icy air.

I cursed the day I'd stopped swimming for exercise.

Slowly—slower than I would have believed possible—I swam for the bank and for my lights that beckoned like a lighthouse to a shipwreck.

If I ever got out of this, I would buy a weight bench.

My eyeballs felt cold. My sight blurred. I should have put on eyeball cozies before diving in.

I knew I was alive only because I hurt in more places than I'd ever known I had. Muscles I'd never had came to life for the purpose of hurting.

If I survived, I would exercise ten hours a day. I would be featured on the cover of muscle magazines as the most in-shape literature professor ever. They'd ask me to teach muscle literature. Iron abs poetry.

The bank was an unreachable promised land, always farther than my stretched arm. The body I tugged beside me weighed at least a ton. Maybe more. I'd never make it. Better go under now, save myself the effort.

Still, my arms and legs pumped mechanically, propelling me toward the bank.

I'd never thought I'd actually be glad that my mind and body didn't communicate. Of course, usually their misunderstandings involved ill-lit spots and good-looking strangers.

My reaching arm touched a muddy, slippery bank. I dug my fingers into the mud to the knuckle, braced myself against the squishy stuff, and pushed against the pull of the current.

Since then, I've seen this maneuver a hundred times in action flicks of all descriptions. Still, I have no memory of how I managed to pull myself up onto the bank, much less how I pulled the other guy along without losing my grip on him.

And all I have are these images that look like scratchy black-and-white slides and explain nothing.

Click, picture of someone that looks like me lifting him up by one arm onto the slippery, muddy riverbank. Impossible. I could never lift myself up onto anything by a single arm, or leg, or anything else for that matter.

Click, close-up of my other arm, convulsively clenched around the man's chest, pulling him up along with me.

Improbable. Awkward, too.

Click. Me, leaning down from the bank, both arms extended downward, pulling him up, out of the rushing water.

Ridiculous. This particular body weighed upward of two hundred pounds, compared to my hundred and eighty five. Besides, he was almost a head taller than my respectable six feet.

Tired as I was after the arduous swim in freezing water, I couldn't have lifted a newborn kitten by the tail out of a sewer drain, much less a giant out of a raging river.

All I can swear to, all I remember with any certainty, is that I lay on ice-covered grass, some feet from the rushing river, dripping and gasping and coughing, choking and trembling and crying from sheer tiredness, for I don't know how long.

Little by little, cold and pain from my hands and feet nudged me to full awakening.

My arms tensed in a tight, aching spasm. Snow that had piled over me, like a cold down blanket, scattered in all directions as I sat up.

My own groan of pain and effort startled me.

It wouldn't do to die looking like a Popsicle in Elizabethan costume.

My father had always said I'd die in the gutter. This didn't even rate that high, and since when did I want to prove the sonofabitch right?

All my life, until my father had died five years ago, he'd controlled my every step.

He'd chosen my degree and the college at which I pursued it. He'd purchased my current job for me. Under the impression that I could be turned into a chest-pounding macho man, he'd bought me a wife, too, when I was little more than sixteen.

But after my father's death my wife had left, pleading irreconcilable similarities.

I was free. I was on my own. My life might not be wonderful, but damn it, damn it, it belonged to me. I wouldn't die now.

I drew myself to sitting with stubborn effort, then to standing with panting persistence. Upright, I looked around, found my car. Much too far away—upstream—but close enough for me to walk to. The idea of warmth beckoned me on.

I trudged to the car, fighting my own body every inch of the way. Reaching it, I walked around, holding onto the hood, holding onto the doors. I opened the trunk, reached in, found the overnight bag I'd taken with me, in hopes the blond would want to go somewhere after the Halloween party at Bad Boys. I searched inside it, till I found my sweater. Pulling it on over my wet clothes helped. The wind no longer felt so cutting. My teeth still chattered, but not as fast.

I took slow breaths, cold air stinging the inside of my nostrils, while I tried to get my bearings. Now, why had I taken a midnight swim?

The memory of the body falling from the bridge returned, clear-cut.

My breath caught. I coughed and tasted brackish river water. Had there been a body? I turned around.

A white shape lay on the riverbank, near the road, right by where I'd crept out. It might very well be a body covered in snow. I blinked. The body-shaped bulk refused to disappear. It must be real, because I could see no tutu, no high heels. Nor did it show any signs of intending to dance.

I got back in the car, took the brake off, and let it coast down the road, the way I had come, swerving to stop near whatever it was I'd pulled from the river. Of course, it might easily have been a blanket, or a trash bag. I remembered the body and the moan, but it was hard to believe. For the ten years I'd lived in Lythia Springs, the worst crime I'd heard of had been a purse snatching. Who would drop a person into the Nugget in the middle of a Halloween night? And why?

Getting out of the car, looking at the white shape, stopped the questions racing through my mind. Actually, it stopped my mind altogether.

It really was a body that lay by the road side, and it looked like what I'd been hoping for in my stocking every Christmas morning since I'd turned fourteen.

Six-foot-four or five, give or take one or two inches, he probably wouldn't make the cover of muscle magazines because he hadn't cultivated his physique to the point of deformity.

Still, he obviously had spent more time exercising than I had. The results of his effort were covered in a nice skin from which even the cold and the river hadn't erased the light golden tone of well-buttered toast.

His short, curly hair looked to be the same tone as his body. It would probably look lighter when dry. As for his features, they'd been cribbed from one of the nicer ancient Greek statues. If I'd had him made-to-order, I might have made his nose somewhat less aquiline, his chin less square, but who was complaining?

I remembered a face like his, or very much like his. Somewhere. The memory escaped my efforts to pin it down. It must have been a picture, a TV broadcast, or one of those pesky Greek statues.

Anyway, I was *sure* I didn't know the man any better than that. I'd never seen that broad chest, that narrow waist, that flat stomach. Nothing short of lobotomy could have made me forget that, or the long, bare legs, with their powerful, sculpted muscles.

He wore nothing except thoroughly soaked wine-colored shorts and a light coating of snow.

Falling to my knees beside him, I realized I'd just pulled Bacchus out of the Nugget and solved for posterity the question of whether classical gods wore boxers or briefs.

No.

An immortal's skin wouldn't feel so cold, nor would his breathing gurgle out of blue lips.

Calling to mind what scraps of life-saving technique I'd picked up from movies and books, I thought I should be pushing on his stomach or something. Of course, wouldn't it do wonders for my reputation, if this stranger woke up and found me in Shakespeare costume, straddling him? Lythia Springs was a small, quiet western town. Bile College was a small, conservative college. They didn't cotton to that sort of thing around here.

Tentatively, I grabbed the man's shoulders and, with much huffing and puffing, got him turned sideways.

Pushing with both my hands and making sure I touched nothing more incriminating than his ankles, I folded his legs up against his stomach, with his knees toward his chest.

He shook, took a breath, and made a loud gagging noise that resolved itself into a dry cough, that became very, very wet as he spewed forth vast quantities of river water.

"Well," I said, my voice little more than a raspy whisper. "I'm glad we fixed *that.*" I swallowed hastily as the river water *I* had drunk tried to make its way upward.

The man coughed and choked and coughed again.

I got back to the car, found a blanket, lugged it back to him.

He had stopped throwing up water, but remained unconscious.

I lay the blanket on the relatively dry rock by his side, and rolled him into it.

Then I grabbed him by the shoulders and dragged his blanket-encased bulk over the rocky ground, the three or so feet that separated us from the car. Opening the passenger door, I lifted and pushed him in.

He fell, draped over both seats.

I leaned against my car, panting.

My ears whistled, whirred, and popped like the least restrained of breakfast cereals.

Going around and into the driver's door, I used strength I no longer thought I had to shove my passenger more or less upright in his seat. He left streaks of river water on my white upholstery.

No one had ever told me that saving lives would drive up dry cleaning costs. Another of those little things in life that no one tells you about.

I returned to the passenger side to deal with the problem of my unconscious passenger's legs.

Whoever designed the passenger seat of the MG, hadn't thought about the logistics of folding a very tall, unconscious blond into it. Lack of planning.

I gathered and bent his legs, shoved and kicked his feet into the car, and hoped he wouldn't die on the seat. If rigor mortis set in, they would need a can opener to get him out again.

I slammed the passenger door, relieved that it closed completely.

There had to be a better way of meeting men.

Stumbling around the car, I fell into the driver's seat, closed the door, closed my eyes, and cranked up the heat full blast.

The heat hurt like hell, hitting my skin, and bringing circulation back to my protesting extremities. I shook and fought back nausea.

My body insisted that dying would be easier, that all I had to do was open the door and run out into the snow and I would die, painlessly. I told my body to shut up. I'd give in on the next good-looking stranger, but not now.

Putting my head on the wheel, I closed my eyes and concentrated on not dying of pain.

After a long time, I started feeling better and the heat from the vents stopped hurting when it hit my skin. My hands resembled hands again and my toes existed as something more than pain. I thought I might yet be human again, sometime in the distant future.

"Who in hell are *you?*" It wasn't quite a voice, but a low, low rasp, only slightly louder than the hiss of the air pumping into the car.

II

You Intoxicate My Soul with Your Eyes

I turned around, opened my eyes.

My passenger obviously hadn't recognized me, but with his eyes open and quasi-focused, I *knew* him. Much too well.

His long, long legs and innocent-looking jade-green eyes had led me to think of him as "Bambi." He signed his brilliant papers *B. Quick*, and attended both my Advanced Creative Writing and the second year of my Shakespearean biography classes.

My heart sunk.

Bacchus was Bambi. He was someone I knew. One of my students.

I could only plead tiredness and rampant stupidity for not having recognized him earlier. That and the fact that he never came to class in his underwear.

Besides, I hadn't fully looked at him since the first day in class, when I'd taken a glance and decided it was dangerous for my sanity and career to take a second. Since then, I'd made it a point of looking at his feet whenever I needed to talk to him.

I'd never even asked him his full name.

I stared on, bewildered. He was a student of mine. Out of bounds. Even supposing Bacchus was stupid enough to go for middle-aged college professors with black hair fast going white and unremarkable Anglo-Saxon features.

But his being my student put the thing in a wholly different light. What were the chances of someone I knew—someone I felt attracted to—being dropped in the river just as I drove by?

This had to be a setup. And I knew who had set me up.

Sherry, the wife my father had bought me—his being convinced that the great Western sky and marriage would be the cure for what ailed me—had entertained a never-ending string of affairs during our five-year marriage.

The most constant and annoying of her ex-lovers was Elderman, Bile Dean of Literature and my boss.

Elderman still blamed me for Sherry's decision to move to California. He made no secret of thinking I was a spoiled little rich boy who'd not have a job save for his father's money having bought him one. And he'd love to have an excuse to dismiss me.

Of course, in these enlightened times, my sexual orientation wasn't enough.

But if I were caught assaulting one of my students, say, on a Halloween night, and while I wore a bizarre costume . . . ?

Frozen with horror, I stared at B. Quick, waiting for a camera flash.

When none came, I let myself fall forward until my head rested against the steering wheel again. "I should *know* not to trust green-eyed blonds."

"What?" B. Quick asked or rather croaked, puzzled wonder in his hesitant approximation to a voice. "Who are you? Where am I?"

I lifted my head. No cameras flashed. "I—We—are just outside Lythia Springs. By the Nugget. You know me."

Didn't he know where he was? Wasn't he in on the plan?

Or *hadn't* this been a setup? Did this mean Bambi really had been dropped, unconscious, into a flooding river? Did he remember anything? Would he think *I'd* bumped him on the head, dropped him in the river, pulled him out again? Why would I? Playing Pooh sticks with him, from the bridge?

I looked at his pale-gold skin, his chattering teeth, the look of utter bewilderment in his sunken green eyes.

Yeah, yeah, tell it to the police, professor.

Still no flashes.

Could he be wired for sound? Have miniature cameras somewhere? *Like where, for instance, Bill, the way he is dressed?* Cameras there *would* **hurt**.

I stared at the bewildering jade-green eyes that bulged out in an I-don't-believe-this look, while the mind behind the eyes probably labored under the delusion that English professors didn't go traipsing about late at night in tights and lace.

He cleared his throat. "Please . . . please tell me you're *not* William Shakespeare."

He'd gone around the bend.

My wig had been lost and my own dark curls were shorter than Shakespeare would have worn them. The false beard and moustache had to be soaking wet. And I was wearing a sweater. I couldn't look that much like Shakespeare.

"Of course not. Don't be ridiculous. I'm Mary, Queen of Scots. The beard is false."

His eyes widened. His hands, confined as they were within the tight folds of the blanket, yet made a noticeable effort to reach the door handle.

What did I think I was doing? Administering shock therapy?

Mentally kicking myself, I cleared my throat again. Just because he was nuts didn't mean I had to match it. I made my voice as dry as I could. "My name is William Shakespeare Yates. I'm a professor at Bile."

His eyes widened again, but then resumed normal proportions as his features relaxed. "Oh," he said. "You're—Oh."

He glanced away. A noticeable pink infused his cheeks, under the gold of his skin. It was an effect much like the rosy-orange of a sunset. He looked back at me, peered at the Elizabethan collar. "Is it still Halloween?"

"Um. Halloween. Yes." With my luck, his next question would be if the Armada had attacked yet.

I was wrong. His next question was considerably stranger than that. "The Green Rapture party? Did I ever get there?"

"The what?" I asked, even as my synapses fired obligingly, putting two and two together. Green Rapture: the militant environmental group at Bile. Well, as militant as Bile got. They made signs and on fine spring days camped out by the roadside chanting *meat is murder*. Party. Halloween party. Booze, possibly drugs. Student dropped from bridge, presumably by another partygoer. Student who didn't remember where he was or how he got there.

Hooheeeee.

Apparently someone had a better time than I had. A *much* better time must have been had by at least two people.

B. Quick had obviously drunk enough to pass out.

And the other guy must have mistaken B. Quick for an empty bottle or a party leftover.

"I don't know anything about a party. I just saw someone drop you in the river and I pulled you out."

Said that way, it seemed much too easy. My aching arms

demanded a recount. I hadn't pulled him out, I'd dragged him out using strength that I didn't have and muscles I only planned to grow. "Don't you remember anything? The party? Drinking?"

He frowned. "I don't drink."

Ah, well, nobody was perfect. "A fight, maybe?"

He shook his head and flinched as if this hurt him. "No. I don't—I don't really fight. I just remember being in my room. It was about five p.m." He touched each finger of his left hand with his right index as he enumerated his actions. "I set my alarm for seven, so I wouldn't miss the party, then I took an aspirin. I lay down for a nap. And—" He stopped the finger-counting, opened both his hands and spread his arms, as though letting go of it, shrugged. "Nothing, until . . . now."

He looked down at the blanket, frowned at the dashboard of the MG, and glared at the windshield with its ever-growing covering of snow, as though all of these had done him personal harm.

His gaze came back to meet mine. He narrowed his eyes and looked like he was appraising me as a potential basher-kidnapper-and-dunker of innocent blond students.

Conscious of what I must look like, I ran a hand through my hair, tugged nervously at the soaked remains of a lacy Elizabethan collar that was drying into a droopy sagging version of itself. Not exactly your beauty parlor makeover.

"I didn't do it," I said in a tone I didn't remember using since my father's death.

His eyes rounded. His eyebrows, pale but abundant, raised in a query. "Didn't do what?"

"Drop you in the river," I said. Damn it, why did I sound so guilty? I wasn't guilty of anything. For once.

He shook his head, still frowning. "Chris," he said, as if this solved everything.

I restrained an impulse to reach for the door handle myself. Who was Chris? Did he think I was Chris?

"My name is William Yates, Professor Yates. I—"

He shook his head, and really flinched as though the movement hurt. "No. I mean, it has to have been Chris who threw me in the water."

He took a deep breath. "Chris. My roommate. The aspirin I took. It had to have been . . . laced with some drug. You couldn't have done it. You don't have a key. My house. I lock the door. And you . . ." He looked at me, wide eyed and puzzled. "Why would you kill me? Drug me?"

All right. So the wild rumors about me had bypassed someone at Bile.

Quick didn't look at me. He looked at the steering wheel. "You see," he said. "Chris Hogg is my roommate and he is not—"

"Chris Hogg?" the whine fled my voice, pushed out by full-fledged surprise. "Not a-thousand-ways-with-a-slightly-used-father Hogg?"

Chris Hogg had been my student for three years now, and promised to remain my student and Bile's plague as long as his parents' money held out.

He needed a psychiatrist, not a college degree. Only, of course, his father was a psychiatrist and the star attraction—as victim—in all the assignments that Chris inevitably managed to turn into stories of murder and mayhem.

Quick looked up. "You remember him?"

I nodded. Once, in despair, I'd given the class *the manufacture of bread* as a writing assignment. My stomach still churned at the memory of Chris's effort. "What's a nice boy like you doing with a roommate like Hogg?"

"I needed a roommate or I couldn't keep my house. I like my house. I advertised late and couldn't get anyone else."

He looked back at me. "I'm sure he fed me some strange drug. Dumped me in the river. And all so he could eat all my cereal and drink all my coffee. It's the type of thing that would seem natural to him."

I frowned. But it couldn't be Chris who'd dropped him from the bridge. Chris Hogg didn't have long, light-colored hair. He had short mouse-colored hair that went surpassingly well with his sharp ferret-like face. But then, what did I know? Perhaps the long hair had been a hallucination. Perhaps Chris had worn a fright wig. It *was* Halloween.

"Would you help . . . I mean, I hate to bother you. Ruined your costume. I didn't mean. I mean, would you . . . ?" He looked intently at my tight-covered—and itchy—legs.

"Yes?" I asked. Anything to disarm laser-gaze. Another three seconds of that stare and my legs would start smoldering.

He glanced up.

"Would you . . . Would you take me home?"

Oh, I'd take him just about anywhere he wanted. "I'd be glad to," I said.

"Oh," he said. "If it's not too much trouble."

Too much trouble. What did he expect me to say? *Off into the snow with you, young man. Barefoot and naked.*

I would never make a creditable Victorian villain. I lacked moustaches I could twirl. Not to mention a black cape. Oh, what I'd give for a warm black cape.

I cleared my throat and looked away from his grateful expression. "But you know . . . Perhaps you have a concussion. Perhaps we should go to the doctor."

He made a face. "Bad idea. The drug Chris gave me

might be illegal. Don't want to get in trouble. Would break my mother's heart." He tried a smile that came out crooked. "My brothers' too. And all my sisters' hearts while I'm at it."

"Right," I said, my relief at avoiding emergency room explanations quarreling with my guilt at letting the kid go home without taking him to the doctor first. "If you feel sick . . . later . . ." I cleared my throat. "I mean, you probably should try to get seen by a doctor in the next few days."

He nodded, minimally.

Um. No point beating the subject to death. "Where do you live?"

He broke eye contact, looked at the snow fast accumulating on the windshield. "Two thirty," he said. "Calamity Jane Way."

His address was solidly in the middle of what had been the whorehouse district in mining days and had now changed—perhaps not substantially—into student housing.

The snow picked up speed, accumulating on the windshield.

"Right," I said. I stumbled out of the car, knocked most of the snow off. The visibility didn't improve much and I'd have to find the bridge by guesswork and sense of smell.

Ah, what the hell, I had to take the blond home and then . . . who knew what might wait there? Chris Hogg? Or someone else bent on ridding the world of long-legged green-eyed blonds?

Who said my life wasn't interesting?

III

I Shrug My Shoulders at the Whole Affair

Forty minutes, countless under-my-breath curses, and a few scares when the snowfall cleared just in time to let me see a huge boulder right in front of the car, we drove into the maze of tiny streets and Victorian housing relics that constituted Bile College's choice for off-campus housing.

I smelled the area's permanent stink of cheap beer and cheaper grass before I could even read the street signs through the on-again-off-again snow.

After we passed Hangman, the local twenty-four-hour hamburger joint in a small western city devoid of McDonald's franchises, B. Quick directed me. "Left on Kit Carson. Right on Billy the Kid. Turn on the second to the right and you'll be on Calamity. I live in the purple house."

I tried to make a pun about calamity but my brain refused to cooperate. It always did when there was a blond to impress.

I felt too tired to drive. My eyes kept closing. I couldn't master the will to speak. Until I saw his house, when my voice found its own way out. "My God."

The narrow three-floor structure, pasted with every sort of gingerbread gewgaw available to the Victorian mind and wedged between two much larger houses, had been painted a color that could only loosely be described as purple. Or radioactively bruised pink.

Quick sighed. "Rental company," he said. "They used leftover paint." He sounded embarrassed and exhausted. Mostly exhausted, though.

With his blanket-wrapped hand, he managed to open the passenger door. He stepped out. Standing by the car, he shifted the blanket so that it wrapped around him like a cloak, making him look like an incongruously blond Zorro.

I'd been right about his hair. Despite the effects of the muddy water, it had dried two tones lighter than his skin, glowing almost white—with a faint muddy tinge—under the streetlights.

He bent to speak to me through the open passenger-side door. "I'll bring the blanket back to you after I launder it," he said.

"Please, don't bother." I could very well imagine him returning the blanket to me in the classroom. Wouldn't *that* start a pretty round of gossip? "It's an old blanket."

He looked odd, neither frowning nor smiling, but with a suggestion of both on his features. "I don't know what to say." He looked away from me and down at the fraying fringes of the blanket around his ankles. "*Thank you* seems so inadequate when you saved my life."

"Don't say anything." I felt my cheeks heat and couldn't remember when I'd blushed last. His gratitude made me feel like a tinfoil super hero. *It's Boozeman. More caustic than cheap bourbon. Faster than frat-party beer. Drunker than a skunk. He changes identities inside a convenient barrel.*

"Just try not to get dumped in the river again. Get another roommate. A sane one."

He nodded. "Right," he said. He closed my passenger door with a decisive bang, patted it as if to apologize and, with less than a steady gait, headed for the lavender door to his purple home.

He tried the doorknob, then reached to the side, to pull a brass ring that, presumably, activated the doorbell.

The door remained closed long enough for me to think of what would happen if Chris Hogg answered.

What if he hit B. Quick over the head? What if he didn't take kindly to Quick's being alive? What if this had been a rehearsal murder or a transference of Chris's obvious hatred for his father? What if—

The *what ifs* grabbed what remained of my rationality by the scruff of the neck, shoved my hand onto the door handle, brought my body out of the car and held it upright and propelled me at a fast step to stand beside Quick.

My mind worked overtime, if not rationally.

I'd take him home with me where he would be safe till the morning, when we could figure out what had got him into deep—and fast-running—water.

I'd take him home with me and feed him and take care of him and clean up after him.

Oh, please, please, please.

I put my hand on his arm, and he turned around to look at me. Not so much surprised as expectant.

My words raveled together before I pronounced them and I had to struggle to form a sentence in my mind. I'd got out no more than, "Listen, Quick—" when the door opened.

Right then I knew that B. Quick's first name really had to be Bacchus because the man who opened the door was none other than Apollo's better-looking brother.

His curly black hair, olive skin, and perfect features went well with his just-stepped-out-of-a-fashion-magazine broad-shouldered, narrow-hipped shape. You could have cut diamonds with the parallel creases on his gray wool trousers. Several sheep had stood in line for hours for the privilege of donating wool to the red sweater he wore.

"Brian," he said—an explosive sound, halfway between relief and shock. He looked from Brian—since that must be the B. before Quick—in his borrowed pseudo-cloak, to me in my ruined Elizabethan finery. His mouth fell open. His eyebrows gathered in a disbelieving frown.

Boyfriend? Somehow it didn't strike me that way. I tried to remember the essays and short stories B. Quick turned in. Conventional. Almost traditional. Certainly no signs of interest in the male of the species.

Brother? Possible, if the family ran to divergent coloration.

"Tony?" Brian asked. He frowned at the handsome face level with his, a few inches above mine. "What are *you* doing here?"

Tony looked cornered, as though Brian had asked him to explain why he liked sex or how he'd lost his virginity. His Adam's apple bobbed up and down. "I . . . I had a phone call. They said you—" He cast a doubtful glance my way. "You needed help. And I came . . . to check . . ." His voice lost force throughout the sentence, ending in a feeble meandering, like the lies of a child or the justifications of an adult who didn't expect to be believed.

Brian stood his ground, his blanket hanging in deep folds around his shoulders, like a judge's robe. "No. What are you doing in Lythia? And don't tell me you came all the way here from Cleveland just to check on me on the off chance I needed help."

I forgot my wet and uncomfortable clothes. I forgot that I looked like nothing in the world. This was better than the soaps. Or for that matter Shakespeare's more lurid comedies.

What brought the dreaded Tony to Lythia? What was the problem between him and Brian? How had he got into Brian's house? And . . . more importantly, who had called and told him that Brian needed help?

Tuned in for the next episode, I peeked over Brian's shoulder to watch Tony's reaction.

Tony opened his mouth, closed it, straightened himself and squared already nicely square shoulders. "I'm the Chief of Police of Lythia."

Oh, goodie. It wasn't a soap. It was a police procedural. Or a western. This was the man with the star, though in more mollified twentieth-century attire. There would be a duel at high noon and someone would be run out of town on a blanket.

Ye gods, how had I managed to miss a Chief of Police that looked like this? I had to start reading *The Conspirator* again.

Brian started. "The *Chief of Police?*"

"Well, yeah." A noticeable if diluted Italian accent crept out of nowhere to taint the Police Chief's impeccable English. It sounded like the remains of an affected accent cultivated and lovingly maintained by someone who had grown up in an Italian neighborhood.

"I found this job last November. I came here on a fishing trip, the year before last. They were looking for a Police Chief. Pays next to nothing. Still, I thought, hey, what the hell, fishing is great around here, right? And the crime rate next to nothing. AND it gives me some credibility to write mysteries, right? And I'd taken a community college law-enforcement course, just as research for writing and I'd just got out of the computer field because it wasn't fun any-more, so—"

Right. Whatever. I hadn't understood much more than

the bare facts that, in old western fashion, Lythia had snagged the stranger passing through and told him to clean up this here town.

Brian seemed to take almost as long as I did to digest the policeman's speech. "You write *mysteries?*" he finally asked. And, before Tony could do more than assume a defensive expression and open his mouth, he said, "No. Never mind. Forget it. Just tell me what you're doing in my house. I thought you weren't going to talk to me ever again. You didn't answer my letters. And who told you I needed help?" The same spurious Italian accent had taken over his speech.

Tony opened his mouth again.

"No. Forget that too." Brian held up his hand for silence. Apparently the accent virus induced compulsive hand movements. "How did you get in? And *why* did you get in without my permission?"

Tony had given up on opening his mouth. He stepped away from the door, leaving the doorway uncovered and revealing the inside of the purple house.

I'd seen the insides of a lot of college student pads, since I'd lived in one myself. Piles of dirty clothes obscuring the carpet wouldn't have surprised me. Beer cans amid the clothes, decaying furniture, and the occasional torn book would have left me cold.

The mess that made my jaw drop and caused Brian to take a step back fell into a different scale of magnitude. Every piece of furniture in the house, including a large sofa and a massive armchair, had been overturned. Every book, and there seemed to have been quite a few, had been thrown out of the three bookcases, torn page from page and strewn all over the brown vinyl floor. The bottom and cushions of the sofa and armchair had been slashed. Woolen white upholstery stuffing littered the floor.

Brian took two steps into the house, hesitantly, trailing his blanket.

I walked in behind him, uninvited and probably forgotten, but curious and more worried than ever about Brian's safety.

"The door was unlocked," Tony said, standing in the middle of the wrack-and-ruin like a victorious conqueror. "Still, I didn't come in until I heard the back door slam and a car start up in the alley out back.

"Then I opened the door and ran through the house, just in time to see the car disappear down the alley. I was afraid that you—"

"A VW?" I asked. "A VW driving off?"

Tony glanced at me, shook his head. "No. It was a sports car. A convertible. But it was burning rubber out of here."

All right. Had I hallucinated the VW out of a more unfamiliar type? Unable to swear that I hadn't—what with pink elephants, tutus and all—I kept my mouth shut. I wasn't exactly what you'd call a reliable witness. Not in my secret Boozeman identity.

"And the house looked like this?" Brian stooped, picked up a book, smoothed its pages, set it carefully atop an overturned sofa.

"Yeah. The two bedrooms upstairs and all." Tony shrugged. "I got worried about you. The call I got said—Well, they said you were—" He gave Brian a wide-eyed look, then glanced at me, shrugged and looked over my head as he said, "I guess—Someone took you out for your birthday?"

What? Someone took Brian what? Forgetting gender for the moment, did Brian/Bacchus normally drag home aging English professors in outlandish clothes? And did he often go out wearing a blanket and underwear?

If I'd missed both *that,* and the sculptural Police Chief, I was a lot more out of touch than I'd thought. And Lythia must be a lot more interesting than I'd realized. Or my vision must be getting worse. Time to get glasses.

"No." Brian frowned at his—friend? Brother? Acquaintance? I wasn't going to attract the likes of him by wearing wet lace and tights. So much the worse.

"No," he repeated, when one denial had been quite enough. "He—I fell in the river. Or was pushed. Or something. He—" Another look at me, this one marginally less than disapproving. "Professor Yates rescued me." Another look at me—a defensive stare at his friend. "He was at a costume party."

Tony stared at me for a moment. "Professor *Yates?*"

Not sure of the reason for his emphasis on my name, I responded with a glare. I'd just realized that, what with the sweater over the Elizabethan tunic, it looked like I wore a mini-skirt, tights, and a frilly lace collar. All I needed was a fashionably tiny snakeskin purse and I'd be the belle of the ball.

I looked away.

Tony silently declared himself victorious in our glare tug-of-war and turned back to Brian. "What do you mean, you fell in the river, or were pushed, or something? Don't you know?"

Brian opened his mouth, closed it, shook his head. "No. I was out. I think my roommate gave me something. Some drug. Changed one of my aspirin tablets with something, probably. I don't remember anything, except laying in bed and then waking up—" He frowned. "I remember water, I think, and someone dragging me. I must have gone out again, because I only woke fully in Professor Yates' car."

Tony made a face that could only be described as *it's another fine mess you got us into.* "You know, Brian, this qualifies as breaking and entering and vandalism, which is the most serious crime in the history of Lythia Springs, at least since the thirties." He crossed his arms on his chest, in a gesture of *now what are you going to do about that?*

"So?" Brian asked. His eyebrows gathered together, a vertical frown creased the space between them. "What do you mean by that? *I* didn't do it."

I started edging toward the door. Friends or foes, it was obvious these two crazy kids had something or other to solve among themselves. And, as my father had often told me, I was really bad as a dispute mediator.

Feeling all the tiredness of the last few hours, I longed for my nice warm bed. First, though, I would take a shower, and get rid of the tights and whatever remained of my false beard.

Behind me the argument raged as I retreated.

"It's not my fault," Brian said, sounding much like I had in the car.

Something like altruism tugged at my conscience, but I told it to take a hike. If Brian wasn't safe with the Chief of Police, whom would he be safe with?

IV

All This Foolish Prattle

I don't remember driving across town to my home in the building that its architects had christened Lockmaster. No one ever used the name, of course, except for real-estate agents when they were re-selling one of the ten condos in it. The five-floor, green, reinforced-cement-and-tile structure had been called *The High-Rise* by everyone in town ever since the first inhabitant moved into it sometime back in the fifties when Bile College had first purchased what remained of this mining town from the one or two holdouts who'd stuck around since the silver boom.

I'd moved in during the late eighties and lived there for the last ten years. The building had become a part of me.

That Halloween night, after leaving B. Quick's house, I remember driving into the ill-lit underground garage, and I remember how chilly the air felt when I got out of the car. The sound of my car door closing woke resounding echoes from the cavernous concrete structure. The garage smelled of motor oil and gasoline and the must of damp, underground places.

I crept across an access ramp to the door of the elevator, all the while expecting to hear a car accelerating toward me to run me over, as it would have in a bad thriller. This garage was not secured, something that had never bothered me before. It was open to anyone who might drive into it.

And the mood of the evening was paranoia with shades of adventure and failed romance.

None of this would have happened if my would-be date had only kept his word and shown up. So, why was I not sorry he'd failed to show?

In the elevator, I pushed the button to the fifth floor, where I had my condo, then looked around and groaned.

Back in the fifties, when Lockmaster had been built to house the prestigious faculty of Bile, some sadistic fool had tiled the walls and ceiling of the elevator in mirrors.

Which gave me the inestimable pleasure of riding up in the company of not one, not two, not three bedraggled Bills, but an endless number of them, each reflecting multiple times off each side of the elevator and each one looking more battered and socially unacceptable than the next.

My water-stained green cashmere sweater hung, begrimed and limp, from my sagging shoulders. A soupçon of black tunic, looking like a velvet mini-skirt showed beneath. My torn and tattered lace collar that had lost all its starch surrounded my neck in drooping frills.

Most of my false beard remained in place, but the left half of the moustache had migrated toward my left eyebrow and—attaching itself to the end of it at a rakish tilt—gave me an expression of Mephistophelian skepticism.

I closed my eyes and rode most of the way up with my eyes closed opening them only when the chime announced that I'd arrived at the fifth floor.

The elevator door yawned open and I stared into the baby-blue eyes and fluffy white curls of Mrs. Murphy, my neighbor across the hall. Her husband was a retired professor of political science. We usually exchanged friendly if casual hellos in the hall.

Now she looked neither casual nor friendly. She glared up at my face. Her eyes widened in staring panic. Her mouth made an O of astonishment.

"Halloween," I mumbled in her general direction as I swayed past her out of the elevator. Catching a final glimpse of myself and realizing that my still soaking-wet clothes kept dripping clay-stained water, I added, "It's snowing."

She crept by me in a waft of mothballs and lavender, cringing away, lest I might reach out and soil her pink skirt suit with my touch.

My last look back showed her pounding the door-closing button with force quite unbecoming of an old lady.

I staggered across the faux-marble–tiled hall and leaned against the wall, right next to the plastic rubber plant that stood guard beside my mahogany door. It wasn't fair.

Mrs. Murphy probably thought I was stinking drunk, and God, oh, God, I wished I was. But for once I had got this horribly disreputable-looking by not doing anything more terrible than saving someone's life. No good deed would be left unpunished.

I slid the key into the lock, shoved my door open and staggered into the long, multi-purpose room that ran the entire length of the condo.

The polished mahogany doors to the two bedrooms, the laundry room and the guest bathroom punctuated the left wall at even intervals, giving this area the look of a waiting room to a series of offices.

Depression and Failure and Associates, maybe. Or *Boozeman, Inc.*

Closing the door and pulling my soaked shoes off, I sighed, in relief. Despite all the strange events of this night, I'd made it home. Home safe. Only this didn't feel like home, had never felt like home.

The heat was set at ten degrees below comfort, because I'd fooled myself into believing I wouldn't be sleeping home tonight. And the condo had that curious shut-off smell of abandoned and empty places.

When you get home, there should be someone to welcome you, someone to acknowledge that you've reached a safe haven. At the very least, the place should reflect your personality; there should be a feeling that you are amid your favorite objects, things that belong to you only.

I walked in my stocking feet across the virulently green shag pile carpeting to the tiny "efficiency" kitchenette that took up the rightward corner of the outside wall. The leftward corner was taken by patio doors that opened onto a square concrete balcony overlooking the tops of the trees—all five trees—of Lythia Springs Central Park.

I set the thermostat on the wall to defrost. Finding the remote, I turned music on. Billie Holiday. My preference for old-fashioned blues probably meant something, but Sherry no longer lived with me, and I didn't want to psychoanalyze myself.

While the strains of *My-Mother's-Son-in-Law* soothed some lonely, bruised place in my soul, I got myself a cup from the upper cupboard, a bourbon bottle from under the counter.

I poured myself two fingers of Kentucky's excuse for existence, because the body must be soothed, too.

Bourbon smelled good, caustic and clean. Better than I smelled. A distinct smell of river water clung to me, not a scent I could define, except that—I decided—I smelled like trout. The sweat from my exertions and my too-fast reheating mingled with it. Somewhere, I must have come across evergreen, too because a scent of cedar gave the whole unholy reek a cheery Christmassy feel.

Ho, Ho, Ho and a bottle of rum, and a dunking in a freezing river to you too, Santa Claus.

I raised my glass to the old elf, tossed my drink back, waited five seconds for the warmth of it to reach my toes, and, still swaying to that old-time music, started undressing while making my way to the shower.

Taking off my sweater, I dropped it on the floor, precisely between the kitchenette and the door to my bedroom, not far from the great brown leather sofa that took up most of the area near the kitchenette. What, under normal circumstances, would be a dining room.

Normal circumstances had ended for this condo when Sherry, my ex-wife, had moved out, taking with her all the furnishings she'd bought when we'd gotten married.

My father having—not coincidentally—passed away a few weeks beforehand, I'd simply replaced her furnishings with his.

He didn't have a dining room table in his apartment because after my mother's death he always dined out. So did I.

So the whole room had become a living room, furnished in five gigantic leather sofas and chairs and an enormous, round coffee table, still ornamented by a giant cut-glass ashtray which, since I didn't smoke, I used for paper-clips. With hunting prints on the wall and green shag carpeting on the floor, it looked much like a hippie pad taken over by an English gentleman's club.

I pulled off the soggy mess that remained of what had been a pair of perfectly good black tights at the door to my bedroom; tore off the black velvet tunic—and its attached lace collar—just inside my bedroom, where the gentleman's club turned into colonial gentleman's abode, furnished with my father's single sleigh bed, and his plain tall-boy dresser.

I walked through the bedroom and into the attached avocado-green but otherwise quite acceptable bathroom and set the shower temperature at blistering hot and the spray at full blast before divesting myself of my underwear and diving under.

The remainders of beard washed off my face to cluster near the drain like mutant caterpillars ready to hatch butterflies that would attack New York.

Under the shower, I tried to think through my puzzlement of blonds and not so blonds.

What was going on in Lythia? Why had my date stood me up after practically begging me to meet him at Bad Boys on Halloween? And what was his name, anyway? I tried to remember, but couldn't. Weird, because I'd really liked him.

But after pulling Brian from the river no other green-eyed blond seemed to matter.

And I should know better than even thinking of Brian. *There* was breathtaking heartbreak, walking—unsteadily—on two long legs.

I turned the shower temperature down two notches. No use inviting spontaneous human combustion.

I turned the water temperature lower and changed the subject of my thoughts forcibly.

Who could have thrown him in the river? A member of the Society for the Elimination of Good-Looking Blonds? Had they got my would-be date, too? I didn't have the strength or the stamina to go fishing for whatever-his-name-was this late at night.

And then there was Tony-whatever-his-last-name-was. Why had he been in Brian's house, waiting? Was there more to their relationship than they'd let on?

I couldn't decide if that would be good or bad. If Brian

was involved with a male, it would mean I had a chance. But what could my chance be, when the male happened to be a demi-god?

I shook my head. Nothing I could compete with there. I lowered the shower temperature some more.

What had brought God's-gift-to-the-police-force clambering to the home of a near-drowned blond? Had Tony in fact thrown Brian in, and then just rushed back to try again?

Should I go back to prevent the murder? Should I shut up and mind my own business? And, while I was at it, what could I tell my neighbor to keep her from thinking me a dangerous lunatic?

I washed three times, in progressively colder water, until I didn't smell of liquor, or river, or sweat anymore, and until my mind had stopped spinning around the two quasi-deities—the blond and the dark one.

The bard had similar problems, of course, or worse ones, since they involved both genders. I'd never been so creative. Women were okay. They just didn't do that much for me.

I dried myself vigorously; splashed myself liberally with the bottle of cologne that Sherry had sent me for Christmas. *Athos, the scent for the brooding man.* Not to mention the truly smelly one. In this case, however, Athos served quite well to mitigate the clinging stench that had survived hot water and lots of soap.

I don't remember walking to bed, nor crawling in, naked, between the sheets.

Which is where and how I was when I woke up with a bell.

The doorbell had hardly rung since Sherry had left me. Still half asleep, I stumbled around looking for the phone, got it, turned it on, screamed "Hello" into it for a few seconds, until I realized that I could hear a dial tone.

Still, the bell rang.

"Mrs. Murphy," I muttered to myself. She'd come to ask me for a recommendation on mini-skirt tailoring. I dragged myself to my closet, threw the mirrored door open, got hold of one of several robes that Sherry had given me for Christmas during our married life. Since their patterns ranged from the bizarre—naked couples frolicking in a Renaissance landscape—to the outrageous—pink polka dots on a yellow background—I rarely wore them. But there are occasions for everything, and one of those occasions definitely involved not mooning your next-door neighbor.

Wrapping myself in the first robe that came to hand, I hurried to the front door.

Halfway there, I woke up enough to register that this was the blue robe with the golden paisleys, that looked exactly like a Chinese royal robe only infinitely more swishy. Still, what the hell, it was better than what Mrs. Murphy had seen me in last. I thought.

I threw the front door open.

Mrs. Murphy's eyes weren't where I expected them—slightly below mine.

I looked up, then up again, and still further up, into the dark, menacing eyes of Apollo-Tony-Chief-of-Police-of-Lythia-Springs.

Straightening up, I squared my shoulders and started, "Mr. Police Chief, why it's an unexpected—" then stopped, just in time, because if I said it was an unexpected pleasure—wouldn't you know it—he'd probably take it wrong.

He looked like Attila the Hun with toothache.

I thought I could hear western music in the background. Not friendly country western, rather the sort of ominous birdcall that announces a challenge for a duel.

I grabbed the handle, ready to slam the door shut if he should draw a gun. "How may I help you?"

He frowned. "You can start by telling me what you think you're doing."

I did. "I'm standing at my door, in the middle of the night, talking to the Chief of Police of Lythia Springs."

It seemed like a pretty good guess but it failed to satisfy him.

His frown worsened. He drew in a deep breath and took a step forward, edging his foot into the doorway, so I couldn't close the door if I tried to. His voice boomed up an added note. "What did you do to Brian? What about the corpse? What the hell is all this about?"

I'd saved Brian's life, that's what I'd done to Brian, but by this time I had a pretty good inkling that *Tony* wouldn't be happy with that answer. Corpse?

I looked up and said, in as quiet and polite a voice as I could muster, "Won't you please come in where we can talk about this without disturbing my neighbors?"

I didn't expect it to work. I expected him to go on screaming and yelling about my supposed misdeeds, until the entire population of the high-rise gathered at my door pointing fingers at me.

My—unfortunately limited—philandering had never earned me the ire of outraged fathers, wives, or for that matter, boyfriends, so I didn't know how to deal with this.

Was he a boyfriend? And what exactly had aroused his ire? Did I even have a chance?

My heart beat near my throat, despite my knowing it was foolish.

He lifted his hand and for just a moment I thought he would punch me. He probably thought so, too, but he didn't do it. The same lovely police brutality case that crossed my mind must have flashed through his. Instead, he took a deep breath. A muscle worked in his cheek, in a spasmodic tic. He shrugged, and said, icily polite, "Thank you, I think I will," before stepping into my living room, far enough for me to close the door behind him.

That, of course, got me to be in a closed room with a large, angry man. "Please sit down," I said. "I will get us something to drink. What's your poison?"

"I don't drink," he said.

He apparently also didn't sit. He hovered near me, much too close for comfort.

"Coffee?" I ventured. Damn, I *needed* bourbon. This was going to take *a lot* of bourbon. What the hell did he want with me?

I had a vague memory of seeing a jar of instant coffee in the pantry. A very vague memory. Though I had done most of the cooking during my marriage, I hadn't cooked since Sherry had left. For the last five years, my meals in the house hadn't gone much beyond those two fingers of bourbon in a cup. "I think I have coffee . . ."

He frowned again, as if trying to decide what this alien beverage might be, and what it would do to him. "Coffee will be fine, thank you." He didn't show any interest in sitting down, but also didn't punch me. Bad news, good news. Instead, with a bewildered look at the trail of wet clothes that crossed the living room, he followed me to the kitchenette.

Of course, I couldn't pour myself another shot of bourbon with him right there. Or rather, I could, but in the mood he was in, he might very well run me in on some obscure Lythia Springs regulation. Such as it's illegal to drink alcohol while wearing a blue robe at three in the morning on the first of November.

I opened my pantry, spotted the small, brown coffee jar, dusted the top, turned around to get coffee cups from the cupboard, and found Tony staring dubiously at the used cup I'd left on the counter. Its bright pink side demanded in big yellow letters *WHO ARE YOU CALLING A GIRL?* Sherry's. Feeling my cheeks heat, I picked up the cup and put it in the sink.

The two cups I got out of the cupboard were only marginally better. The dark blue one proclaimed, in gold letters, *IF I WANT YOUR OPINION, I'LL GIVE IT TO YOU.* My father's. The purple one, my own and bought during one of the crazier times in my marriage, read, *BAD BOYS DO IT IN STYLE.*

Tony stared at the blue one, frowned at the purple one. He crossed his muscular arms on his broad chest.

"I want to know why you ran over someone and put him in your car and whether you were drunk at the time and what you did with the body and if that's the body that Brian saw in his kitchen."

"Beg your pardon?" I stared, my mouth falling open at the magnificent rolling confusion of questions.

He didn't answer, just frowned at me.

To diffuse tension, I grabbed the pink teakettle, rinsed it to get rid of any spiders that might have crawled in over five years worth of disuse. I filled it with water, set it on the stove, and looked up at Tony.

He frowned. "I went to the station after I left Brian's house and I had a phone call from some students, who said you ran over someone down by the river, and then put him in your car."

I thought about it. I had swerved, stopped near Brian. What would it look like to a passing student in a snowstorm? "I rescued Brian from the river," I said. "As he told you. I had to drive up to where I'd pulled him, so that I could put him in the car. I didn't put anyone—or anything—else in my car tonight."

He continued to frown at me. "Look, it's no use. You're clear with the law. Brian is painfully young, but he is legal, turned nineteen today. But, damn it, he is very young. Much younger than you and damn it, why would *anyone* call me and say you killed him?"

I stared, flabbergasted, mouth open wide, unable to think of a sound I might make, much less a word to protest.

He sighed and glowered. "And do you and Brian really expect me to swallow a corpse on the kitchen floor?"

"Beg your *pardon?*" I repeated, the ghosts of my much-too-well-bred New England ancestors conspiring to put outraged incredulity in my voice, even as I tried to banish the luridly vivid, unlikely image conjured up by his words.

He hissed out breath through his nose, the same sort of noise, halfway between snorting and spitting, that an annoyed dog would make. "Fine. Just fine. If you're going to be that way, why don't you tell me your version of last night's events? All of it. All you did."

All I did? My turn to clear my throat and look at him in outraged disbelief. Did he really need to know about the party at Bad Boys? Should I describe the costumes and who had hooked up with whom, or was that to be left to his imagination?

He had no legal authority to ask me this. On the other hand, he had the muscles, the size, and almost for sure more energy than I could muster at the moment. "I went to a costume party," I said, icily polite. "With a few friends. And I drove home late and pulled Brian from the river." A few friends, or rather a few acquaintances, and about two hundred strangers and free spirits, coming from all the little mountain towns scattered within five hours from Cowpatty, but that was hardly the Police Chief's business, was it?

I looked away from his stern glare that was starting to remind me of my father's, to open the coffee jar and rummage in a silverware drawer for a spoon. I only found a soup spoon. Since Emily Post wasn't looking, I used it to dig into a stratum of fossilized instant coffee halfway up the jar. Digging out two golf-ball sized lumps, I put one in each cup, got the kettle that had just started whistling, filled the cups, and stirred furiously.

The Police Chief snort-hissed again. "And?"

"And what?" I asked. "Look, Mr. . . . Police Chief, is this an enquiry into something, or are you just having fun? Who died and made you my father confessor, anyway? I just want to go to bed. I'm very tired. Could you tell me exactly what you want to know?"

"Someone called me," he said. He looked very tired. "And told me you had killed Brian and dumped him in the river. And then the students called . . . and I went to his home and you came in with him . . . with Brian."

"Who called you first? Who told you I killed Brian?" How could someone except the guilty person to even associate me and Brian and a river, tonight of all nights? I'd never exchanged more than a few words with him before, in the two years of our acquaintance. Even I hadn't known I'd run into him. Even I hadn't known I'd drag him out of a body of water. Even I would never have guessed the heroic depths of Boozeman.

Tony frowned. "Who called me is not the issue. The issue is that someone said you'd killed him and dropped him in the Nugget, from the bridge just outside Lythia, and then, here you are, all wet and bedraggled and Brian says he was hit on the head and dropped into the river and you rescued him. And then someone else called and gave me your license plate and said it looked like your car and someone dressed funny putting a corpse in it. So I went to check on Brian, and there you were again. If I hadn't been . . . If I'd noticed you leaving while I was talking to Brian, I'd have asked you to explain it then. But I didn't and now I'm here. Would you care to explain it?"

I didn't want to explain anything. I thought that this might, after all, really have been a conspiracy, that Brian might have been the bait, and the police the mechanism to run me out of Lythia Springs on a rumor.

"Look," I said. "I didn't do anything of the kind. I mean, dunking Brian. I obviously didn't kill him. And would anyone *choose* to do this stuff in Elizabethan attire?"

Tony's eyes glimmered with an *oh, so that's what it was,* only to harden, immediately thereafter, with an expression of searing disdain that said, much too clearly, *you perverts might do anything.*

"Look, I was at Bad Boys all evening," I said. I pointed at the cup on the counter. "It's a gay bar, in Cowpatty. It . . . ahem . . . serves all the small mountain towns around here. I'm well known there. The bartender, Ivan, will remember me. I was stood up, my date never showed." I shrugged. "So I drank a lot. And when I left I saw this thing being thrown from the bridge."

"Your date?" Tony raised an eyebrow. "Could I have er . . . the name?"

I shook my head. "Sorry. Can't remember. He's blond, much shorter than Brian and much—Much—" Much less attractive.

I bit my tongue before adding that bit of information to the story and segued into the tale of the body falling from the bridge, including, "I grabbed him under the arms, dragged him out of the water, rolled him in a blanket—" Then I proceeded all the way to, "I thought I'd better leave you two guys to argue whatever it was you needed to argue, and come home and get some sleep, which, incidentally," I added, with a significant look at the grandfather clock in the corner of the living room, "I didn't get much of, and I have to give a lecture at seven-thirty."

Wouldn't you know that he'd ignore the hint? He grabbed blindly for the cup nearest him—the Bad Boys one—took a swig.

His eyes opened wide and, for a moment, I expected smoke to come billowing out of his ears. He swallowed with visible effort, made a face, coughed, set the cup down, swallowed again. "You mean, that's all? But why would someone tell me you killed Brian?"

"Look, does he look dead to you?" I didn't even want to think who might have called the police to say I'd killed Brian. It had to be a Halloween prank, the names picked out at random for their unlikelihood but—I looked at his flashing eyes and taut mouth—the Chief of Police would never buy that. I wanted to go to bed. Or to sofa. Or, at this point, to living room floor. Anywhere, anywhere at all as long as I could sleep there. "Look, why would I kill him? Kill Brian?"

He frowned and snorted again. "You are gay." He had the grace to blush at such blatant bigotry, but didn't give any hint of apologizing. "You could have a crush on him, or something."

Oh, yes, sure. All gay professors ran around killing their good-looking students, all day. Known fact. Heck, there must be whole cemeteries devoted to the victims.

If I hadn't been so tired, I would have tried to throw a punch at the Chief of Police's square chin, and damn the fact that he was taller than I and younger than I and probably more adept at punch-flinging. My voice tightened with anger as I said, "I barely know Brian. He's just in my classes. And he's a good student, never writes about killing his father or anything dumb like that."

Tony's eyes widened and he shook his head gently, as though to clear it. "What about the corpse?" He picked up his coffee cup, looked suspiciously at the dark liquid, set it gently back down on the green-gold laminate. Glared at me. It was obvious he thought he'd pulled a hidden trump from his sleeve. "The corpse on the kitchen floor. Is he alive, too?"

"What?" Had I said anything about a corpse? Was I still drunk? No wait, the Chief of Police had said—"I didn't put any corpse in the car," I said, appalled to hear the it-wasn't-me whine creep back into my voice. Still, it wasn't fair. I just wanted to sleep. Oh, boy, did I ever want to sleep. "I saw a body, not a corpse. It was Brian's body." I shook my head in a vain attempt to clear it. "It was Brian and his body. I mean, Brian is alive, so he has his body with him. At all times." I bit my lip and felt my cheeks heat.

"And the corpse Brian says was in his kitchen? The cut-up corpse?" Tony almost smiled, like a man who'd not only just pulled out a winning ace from his left sleeve but knew his partner was hiding outside the window, ready to shoot the patsies if they objected.

I wanted to run screaming through the night, but I was too sleepy to take a step. And then there was Mrs. Murphy, who was likely to take umbrage to a man in an exceedingly swishy robe running screaming up and down the hallway between our condos.

So here I was, locked in this B-grade whodunit, discussing a corpse I'd never heard of, a blond I barely knew, and an anonymous denunciation I couldn't even guess at. "Look, I've seen no corpses."

Tony glowered. He did it extremely well. Practice made perfect. "Brian said he saw a cut-up corpse on the kitchen floor, just before someone hit him on the head."

"I didn't hit any corpses on the head. Nor any Brians, either. And I didn't even see his kitchen. Brian's kitchen. Or the corpse's. Whose kitchen are we talking about, anyway?" I waved my hands around, wildly, not sure of what I was saying, much less what I meant.

I'd been captured by a psychotic policeman who'd break me through lack of sleep, until I admitted to hitting a corpse on the head in the kitchen of my car. It sounded like beat poetry. "Did you look in his kitchen? The corpse's kitchen? Brian's? Was a corpse there? Help me out, here. You're in a better position than I am to know what happened."

Tony nodded. He looked at the ceiling and appeared to appraise the molding. "There was nothing on his kitchen floor. Brian's. I mean, there were pots and pans and stuff, but no blood. No traces of blood," he said. "It was clean as a whistle. As Brian would keep it. He always was a neat freak. And there wouldn't be any corpse. Damn it, there just couldn't. It doesn't make any sense. I researched this city very carefully before I applied for Chief of Police. Since it doesn't pay a real salary, I didn't want to have to work at it full time. There was only one murder in the whole history of the town, and it was back in mining days, and it might have been a duel. Other than that, the only crime was a rape in the thirties, and even that was committed by a transient. There just can't have been a corpse in Brian's kitchen. In *Brian's* kitchen, yet."

I didn't want to think why the thought of murder in *Brian*'s kitchen galled him so. I'd gleaned that the man wanted me to tell him there had been no murder. And if I did, he would let me sleep. "Well, you know, Mr. . . . huh . . . Police Chief—" I fumbled.

"Marssano," he supplied.

"What?"

"Police Chief Marssano. Or Mr. Marssano, if you prefer. It's all the same to me." He shrugged. He looked calmer.

It was all the same to me too. I just wanted to go to bed. I was so far gone that I didn't even want company, blond or otherwise. I kept a hand on the counter to steady myself. "Right, Police Chief Mr. Marssano, you know that Brian had a shock. I mean, being dropped in the water and all, and probably being doped beforehand. He probably dreamed it all up. The corpse and . . . and the kitchen and all."

Tony nodded. His face relaxed. I could almost hear my words click neatly into the space open to receive them in his mind.

I realized, with a start, that this was what he'd wanted all along. He'd wanted me to tell him there had been no murder, so he could go home and go to sleep.

But he sighed, and returned to the attack. "I've thought of that. Then why would anyone call me and tell me you'd killed Brian? And what about your license plate and the corpse?"

"I don't know," I whined. License plate? Was there a license plate on the corpse? Did he think I had killed someone with a license plate? Was he not making any sense, or was I really, really beyond drunk? "I just don't know. I'm tired. I want to go to sleep. It was probably a prank; that's all it was. Someone dropped Brian from the bridge just when he knew I'd be coming by and then called you to make life more interesting for both of us."

Several things were wrong with this theory, the first one

being that no one could exactly anticipate when I'd decide to drive back from Bad Boys. And certainly no one would risk Brian's life over a mere prank. But hopefully the policeman wouldn't notice, right? "Look, it's late and I'm tired . . ."

I didn't even want to mention the possibility of a plot against me. Then Tony would think I was paranoid, and from that to the dreaded psychiatric evaluation and God only knew what else, would be just a step. That was probably the reason behind this whole mess. To force me into a mental hospital. So I would have to leave Bile and Elderman would no longer have to look on my smiling face every morning.

You're not paranoid when they really are out to get you.

"Fine," Tony said. He tried to practice his glower, but it ended in a yawn. "But I'm still keeping an eye on you."

I nodded. Fine with me. Worse things could happen than being followed by Apollo. I essayed a smile.

He frowned more intensely, pivoted on his heels and walked to the door.

I followed, in sleepy bewilderment.

He must be very sleep deprived, too. And terrified, I thought, at the awful prospect of actually having to do the job of a Chief of Police.

At the door, he turned around. "You know, Brian is very, very young. Turned nineteen today." He glanced at his watch. "Well, yesterday, technically."

Leaving me to ponder this odd bit of vital statistics, he walked out of my condo, banging the door behind him.

"So you'd told me," I reassured the closed door.

I leaned against the door, pushed against it to get myself moving and moseyed on to the safe harbor of my bed.

I woke up with a bell ringing.

"Oh, crap, not again," I muttered into the pillow.

My mouth tasted like the inside of a stale instant coffee jar, and a malicious sprite had wedged sand between my eyes and my eyelids. My head throbbed with each ring of the bell, like a well-tuned violin under a master's hand.

Fortunately, I hadn't taken my robe off. Sort of tightening the belt and smoothing down the rumpled cloth, I lurched to the front door, threw it open.

Mrs. Murphy, a harassed, beaten-down-looking Mrs. Murphy, her suit rumpled and her shoulders bent, stood across the hall, her hand on her polished brass doorknob, her shoulders sagging in tiredness or discouragement.

"Mrs. Murphy?" I muttered, and attempted to smile. I knew I hadn't succeeded because my skin felt tight and brittle and my lips insisted on pulling downward at the corners. "How may I help you?"

She looked back over her shoulder, with the gaze of a deer caught in the headlights. A slow blush spread on her cheeks, she yelped, opened her door, jumped into her living room, slammed the door shut behind herself.

You'd think at her age she'd be past ringing doorbells and running away. I stared at the blank mahogany door across from mine.

The bell continued to ring.

Damn. Telephone. Wouldn't you know it?

Slamming the door shut, I foundered toward the kitchen, grabbed the unit there. "Yes?" I yelled into the phone.

"I want to know what the hell you think you're doing," a voice blared in my ear, setting off unholy echoes inside my cranium.

"Listen, Tony, Mr. Marssano, sir, I didn't see anything suspicious. Nothing suspicious. Ever. Forget everything I told you, little as it was. It was a joke. Big joke, haha. All right? May I go to bed, please, now? Please?" The clock showed five o'clock. Much too damn early to be playing *guess the question* with police officers. Didn't the man ever sleep?

"This is not your boyfriend, Yates," the voice yelled, acquiring an oily, officious tone I knew all too well.

Elderman. By-the-bottle, Elderman. "I saw you drive past my house just a couple of hours ago, and I want to know how you expect to be at your early class, when you're obviously out at all hours of the night."

Elderman. Dean of Literature, and, obviously, a rapidly degenerating psychotic. He'd annoyed me in various ways before, but never, never, never in the past had he even hinted at monitoring my bedtime. What was next, would he come over to make sure that my teeth were brushed? Or that I had my pajamas on properly? Perhaps give me my favorite teddy bear and kiss my forehead before I went beddy bye. I shuddered at the thought.

Was everyone possessed of my father's spirit tonight? Were they dragging me out of bed at unholy hours in order to make a man out of me? Would they make me run barefoot through the woods next? Or arrange a second marriage for me?

"I was in bed, Dr. Elderman," I said, as coldly as I could manage. "I was asleep, attempting to ensure that I got up in time to teach Lives II."

"How long have you been in bed?"

He sounded odd. The question was odd. Of course, I remembered odder behavior from Elderman. I remembered, back in the early days of my marriage, when he and Sherry had experimented with . . . ahem . . . mind-expanding substances.

Once I'd come home to find them trying to catch the elephants that lived in the fridge and left footprints in the butter. Perhaps good old doctor Elderman had just found his long-lost stash.

I very badly wanted to call the Police Chief back and set him on Elderman. Tell him Elderman was on drugs.

But I couldn't because, for all our hatred of each other, Elderman and I had kept an unspoken pact through all the years of our acquaintance. He didn't divulge what he knew of my binge drinking and my sex life, and I didn't divulge what I knew about his stupidity and his sex life.

So all I could say, with controlled rage, was, "I haven't been in bed nearly long enough to understand this conversation. May I go back to sleep now?"

"Have you seen Joanna?"

Joanna Zimmerman, the modern-lit professor, was a beautiful redhead with the body of a fashion model, the mind of a nuclear physicist and the romantic inclinations of a Russian roulette player. She was also, if the college gossip had it right, Elderman's current lover. I wanted to tell him that if he'd misplaced his redhead, it was hardly any of my business.

All I'd found was a blond. Definitely male. Damn. Where was the cold-water faucet when you needed it?

I didn't want to argue. The whole point of this exercise was to get to bed and to do that, I needed to treat Elderman as I'd treated the Police Chief.

Tell him exactly what he wanted to hear, and never mind if I didn't know why he wanted to hear it. "No, I haven't seen Joanna," I said, thinking only of my nice, comfortable bed, my clean sheets, my warm blanket.

"I haven't seen anyone. I've been in bed since I got home from the college." I told the absolute truth, since I'd gone from class to Bad Boys and changed in my car, so I'd only got home from the college after Bad Boys and Brian's rescue, and taking him home.

The sound normally transcribed as "harrumph" came from the phone. "That's good," Elderman said. "Very good. That you've been in bed, I mean. Although I had a call from some students, saying you ran over a student down near the river and—"

Not that again. Had delusional students called all of Lythia Springs? "It was some other MG. I don't feel well. I'd like to go back to sleep."

Elderman paused, for a while. "Um. If you don't feel well, perhaps we can get your assistant to substitute for—"

My assistant, Daphne Mallard—who *wanted* to be called Daphy—would have cardiac arrest if I called her at five thirty in the morning. She'd be incoherent if I gave her less than twenty-four hours to prepare to teach a class. Not that she was ever coherent. I inflicted her on students as little as possible.

"No," I said. "Thank you. I'll be fine. See you tomorrow." I tried to hang up the phone, pressed some other key instead, got a sharp beep, and lowered the phone to look for the off button.

Some noise issued from the receiver.

I took the phone back up to my ear. "What?"

The answer turned out to be the most outlandish question of the evening, "Do you know who in town has a Karman Ghia?" Elderman asked. He cleared his throat when I didn't answer immediately. "I'm thinking of buying one."

So, of course, he mistook me for the auto trader headquarters. Which I did, as a sideline, along with my full-time job of murdering good-looking students. "No," I mumbled into the phone. "I don't know who does." I hung up the phone.

My arms still ached and my legs hurt with throbbing pain. I'd gone swimming in the river the night before, hadn't I? Pulled a blond out. Best catch in years. Best catch *ever.*

I was getting too old for this.

From this day on, I would fish for blonds no more. If I survived another day.

Back in the bedroom, I set the alarm clock for six-thirty. Plenty of time to wake up, get a shower, get dressed, cross the main plaza of Lythia to the college, right? Plenty of time. As long as I didn't mind foregoing breakfast.

Only I couldn't sleep. Tired as I was, my body aching and my eyes closed, I found my mind racing in circles.

I remembered someone who had a Karman Ghia. The blond who'd agreed to meet me and never had. We'd stood by his car when we'd made the date. He had a nice, red Karman Ghia.

Why hadn't he shown up? If someone was going around Lythia dunking blonds, could the other blond have got dunked too?

Was he the corpse on Brian's kitchen floor?

Right. Try as I might, I couldn't believe in that corpse any more than the Police Chief could.

I turned and tossed until the upper sheet wrapped around me like a shroud.

While I fought free of it, I wondered what this sudden obsession with cars was all about? I didn't remember hearing so many cars mentioned in so short a time. I'd seen a Beetle and Tony was searching for a Viper and Elderman . . .

Could Elderman have gone by Brian's house at about the same time Tony had? Could he have thought that the convertible driving out of Brian's house was mine? Was that why he'd called? But, a Beetle didn't look like an MG. The

Beetle wasn't a convertible, either, if I remembered correctly. Then again, perhaps the law was less than eagle eyed? Or . . . a secret drunk? Was that why he wanted to know where I'd been all night? Why would he wait so long to call? Brian must have been taken out of his house, in that car, or the Beetle, or whatever, around midnight.

Why should Elderman care who drove out of Brian's back yard? While we were at it, why did the Chief of Police want me to know that Brian was nineteen? Informing me that he was of legal age? No. Then what? Informing me that Brian wasn't old enough for me, more likely.

Why should he assume that Brian and I had been up to something?

Brian and I—the thought bordered on bizarre. Bambi-Bacchus himself, and a middle-aged professor who had seen better days and who, even in those days, had never been God's gift to men, women or small furry animals.

I must have fallen asleep between a turn and a toss, because I woke up with a bell ringing.

"Not again." This time, I wisely picked up the phone, although I sat up, ready to go to the door if it were required.

"Professor Yates," I told the phone.

"William."

There were only two people who *ever* called me William. My mother and my ex-wife. My mother was dead.

"Sherry?" I looked at the clock. Six in the morning. What the hell was Sherry doing awake at six in the morning, when her routine included husband hunting till two or three a.m.? Or was she married right now? Try as I might, I couldn't remember. She'd been married five times since our divorce, and sometimes it all ran together, not helped by the fact that all her husbands after me had been named Henry.

"William, what do you think you're doing?"

I groaned loudly. "I think I'm trying to sleep, but I obviously am not doing too well at it, so tell me what I should be doing. Just tell me." I needed to know what *she* wanted to be told, so that she too would leave me alone, and I could sleep. "Just tell me what you want me to say."

"I want to know what you've done to Joanna." Each of Sherry's words rang through my cranium like a cursed bell peal.

Joanna? Joanna? This was getting to be an obsession. "What?"

"William? Did you hear me?"

"I heard you," I said. "But—Joanna? Wh—Why?"

"She called and she was crying. She left a message on my answering machine and said something about a man being scum."

"Did she say who was scum?" I asked, tentatively.

"Don't be silly. She said *him* so, of course, it had to be you."

Oh. Of course. If a man were scum, I must be it. That made perfect sense. In a Sherry sort of way.

I sat on the bed, aching and tired. I tried very hard not to cry, myself. Big scum boys didn't cry. "Look, I haven't seen Joanna in more than a week. I haven't heard from her. I don't know who did what to Joanna, but I wasn't the lucky fellow, okay?"

Sherry sighed, a histrionic sound. "William." She sighed again. "I don't understand why you'd want to borrow her car. You know very well that she's always having problems with it, and if you borrow it, the least you can do is give it back clean and maybe fill the gas tank."

I hoped she was talking to her new husband while on the phone with me, because this made even less sense than the foregoing.

"Sherry?" I asked. "What the hell are you talking about?"

"That's rude."

Probably. What was the etiquette for answering in a conversation you couldn't understand at all? However, with Sherry, the *yes, dear* tactic had always stood me in good stead. "I know," I said. "I have to go now. I'm going to fall asleep." Without waiting for her answer, I hung up the phone.

I managed about a half hour's sleep until the alarm rang and, still tired, still sleepy, still aching, I dragged myself out of bed, into clothes, and out to the college.

I have no idea what I told the seven-thirty a.m. class on Shakespearean biography. What's more, I would swear they didn't either.

The class, assembled in the small amphitheater—a ten-by-twenty room, with oatmeal colored walls and a hundred-and-fifty battered old wooden seats—had to be Elderman's idea of a practical joke. He probably thought no student would sign up for a seven-thirty a.m. class.

If so, the joke was on him. Shakespeare's Lives was one of the easiest classes that filled the humanities requirements for science degrees. All you had to do was memorize information and spill it on the test. It attracted science majors far and wide, and also a few genuinely bookish souls from humanities.

So the two-year class had an enrollment that held steady at a hundred plus.

Still, when I entered the amphitheater and turned my attention to the glazed-eyed ranks, I noticed right away that a seat on the front row center had been left open. B. Quick's jade-green eyes with his oh-so-attentive stare weren't anywhere else in the room, not even in the far-off seats near the ceiling. Chris Hogg was also conspicuously absent.

I have no idea at all how I managed to make it through the rest of the hour and a half. I'd hear my voice say well-rounded, profoundly professorial phrases, like, "the Anne Hathaway, William Shakespeare forced marriage versus love match question," or "the question of the lost years and the *killing the calf* reference," all the while wondering if I'd gone mad. Who cared about people who had died centuries ago? What did it matter if Shakespeare had been a schoolmaster, a law clerk, or a butcher's apprentice? Or all of those together and a mercenary soldier in his spare time besides? Why were all these idiots here? What did they care? What did I care?

Where *was* Brian?

I'd saved him. Had I let someone else kill him immediately after? And who was it? His so-called friend, the Chief of Police?

V

An Indiscretion on Someone's Part

"Professor Yates?" someone asked, as I left the classroom.

I was looking over the heads of the usual throng in the hallway for Brian.

Instead I saw a skinny girl with stringy hair in a bad home perm. Despite skinny arms and legs and a toothpick-body, she had a big, protruding belly.

She was looking intently at me, as though she were expecting something. Wanting something. Of me?

I tried to walk past her, but she walked in front of me. "Professor Yates?" she said.

I stopped. "Yes?"

"I . . . I am Tiff Morden. I was wondering if I could transfer into Creative Writing."

"Now?" I asked.

"Um . . . Yes." She twiddled a bit of hair between her fingers.

There were always a certain number of transfers, and I didn't think that she would be any worse a writer than the people already in it. "If you want to," I said.

And again, I tried walking past her.

"Professor Yates," she said again.

"Yes?" I turned around.

She was still looking at me with an anxious, all-expectant gaze. "Will . . . will Brian Quick be in the class?" she asked.

Brian? What was going on here? "Brian is in creative writing one-oh-two. I assume you'd be in the beginner class, so probably not."

"But Brian is okay, right?" she put her hand on my arm. It was a small hand, very hot. "Brian will be in your class, right?"

Dumbfounded, I opened my mouth and was ready to tell her that Brian had been all right last I saw him. But before I could speak, another voice—a male voice—said, "Doctor Yates?"

Bringing my gaze closer at hand with an effort, I saw Tony standing right next to me in the pose of a policeman avoiding a suspect's escape.

He looked at me intently. "Is there somewhere we can have a word in private?" he asked.

I nodded, dumbly. He looked just as good in the faint light of day coming in through the dingy windows as he had late at night, under artificial light. He wore a new pullover, this one in manly-man pine-green and dark green pants, carefully creased down the front. His curly black hair was combed back, not a single one out of place. But dark circles around his dark eyes betrayed a sleepless night.

"We'll go to my office," I said, and led him down the hall, amid the crowds of rushing students.

What was he doing here? Did he suspect me of something? Or had he come, once more, to remind me that Brian was now nineteen? Or hadn't been nineteen before?

Perhaps he'd come to check for the bodies of all my previous good-looking students.

I sighed. He'd be very disappointed. The only corpus delicto in my office was the murdered corpse of literature, in the form of essays and more essays written in barely literate English.

My office was down the hall from the block of classrooms devoted to English literature. A small room, barely large enough to contain a battered regulation black-metal desk, two stackable file cabinets and two creaky roll-away chairs, it was my understanding that it had been a broom closet before my father had bought me my position with Bile. Which was, probably, much too appropriate.

Afraid that Tony might sit at my desk and interrogate me from a position of authority, I scurried behind the desk as soon as I opened the door.

Dropping down on the chair, I looked up and said, as professionally as I could, "You wanted to talk to me?"

Tony tilted his head to the side. He looked around at my office, cramped as it was, each flat surface covered in piles of essays, then raised his eyebrows at the pencil holder on the desk—a porcelain container in the shape of a pink kitten who must have suffered a radical trepanation.

"My assistant—" I started to say, intending to explain that my assistant, Daphy, had picked that particular office accessory and I endured it because it beat some of her other homey touches.

But his eyebrows climbed even higher when I spoke, and I decided that I didn't owe him any explanation. I glared at him.

He smiled, a tight smile with closed lips, and he closed my office door with his foot, as he advanced toward my desk.

He set his fingertips on my dusty, paper-covered desk and leaned forward as though the tips of his fingers were the only things that prevented him falling forward onto my desk.

"Doctor Yates," he said. "I know what's going on."

He did? I raised my eyebrows at him in turn.

"I know what you've been doing with Brian."

I sighed. "The pulling him out of the river part? Or the giving him a ride home."

He smirked.

I sighed. "I haven't got the slightest idea what you might be talking about," I said.

"Don't you now?" He walked around the desk, slowly, staring at me, his hands behind his back in the best cop-flick style. "Yesterday night, after I talked to you, I thought you might be feeding me a line—trying to get me to calm down and go home."

Really? I looked up at the perfect features. All that and a brain too. Who'd have guessed?

"So I went back to Brian's house. That and—" he hesitated. "And I was afraid something might have happened to him. Someone might have killed him. After those phone calls and his talk of seeing a corpse on his kitchen floor. So I went to his house and woke him up and I looked around. Just looked as I would in a crime scene. And . . . well, you know what I found."

"I wait with bated breath," I said. To be honest, my breath had pretty much smelled of bait the night before, with all that river water. I laced my hands on each other on the desk, in a position of perfect expectation.

He sighed. "The drugs, Doctor Yates."

"What drugs?" Brian had said his roommate might have fed him some drug, but I was at a loss to know what.

"Oh, I don't remember their names, but they were all prescription drugs, available to psychiatrists: depressants, mood altering substances, anti-depressants." He smiled at me. Or rather, he showed me his teeth in a feral grin, similar to an animal's baring of teeth. "These were samples, given to psychiatrists by pharmaceutical companies. And looking at your record, I find that your ex-wife, to whom you're in the habit of sending large sums of money for no good reason, since you stopped paying alimony years ago, is a psychiatrist in California. So I'm willing to bet those compounds that the lab in Denver is still analyzing are the kind that causes the sort of hallucination that makes someone imagine a corpse on his kitchen floor. And jump from a bridge to a raging river."

"What?"

"You have drugged Brian, have you not, Doctor Yates? To get what you wanted from him?"

I rose. "What could I possibly want from him? Essays? Short stories? He turned them in on time, thank you so much. Without being drugged into it. Most students do, mind-numbing though the course might be."

Tony laughed and shook his head. "Sex," he said. "Weird sex."

Anger warred with incredulity in my mind. "You're out of your mind," I said. "Why . . . why . . . why . . ."

I wanted to ask him why he thought even I would be hard up enough to need to drug someone into sex. I wanted to ask him how he dared tell me this in my own office, after knowing me for less than twenty-four hours.

But I couldn't talk. For the first time in my life I was genuinely speechless.

Tony made a gesture with his hand, dismissing my protest. "Oh, you can be at ease. I couldn't prosecute you. Brian said he never saw the drugs before even though they were right under the sink in his bathroom. He said you haven't done anything to him. He said he didn't know you except from seeing you in class until yesterday night. But your picture was in his bedside drawer and I know Brian well enough to know what that means."

He stood against the door, his arms crossed on his chest, smirking. "So I'm just telling you that I know what's going on and that it had better stop. Brian is too young for this, too good for your schemes and amusements. Leave him alone. Or else."

He opened the door and left, closing it behind him.

I closed my mouth by an effort of will and swallowed.

What the hell was going on here? What was wrong with the Police Chief? What was wrong with Brian that he induced this sort of behavior in people?

Someone had dropped him from the bridge and now the Police Chief was threatening me because of him.

I heard my own mouth say, "Was this the face that launch'd a thousand ships and burnt the topless towers of Ilium?" and frowned at my own stupidity. Yeah, quoting Marlowe was going to be a big help, just about now.

Any minute now, Boozeman would burst out of Bill Yates' unassuming self and, with a quotation and a pirouette, set everything to rights.

A typical English professor reaction, quoting something at a baffling situation, I thought. It made me feel smart and superior, but, of course, I wasn't either.

What I needed here was cold rationality, I thought, glaring at the pink kitten with the hole in the head from which pencils protruded. But cold rationality was not one of the things they taught us in literature courses. Or hot rationality for that matter.

Similes, metaphors, images, but no rationality.

I frowned at my hands, still entwined on top of the desk. Psychiatrists. Chris Hogg. Brian had said Chris might have drugged him, as if this had happened before and might happen again. And Chris Hogg's father was a psychiatrist.

And I hadn't seen Chris Hogg in class, just as I hadn't

seen Brian. I drummed my fingers on the desk.

I should go to Brian's house and ask him where Chris was, what might be happening.

But if I went to Brian's house, the policeman was likely to follow me and . . . arrest me?

What for? Gawking and longing?

No, but he might contrive charges. The policeman could make it damn unpleasant for me. Any excuse would do for Elderman to fire me. My being arrested would surely be enough of an excuse. He could tell the college that I'd defiled Bile's good name, or something.

My fingers still drummed on the desk and I glared at my door.

I couldn't let the policeman keep me from going to see Brian. Brian might need me.

What for? Hopefully not to drag him out of the river again.

And then again, if his friend was so crazy as to construct this entire conspiracy theory out of my having been with Brian last night and out of Brian's having my picture in his bedside drawer—

My brain stopped. Blood whistled past my ears, very fast. I heard my mouth suck in air, desperately, like a drowning man's last gasp.

Brian had my picture in his bedside drawer?

Why? Where had he got it? And why would he keep it? Why?

Suddenly, the drugs, the picture, the attempt to kill Brian, all of it tied together into a knot that had become vitally important to me.

The center of it all was the picture. Oh, I suppose in some thriller novel, a killer might keep a picture of his future victim on his bedside or in his wallet for years, to sharpen his purpose and concentrate his wrath. But it didn't happen in real life, did it? People didn't keep pictures of other people they hated, right?

And there was Brian. What might be happening to Brian right now? What if he wasn't even alive? What if his friend was so jealous of finding my picture in Brian's bedside table that he had to kill Brian? What if . . .

I looked at my watch. Despite what I'd told Tony-boy, I didn't have any other classes for the day.

And I needed to go see a man about a picture.

So, at nine fifteen, I hurried to the parking lot of Bile, under gray skies and a renewed bout of white flurries. I tried to talk myself out of going to check on Brian.

What would he think? Would I look like an idiot?

I kept thinking that Brian might very well be dead on his kitchen floor. In which case, he would be past thinking.

And I might be left to pay for the crime.

And Brian had my picture in his bedside drawer. At least if his friend didn't lie.

As for my looking like an idiot, since when was that a new experience? Good Lord, if I didn't look like an idiot, no one would recognize me. How would I even know I was myself without the stupidity factor?

I thought of how I'd looked in that elevator, thought of Mrs. Murphy's bewildered look the night before, and groaned. Couldn't beat that.

Driving cautiously because my lack of sleep left me more wavering than any drunk, I made my slow, painful way to Calamity Jane Way and parked in front of the unholy purple house.

A knock on the lavender door produced nothing. I thought of what I'd say if Chris Hogg opened the door, if everything was back to normal. I thought what I'd do if no one opened the door, if the only thing in the house were a corpse. Brian's corpse. Should I call the police? And get arrested for my pains? Should I try the lock? What if Brian was bleeding on the kitchen floor and I could rescue him by breaking the door down?

I thought of Brian standing by the door, wrapped in the blanket, leaning down to thank me for saving his life. Brian just couldn't be dead. He simply couldn't. When I saved lives, they damned well should stay saved. It was the principle of the thing.

My palms sweated, my head pounded. I felt nauseated with tiredness, gorged with it, as if exhaustion were a food I had eaten too much of. Incongruously, my stomach bit itself in acid pains of hunger and nervousness.

I knocked again.

Sounds came from the inside, soft footsteps as of bare feet approaching the door.

Brian's voice called out, "Just a moment."

A dead bolt slid. The door opened.

Brian stood, barefoot, in the doorway. His feet were long, very pale, and had the sort of long, thin toes my mind associated with being well born and well bred.

He wore ratty jeans so faded they looked almost white, and an eggplant-colored T-shirt so torn and tattered that it was held together solely by the power of his imagination. Here and there, interesting bits of Brian peeked through. Some chest hair, and, oh, I'd been kind of busy to check the night before, but, yes, he did have a belly button. A nice inny.

One less worry. He isn't a space alien.

On his right hand he held a hammer, and a bunch of large nails in his left hand. " 'Fessor Yates?"

"Thank God, you're not dead on the kitchen floor," I said.

His eyes widened. He opened his mouth.

"I mean—" I stopped.

"You mean you're glad I'm not dead on the kitchen floor." He closed his mouth; his lips twitched upwards. "I appreciate the thought." He stepped aside, against the door, so that he left a passage into the house wide open, and he motioned with the hammer for me to enter. "Tell you the truth, so am I."

I went in. If the policeman found out—If he'd followed me—

But I could no more keep myself from going in that house than I could keep myself from breathing.

"I'm sorry," I said. "I should have known you were fine, but when I didn't see you in class, I thought—Well, I thought I'd just come and look." I wanted to tell him about his friend's visit, but at the same time I didn't want to.

How long had he known Tony? Would he believe me if I said how strange the man was? Or would he believe Tony and think I was some sort of a dangerous lunatic bent on drugging good-looking students and having sex with them?

He shook his head, smiled, closed the door. He looked fully rested, not at all like he'd spent the night being thrown in and dragged out of a body of water or standing by while a policeman searched his house.

Ah, to be nineteen again.

"Please, don't apologize. It's nice to know someone worries." He gave me the sudden benefit of his intent gaze, before turning away. "I don't have many friends here in Lythia Springs. Sometimes I wonder if I could just disappear and no one would notice. But I'm fine, really."

The room I entered, now cleared of debris, revealed itself to be L-shaped, the entrance proper a ten-by-ten space, after which the stairs took up some room and left only about a ten-by-five strip.

The entrance was furnished with a large garage-sale sofa in an earth tone floral, and a red armchair, probably of fifties vintage. The narrower strip contained a magnificent walnut dining room table, with eight chairs and a matching sideboard.

Brian headed for the dining room, set his hammer and nails down on the sideboard. "It's just that I've never missed a class and today I thought I'd take the day and fix up the place. The way it looked bothered me."

He'd done a lot, for it being as early as it was. Books were either back on three bookshelves against the entrance-room wall, or neatly stacked on the right-way-up dining room table. One of the bookcases lay on the floor, open side up. Most of the stuffing had been gathered and put back inside the sofas. Only a wisp here and there marred the vinyl floor, and the sofas and chairs looked decent.

"I put duct tape on the backs," he said, stepping around the sofa and touching it lightly with a long-fingered hand. "Can't sew to save my life." He headed to a narrow space behind the stairs, where a blue denim curtain covered up what I assumed was a doorway. "I can refinish stuff, like the table and chairs and bookcases, but I can't sew."

"Beg your pardon?"

"Thought I saw you looking at the cushions," he said. "I put duct tape on the backs. I can't sew. I'll have to wait till my sister Lou visits and ask her to fix them."

I nodded. "I hear sisters are very useful that way."

My voice sounded distant. He was alive. I'd worked myself into a frenzy over nothing. The police couldn't think I killed him if he was alive, and besides, I barely knew the kid. The police chief was damn right he couldn't prosecute me. I'd done nothing wrong. No one could hurt me. No one had hurt Brian. I felt as if the strings that had held me upright and walking had been cut, letting me droop with fatigue.

What did he really think of my dropping by unannounced? What did he think of me? Did it matter?

Why would anyone think I'd killed Brian? Why would anyone tell the police that I'd killed him? Why would the policeman think I'd drugged Brian and had my way with him? Did Brian truly have a picture of me on his bedside table? If this wasn't a plot against me, how could everyone have misjudged me so badly?

"I don't have any sisters," I said. He was all right. He wasn't in any danger. I wasn't in any danger. I should leave him alone and go back home. I should get a little sleep. Ten hours or so. Maybe twenty.

He turned around and grinned. "I'd rent you one of mine. I have five. Would you prefer a sweet, demure nun or a foul-mouthed professional mechanic?"

"Beg your pardon?" He *rented* his sisters?

He must have read my thoughts because he blushed. "As a sister, rent you a sister, not—You said you didn't have any. I meant that I could—" His blush intensified. "It was an attempt at a joke. Joke, ha ha, you know. Look, would you like some coffee? I just made some."

"Yes, thank you." I should go home and leave him alone. But he was being friendly and I hadn't had any breakfast and my stomach hesitated on the narrow ledge between nausea and ravening hunger. I felt dizzy too. Probably the lack of sleep.

He pulled the curtain—a piece of denim hemmed with duct tape—aside, leaving a doorway uncovered. Through it, I saw a kitchen.

Or, at least, something that could be called a kitchen. Smaller than my tiny kitchenette, it contained exactly three cabinets, painted an offensive shade of green, an apartment-sized stove, a bathroom-type sink, and a battered refrigerator that someone had painted a glowing pink.

An incongruously complex and modern coffee maker sat on the one square foot of counter space. It looked like one of those intimidating machines that makes coffee, espresso, cappuccino, hot chocolate, clam chowder, diapers the babies, feeds the cat and walks the dog.

Brian got two red enamel cups from the cabinet nearest the door, filled them with coffee from the carafe, asked, "Sugar? Cream?"

"Two teaspoons, a drop, but—"

Before I could offer to get my own coffee, Brian had done it, getting sugar from another cabinet and milk from the pink fridge. He handed me the cup.

I tasted it. Hot, divinely smooth. "Good coffee."

He grinned, blushed. "Cafe Roma. I get it from the health food store near the college. It's my one vice." He patted the machine affectionately. "My brother Iggy—Ignatius—sent me the coffee maker from Italy. He's a Vatican attaché—I mean, at least, that isn't right because that's something like an ambassador or something. But he works for the Vatican."

Iggy was a Vatican attaché? *What* was a Vatican attaché? It must be some sort of ecclesiastical briefcase, but surely that couldn't be it. Iggy sounded like a human. Damn. I knew I shouldn't have skipped undergrad Catholicism 101.

And . . . Iggy was Brian's brother? So he had five sisters and a brother. Hadn't his parents had any hobbies? Not that I minded, if the results of their efforts were all as aesthetically pleasing as Brian. Sure as heck beat clay ashtrays and papier-mâché trays.

I drank my coffee and ogled and longed, which, after all, were not crimes under any known statute.

"You'll forgive me," Brian said. "I'd like to know what made you think of a corpse on the kitchen floor? I mean—"

I looked down at the floor, in reflex. Vinyl ineptly pretending to be red clay tiles. No sign of blood. Big gashes, here and there, but of the sort that could as well be the result of the house having been occupied by students for years on end as of an ax hitting the vinyl.

Why had I said anything about the corpse? Brian hadn't told me about the corpse. Apollo's meaner brother had told me about the corpse. Now Brian would think I knew about it because I had also seen one. Or I'd killed someone in his kitchen. "Apollo."

Brian stared, his eyes big as plates.

I bit my tongue hard. "I mean Tony."

Brian opened his eyes yet wider.

"I mean the Police Chief, what's his name?"

Brian chuckled, looking relieved. His eyes shrank to normal proportions once again. "Marssano." He turned toward the counter, refilled his cup.

I was trying to figure out how to explain to Brian why I had mentally filed the Chief of Police under the name of a Roman god.

Brian didn't ask. He smiled. "Anthony Marssano. Anthony Mark Marssano."

"You know him well." It wasn't a question.

Brian nodded. He made a face. "Oh, yeah. For years and years. He lived two doors down from my family. Dated my sister Lou for a while between her third and her fourth marriages. But he was five years younger than her and it didn't work. Most of Lou's relationships don't." He made a face, looked at me with disarmingly intent green eyes. "Did he tell you? About the corpse, I mean? And why? I didn't remember it when I talked to you. It came back to me when I was telling him about it. And then he left here at three in the morning. Then he came back, like a bat on speed, and searched the whole damn place. Found Chris's stash."

I took a sip of my coffee. "He got to my condo by four."

Brian looked puzzled. He poured himself another cup of coffee, frowned down at me. "You know him? I mean, did you know him before yesterday?"

I took a deep breath. How could I explain the Police Chief's odd behavior to him, when even I didn't understand it? "No, but he—" I stopped. If I told Brian what Tony had said about an anonymous call, would Brian suspect me? Or would his reaction to the information reveal whether or not he'd been in on whatever this was?

I was too tired for this labyrinthine a calculation. "He said someone had called him and told him I'd killed you and dropped you in the river."

He stared at me, eyes wide open. "What?"

"Tony said the reason he came to your house was that someone called and said I'd killed you and dropped you in the river."

"What?" He stared, his eyes closing a bit, while his blond eyebrows lowered over them. "You? Why would you do that?"

What did he mean why would I do that? I obviously hadn't. Had he forgotten that? "I didn't kill you," I said. "I mean, I didn't drop you in the river."

He opened his mouth, closed it, squared his shoulders, looked at me suspiciously. Not so much as though he suspected me of attempted murder. More as though he suspected me of gross stupidity. "That's what I meant," he said. "Why would you? Why would anyone even think you had? Didn't the caller tell Tony that? Didn't Tony tell you why he believed it?"

"I think he thought I'd done it for kicks. Tony, I mean. I think he assumed—He seemed to think—"

I stopped short of telling Brian that Tony seemed to think he and I were an item, or at least that I had a morbid fixation on Brian, and that, of course, a man who wore mini-skirts might very well do anything. But I had to explain myself, or Brian would think I was even more of a crazy lunatic than he already did.

"He came to my office today. After my Lives' class. He said that I had been giving you drugs. He seemed to think . . ." I felt my cheeks heat with a blush. How could I tell Brian what Tony seemed to think?

Oh, sure, Tony had said that Brian had my picture in his bedside drawer, but what if that was no more than the policeman's overactive imagination? And if Brian was straight, if Brian had never had any interest in me—the second an overwhelmingly likely possibility whatever his orientation—how could I explain to him what his friend thought?

He wouldn't believe it. He would think I was the crazy one.

Brian was still looking at me, bewildered, as though none too sure of my sanity.

"I think he was just trying to protect you . . . from me," I finished lamely.

Brian must have caught the idea, anyway, because he choked on his coffee and spluttered helplessly. He took a deep breath.

"What the hell does Tony think?" he asked, loudly. "Just because . . ." He put his coffee cup down, lifted his hand, punched the wall behind the counter hard enough that if it had been modern construction he'd have made a hole in the drywall.

As it was old, solid, probably lath and plaster construction, it made a hard *thunk* sound and Brian shook his head.

He bit his lower lip, looking incongruously like a sulking little boy. Taking another deep breath, he said something odd and foreign-sounding, that carried the sound and feel of an expletive.

My mind hung suspended from the sentence he hadn't finished. Just because . . . what? Just because Brian had had an affair with Tony? Just because Brian liked middle-aged professors and didn't much care what gender they were? Just because Brian's dream was to meet a man in tights, frilly collar and ruined wig? What? What?

But Brian shook his head and swallowed hard and muttered something under his breath and it wasn't my business to quiz him, anyway.

I'd overstayed my welcome.

I set my cup down on the counter. "Thank you for the coffee. Great coffee, really, but I must go home."

Brian looked at me, blinked.

I realized that for a few seconds he had completely forgotten my presence. "I mean," I said. "It's getting late. It's after nine and I—"

His face fell. He looked like a little boy whose birthday party had just been canceled.

"No," he said. "No, don't go." His hand grabbed at my arm, then let go. "You don't have to. I'm sorry." He opened his hands in the ancient *look, ma, no weapons* gesture. "I was mad at Tony, not at you. He—It's an old grudge. Yesterday was the first time I saw him in about two years. And he was just as much of a prick as—It wasn't up to Tony to guess about my private life or yours, that's all. I can't believe Tony hounded you. Did he threaten you?"

"No. Well, yes, but nothing . . . It was nothing," I said, and strived to look confident and self-assured.

I wanted to guess Brian's private life. I wanted—

I stopped my thoughts short. I wasn't going to and that was that.

He looked sad, forlorn, lonely. He'd said he didn't have many friends in Lythia.

I'd been lonely most of my life. Tired as I was, I had a lot of trouble keeping from doing the first thing that crossed my mind. And the things that crossed my mind, right then, might very easily earn me the sort of punch the wall had just got, and all would certainly draw me further into the shadowy plots woven around Brian's bright green eyes.

"I really have to go. I haven't had breakfast and I'm—"

He clutched my upper arm, brought his face close to mine. "You haven't had breakfast?"

I might as well have told him I had terminal cancer.

"You've been up since—" His hand still tight around my upper arm, he glanced at the white plastic clock on the wall, "Six or so?" He led me, by the arm, to the dining room, pulled a chair, dropped me into it.

I couldn't really have fought it, even if I'd tried. He was taller than I. Undoubtedly he was also stronger.

"No wonder you look ghastly," he said.

I did? How polite of him to inform me of this.

He looked not so much solicitous as outraged, as though I'd violated one of basic rules of civilization by spending half the morning on an empty stomach.

I looked up at him, tried to extricate myself from the coils of his hospitality. If I accepted breakfast with him, then I would accept . . . what? Would anything else ever come of this? Or was I heading for heartbreak full speed again? "Hangman's is just around the corner. I can stop there on the way home."

"And get a plateful of coronary with a side of indigestion. Don't be silly. Sometimes I drop by there for coffee, but that's it."

I'd been called many things by many people, but I hadn't been called silly in such an indulgent, affectionate tone in . . . oh, centuries it seemed like.

That one word held me in place, quieted me down, made me forget Tony-Apollo and his suspicions. It also made me forget my hard-won life experience, my mistrust of people in general and blond male people in particular.

Before I could say anything else, he went into the kitchen, came back with my refilled coffee cup, and a giant muffin on a small plate. Another trip and he gave me a jar of jam, a ceramic container of butter and a knife.

"I baked the muffin yesterday and it's been in the fridge," he said, apologetically. "So it might be a little stale. Still, it has to be better than Hangman's fare."

Whole-wheat muffin, with fruit and nut filling. Peach jam.

For a moment I couldn't speak.

He stood anxiously by the table and looked a question at me.

"Oh, it's fine," I said, looking up. "Just fine. Wonderful, in fact. *You* baked it?"

Man looked like that, could cook and wrote grammatical English. The tune to *Oh, where have you been all my life?* ran through my head.

Then I remembered he had homicidal friends and that there was some plot, linking both our names and drugs and, possibly, just possibly, a dismembered corpse on the floor of the kitchen where this muffin had been baked.

"I bake okay," he said. "Lou had me learn to cook because . . ." He stopped, blushed.

Some primitive part of my mind made comments about beautiful blonds who could cook and incited me to hit him over the head with a club and drag him home to my cave.

However, besides the fact that I was fresh out of clubs and I'd have to stand on a step stool to hit him over the head, he might very well hit back.

And the part that passed for rationality in my English-literature trained brain told me that this beautiful blond was trouble. He'd been dumped in the river. I didn't need to get involved. My mouth worked, despite myself.

"Police Chief Marssano said that you remembered seeing . . . a corpse," I said. "And that you'd been hit . . . on the head?"

Brian nodded. He'd grabbed hammer and nails from the sideboard. Thought made a vertical wrinkle on his forehead, between his very straight pale eyebrows. "I think I remember a corpse, all in pieces—" He turned green around the gills, swallowed. "But the kitchen floor is clean and I probably—" He shook his head. "Perhaps I dreamed it all. As I said, Chris is likely to have given me some drug and dropped me in the river. He's likely to have called the police and complained about you, too. He . . . he was mad at you. He thought you might fail him in Creative Writing again."

He thought right. I didn't speak.

Brian went on, "It would be his idea of a practical joke. He didn't like me and he hated you. It would never occur to him I might die. Or that you might actually find me and lend credence to his crank call to the police. Not that he'd care about either of those, I don't think. He's so self-centered, it would never occur to him that any of his plans had an unintended consequence." He shrugged, again. "In any case, the house does look as it would if Chris and his friends had a party here." Another shrug. "He hasn't come home yet."

"What if he comes home and tries to kill you, again?" I asked. I pushed my plate away. Having eaten, my body had decided it was time to sleep. So much for evolution. Gorg eat. Gorg sleep. Gorg hit hunky blond on head and drag him into cave. Gorg do no such thing if Gorg have self-preservation instincts.

I fought to keep my eyes open. What if Brian showed up dead? This time, I'd spent time with him. This time . . .

This time someone might think I'd killed him out of spurned affection. Would my affection be spurned? Did I feel affection for him?

Brian smiled. "Unlikely. I intend to tell him that if something happens to me, my sister Lou will kick his butt across the state. Chris met my sister once. She scared the crap out of him."

His smile flickered off and he looked tired and not amused. "She scares the crap out of most people. More coffee?"

"I don't want to give you trouble." I wanted to leave. I badly needed to leave. I was too tired. I was too vulnerable.

But Brian was being kind and I'd reached that time of life when very few young men were kind to me. Much less outrageously handsome blond young men with dark jade-green eyes.

"Oh, please." He smiled. "You saved my life. You came here today because you were worried about me. You're not giving me any trouble."

He set hammer and nails down again, got me another

cup of coffee, again with just the right amount of sugar and milk. He took up hammer and nails again, went back to the upended bookcase on the other side of the room, started nailing down a strip of molding that had been ripped from it. "So, anything interesting happen in Lives today?"

Was that irony in his voice? Spectacular blond who could bake and had a sense of humor?

I had to prevent my mouth from hanging open in amazement. And drooling.

"I don't know," I said. "I was only half conscious."

He grinned. "No offense, but you often look that way in Lives. I like you in Creative Writing much better. You actually pay attention to what people are doing." He looked up at me. "You've improved my writing a lot."

"I have?" His writing had been pretty good to begin with. I didn't remember telling him anything earth shattering.

"Yeah. You keep me writing for one." He was quiet for a moment. "Tony told me yesterday that he just got his first book accepted. Mystery. Big advance."

I wanted to wag my finger at Brian and tell him not to dream. Big advances in genre literature these days didn't often fall to first books. I was too tired to lift my finger.

"He's getting married," Brian said. "Gina, his fiancée, told him to invite me to their wedding." He was quiet a while.

"We used to hang out together, the three of us, though they're about ten years older than I. Then, Gina married some clown—she's divorced now—and Tony—" He shrugged.

"Tony and I had a falling out." He hammered a nail into the side of the bookcase with some very loud, rapid-fire bangs, then looked up. "But he—He wants to be friends again. I'm sorry he bothered you, really sorry. He has this—

My mother is Italian and I grew up in a mostly Italian neighborhood. I think Tony thinks of himself as a cross between my older brother and my father. My oldest brother, Iggy, was out of the house by the time I was born, and my father died the month before I was born, so—I don't know. I think Tony really thought you tried to kill me. I don't know why."

He nodded, while he fixed his bookshelf and spoke above the hammering. "Do you have any idea who would have called him? If it wasn't Chris?"

I shook my head. My vision was fuzzy. I needed to sleep.

The early morning sun came through the window next to the shelf, painted a pattern of squares on the wood of the table, and made Brian's hair shine like a halo around his head.

Brian's voice drifted into a haze. I sank into a warm, comfortable slumber.

Thoughts ran through my sleeping mind, disconnected, like pieces of a puzzle flashing on a television screen.

Tony had dropped Brian in the river because he thought Brian was insane. He'd called himself and told himself that I'd killed Brian. But where did Tony know me from, and why would he be after me? What did he or didn't he want with Brian?

And why was Brian being so friendly? Did Brian like me? No. Impossible. Brian didn't have my picture anywhere. That was just Tony's craziness.

But . . . What if Brian liked me?

" 'Fessor Yates?"

I felt a hand on my arm, tried to open my eyes. They wouldn't open.

My head was lifted and something soft stuck under it.

"Another fine mess, Brian Quick." He chuckled. "Well, at least *he* didn't laugh."

I wanted to protest that I had no intention of laughing. A corpse in the kitchen was no laughing matter. But my dream called, and I fell deeper and deeper into it.

All of these tied themselves into a nightmare, in which I floated down a fast-moving muddy river, while hands clutched at me from every side and a voice kept repeating over and over, "Oh, no. Shit, Chris, no."

I woke up, realizing Brian had spoken those words.

VI

Can't You See that It Never Can Be

I woke up, opened one eye. My head rested on a small orange cushion. Right by the pillow, a small notebook page had something written on it that started, *Dear Dr. Yates.*

I lifted my head. Great. Judging by the wet spot, I'd drooled on the cushion. Impressing strangers and making friends with my astounding savoir-faire again. I brushed ineffectually at the wet spot, flipped the cushion over, guiltily.

The sun had set. The window I faced was dark and reflected my own image back at me—short hair just long enough to look like a disarray of dark curls, round brown eyes looking stupid and unreflective, cheeks pale and skin wrinkly, the way it got when you slept in an odd position. It made me look about a hundred and I felt like Rip van Winkle. How long had I been asleep?

I'd heard Brian talk. I looked around.

Brian stood by the floor lamp in the living room, so absorbed in reading a little black notebook that he didn't even glance at me when I moved.

I blinked.

He'd dressed up. At least the pair of jeans he wore looked intact and his eggplant colored shirt had no holes, even if it read *Lou's Tinker And Lube* in large green letters.

And where was Chris Hogg? Brian *had* talked to him. Hadn't he?

I sat up fully, looked around.

The note by my head, written in Brian's familiar angular hand, read: *Dear Dr. Yates, You looked really tired and I couldn't wake you, not even to get you to move to the sofa. So I'm leaving you asleep. I have two classes in the afternoon, but I'll be back around six. If you have time, wait and I'll make dinner for us.*

He'd signed it B. Quick and it was a far cry from the *I've taken a taxi home. Don't call or I'll get a restraining order. Let's do this again on some unspecified February 30th* notes I usually got.

But why was it different? Why was Brian being so nice? Trying to get something on me? Perhaps material for a lawsuit against the college? Or was he just a good person? Was he that unusual thing, a decent human being?

Well, if he were, then surely he'd never be interested in me. Even if he leaned that way.

I attracted scoundrels, scam artists and suicidal idiots. It was a specialty, if a strange one.

On the other hand, no one had ever been this nice to me when I fell asleep at his place. Of course, I'd never fallen asleep on a dining room table, before. Maybe that was what I'd been doing wrong all along. No more beds for me, from now on. I'd sleep with the silverware.

I looked up. Brian continued to read, obviously not aware that I had awoken. And Chris? *Had* Brian talked to Chris? Or about Chris?

"Brian?"

He looked up, his face creased in an intent frown.

"Look at this." He crossed the space between us in three elongated steps, dropped the notebook in front of me.

The writing on the ruled pages was green, and it looked like someone had dipped a spider's legs in ink and encouraged it to traipse up and down the pages. I'd recognize it anywhere.

It was Chris Hogg's writing. I scanned it quickly for the words *father, murder* and *death*. I didn't find them. Maybe it wasn't Chris's. I looked up at Brian, bewildered, then looked at the note again.

Yes, it was definitely Chris's. No one else could write in a hand like that. I read a few entries. It followed a format consisting of names, a long string of letters and numbers, and then dates with a dash and more numbers in front of them. For example, there was, Mrs. Jane M. Murphy APT2345, and then 11-20 5;2-28 10;6-31 15, etc., etc. Jane Murphy. My neighbor's first name was Jane. "What is this?" I asked.

"I figure Chris's little black book," Brian said. He held a gray, vinyl jacket in his hands and showed me a large gash on the inside lining. Down spilled through. "What I want to know is why he hid it inside my jacket. I didn't even notice it until I took the jacket off and went to hang it up, and I saw the down spilling, and then I felt this lump. Can you believe it? He cut into my jacket. The little bastard. You might be right. I think I need a new roommate."

Dumbfounded by Brian's ignoring peril to life but getting alarmed when his clothing was spoiled, I just flipped through the black book. Mrs. Murphy? Could it be my Mrs. Murphy? "What do you think all the dates and numbers mean?"

Brian put his jacket on the back of a chair next to me. "I don't know. My guess would be dates and the rating for each."

So, definitely not my Mrs. Murphy. The younger, racier

model, maybe. I flipped through the book, absently.

"There have to be about fifty names," I said. "Men's as well as women's. It can't be Chris's dating book, really, can it?" The last page read Joanna M. Zimmerman, Phs/rw 89076890. The entries beneath ranged from fifty to a hundred. "I mean, there seem to be all sorts."

"Yeah, and this is Chris we're talking about." Brian walked off to the living room. "Lou gave me this jacket and she's not likely to give me another before next year. Damn." He opened the coat closet by the door. "What have I done with the duct tape?"

I'd stumbled on an entry for Paul Hogg, I/P78&9. Underneath copious entries, with numbers starting at twenty and progressing all the way to fifty.

"Brian, is Chris's father named Paul?"

He came back to the table with a roll of tape, bit into it to tear it, glued a piece over the cut in his jacket. "I don't know—No, wait, his *brother* is Paul. I know that because he's an artist, big time artist, you know, internationally famous and all that stuff. The local paper runs articles on him all the time and all. And one day Chris asked me to drop him off at Paul's studio, and Paul asked me in to look around. He had some pretty neat stuff, sculptures and paintings. Representational, mostly. Not bad at all."

He frowned at the newly patched tear on his jacket. "Not bad looking either, though the dainty type. I mean Paul. He's a pale blond. Nothing like Chris. Chris said something about being the son of his father's second marriage. Paul and John—Paul's twin—are the sons of his father's first marriage."

I flipped the page. The book was alphabetized and the page before Paul's read John Hogg, IPhFSD 3456. I hoped that this *wasn't* Chris's little black book, or a rating of dates, but felt vaguely nauseated, all the same.

I closed the notebook, pushed it away. I wasn't about to vent this to Brian.

Golly, Gee, wide-eyed just-turned-nineteen presumable virgins or close to it weren't ready for raunchy reality.

What was Chris doing writing this stuff up and putting it in Brian's jacket? Was there more between Chris and Brian than there appeared to be? A picture formed in my mind and I gagged.

I grabbed the book again, flipped to where Quick should be. Nothing. Wondering at my own obvious relief, I puzzled over how Brian could be involved in the fetid pool of Chris's personal life. Was it just physical proximity?

"Why do you want to know?" Brian asked. "About Chris's family."

"Nothing, really. I'd just heard the name Paul Hogg somewhere and I wondered."

"Oh," he said. He looked at me, for a while. He opened his mouth, closed it. "Is he in there?" he asked, staring at the book.

Before I could answer, he shook his head. "No. I really don't want to know. Look, I don't have much food in the house. I thought I'd wait to see if you were still here before I bought stuff for dinner. If you tell me what you'd like, I'll take Bucephallus to the grocery store and will be back in a moment."

"Bucephallus? Alexander the Great's horse? You'll take a dead horse to the grocery store?" Was it a mob joke? He'd said he had been brought up in an Italian neighborhood.

He smiled sheepishly. "Bucephallus the iron horse. It's my bike—motorcycle—a dying Honda. Terminally rusty, but at least it has a cool name, right? So, what do you eat? Are you vegetarian? Something like that?"

I shook my head. "Omnivorous."

His smile became a grin. "What a coincidence, so am I. So, what should I buy?"

I looked up at him, all the way up to the tousled pale curls and repressed a sigh.

Staying here, having dinner à-deux, might not be the best plan in the world. "Tell you what, you fed me breakfast, let me take you out to dinner. You've already told me you don't like Hangman's, so how about Buffalo's Roam?"

Buffalo's was a medium-priced restaurant, halfway between Hangman's and the Lobster Trap in price as well as distance from Calamity Jane. It did a brisk business of steaks and televised sports and catered to middle-aged professors, middle-aged computer wizards, middle-aged tourists.

Brian looked puzzled. He shifted a foot. "I can't afford Buffalo's Roam."

"I'll pay," I said, and before he could form the protest his frown pre-announced, "Look, you fed me breakfast and allowed me to sleep on your table, and—" I picked up the orange cushion and held it up, as exhibit A. "I drooled all over your stuff. It's the least I can do, taking you out."

He stared at the cushion, frowned. "You're sure? Buffalo's is pretty expensive."

For students, I supposed. "I get paid good money for boring young people in Lives," I told him. "Come on. Go out with a middle-aged professor who isn't even wearing tights. Live a little."

He looked shocked, then laughed, gave me a sheepish glance, blushed. "All right." He put his jacket back on. "Your car or Bucephallus?"

"Young man, I've never ridden a motorcycle and I have no intention of starting now." I got up.

"Aw, come on." He grabbed my upper arm and shoved, lightly. "Live a little."

But in the end we took the MG, though Brian insisted on riding with the top down, since it had stopped snowing just then.

I had trouble thinking of this carefree, almost obnoxiously ingratiating young man as a potential player in a conspiracy against me. Which was strange enough. I'd never before had any trouble conjuring paranoia on demand.

"So, do you have a lot of problems with it?" Brian asked.

Thoughts ran riot through my head. I cleared my throat. "With what?"

He patted the dashboard, threw his head back, his pale hair blown around by the wind, his eyes closed. "The car."

"Huh?"

"Does it break down a lot?"

"Sometimes." I was sure I looked purple with cold, but Brian looked good, his skin paler than usual and his hair golden will-o'-the-wisp glowing in reflected headlights.

"So, where do you take it?"

"Huh?" I concentrated on keeping my nose from freezing by sheer willpower, while biting icy air rushed around us, and we drove the expressway as a fast route to the other side of the city.

Why hadn't I told him we would have the top up and that was that? Well, for one because this made it less private, afforded fewer opportunities for my body's overriding my brain and leading me into misguided attempts at seduction. I looked over at him. Well, that and because he'd asked *so* nicely.

"To get repaired." He looked at me. "The car."

"Oh. Carriage Express."

"No." His look turned incredulous. Green eyes opened

wide. "They're bozos. And they're way too expensive. Next time you have problems, come to me. I'll take care of you."

I tried to look straight ahead and keep a steady course on the road. My hands shook.

God, why am I tempted this way? I am not a good man. There's no reason to try me. I've been found wanting long ago. And, God, oh God, am I ever wanting. Is he in league with Elderman? Is the plot, really, to drive me to a madhouse? And how can he look so nice and wholesome, if he's involved in something like that?

"My sister Lou taught me."

"What?"

He stared at me, sweetly puzzled. "To fix cars. She's a mechanic. She owns her own garage."

"Oh."

It went on like that all the twenty minutes it took us to take the expressway that surrounded Lythia to the other side of town, the new development side, with all the better restaurants and the modern bookstore.

In fact, his eager questioning about my car and the horrendous double entendres in my mind continued till we sat down at a corner table in Buffalo's, I with a beer and Brian with a soft drink. Which brought home to me that the man wasn't even legal to drink full-force drinks, and what the hell did I think I was doing?

Taking him out to dinner. Just taking him out to dinner. It was all I intended on doing, honest.

What the hell, he was my student. And he was, maybe, involved in a murder. What type of scum did I think I was anyway? Did I really think I'd seduce a student? Didn't I know myself better than that?

Besides, this kept it public and impersonal, right?

Public and impersonal.

He had turned nineteen. Why couldn't I try? What could he do? Say no? Scream bloody murder? Punch me to a bloody pulp? Sue the college over sexual harassment?

I'd been turned down before. I'd been punched before. And was my job really that important?

He turned away from me, said hello to a beautiful red-headed woman.

It took me a few seconds to recognize her waist-length dark-red curls and the shapely body, contained but not exactly hidden within a cobalt blue sheaf dress. I had ogled her for a good five seconds by the time I recognized Joanna Zimmerman. Which just proves I was temporarily insane.

"Oh, hi. We missed you at the party, Brian," she was saying as I came to my senses. "I heard you had some problems at your place." She stopped by his chair, her hand on his shoulder.

Her nails were painted dark red, like dried blood.

"You heard?" Brian asked. "Oh, it was nothing. Just one of Chris's crazy stunts, I'm sure."

"Joanna," I said, wanting into the conversation, wanting to keep my mind from Brian, wanting someone else to witness my good behavior, here, in public, with Brian. Wanting to prove I recognized Joanna, maybe. I didn't know.

My brain had stopped functioning long ago. "Sherry was worried about me—I mean, you—I mean, me having done something to you—I mean—She seemed to think you were in trouble. Are you?"

She looked from Brian to me, and frowned before smiling. "Oh. Hi, Bill. You know Sherry. She just makes these big dramas up." She looked at Brian again. "Have you guys known each other long? Are you friends?"

I kicked him under the table. Joanna was Elderman's

girlfriend and I didn't want to hear about undue fraternization with students. If Brian wasn't in cahoots with Elderman, Joanna certainly was.

Brian stared at me, shocked at the kick.

"No," I said. "I just went over to take him the notes from Lives Two. And we thought maybe we'd go out to dinner, watch some—" I looked over at the television, to see what sport was playing, and my thoughts stopped, while I stared at the image on the screen.

I was vaguely aware of Joanna's saying, "Well, have to go. Bon appetite," and of Brian's leaning forward and asking in a whisper, "What in hell was *that* for?"

But I couldn't answer because the large screen television, that no one else in the bar seemed to be watching, was displaying, in glorious color and full-fledged realism, the picture of a severed head.

Chris Hogg's.

VII

He Treats Me Badly Each Time that We Meet

I whimpered.

Brian looked up, made a gagging sound. He stood up, throwing his chair down in his haste.

People around us reacted with varying degrees of disgust and alarm. People yelled. Plates overturned. Crockery and glass broke. Indisposed diners stampeded for the restrooms or the door.

I heard someone say something about student-run TV stations and Halloween pranks.

After standing up, Brian had remained motionless, staring.

As I looked up at him, his gaze slowly deviated from the TV to me, and he nodded almost imperceptibly, and bent to grab his mangled jacket from the back of his toppled chair.

I got out my wallet, counted enough money to cover our drinks twice over, dropped it on the table.

We elbowed our way through the gawking, talking, moaning crowd to the entrance, where we had to push our way through people who were throwing up into every patch of greenery they could find.

The crowd outside was larger than the one inside and, other than the ones throwing up, they talked more, too. I cut through the melee, shoulder forward, like a transatlantic through stormy waters. Disjointed sentences reached me.

"God, can you believe that?"

"Must be a Halloween prank."

"Looks *just* like someone I used to date."

"Hell of a realistic prop."

"Those damn students."

Brian, my own parcel of the cursed student body, stood by my car, waiting.

He didn't talk until I'd got us out of the parking lot, which involved still more careful navigating through milling crowds.

As we turned right, out of the parking lot, he said, "I suppose we ought to go to the police."

I supposed so, too, though I'd been trying very hard to think of something else to do. "Your friend, Tony, isn't going to be happy." He was going to think I'd done it.

He was going to think it was part of that gay professor killing attractive students for fun and pleasure thing. Of course I'd never considered Chris attractive, but maybe Tony would. All I knew is that some way or other this would come to rest at my door. I bit my lip. He couldn't. He just couldn't. I had an alibi.

I didn't do it, my mental voice whined.

Brian set his lips in a straight line, made his jaw so square that you could have cut paper on the corners. "I don't give a damn about Tony's happiness."

All right. I wasn't about to argue with a man who could square the bone structure in his jaw. I pulled into another parking lot, next to the restaurant, got out. From the trunk of my car, I got the phone book I kept there, for just such instances. I looked up the Police.

It turned out the police station was across the park in the same central street—Main Street—where it probably had been since the days of shoot-outs at high noon. I'd just never noticed it. It had been a long time since knowing the whereabouts of the police, and avoiding it, had been a necessity for me.

I put the phone book back, got into the car, started it.

Brian sat, with his fists balled up, his jaw more square than ever. Through clenched teeth, he muttered what I thought was, "son-of-a-bitch-son-of-a-bitch-son-of-a-bitch."

I didn't ask; I didn't want him to tell me whom he was talking about.

Probably not me. I mean, it *shouldn't* be me. But then, I really didn't want to *know*.

To get to the police station, the highway was far from the best way, so I stuck to the land route, traversing the wilds of suburbia, then the deserted warehouse district, finally small downtown roads, until I hit Main Street.

Brian had stopped muttering. He sat back in his seat, his features slack.

As I parked in the gravel parking lot of the tiny building with the big Lythia Springs police station sign, I wondered if Brian had fallen asleep.

But he opened his eyes, looked at me and said, "So there was a corpse in my kitchen."

"Yeah," I said. It seemed too much of a coincidence to believe that Chris might have got killed elsewhere and Brian have hallucinated a corpse on the very same night.

"Who do you think killed Chris?" Brian asked.

I shrugged. "You knew him better than I did. Who do you think?"

He chuckled, a nervous sound. "The problem with

Chris," he said, slowly, "is that practically everyone who knew him wanted to kill him. Except Tiffany."

"Tiffany?" I asked.

"His girlfriend." Brian groaned, as though he'd just remembered something and squinted as if in pain. "She's pregnant, too."

The scary thought of Chris having reproduced stopped me from answering. I got out of the car.

Brian followed.

We shouldn't have bothered. The door to the police department was firmly locked and there was nothing to tell us why, not even one of those "gone fishing" signs.

It seemed wrong for the police station to be closed, but it definitely was.

Nothing we did, from skinning our knuckles drumming on the door, to honking in the parking lot, raised a living soul.

We returned to the car. "What now?" I asked.

"My place, I suppose," Brian said. "I should call Chris's next of kin. I have the numbers at home."

"Brian, I think by now everyone in town has been informed."

He groaned again, a *please don't tell me that* sound. "I know," he said. "But they still need to . . . I should make personal contact. They have a right to dispose of his things, and . . . and of the place. Rent will be due soon. I'll need to find a new roommate."

Not quite sure whether to be glad or shocked that he was thinking so rationally, I started the car toward Calamity.

The purple house looked more ghastly than ever. A TV truck had parked just in front of it, its lights playing with unholy relish over the ornament-burdened facade, putting fluorescent patches on the atrocious color.

An old red Porsche convertible had parked right behind the TV van.

As Brian and I came out of my car, the TV cameras and their light trained on us.

Great. So much for keeping undue fraternization a secret.

Seeing the pained expression on Brian's face, I decided that if this were a plot to make me lose my job, then so be it. Brian had the type of personality that couldn't take this harassment, while I had gone beyond embarrassment many years ago.

I could leave now, and lose self-respect and any chance at Brian's friendship.

On the other hand, I could stand by the man who let me drool on his pillow.

There was no way to do that without being caught in the glare of the cameras.

I sighed. Lessons learned from my days in the closet still applied. When you can't hide it, flaunt it. Chances are no one will believe it if you flaunt it broadly and loudly enough.

Silently kissing my job goodbye, I bravely interposed myself between the camera and the blond.

I waved cheerily and sang out "Hi, mom," to the fury of the cameraman who jerked the focus away from me and toward the ground. But his co-annoyance, a much-too-scantily attired young woman with the bodily charms of a string bean thrust a microphone in my face, yelling with some glee, "Professor Yates."

I glowered at her, then blinked as the focus of the camera and the light that accompanied it came to rest on me, once more. I vaguely remembered seeing the woman in Lives, but I'd be damned if I remembered her name.

"Guilty as charged," I said. "You can turn off the interrogation lights."

"You're confessing? Like, to the crime?" the girl asked in breathless wonder.

"Oh, yeah," I said. "I shot the bastard."

"Shot?" the cameraman asked.

"Poisoned, shot, drowned. Rasputin, you know. Damn hard to kill." Grinning inanely, I climbed the steps to the front door, one step behind Brian, keeping my back to him and my front to the camera.

"Ras—What?" the girl asked.

"Rasputin. I confess. I killed him. It was a tough job, but someone had to do it for the good of the monarchy. Someone had to save the tsar. I've also slain several essays turned in by hopeful students and—" Brian got in the door, closed it. I heard the latch click home.

After a betrayed glance back at the closed door, I stood there, facing the camera. Maybe he really had set me up. Maybe he just wanted to get me in trouble. But, wasn't killing his roommate a little over the top, just to discredit me?

"No, really, Doctor Yates," the brunette persisted, pouting unlikely cherry-red lips in my general direction. "What *are* you doing here?"

"Visiting a friend," I said, on automatic, not really caring, listening, hoping that the door would open again. Had it latched because it was automatic? Or had Brian locked me out? I tried to remember. "I'm afraid he's lost his head."

The door opened, a hand grabbed me by the back of the jacket and forcefully pulled me into the living room.

The door closed again. A quick look down showed me that latching was, indeed, automatic.

"Took you long enough," I said, whirling around, expecting to find Brian and finding, instead, Tony's none-too-amused glare.

"What, exactly, did you think you were you doing, Doctor Yates?" Tony asked. "Your stand-up routine?"

Everyone asked me what I thought I was doing these days. But no one left me alone long enough to think about what to do.

"Protecting the blond," I said, and attempted to amend, "I mean, the Brian. I mean, getting into Brian's hou— Getting Brian into the house unnoticed."

Tony cleared his throat, shook his head. "How many crimes did you confess to?"

I didn't answer. I'd found the blond. He sat down at the dining room table, looking around with an appalled expression. The expression was justified and might even excuse his leaving me outside to face the limelight unaided.

All around us, the books he'd so lovingly set in place littered the floor. The hall closet had been ransacked, every item pulled out. The sofas had been gutted, once more. This time some creative searching genius had cut long gashes in the hundred-year accumulation of wallpaper on the walls and not much newer vinyl on the floor.

Brian, still seemingly unaware of my presence, looked up at Tony. "I hope to hell you have a search warrant."

"What?" Tony turned from me to Brian. "A search what? Brian, I do have a search warrant, signed by Chris's parents, but I didn't search. I didn't do anything except come in, and that's only because the door was open. I heard a car drive away at the back again, but this time I didn't even see it by the time I opened the back door. The TV van showed up about that time." He squared his jaw. Had he learned it from Brian? Or Brian from him? "Those damn idiots. Putting the head on the air, moving it, if you please, to the studio, before alerting the authorities."

Brian looked up, horrified. His Adam's apple bobbed up and down. "Did you—I mean, you've taken it into custody, right?"

Tony nodded. "Oh, yeah. Damn right I have. But my department consists of me, a full-time officer adept only at writing traffic tickets; two part-timers who mostly fill in for street festivals; and a coroner whose real job is as a surgeon in the hospital. I had to close the police department, send a part-timer down to keep an eye on the head, go locate the coroner, get him out of the Lobster Trap, where he was treating his wife to their tenth anniversary dinner, send him to the TV station to take possession of the head, and then escort him to the creek, where the head was found, and where my two part-timers are combing the creek bed with a net. We've found an arm and two hands. I left the doctor and the part-timers with it. I came here. And I found this." He looked at Brian. "Any idea who has been turning your place upside down, or what they might be looking for?"

Brian shook his head.

I noticed the black notebook I'd left on the table was gone and wondered if it was part of the torn and tattered piles on the floor, or if the burglar-and-ransacker had taken it. But if that was all they wanted, why tear the house apart? It had been sitting in plain view.

"Chief?" A nasal voice called from the kitchen. "You've got to come and look at this."

At the time, I thought Tony said, "Damn."

In retrospect, I think he said, "Ram." He tended to pronounce the two much the same way. He hustled toward the kitchen, with me in close pursuit.

I heard Brian drag his chair back and, as I leaned in at

the kitchen door, felt his hand on my shoulder.

A thin man, who gave the impression of having sagged into thinness from some much greater stature—an impression emphasized by his wearing Salvation Army rejects at least five sizes too large for him—stood in the middle of the kitchen. He held a spray can in one hand and a black light flashlight in the other.

As he played the light over the walls, they fluoresced, all over, in a pattern that made me think someone had turned a hose on the wall. He looked at Tony with a silly grin. "Jackpot," he said.

"Ram," Tony said. "You weren't supposed to have touched anything. Besides, you shouldn't be doing anything without me as a witness that you didn't plant the evidence. You—"

Brian reached over my shoulder to tug at Tony's green pullover. "I'll sign the search permission, Tony. I wouldn't think the lack of a witness would matter. What could he have done? Planted all the residual blood?"

"Well, yes," Tony said. He turned to his subordinate. "Ram, do me a favor, keep your hands behind your back and come with me."

"But Chief there's—"

Tony glowered. "Yes, yes, I'm well aware what there is. We'll look at it together, later. Just don't touch anything." The last was a scream, as Ram tentatively prodded a handle on the coffee machine.

"Blood?" I asked Brian.

"The spray is a special compound that causes residual blood to fluoresce under black light," he said, then looked at what must have been my astounded expression. "What? I write mysteries. For fun."

Tony walked into the dining room, with Ram lumbering

close behind him. Up near the lowest step of the stairs, lay a conglomeration of black bags that I hadn't seen before. Tony's.

Tony conducted a thorough search of his own bags. He pulled out plastic bags of all sizes, sprays of indeterminate use, mysterious little packaged kits, bottles and lenses, cameras and a seemingly never ending supply of film that he stacked on the vinyl beside the bags.

I wondered if he didn't know what the bags contained or if he thought, perhaps, that the criminal might have smuggled an ax inside the bags while he wasn't looking.

When Tony got out a hand-vacuum, I felt my face freeze into a mask of shock.

Brian chuckled, touched my arm to call my attention. When I looked at him, he explained in a loud whisper, "It's for vacuuming around the crime scene. To get small evidence you might not get otherwise. Hair and such."

Tony stood up, with a flourish. He pushed a little printed form in front of Brian, handed him a pen that said, *Lythia Springs Police Department*. "There, if you'd sign that. Technically I have permission, but I'd feel better if I got it from all parties."

Brian did.

Tony, obviously encouraged by the ease of his autograph-collecting, handed us a yellow pad of paper apiece. "Now," he said. "I should take you to separate rooms and interrogate you, but there's only Ram and I, so if both of you would be so kind as to write down what happened last night without talking to each other." He gave me a jaundiced eye, as I opened my mouth to protest. "All the *relevant* events," he said. "That might have anything to do with the crime. Truthfully, this time, please, Dr. Yates."

All right, whatever that meant. Did he really expect me

to write down that I'd killed Chris Hogg and thumped Brian on the head, before dropping the whole kit-'n-caboodle into the Nugget? Or did he just want us out of his hair while he searched the crime scene? I looked up to see him measuring things, snapping pictures.

Either way, I'd start with getting Brian out of the river.

As I wrote, I wondered why Brian hadn't been killed, also. What was the point of dropping a dismembered body into a river with a still-alive one? Why had anyone gone to the trouble of making itsy-bitsy pieces of Chris Hogg? Hatred? Possible, but why? Why, while they had the ax on hand, didn't they make mince-Brian too?

Not that I was complaining. I looked over at Brian, who wrote very fast, with fierce concentration, biting the lower left corner of his lip as he worked. No, I wasn't complaining at all. Better a whole blond than separate pieces.

But should I assume the murderer had an undue respect for green-eyed blonds? Or was he just an aesthete, refusing to destroy a biological work of art?

I finished my meager account, which included a lot of *and then I guess I,* signed it, dated it, handed it to Tony, who had come to stand near the table.

He scanned it, as though to make sure I hadn't confessed to any mass murder of essays, then looked at me, "So, Dr. Yates, where were you and Brian tonight?"

"At Buffalo's Roam," I said. "We'd just got in, when I saw . . . on television."

He nodded. "Do you often take Brian out to dinner?"

"I don't see where that's any of your damn business." Brian looked up from his writing, still clutching the pen in his hand.

He'd squared his jaw again, and this time his eyes were flashing green light, something that shouldn't be possible without the help of a special-effects crew.

"It could be," Tony said. "If Dr. Yates here contrived to take you to dinner so that his accomplice could search the place while you were gone."

"What?" Brian asked, staring at me.

Oh, sure. I'd faked the drool on his pillow, too.

"Which would also explain how he came down that road just in time to fish you from the river," Tony said. "Awfully convenient, don't you think?"

"Wouldn't it be easier not to have thrown him in?" I asked.

Tony grinned. "Not if what you wanted to do was gain Brian's confidence."

All right. "Police Chief Marssano, you should be writing mysteries. No, wait, you are, aren't you?"

His expression soured. "Dr. Yates, why did you lie to me about when and how you left Bad Boys?"

Brian's eyes widened.

He mouthed silently *Bad Boys?*

I stared. "I didn't," I said. "Not if I remember correctly, and I think I do. I mean, I wasn't *that* sloshed."

Tony grimaced. "No. According to Ivan, the bartender, you weren't sloshed at all. If you weren't drunk, why did you leave Bad Boys at ten and supposedly get to the bridge by midnight?"

"I took back roads," I said. "I told you—"

"Yes, you told me you were drunk. But Ivan, who is a bartender and should know, said you weren't. So, what were you doing with your extra hour, and why were you near that bridge at all? Why just in time to get Brian out of the water?"

He looked paternal. "What was it, Doctor Yates? Second thoughts? Early repentance? Or a desire to worm into Brian's confidence?"

I sighed. Even I never took fishing for dates to that extent, but try and explain that to the police. "Are you going to arrest me?" I asked.

"Are you confessing?"

"No." I pointed at the paper. "All I know is on that page. But you seem to think I'm a murderer. So, are you going to arrest me?"

He grinned. "Not yet. All we have is circumstantial. We don't even have a motive yet. But we will, Doctor Yates, we will. There's always that caller who tipped us. As soon as we find him, I bet he'll have a lot more to say about the case."

I felt my reason dwindle as my gorge rose. "Look, Napoleon, the call was anonymous. You can't—"

"Hey, Chief you've got to come look at this," sounded from the kitchen, again.

Tony took a deep breath. Still standing, he clutched his hands into fists so tight that the yellow sheet of paper I'd just handed him got crumpled at the corner.

"Ram," he said, this time distinctly. "I swear. I hired him to write parking tickets. I should have known what he'd be like with a major crime. But, damn, I didn't think there would be any major crimes here."

He turned and marched stiff-legged to the kitchen, with Brian and I close behind.

Ram had removed the vinyl from the floor. One layer of it, at any rate.

Underneath, the kitchen appeared to be paved with glossy black stones.

"Dried blood," Brian said. His voice caught. He sounded sick. "I told you there would be—"

"Damn." Tony said. Or Ram. "I'll have to pull out the cabinets, do a whole work-up on the place. Fingerprints and all. Sorry, Brian, I don't think you can live here for a few days."

Brian looked pale and angry. He took in a deep, sharp breath. "I don't know if I want to live here," he said. "Ever."

"Right," Tony said. He got some index cards from a bag, and an inkpad. "Why don't I fingerprint both of you, and then why don't you call a friend, Brian? See if you can stay for the night somewhere."

I should have caught the implication. I did catch the implication. But hope springs eternal and, hell, having saved the blond's life, not to mention having shielded him from the mean, evil TV cameras, perhaps I expected, if not gratitude at least trust. So I tried my hand. "You can stay with me. I have a very long sofa—" I stopped.

The chill in the green eyes could have formed icicles in the soul of someone who had one.

"Right," I said. "If you have a place to stay, I'll go, then."

I let them take my fingerprints and left.

That drive home was the loneliest journey of my lifetime.

VIII

Until the Real Thing Comes Along

At home, I went to the kitchen cabinet, got out a new bourbon bottle and a cup—this one pink and lovingly tagged with *Marriage is Forever.*

I remember the first cup I drank, and I remember the second, caustic on the tongue, warming me inside.

I do not actually remember lying down on the kitchen floor, with the cup by my side and the empty bottle lovingly clutched to my heart, like the dearest of friends.

That's how I woke at first light, however, and first light had never seemed like so much light as it did just then.

I opened my eyes, saw nothing but white glare that made my head throb. "I'll talk, I'll talk already," I muttered.

Little by little, all that light resolved itself to meek rays of sunlight coming through the half-open blinds in the living room.

I sat up. Would my head stop pounding already?

The digital clock on the stove showed seven o'clock.

Grabbing onto the side of the counters, I pulled myself upright, did some complex calculations and determined that it was Wednesday. It being Wednesday, I taught my first class—Creative Writing 101—at ten.

Time enough for me to get up, buy myself a new head, shave my tongue, and steal a functional brain.

Gaahhh. I didn't remember drinking this much in a long

time. Not since Sherry had announced that she had found a nicer, more convenient home in California and was leaving me.

Under the ice-cold shower, things started coming back to me.

Brian first. The blond was starting to take much too prominent a place in my thoughts. Especially since I still wasn't sure what role he played in this murder plot. Not that I was sure it was a plot, anyway. But if there was a plot, was it against me? And if it were a Bill-trap, was Brian the cheese or the clamp? And was he aware of it, in either case?

I did remember going to Brian's and falling asleep on his table, and attempting to take him out to dinner and—

The head. Chris's head. Halfway through rubbing shampoo into my hair, I stood, stock-still. Shampoo ran down, stinging my eyes.

Someone had killed Chris Hogg. What was more, someone had killed Chris Hogg in a way worthy of his many fictional murders of his father. Um . . . what had Chris Hogg's father done for Halloween? Trick-or-axing? Did he, for some reason, hate me? Did he call Tony?

I finished washing and dried myself.

Tony. How could he believe I'd thrown Brian in the water? How could he think I might have tried to kill Brian? All based on that one, anonymous call and a bartender who didn't want to admit he'd let a sloshed costumer drive home.

It was not to be believed.

Yet Brian had believed it.

Well, Brian didn't know me that well.

Maybe he thought dunking blonds and pulling them out again was one of my hobbies. Playing Pooh-sticks with blond young men.

What did I expect?

I expected the man to have more sense than to think I'd carry on such a plot while dressed in tights and an Elizabethan collar, that's what I expected.

I stomped out to my bedroom, dressed—in an approximation of Hamlet and in reflection of my mood—in dark-gray slacks and a black pullover, and marched all the way out to the kitchen for the dregs of that instant coffee.

I couldn't wait till I made it to Hangman's or to Flapjack Follies for my daily dosage of caffeine. I needed to go and talk to Tony Marssano, by the grace of God Napoleonic Chief of Police of Lythia. I would talk some sense into his thick Italian skull.

I grabbed a cup—emblazoned with **IT'S NOT AN ATTITUDE PROBLEM, IT'S A STATEMENT**—from the cabinet. Having dropped the rock of coffee into it, I filled it with hot water from the tap, swirled the whole around until it formed a thick paste, opened my mouth, closed my eyes and swallowed.

Half an hour later, in my car, driving down Main Street, I felt the taste in my mouth subside. By then I had awakened enough to realize there was no use going to see the Chief of Police.

He couldn't pressure Ivan into telling him the truth. No bartender would ever admit a client was less than sober when said client had left the bar counter and headed for a car. But I had no proof of this and no wish to attempt to use it as a defense in a trial where I would be the star attraction. Worse, I didn't even have a way to explain it to Tony if Tony chose not to believe it.

It had snowed during the night and, though the plows had done their job, a shiny white carpet covered everything but the center of the roads. If Brian were with me, he'd probably have insisted on having the top down anyway.

Only Brian wasn't with me. Brian thought I'd helped kill Chris. The Chief of Police thought I'd conspired to kill Brian. I had no proof that I hadn't done either one and the only thing keeping me out of the slammer was my complete lack of motive. That would shield me until Tony figured out I had a history of psychiatric problems and that I had once—supposedly—attempted suicide by very messy means. Not a second after that.

Hissing my frustration out between clenched teeth, I stopped the car in the parking lot of the United Church Of All Hallows.

Well, what now? I had a good two hours before I was due at the college and the thought of breakfast turned my stomach.

I found myself thinking that the best way to prove I hadn't killed Chris was to find out who *had* killed Chris. Closing my eyes, as the headache started up again, I whispered to myself, "Yes, that's right. Boozeman to the rescue." But the idea persisted.

Thinking came back to me slowly, hesitantly, like an elephant in ballet slippers tiptoeing through a cardboard landscape.

People who might have killed Chris. Well . . . Just about anyone, Brian had said.

However, the person most likely to have killed Chris was his father and, for that matter, every court in the land should consider it a case of straightforward self-defense.

It would also explain the axing. If the man had read even one of Chris's essays, he was more than justified in any excessive violence and malice toward his wayward and seriously deranged son. However, Chris's father would have no reason at all to kill Brian, would he?

So, just dropping him unmolested into the Nugget made

sense. Maybe he figured Brian would recover and swim away. Then again, no, surely whoever did it meant to kill Brian too. Maybe the doctor had reasons to want to kill Brian though. Well . . . If Brian had seen the body in the kitchen that would be reason enough. Just not sufficient reason to chop him to pieces with an ax.

From the trunk of my car, I pulled the phone book. A Dr. Byrnum Hogg, Mental Health Specialist, was listed. I drove to the pay phone outside Hangman's and called.

A cheery female voice assured me that Dr. Hogg would answer his phone at eleven a.m. weekdays, further informed me that if this was an emergency I should call another number, and if it wasn't, I should leave a message.

I left a message asking about the availability of an appointment.

Making an appointment with a shrink choked me but, hell, I'd been married to one and survived.

I was Boozeman and could survive anything. Except maybe a Chief of Police who, from subconscious motives best left unexplored, *wanted* to prove me guilty of murder.

I still had an hour and a half remaining on my schedule before class.

On a whim, I looked up Paul Hogg. He lived on the other side of the ex-whorehouse district, where the brothels must have been larger, or the mistresses indentured to more affluent masters, because the houses ran to sprawling dimensions.

I drove there, through the maze of little streets, all the while fighting a wish to go back, to look at the purple house, to see if someone around there might know where Brian had gone. To a friend. Who were his friends?

Try as I might, I didn't remember him hanging out with anyone in particular, spending time with any group of students.

Paul's house, 789 Gangbusters Avenue, sat far back enough from the road to be no more than a white blur amid tall juniper trees.

I walked the spacious winding pathway through the immaculately kept yard and rang the doorbell beside the gleaming oak door, with its raised, carved panels.

Silence.

At length, a voice from the other side: "I do not give interviews."

"I don't want an interview," I said. Well, not technically. I had no intentions of writing it down. I just wanted to save my humble neck. The voice sounded familiar. Could this be an ex-student? "My name is William Shakespeare Yates and—"

A gasp sounded, loud enough to be heard through three inches of oak.

The door opened, so quickly that I jumped back, startled.

In the doorway, in a white robe, his shoulder length hair a mess, his eyes wide with surprise, his oval face frozen with shock, was green-eyed blond number one. Or perhaps number two.

Paul Hogg, a.k.a. the fair youth who'd stood me up on Halloween and left me all alone in my Shakespeare costume.

"Paul Hogg?" I asked.

"You found me." He smiled. By his side, a very large black dog displayed mad, tail-wagging joy. "I couldn't remember if I'd given you my address or not."

I nodded to him. Hell, he hadn't given me his *name*. And he'd stood me up, damn it. Stood-me-up. I had to remember that, no matter how big he smiled, nor how endearing he tried to be now.

He'd stood me up on the night his half-brother was killed. Had he been out axing Chris? Too busy to keep our date?

"I didn't have your phone number," he said. "I had to look in the book and when I called you, you didn't answer."

"You didn't leave a message," I said.

"I didn't know if you lived alone. Messages can be so embarrassing." He winked. "My car wouldn't start. I found out later someone had stolen the battery. Strange, isn't it?" He grinned. "Must have been a student whose battery failed. Lythia Springs. You've got to love it, though I sometimes wonder why."

He ran his hands through his straight, shoulder-length hair, pulling it back from his face. Icy blond hair, I thought, shiny and lank, two shades lighter than even Brian's, which is to say almost transparent.

"I'm being awfully rude, aren't I?" he said. "Move, Faustus," this he addressed to the large, tail-wagging Labrador. He grabbed the dog by his thick leather collar and pulled him aside, which had to take effort, considering the dog must have weighed as much as he did.

Paul smiled at me, "Come in."

Said the spider to the fly, I thought.

Paul and the dog preceded me into a white marble-tiled hallway, with white walls all around.

The inside of the old Victorian had been gutted and turned into something its own creators would not only not recognize but also have nightmares about. To the left, a broad spiral staircase—painted shiny white—climbed to a half-open upper floor. I got a glimpse of a massive pine bed. The way sheets and a white duvet were piled on it, I couldn't tell if someone might be in it.

Great set-up if you wanted your every guest, salesman and Jehovah's witness to be intimately acquainted with your sex life.

To my right, a wide arch opened to a white-on-white

living room. Ahead of me, another broad arch gave way to a white-on-white dining room, furnished with chromium-and-white-lacquer table and chairs. In the middle of the table, a tall glass vase held white calla lilies. Up on the side-board, in a silver frame, stood a picture of two boys. They looked exactly alike except that one wore blue beach shorts and one white beach shorts. One had his arm over the shoulders of the other and both smiled at the camera, smiles full of braces and freckles. Both looked like Paul, a thirteen-year-old Paul.

"What will you have?" Paul walked ahead of me, while his dog smelled every inch of me that it could reach. "Coffee? Tea?" He turned back, grinned and winked again.

"Coffee," I said, to forestall bad jokes.

We walked through the dining room and under another arch, into a white-tiled kitchen with white cabinets and all the latest in white appliances. Paul walked noiselessly on bare feet.

His coffee machine looked only slightly less complex than Brian's, but it was, like the rest of the kitchen, white, so that it almost disappeared against the counter top.

He waved me onto a—white, of course—wrought-iron chair that, with its mate, flanked a tiny wrought-iron table of the sort associated with old time ice-cream parlors.

I sat down, uncomfortably, watching Paul make coffee. What was I doing here, anyway? Oh, yeah, trying to find out *anything* that might get the Chief of Police off my case. And maybe, just maybe, something to prove to Brian that I wasn't a murderer.

Not that there was a hope; not that anything would ever happen between Brian and I. But I still would rather he didn't think of me as a murderer.

Faustus put his head on my knees and looked soulfully up at me.

I never had pets. My father wouldn't allow them, and neither would the various boarding schools to which he farmed me. But I liked dogs. And cats. I'd learned their protocols long ago, with strays and the dogs of friends and casual acquaintances.

I scratched behind the furry black ears. Faustus' heavy black tail thump-thumped the floor.

"He likes you." Paul smiled. "Weird. He usually barks himself hoarse at anyone who comes near me. Even Chris's roommate when he—" He stopped.

My attention hung suspended. Brian had mentioned Paul's good looks. I felt a quite unreasonable nettle of jealousy and looked expectantly at Paul, but he wouldn't finish the sentence. He turned his back to me, got two cups from the cupboard. White cups, with no sayings on them. He filled them, got a creamer and a sugar bowl, brought the whole to the table on a white tray.

"I'm sorry," I said. "About Chris."

He didn't have the hypocrisy or the decency to fake bereavement. "Yeah. I always knew someone would kill him, but that was over the top. An ax, and all." He handed me my cup and a spoon, shook his head. "Poor Chris. Born a fuck-up, always a fuck-up. Did you know him? Personally, I mean?"

So far he didn't sound like he was all broken up over it. Did that make him more likely to be the murderer? Or would the murderer take great care to sound distraught?

"I had him in Creative Writing. Four years in a row."

Paul flinched, opened his eyes wide, looked earnestly sympathetic.

His eyes fell short of the intense green of Brian's. Instead of deep jade, they looked moss green. A softer, less forceful color, infinitely less probing. "You poor thing. Did he still write about killing our father?"

I nodded. "Do you have any idea why?" I stirred my coffee. He'd brought out silver spoons with a PH engraved on the handle. "I mean, why he would want to commit parricide?"

He shook his head, shrugged. "Not really."

His eyes dropped to the table, he traced round and round the sugar bowl with his long white finger that ended in a perfectly sculpted oval nail, with a big tear in the center.

"I mean, my father is not wonderful but . . . It's just that Chris . . . Well, Chris doesn't look—Didn't look, like either his mother or my father. My father's second wife is quite decorative, thank you, but . . . she produced Chris. I don't think my father ever forgave Chris for being so homely. It looked bad on Christmas cards and all. Then he decided Chris would be a genius, but Chris wouldn't play along with that, either. So, my father just wrote him off. Didn't ask him to pose for the family picture, didn't mention him to acquaintances. You know, that sort of thing. If it were a century ago, he might have paid Chris to live in India or somewhere like that and send him his allowance every month, on condition he didn't show himself."

He sipped his coffee. "You see, I'm the distinguished artist." He grinned impishly, over the rim of his coffee cup. "And John, my twin, is the financial wizard. Trisha, my sister, is the star student. Chris . . . Chris was just a fuck-up."

It seemed like a stupid reason to hate a kid, but then my father had despised me with far less reason.

I had been a fairly precocious child, and entered college

just short of my fifteenth birthday and with high grades. Heck, even while I was doing drugs and laying anything that moved or even waved in the wind, my grades had remained top notch. Still, the old bastard had hated me. Because I took after my mother, he said.

I looked up at Paul.

He smiled at me.

He looked exactly like a cat contemplating what to do with a fat bird.

A sudden chill ran up my spine, as I thought of him holding an ax, of that beautiful, delicate face contorted in a murderous rictus. It didn't seem possible, but who knew?

"Would you like to see my work?" he asked.

I cleared my throat, drank my cup of coffee at a gulp. "I have to go teach a class. I only wanted to—I mean . . . I wanted to express my condolences."

"Oh, don't bother." He waved his hand, dismissing condolences. "I'm not bereaved. Not really." He looked pensive, and gave me a look just out of the edge of his eye. A cat about to pounce. "But I do think the police should have a talk with my brother's roommate."

"Brian?"

"Oh?" Paul's eyebrows shot up. "You know *her?*"

The hissing, scathing reversal of gender pronoun applied to Brian of all people made my tendons bunch up and I had to make an effort to avoid clenching my fists.

Instead, I shrugged, as though Brian Quick and the works thereof were the least of my concerns. "Not intimately," I said. "But I have *him* in two classes. *He* always seemed singularly mismatched with your brother. As a roommate, I mean." As if I'd even known he was Chris's roommate until the night before last.

Paul frowned at something in the mid distance. "Ah,

well." A small smile turned the corners of his pale pink lips upward, even as his eyebrows remained contorted.

"Yeah. Brian is a nice looking piece," he said. "I could have *got her,* too." The smile turned to something vaguely unpleasant, the sort of expression that made one want to wash his hands. "I asked Chris to bring *her* over and I invited *her* in, but . . . Faustus went nuts. So *she* only got to see the studio and left, as untouched as *she* came in. Just as well, because if someone axed dear old Chris, I'd lay bets on Brian . . . and it wouldn't look good to have laid Brian. It might very well come out in court and my daddy dearest would have a whole herd of cows."

He sighed. "All the same, I remember thinking that Brian didn't act as if *she* liked my baby brother all that much. Chris had to have cramped *her* style. Chris . . ." The frown deepened. "He liked taking someone's secrets, and using them. Emotional sadist. I guess it was his way of getting a piece of his own back."

He bit his lower lip, then caught my eye, smiled and ran the tip of his pink tongue along his upper lip. "Little Brian looks like *she*'s hiding all kinds of *nice* secrets." He gave me a half-veiled look from under his eyelids and the smile crept slyly up his face. "Nice *girl* like that could be very popular."

He stared at me, with obvious eagerness.

I picked up my coffee cup, pretended to drink, even though the cup was empty. I had to hide my face. I had to hide the glare-of-death forming in my eyes.

His eagerness diminished, replaced with a smug, self-satisfied look. It pleased him that I didn't rise up in defense of Brian.

I felt torn. Why did Paul think that Brian had killed Chris? Could it be true? But then, why had Brian been dropped in the river? A fall out amid thieves?

I looked at Paul's assured smile. He sounded like he knew lots and lots of things. Nasty things. Creepy, crawly things that hid beneath rocks in his lime-encrusted, slimy mind.

God, I had to remember not to make dates while I was sloshed and I must learn to think beyond a pair of nicely stuffed tight jeans.

He shrugged, patted Faustus. "Either Brian did it, or Dr. Joanna Zimmerman."

I jumped. "Joanna?"

His eyes opened wide. He hadn't counted on that one hitting any mark.

His voice sounded baffled and calculating—a unique Paul mixture—as he said, "At least . . . I saw *Dr. Joanna* hanging around in Chris's house a lot. I'd go in and she'd be there. Anyway, Chris had decided to marry the airhead . . . what's her name? Tiffany? Yeah, I think that's it, Tiffany or Crystal, or one of those vitreous names. Chris actually believed she was pregnant by him and was going to marry her. Well, that and the way I figured it, Chris wanted to spite the entire family by marrying such an obvious idiot. Maybe good old Joanna got jealous and took an ax and gave Chris forty whacks. Or however many."

He stood up. "So, wanna see my studio and then, maybe, stay for lunch?" He leered.

Another time, another place. Two days ago, I would have jumped at the chance, called the college with some excuse. Whatever Paul might be, he was no wide-eyed innocent like Brian. I could get what I wanted, plenty of it, no questions asked, no commitments demanded. Besides, he wasn't my student.

But his eyes were not exactly green, his shoulders weren't broad enough, he was, for crying out loud, two inches shorter than I.

Besides, there was something about him—a slinking, sneaky quality that made me queasy and gave me an intense desire to shower. This whole business was murky. We were dealing with crime and he had been in Chris's little black book, which sounded less and less like a date book and more and more like something else. A record of things Chris had on other people?

Paul might—he might very well—have taken an ax to Chris himself. That thing Paul had said about Chris using people's secrets . . .

I remembered the way Paul looked when he said it, with his tiny, regular teeth clamped onto his lower lip. I wondered about Chris's notebook, the page on Paul.

What had Paul done? What had Chris done to Paul?

I made my excuses, truthful ones. I needed to go look over my notes before I taught my next class.

He smiled, graciously.

He walked me to the door, accompanied by an overfriendly Faustus.

At the door, he paused.

He grabbed me by the back of the neck, pulled my head down, kissed me, pushing his body up against mine. His tongue probed for my tonsils.

I pushed away, fought for air.

"I have to go," I said, my voice odd.

God, it had been a long time since I'd been attacked by a blond of any description. I had to keep in mind that we were in the middle of a murder investigation and that Paul might have been the murderer, just to steady the shaking of my hands and slow the blood that rushed through my veins. "I really have to go."

He pulled back, licking his lips. "Come back when you have more time," he said.

I nodded. He'd arranged for his robe to fall open. I didn't want to look.

But it was hard to avoid seeing the huge blue-black bruise on his left shoulder.

When he opened the door, I noticed that he had a blister on the palm of his white hand. A large blister that had burst into a patch of sore, skinless flesh.

The kind of blister that someone with delicate skin might get from hefting a large ax.

IX

What Can I Hope For; I Wish I Knew

I got coffee at Hangman's, with a side of pensiveness, an awful lot of rumination, and a sprinkling of self-recrimination.

He'd wanted me. Or at least, he'd been willing to fake it.

He was young, nice looking, seemed to have all his own teeth, his own hair, and he kept both teeth and hair clean. He had a career, his very own home and a nice doggie. These qualities alone made him better than anyone I'd even got close to sleeping with in the last seven years. At least if you didn't count anonymous strangers and ill-lit places.

I'd turned him down. What the hell was wrong with me? Did I think blonds grew on trees? So what if he might be an ax murderer? Since when did I have standards?

Out of nowhere, I wondered where Brian had spent the night, what he might be doing right now.

Probably doing what you so virtuously turned down, you fool. With some willing friend or other.

The idea hurt and I realized that my feelings for Brian had at least as much to do with my refusal of Paul as did my fear that Paul might be a murderer.

My feelings for Brian. I didn't even know if the man leaned that way. Tony seemed to suspect it. However, clearly, Tony was not the most perceptive man around. And as for Paul Hogg . . . Well . . . He struck me as the sort of gay man who thinks every man is either secretly gay or can be turned.

So what the hell was I doing having any feelings for Brian? What was wrong with me? What kind of an idiot was I?

I'd avoided love successfully for the last twelve years, ever since Lupi had broken my heart and tried to kill me in the process. I was not ready to give my heart to another lover who might abuse it.

Sex was fine, as was the sort of working friendship I'd forged with Sherry, but Lupi—or the hospitalization after what Lupi had been very careful to make sure looked like a botched suicide—had vaccinated me against anything else, vaccinated me for good and all. Or so I'd thought.

Now, I would fall in love again? Stupid, platonic love with no consummation and no hope of any?

Stupid, platonic love of the worshiping-at-his-feet, face-the-cameras-for-him, anything-for-my-man kind with a boy, a child barely out of high school? For a man who might very well be involved in murder? For a man around whom dark currents of danger and deceit swirled? What kind of a fool was I?

An old fool. I made a face at my reflection in the coffee cup. An old fool brooding over a coffee cup and a pile of typed paper, while he got later and later for the class he had to teach. An idiot mooning over a nineteen-year-old who'd never give him a second thought except as a possible ax murderer. Mooning over a nineteen-year-old who might very well be involved in the ax murder as an accomplice or a plotter.

While these thoughts insisted on running through my head, I looked through my notes, wrote comments on the margins. I swear I thought these comments would help me conduct a class, in which I was supposed to expound on the overuse of adjectives.

Mid-class, I found myself staring at things such as: *Brian has much better legs* and *of course Brian isn't an ax murderer. What if I end up in jail? What if all this is a trap to catch me?*

They were, unmistakably, in my handwriting. I started to doubt my sanity.

I somehow managed not to betray anything to the class of ten earnest men and dutiful women who persisted in trying to write despite a complete lack of grammatical understanding or feeling for the language of Shakespeare.

After the class, I stopped by my office to get my notes for the afternoon—Creative Writing 102—class.

I noticed that Brian was talking to the skinny girl who had seemed so worried about him before. She leaned toward him, looking out of balance, like an olive on two toothpicks.

I felt a vague uneasiness. After all, she had asked about him. But I couldn't imagine Brian being interested in the likes of her. And yet, uneasiness remained.

My assistant, Daphy, sat behind my utilitarian wooden desk, brownish pigtails—yes, at forty-something, the woman wore pigtails—a-flutter, gray-blue eyes moist.

"Your psychiatrist called, Dr. Yates," she said and blinked large tears down her concave cheeks. "He says he can see you this afternoon." She reached for the box of tissues I kept on my desk, for those occasions when I needed to explain to overemotional students of either gender why they'd never be good writers.

"I understand." She dabbed at her eyes, blew her nose noisily. "If I had a counselor I'd make an appointment, too. Just to deal with the grief. Poor Chrissy-poo."

"Sherry called?" I latched on to the central puzzling fact and let the other ones go, including her seemingly unwarranted but apparently genuine grief for Chris.

Sherry had rarely called me at work, even while we'd been married. Why would she call now? Unless she were really hard up for money, of course.

"Sherry?" Daphy echoed, looking blank.

"My wife," I said, trying to remember whether I'd been cursed with Daphy on the last year of my marriage. Or had she come into my life after Sherry had departed it, thereby keeping the level of annoyance constant? "I mean, my ex-wife, Doctor Sherry Yates."

Daphy gaped. "Oh, no, Dr. Yates. This was a man. A Doctor . . ." She searched through my desk, which, as at any time when she sat at it for more than ten seconds, had become littered with little purple sticky notes engraved with butterflies.

"A Doctor Hogg," she said, looking at the note. "I remember, because it was Chrissy-poo's last name and—"

Doctor Hogg. So, Byrnum Hogg had called back. And offered an afternoon appointment?

Even given that Lythia didn't have enough heads to shrink—a factor that had impelled Sherry California-ward—this seemed like too open a schedule. Particularly when his youngest son had just been murdered.

I shooed Daphy out of my office, swept her litter of little notes and reminders from the top of my desk, found the one with Dr. Hogg's name.

Gritting my teeth, I prepared to call a psychiatrist and make an appointment, even though everything in me screamed and yelled don't-wanna, throwing itself to the floor like an ill-behaved toddler.

Yet, I'd better. I'd better figure this out before I found myself in death row.

It all seemed surreal.

Murders were not supposed to happen around middle-aged college professors. It was in the rulebook for middle-aged college professors.

I had already lived through interesting times in my college days. Now I wanted to be bored, bored, *bored,* damn it. Any time now.

A pleasant female voice answered my call.

"Dr. Yates," I said. "I left a message and—"

"Oh," she said. "Of course. We can see you at three, if that's acceptable."

My class was at one. Which left me barely enough time after it ended to tear across town to the shrink. While I'd often felt like doing that after teaching either of my Creative Writing classes, this would be my first opportunity.

Brian would be in the classroom with me for a whole hour and a half, and I'd have to act proper and professorial. I couldn't even ask him what sort of fool committed murder in tights and chose to voluntarily plunge into the frozen Nugget to earn the potential confidence of an undergrad. I might very well need a psychiatrist, afterwards.

Doctor, he thinks I dunked him in the river. He thinks I voluntarily swam while dragging him. Mind you, Doctor, my fair swain might be fair and all, but he sure as hell is no lightweight. If I'd planned it, I'd have brought a rope and pulley. And a really large hook.

My arms hurt with remembered strain.

"Doctor Yates?"

"Oh, yes, three o'clock is fine. Ahem, I just want this to be a preliminary interview. I mean . . . I want to interview Doctor Hogg, see how he . . . how we interact, you know?" Hopefully, there would be no reason for them to know I was a professor of English, considering my display of a large vocabulary and smooth usage.

She hesitated audibly. "We still have to charge you for—"

"Oh, of course." Lawyers and psychiatrists, I knew, charged for everything.

Hell, Sherry charged me for time spent on the phone with her, even when she called. It was her belief that just hearing her voice held enough therapeutic benefit to me that I should pay two hundred an hour for it.

I hung up the phone, looked up at the wall clock. Twelve-forty-five. Gathering up my notes into my soft-side leather briefcase, I started toward the classroom.

Only to meet with a very large obstacle on the way.

Large and strangely dressed, in an impeccably cut pea-green jacket and cherry-colored light wool pants. Elderman, Dean of the department of English at Bile stood about five inches taller than I and a good ten inches wider, most of it on the shoulders. With fast-graying light-colored hair and beard, he looked exactly like a Viking who had just visited the more upscale kind of rummage sale. "Yates, I have to talk to you."

I blinked at the green jacket, looked down to find that his shoes, brand-name and expensive, glowed an unearthly burnt orange, looked up again. "What?" I asked.

"I need to talk to you," Elderman said. "In my office."

I cleared my throat and looked toward the door to the little writing lab, where my students gathered, staring eagerly at us. As if they expected us to grow antennae and extra limbs. Or perhaps they just hoped I would wrestle Elderman to the ground and dress him in less offensive clothing.

Brian sat in the front row, his long legs stretched out in front of him, a notebook in his lap, his eyes turned in my direction, looking intent. Perhaps *he* expected me to take an ax out of my pocket and cut the clothing off Elderman.

Daphy appeared behind Elderman, still wiping her tearing eyes with a tissue. From the looks of it, the same long-suffering tissue she'd snatched up in my office.

"Ms. Mallard will substitute for you." Elderman reached back, blindly, and propelled Daphy toward the open classroom door.

Normally, when I called the woman and asked her to take over a class, I had to explain what I'd been doing with the class in excruciating detail and visit at some length exactly what I wanted her to do with it.

Even then, she was as likely as not to tell me that she just didn't understand and to play *poor little me.* But now, under Elderman's influence, she didn't even sniffle. Well, not more than usual.

She glided—as close to a glide as Daphne could make it, considering she walked feet-out like her cousin Daisy Duck—into the classroom and closed the door.

What *did* Elderman do to women? Even the smartest ones, like Joanna, fell for his brand of snake oil. Why? Whatever it was obviously didn't work on males.

I looked up and down his pachyderm-like bulk stuffed into eye stinging clothes and topped by his frowning face with its share of lived-in-lived-a-lot wrinkles. He still wore his hair waist-long as he had in the sixties, even if he tied it behind his back most of the time.

"Now, Yates." Elderman tapped me on the shoulder. "To my office. Follow me."

I followed him. Frankly, given my choice, I'd rather stare at Brian than at Elderman's broad, ungainly back. But hell, this wasn't about my choice, was it?

In Elderman's office—a white-carpeted expanse, large enough to fit my large living room into—he waved me onto one of the woven-leather and metal chairs, while he took his place behind the much-too-large chromium and smoked-glass desk. He flexed his pea-green attired shoulders, took a deep breath and formed his hands into a steeple.

God, please, not the steeple. When Elderman made a steeple with his hands that meant he would wax pompous for at least two hours.

You'd never believe that this was Sherry's mind-expanding partner, if you saw him now. How the man had changed since becoming Dean. Expanded in body if not in mind. Swelled. Like a balloon given too much air.

"Yes?" I asked, taking a deep breath and steeling myself against the onslaught.

It started pianissimo. "Yates, do you realize that the reputation of the school rides on the shoulders of each and every one of its professors, employees and administrators?"

I bit my tongue so I wouldn't say, *Is that what that weight has been all those years? When is it going to start paying a fare?*

Instead, I said, "Elderman, I'm not an idiot." What had he heard? Had he, also, been on the receiving end of an anonymous call about me? What had this one accused me of?

"Really?" he asked. He raised his eyebrows in steep arches toward his hairline. He and the Chief of Police. Were they related? Make a note. Check it out.

There was no point talking to Elderman while he was in this mood. The best thing for it was to let him talk, while you contemplated important realities of life, experimented to see how far you could cross your eyes, saw how many of your knuckles would emit a satisfactory crack, or tried to touch the tip of your nose with your tongue.

While I engaged in experiment number one, Elderman

said, "What do you think Mr. and Mrs. Quick will feel if they see the tape of your performance on TV yesterday?"

I stared. Mrs. Quick? Was Brian married? Would wonders never cease? "Performance?"

"Yes, yes, your clowning and buffooning before the cameras, while obviously hounding a student with who knows what intents." He stared at me, as though he had a clear idea of the intents, even if he didn't, technically, *know* them.

He was way ahead of me.

I stared at him, trying to raise my eyebrows as high as his, feeling incongruously relieved that what he wanted to talk about were misdeeds I remembered and not some nebulous accusation by persons unknown.

"What do you think Brian Quick's parents will think if they see that footage?" Elderman asked. Without waiting for an answer, he went on, "That we, Bile College, are offering up our students to satisfy the perverted lusts of our professors, that's what."

He finished with a flourish and stared at me, all paternal disapproval.

I'd had the original in paternal disapproval and Elderman didn't even scratch the surface. Besides, there was the fact that he didn't accuse me of an ax murder.

Hell, seduction of a student was nothing. I could live with that any day. Even if I hadn't done it. I hadn't done the murder, either. Not that the police would believe *that*.

"I don't see why my lusts—supposing I have more than one at any given moment—are any more perverted than a taste for young girl students, or the wives of fellow professors."

He did a double take. We didn't, either of us, ever allude to Sherry.

"Besides," I said, gratified by the double take. "This is—for crying out loud—the nineties. So I'm gay. Sue me. It's not like I'm in the closet, or at least not so far in that I can't swing the doors wide open for a breath of fresh air. You push me too much and I just might organize a pride parade in Lythia, roust all those students and professors, and maybe a few tourists out of their little airless walk-ins. Get it all over the media, so we become known as a gay-friendly college."

I grinned at him, teeth-only. "Hey, maybe we can start a gay-studies center. You'd like that, wouldn't you?"

He wouldn't. That much became obvious from his scowl, the red rapidly tinting his cheeks.

"Bill," he said, in a hearty, man-to-man voice. He never called me Bill. "All I'm asking is that you keep your hands off those students who are taking classes with you. You might be a special case here in the college, and your father might have donated enough to cover your salary for the next ten years, but certain rules still apply. We don't want it to look like you're abusing a position of trust and confidence. I mean, this boy, Brian, he entered the college last year. I'm not even sure he's legal. You could create some very embarrassing situations for the college . . . I mean, how long have you been seeing him?"

I weighed everything in my mind. Not any of his business how long I'd been seeing Brian. Or anything else.

On the other hand, much as I disliked it, Elderman had theoretical responsibility for and authority over me, professionally.

Why the hell should I get myself fired over something that would happen only in my dreams? My relationship with Brian was above board and about as squeaky clean as it could get. Nothing about the relationship even touched impropriety.

"I went to talk to Brian yesterday," I said. "He'd requested my advice on a personal matter. A personal matter not involving me. Other than that, I've only seen him in class."

Also half-naked, after being fished from the river, but that didn't count. I hadn't really looked at him. Not more than necessary to forever imprint the pattern of his muscles and the texture of his skin in my memory. Nothing Elderman needed to hear about.

"So, you didn't see him—" Elderman stopped, opened his mouth, closed it, cleared his throat.

"This personal matter," he said. "Did it have anything to do with Chris Hogg's murder and their being roommates and all?"

I wondered if he suspected Brian of a relationship with Chris or, alternately, of complicity in Chris's murder.

"It was a personal matter," I said, steadily. I thought of his talk about his multiple sisters and his brother who was a Vatican briefcase. "Having to do with his family and their expectations for him. It in no way concerned the college."

Elderman looked at me out of the corner of a suspicious eye. "That's all you did, advise him on a family matter?"

Well, I'd fished him out of the river. But if I mentioned that, I would have to mention the murder. Which would make Elderman decide that I was a murderer.

I'd also fallen asleep on Brian's table, but I saw no reason to get into that. Elderman might have hunted for elephants in my fridge, but whatever else he'd done with Sherry, I didn't think he'd ever fallen asleep near her. He wouldn't understand.

"That's all I did."

Elderman nodded. For a moment he was quiet. His thick blond brows beetled back and forth, gathering in the middle of his forehead, then spreading out. He steepled his hands again.

I braced.

"I want you to understand, Bill, that you are not above the rules, though. I want you to understand that the appearance of impropriety . . ."

It went on and on and on.

By the time he stopped long enough for me to say, "Thank you, goodbye," I had barely the time to make it to the psychiatrist, and the leather straps that made up the seat of Elderman's chair had formed permanent indentations on my behind.

Running out the door of Byron building, where I taught all my classes, I found myself forcibly halted, my shoulder clutched in a large hand.

"Look, Elderman," I said, whirling around enough to face my captor. It wasn't Elderman. He topped Elderman by a couple of inches, and had green eyes of the sort one could drown in.

"Brian?"

He looked worried. " 'Fessor Yates?"

I nodded. Last I'd checked. Although looking at his eyes made me forget most things, from my mother's maiden name to my birth date, I thought Yates sounded about right. And I was a professor. Almost sure of that.

"Look, I . . . I want you to know. I mean, I don't really suspect you. I mean, I trust you. You're one of the few people I trust." He stopped, blushed. "I just didn't trust myself. I mean . . . staying with you—"

"That's all right," I said. It was more than all right.

Just those words and my heart had already climbed from somewhere near my feet back to its proper position. The power the man had over me. No fool like an old fool. "I have to go, though. I have an appoint—"

He nodded, but didn't let go of my shoulder. "I just wanted you to know that and . . . Look . . . I really need to talk to someone about something, and I don't know whom else I can trust. Would you . . . Can I take you to dinner tonight?"

My heart climbed the rest of the way up and exited, with my brain, through the top of my cranium.

This left me with a happy, vacant expression, and absolutely no idea of where I was, or of anything else. "What?"

"Dinner," he said. "I can't invite you to my place, because I'm staying with Dr. Zimmerman. But I thought we could meet somewhere." He smiled. "Somewhere I can afford. My treat. I want to talk to you."

"Huh . . ." I couldn't think of anything else to say.

When had a man invited me to dinner, last? A nice-looking man, who might, God knew why, have an interest in me?

A nice-looking man who might be an ax-murderer? Well . . . Since when was I that choosy?

"How about the Saloon?" he asked.

The Saloon, one step down from Buffalo's, served fried chicken and beer to students and their dates. A different hangout for me, but what the hell. Live a little. Live a lot.

I grinned madly at him. Definitely not the time to get choosy. "Right."

He let go of my shoulder, patted it, absently. "Six?"

"Six," I agreed, and left Bile, my feet walking so far off the pavement it was a miracle I didn't float away.

X

That's How I Got Cynical

The minute I saw Dr. Hogg's office, I knew he'd committed the murder. He'd killed Elderman. Obvious motive, too. Office envy.

It made so much sense that it took me a few minutes, in the immense reception room with its white carpet and its tiny, battered, gray metal desk, to realize that Elderman hadn't been murdered. Chris Hogg had. Damn. So much the worse. I knew there had been a flaw somewhere.

I approached the receptionist, who, like the office, gave the impression of having seen better days. She was a fine, sculptural blonde with long legs, pale blond hair and the sort of features that say *you touch it, you bought it,* but her hair had a cut-it-myself-at-home look, and her eyes stared out of dark, bruised rings.

"Dr. Yates?" she asked, just a little too eagerly. "Dr. Hogg is anxious to see you."

She sounded a lot like Paul. An awful lot. Now that I looked closer, I could see the same fine tracery of eyebrows, the same high, lofty forehead, the same narrow-bridged nose.

But I couldn't stay and chat and find out how they were related. She stood up and led me, hips swaying just enough to remind me that she had them, into a door lost at the far end, across an expanse of cream carpeting.

Whiter spots on the walls showed where prints must have hung that were now gone. The carpet too, and the building itself, in one of the nice little suburban style office parks just outside Crystal Camp, Lythia's exclusive suburb, all of it spoke of an expensive location, an expensive office. So, why the used desk and the harassed blonde?

She knocked at the heavy mahogany door in the far end, and a voice answered, "Yes?"

"Dad?" she said, then looked like she'd very much like to bite her tongue. "I mean, I mean, Doctor ah . . . um . . . Doctor Yates is here, Doctor Dad, I mean, Hogg Dad. I mean, Doctor Hogg."

The door opened. A middle-aged, suit-clad Paul clutching a pipe in his left hand, glowered at the girl. "Damn it, Trisha. How many times do I need to tell you that in here I am Doctor, not Dad? For that matter, not Doctor Dad, either. You are incompetent."

He pointed the stem of his pipe at her. "You're just like your brother."

She stomped her foot, plastic-looking shoe sinking noiselessly into the high pile carpeting. "I am not like my brother either. I am not a dirty little blackmailer. I would never steal my father's professional files and—" She stopped.

Her eyes grew big. She darted me an alarmed glance, then stared at her father with the look of one expecting doom.

"Patricia Hogg, watch your mouth." Dr. Hogg managed a sideways look at me, and a disapproving little frown that would have made Paul proud.

She looked at me, gave me a frazzled little smile, hysteria pulling her gaze wildly all about the room.

"Well, I'm not," she said primly, turning her back. Almost back to her desk, across the sea of white carpet, she turned to me and said, "At least Dr. Yates can rest assured that his files won't be stolen. Chris is dead, thank God."

"Patricia." He sounded as paternal and reproachful as Elderman.

Untouched, she sat at her desk, opened the top drawer, took out a thick book and sat down with it on her lap.

"Trisha," Dr. Hogg said, almost pleadingly.

She turned back to him. "What? I have a test tomorrow, Dad. I have to study, Doctor Dad. It's not like you're going to support me. And Paul and John wouldn't."

She made a face, returned to the contemplation of her book. "I'm a girl for one. Neither of them, really, has much use for girls."

Dr. Hogg visibly gave it up. His features sagged into disappointment. He looked at me, cleared his throat. "Dr. Yates?" He looked shocked that I hadn't bolted yet.

To be honest, so was I.

Did I need to go through with this? I'd already heard that his files had been stolen by Chris, who had then blackmailed his patients. Probably the reason for the poorhouse furnishings.

Surely enough of a reason for his father to murder him.

Ah, but did his father have an alibi? How could I find out whether or not he did?

I looked at the aged Paul, wondered what he'd think if he knew I'd played tug-of-tonsils with his offspring. I really didn't want to know.

A sane part of me, assuming there remained any sane part in me, insisted that finding the culprit, conducting interviews and what not was Tony's job. Tony's, damn it. Not mine.

But then, Tony thought he had it all sewn up, didn't he? Tony thought *I'd* done it. No question about it. A less-than-charitable part of my mind coiled up and hissed that Tony boy was just jealous because he thought Brian and I were getting some. A wild, cackling part of me replied that I wished. Which was true. I wished.

I wished the murder were solved, Brian and myself safely out of it. I wished it were six o'clock and I were with Brian in the Saloon.

"Dr. Yates?" Byrnum Hogg asked.

I shook my head. "Ah, yes. If you have time, I would like to talk. I mean, I'm conducting an interview for . . . I'm trying to find a therapist and I thought . . ."

He smiled, held his hand out, all smooth manners. "Call me Byrnum," he said. "All this Doctor thing can get pretty old. And you are?"

"Dr. Yates," I said. "I mean, William. William Yates."

His fingers, as white and elongated as Paul's, held mine in a vise-grip for a second.

He stepped out of the way to reveal an office furnished with a frilly white daybed and a small white vanity table that, from the confusion of papers on the top, must be used as a desk. Not what one would expect, but probably brought from the spare room at home when they'd had to sell the original furniture. Only, why were they in so much trouble? Chris? The file-theft? I smelled a motive.

"Please, sit down." He waved me toward the frilly wrought-iron-and-lace day bed, and I sat at a corner of it, looking at him.

He sat at the vanity table, opened the drawer, got out a pouch of tobacco and started filling his pipe with painstaking care. "You must forgive the decor."

He looked earnestly at me, entreating me not to judge the psychiatrist by his furnishings. "We've . . . we've had some financial problems recently and had to bring furniture from home. Nothing to do with the quality of our care, of course."

He waved casually toward the wall, where row upon row of diplomas in neat black frames took up most of the space. Amid them hung the picture of a willowy blonde woman and three smaller pictures: one of Trisha and two seemingly of Paul, which I assumed meant that one was John's.

I nodded. "Yes. I taught your son, Chris."

I thought that Paul hadn't been joking. He'd been literal. His father had thought Chris too homely to be in the family portraits. "Apparently, huh . . . Chris has caused some problems for you."

To my surprise, he shook his head vigorously. "You must not listen to Trisha. She's going through her Electra phase and she resents all her brothers very much, her brother Chris most of all because he is—was—her only full brother."

He crammed more and more tobacco into the already overflowing bowl of his pipe. He pushed his finger hard into the bowl of the pipe, strewing tobacco all over the vanity-desk.

He continued pushing more and more and more tobacco into it, then pushing it all over the desk. "Did you know that in ancient Sparta the father of the family had the choice of accepting or rejecting the infant and if he rejected him, the child was exposed by the side of the road, and it might never live but it didn't matter because it just didn't count?"

The pipe dropped from his hands, rolled from the desk, unattended, fell to the floor and nestled contentedly in the carpet, tobacco strewn between the fibers.

Dr. Hogg's face crumpled, like the face of a very small child who's been sorely disappointed.

"*My* Chris," he said, and gathered up his tobacco pouch in his hands, and held it to his chest. "My baby. I should have accepted him, but now it's too late. Is it too late, William?"

Absalom, my son. My son Absalom. The age-old cry. Would my father have felt like that, if I had died, years ago, in that emergency room? Or would he have said, *good riddance.* I didn't want to know. I leapt up and made for the door. "Ah, yeah. Rather late. For me, that is. I have to go."

Byrnum Hogg nodded, while a thick tear ran down his cheek. He hugged his tobacco pouch.

I closed the door behind me and headed, full-speed ahead, through the reception area.

"He lost it again, didn't he?" Trisha's blasé voice asked. "He really needs therapy, but no one can tell him that."

I turned around, looked at her. "He's very broken up over Chris's death. Understandable, really."

"Understandable, my sore little foot," she said. "Damn it, if I'd thought of it first, I'd have killed him myself."

I took a deep breath, looked at the cheap plastic clock on the wall. A quarter to four. I turned to the girl. She was studying for a test and probably was a student at Bile. But she wasn't my student, and besides, in for a sheep, in for a lamb . . . or was that the other way around? "Ms. Hogg, I don't suppose you'd come have coffee with me?"

She looked me up and down, then up again. "Ah, what the hell." She smiled. "Marriage is a way of escaping this mess, too." To what must have been my look of utter shock, she added, "Yeah, sure, Dr. Yates. I'll go out for a cup of coffee. Or tea. Or me."

I had been trying to avoid that joke.

XI

Sweet Was the Touch of Your Lips

Trisha got in my car, nodding approvingly, as though a gypsy had once told her that she'd marry a man who owned an MG. I hoped not.

In my days I'd raised a few expectations I had no intention of fulfilling, but I hardly thought that inviting someone out for coffee implied a proposal. Or had things changed that much since I'd last gone out with a woman?

Out in the parking lot, I found that the on-again-off-again snow had turned on again. I drove at a snail's pace. I sure was getting an awful lot of training in driving under adverse weather conditions.

She asked, "Where do you want to go?"

I thought about it for a moment. Hangman's seemed safe. Brian had said he didn't like it. "Hangman's."

She did a double take, whispered something that sounded like, "Man who dresses like you . . ."

"Their coffee is good," I hastened to assure her. It was true.

She shrugged.

For the rest of the drive, she kept an admirable silence, abstaining from asking me to name the date or even what china pattern I might prefer.

She'd dressed in a bright red plastic raincoat with a

hood. Her little face peered out from amid the splash of color, looking even more drained and tired. Red Riding in search of any well-dressed wolf.

In Hangman's for once full parking lot, I found a spot near the entrance, escorted the fair Trisha through the door and waited for hi-my-name-is-Bob, an anorectic looking brunette, to find us a table. After he'd wiped it with a greasy gray rag of unknown provenance, and grimaced at our order for coffee-that-will-be-all, he left us to our own devices.

"So, you want to know about Chris for a reason?" she asked, undoing the snaps on her raincoat and pulling it off. "Or is it just morbid curiosity?"

I hadn't realized that my intentions were glass-fronted, and I'd never thought of an excuse for being interested in Chris's murder.

It seemed somehow gauche to say, *Look, the police guy thinks I've done him in, probably because he thinks I've got into his friend's pants, which I haven't but would like to. The pants, not the murder. So I need to clear my reputation, prove I wasn't in on the murder so I can get into said pants. Got it?*

While I tried to think of a tasteful way to express those ideas, my mind, out of touch with the incredibly panicked rest of me, worked smoothly behind the scenes.

I heard myself say, "Well, you see, as a professor I need to publish . . . You know how it goes. True crime books are a good way to get published these days and still keep me teaching Creative Writing. While if I try to break into fiction, it will take me forever. So, I thought with Chris being my student for four years and all, I had a good angle on it, and could probably sell it to the publishers."

I don't think she heard the end of the last sentence. When I said Chris had been my student for four years, her eyes got very wide and she grimaced, just like Paul. "You poor thing," she said. "Four years? You know what, you should have got mental hazard pay."

"I didn't," I said. "So, what you said about Chris stealing your father's files . . . and blackmailing clients?"

"He did." She nodded.

"Do you know this? Have proof?"

She frowned. "I knew Chris. He had access to the files. He worked in the office for a summer. We never heard anything about blackmail until he worked in the office, and then all of a sudden all our clients were being blackmailed . . . you figure it. Not that I was working in the office then. Dad had a real receptionist. But then Chris convinced him that his receptionist was the blackmailer."

She made a face. "That little twerp. I got recruited into working for free. I could have . . . done something nasty to Chris." She looked pensive. "Though maybe not with an ax. That's gross."

Ditto, I thought, as the waiter brought us our coffees. Trisha drank hers plain and black, always a bad sign.

My mind went on: Trisha didn't have proof that Chris had been the blackmailer or the thief of files, and as far as her motives for wanting him dead, they seemed downright trivial. But if he really had blackmailed people, then you'd have a lot of suspects with a lot of motive, and Tony would have to pay attention to them instead of me, wouldn't he?

"Of course he was blackmailing people," Trisha said, as though reading my mind. "How else would he have a million in his bank account?"

"What?"

She looked cool and composed, folding her paper napkin into a tiny triangle. "He had a million in his bank account."

"How on Earth do you know that?"

She smiled. "A friend of mine works at the bank. He told me."

Ah. Cherchez the friend. Still, the mind boggled. If Chris had a million dollars, then he *had* to have blackmailed people or done something illegal, at any rate. That opened up a new and completely different field of speculation about who might have killed him. Would this be enough to get Tony thinking in other directions? Or should I find out more? Who had Chris blackmailed? Over what?

"Do you know whom he blackmailed?"

She looked skittish. "I couldn't tell you that. Not if you're going to put it in a book. I mean, libel and all that. You have to remember none of these people actually admitted—"

" 'Fessor Yates?"

I knew that voice much too well. Looking up, I stared right at Brian's flushed face.

He stared at me, his expression inexplicably wounded and worried, then he frowned at Trisha, looked back at me.

"I thought *we* were going out to dinner," he said, just like a kid denied a treat.

"Ah . . ." I looked at my watch. "That would be in two hours."

He looked at his own watch, a chunky piece of metal on his broad wrist. "Oh. But—" He looked at Trisha again.

I was forgetting my manners. "Brian Quick, this is Patricia Hogg. Chris's sister. Trisha, Brian was Chris's roommate."

Trisha gave Brian the cool appraising look, with appropriate stops at all the points of interest to tourism, and, at long last, decided to smile and extend a hand to him.

"Hi, Brian. My sentiments. About having to put up with Chris, I mean."

Brian nodded and managed a little smile.

He looked back at me. "You won't forget? Tonight?"

Trisha pulled her hand from his.

Why did he look so anxious? I wouldn't forget it short of a complete lobotomy. "Of course not," I told him. "The Saloon."

He nodded, but still didn't look reassured. "I'll see you then." He turned to go.

Which is when I said one of the most stupid things in my life, to wit, "Do you want a ride?"

He turned back, already five tables away, gave me a big grin and shouted, "Nah. I'm on Bucephallus."

And with that, he walked away, leaving me to ponder where exactly I'd intended to stow him in the two-seater, had he accepted my invitation. The fair Trisha took up one seat, I took the other. That left . . . My lap? Nice thought, but it might be hard to drive like that.

Trisha looked nonplused. "He rides Alexander the Great's horse?" she asked, amused.

A woman with a brain. I stared.

"I'm a history major." She smiled. "He's not, is he?"

I shook my head. "Don't think so. At least, he has two literature courses." I watched as Brian—his head visible above all surrounding people—made it to the door and out.

She bit the corner of her lip, in concentration, as she, too, watched Brian's exit. "Too, too bad. Although it explains why I didn't see him before. I mean, if I'd missed that, I ought to have my eyes examined."

I nodded, in agreement, and found her staring at me.

"You two know each other well?" she asked.

"He's my student."

She raised her eyebrows. "*You*'re having dinner with *him?*"

I cleared my throat, remembering Elderman and his *responsibility to the college* speech. An advantage of having grown up with my father was that it had made me a pretty good liar, at least where my feelings and friendships were concerned. "He's having problems with his writing, and I'm helping him, that's all."

She made a little moue with her pink lips. "Not like the tutoring that Dr. Elderman is giving Tiffany, I hope." She looked at me, an eyebrow arched higher than the other. "Nah. You wouldn't."

Not sure what I would or wouldn't do, I smiled, asked her if she wanted more coffee. She had one more cup and our conversation turned to Tudor England. To my surprise, I found the girl really did have a brain. A real one, not just put on for occasions. She had a decent memory too. I felt reluctantly impressed.

"You seem smarter than your brothers," I said.

She looked at me. "Than Chris? That wouldn't be hard."

"And Paul," I said.

"Oh, you know the boy with his pants on fire, do you?" She grinned at me, shrugged. "Don't let him fool you. Paul is smart. He's also talented. In his work, I mean. But he has plenty of brains and quite a bit of low cunning, too. Where did you meet him?"

"Brian knows him," I said. It was the first thing that crossed my mind. I couldn't quite tell the woman who fancied herself my fiancée that I'd met her brother at a gay bar.

Her eyebrow rose, by itself again. "Damn." She looked toward the door Brian had used to leave Hangman's. "I should have known," she said to herself. "All the best looking ones are."

I could have told her otherwise, but that would have involved a long dissertation into how I knew. Perhaps it was just that what you couldn't have always looked better.

"Well, beware, Doctor," she said, with a little, sad smile. "If you see more of Paul, remember that's he's never let either morals or law stand in the way of what he wants."

That last dubious pronouncement was the last mention of her family.

While I wondered if Paul's wanting Brian could have caused him to call the police and accuse me of murder, she changed the subject.

When my mind caught up with her talk, she was smoothly discussing the wives of Henry the VIII and the sociological implications of Queen Elizabeth's putative virginity.

I drove her home, to an apartment not far from Brian's purple house.

The storm had stopped, and the air was bitterly cold but clear under a lowering gray sky.

I got out of the car, opened the passenger door for her.

"You know," she said, looking up at me. "If you kissed me, I wouldn't fight."

"Yes, but it's dangerous to kiss women who are looking for husbands when you're not fully over your own divorce."

She blinked. "Ah. That bad, eh? Well, when you're over it, look me up, Professor Yates. I like the way you talk." She gave me the up-and-down thing, grinned. "The way you look isn't bad at all either. . . . at all, at all."

I nodded, feeling myself blush. Poor girl. I hoped her father's health insurance still covered eye exams.

Getting in the car, I headed for the Saloon under a renewed snowfall.

The Saloon was close enough to student housing that, though the cars in the parking lot could always be counted on the fingers of one hand, the place never emptied.

As I got out of my car, I heard noise from inside. Someone singing what sounded like a drinking song, a lot of loud voices. Arguments and laughter, jokes and poems.

I felt a sudden nostalgic ache for the student life I'd never lived. A dark, dank, B-movie horror quality had tinged my undergraduate years and Sherry and our complex, bizarre relationship, had tainted my graduate time. Not exactly the thing golden memories are made of.

Hesitating by the double glass doors, I read the signs scrawled on them in orange crayon—Happy hour nine to nine; Open three a.m. to midnight; Today's special Deep Fried Cod, all you can eat $1.99.

At the sound of a loud, spluttering motor behind me, I turned in time to see a motorcycle enter the parking lot, half airborne on the speed bumps, seemingly impervious to the patches of ice and snow.

Though Brian wore a polished egg-plant-colored helmet, I knew it was him, even before he parked the red Honda and stood up, removing his helmet.

"Professor Yates?" he said, looking at me.

Well, I did have snow all over my head and shoulders. Besides, the man would never fully recognize me without tights and a rakish moustache-eyebrow.

I shook my head to clear the snow. "Amazing how you don't slide on that thing," I said. "What exactly do you feed Bucephallus?"

"Pardon?" He stole a look back at his bike, smiled. "Oh. Whatever I can afford." He'd parked next to the MG and now he walked toward me, removing his heavy leather gloves and stuffing them in his pockets. "You'd be amazed how much money and time it takes to keep the thing going."

I appraised him, coolly. Why did I fall for men who had a death wish? "I suppose the accidents run pretty high, too, just in medical bills." Try as I might, I couldn't remember any scars in the long, muscular body. I must be slipping.

He looked puzzled. "What?"

"Accidents," I said, pushing the door open and stepping into the small, warm lobby. "The way you ride."

He chuckled. "You're as bad as my brothers. I don't have accidents. Iggy says I must give my guardian angel white hair."

Brothers? More than one. Wait. He'd said five sisters. Did this mean he had more than the one brother who was a Vatican briefcase? I looked at him, as he told the waitress that we wanted a table for two. His roommate had been murdered. Perhaps his family also didn't approve of his roommate.

"Brothers?"

He grinned. "Eight brothers." His gaze lingered on me, curious and amused, as though he couldn't wait to see how I took it.

Oh my, what was I getting into?

Ahem . . . what made me think I'd be getting into anything, anyway? Megalomania.

The waitress—Tiff, the skinny, frazzled-looking girl with a bad home perm on her stringy black hair who had asked about getting into Creative Writing—led us to a table, well ahead of the long line still waiting by the *It Will Be Our Pleasure To Seat You* sign.

As she sat us down at a table fortunately well away from most other diners, I met her gaze. "By the way," I said. "When will you be coming into Creative Writing?"

I don't know why I did it, except to prove to myself that I took an interest in all my students, even those that weren't blond, green eyed and interestingly male.

Tiff looked completely dazed for a moment, as though not sure what I was talking about and then she shook her head. "No. Since Brian isn't and there is . . ." She hesitated.

I waited for her to finish, secretly thanking my lucky starts she'd changed her mind. Her English seemed to be well below the level of even my students.

Brian jumped in. "Of course," he said, directed at her and in the tone of voice that indicated he understood everything perfectly. "Of course, you wouldn't be getting into any more classes just now. Will there be any problems—I mean with the baby and all?"

Baby? Tiff was pregnant? Well, it explained the belly. But, wait, why was Brian so concerned about potential problems with the pregnancy? Was this—?

I refused to think it. Looking up, I saw Brian looking at Tiff with an angel-of-mercy expression. At least, it was definitely not a romantic look.

The girl looked puzzled at his question—perhaps she looked puzzled at every question—then shook her head. "No. No. The baby and I will be . . . we're taken care of. Of course, it was a shock and all."

A shock? Hadn't anyone explained to the girl where babies came from?

Meanwhile, Brian was making vaguely comforting noises. He patted her hand a couple of times.

She looked embarrassed, as if she didn't like receiving the attention. I wondered why. I'd take attention from Brian.

Tiff took drink orders, beer for me, iced water for Brian. Belatedly, it occurred to me that I was his guest and might be straining his budget. Which would account for the intent frown with which he looked at the tabletop.

"I'm sorry," I said. "I'll pay for the drinks, how's that?"

He looked up. "What? No." He shook his head. "No. I invited you. I'm just worried. About something else. I mean, Tiff and all, you know?"

I didn't know, but I was afraid to ask. What would I do if he told me he had fathered the baby? And why would it matter?

Well, okay, I liked to think that he would have better taste, but still it was none of my business.

Brian looked over his shoulder at the waitress as she brought us our drinks precariously balanced in a much too large tray. "But I say we order first, how's that?"

Tiff set the drinks in front of us, water in front of me, beer in front of Brian. Probably according to her ideas of what middle-aged professors should drink.

Brian's long fingers exchanged our glasses, even while he, seemingly absent minded, ordered the cod special.

I opened the menu to the breakfast page as it chanced. Which was fine, because the breakfast special ran only $1.99, and I didn't want to order something more expensive than what my host had ordered.

On the other hand, I shuddered at the thought of deep-fried cod. Golly, Gee, whiz, I must make it a point of being taken out to dinner by guys with a little more money. Right, Bill. How long has it been, six, seven years? Or is it ten? You're going to complain?

"The breakfast special," I said. "Bacon, no sausage. Eggs over easy."

"Grits or oatmeal?" Tiff popped a chewing gum bubble after the question.

"Grits."

She looked shocked. Servers usually did. You can't have

a Boston accent and order grits without getting the startled look. But, what the hell, I liked the stuff. All the fault of Walter Jones, a long-lost friend and occasional lover from my college days.

"Toast," I said, forestalling her next question. "*Not* biscuits." One could take the cross-ethnic thing too far.

She nodded, scrawling it all down, laboriously, in her little green notebook.

As she walked away, I found Brian looking intently at me. "Grits?" He mouthed soundlessly.

Embarrassed, I started removing my jacket, shaking the snow off it, while I answered absently. How long had it been since I'd thought of Walter? He'd been a part of the whole scene with Lupi and I'd tried to forget him as much as the rest of it. Though perhaps he didn't deserve it.

More importantly, how could I expect to ever get anywhere with Brian if, as soon as he started looking at me that intently, I had to look away? "An old friend-slash-lover liked them and I'm afraid I acquired the taste. He was from Georgia."

I hung my jacket from my chair, looked up to find Brian sporting a smile that would have made old Mona Lisa green with envy. "He?"

"Walter Jones. We went to college together. He was journalism major and he—" I stopped.

Oops. Cat out of the bag, meowing ferociously.

Well, it had to get out sometime, hadn't it? Hard to seduce the man without letting him know my interests lay in that general area, wasn't it? But did I want to seduce him?

He was my student, damn it, and so painfully young. Besides there was the murder. What would Tony do if he found me involved with Brian? What would he think? Would he think I *had* killed Chris in a jealous rage?

I blinked, to give myself time, while my thoughts galloped in all directions at once.

Brian's smile could have intrigued a cryptologist.

The waitress dropped our plates in front of us, from about a foot above the table.

I gathered bacon back to its proper place, and stared at the wobbling mound of grits. Just when you thought you were safe, you'd be betrayed by the most ridiculous thing. I had been trying to be virtuous. Virtuous, damn it. Virtuous and paternal, and keeping Responsibility with a capital R in its proper place.

I looked up. If eyes could laugh, Brian's were doing it. He picked up a fry and nibbled it, managing to smile at the same time, even though his face still creased in worry.

"So, how come we got seated ahead of all those people?" I asked, because it happened to be the first thing that crossed my mind.

He frowned. Not what I'd intended, and a little puzzling, but not bad. "Because I know Tiff," he said. "She used to . . . She went out with Chris. Although to tell you the truth I'd forgotten she worked here, otherwise—But she's harmless, anyway. I can't believe . . ." He shook his head. "No. There are people you can't suspect."

Oh, so that's how it was, was it? *Ms. frazzled hair* had some hold on *Mr. I'm not sure of my orientation.* Perhaps he was the father of her baby. I sought out the girl with my gaze. She stood by the order counter talking to a young man within. Her legs had no shape at all. She wore clogs. As she turned and headed for some tables on the other side of the restaurant, I saw that she sported a mess o' crystal pendants around her neck. I looked back at Brian, resentfully. How could he?

He didn't see my look. He stared at the waitress too, as

he removed his jacket, and reached into the duct-taped area for something. He pulled out a yellow manila envelope, pushed it across the table at me. "This was in the gas tank of my bike," he said. "Carefully rolled inside a length of pipe and taped inside a plastic bag."

While he kept an eye on the waitress—possibly watching for the development of some discernable secondary sex characteristics, like maybe breasts—I opened the envelope and pulled out a few pages. Written in green ink, in a spidery hand.

Chris's handwriting. Notes copied from something else, I decided. Looking through a few sample sentences, I realized several things. The notes were coded to the same cryptic combinations of numbers and letters I'd seen in the little black book.

If I remembered the numbers correctly, from the number he'd given her, Not only was Mrs. Murphy in Chris's book, my Mrs. Murphy, but Mrs. Murphy was also a kleptomaniac and Chris had proof. Days, dates, names, incidents, etc., all had been carefully noted in a hand tinier than I'd known Chris could ever write.

I looked up at Brian.

He'd stopped looking at the waitress, stared at me. "There's pictures, too. Here." Reaching into the envelope, he brought out a tiny bunch of negative-sized pictures, about the size that would go into a key-chain.

He pushed one at me. Paul Hogg, coming out of Bad Boys, with someone. Someone who had his back turned and unless you knew his clothes, you'd never identify.

I made a note to throw away that pullover. All I needed was for Tony to find it and he'd decide I'd killed Chris to stop him from blackmailing Paul.

Brian handed me the bunch of tiny pictures. I shuffled

through them, stopped on one, blinked. I didn't even know that Joanna owned any black leather outfits, much less whips and thigh-high boots.

And there was Mr. Fielding, the Classical Literature professor. I didn't think the blonde on his lap was his daughter. Much too young for that. And our mayor, surely he didn't frequent that area of town. What was the hastily wrapped package the young man with the dread locks was handing off to him, anyway?

Elephants in the fridge where you least expected them.

I shoved all the pictures back into the envelope, then the cards. One of the cards fell out. I couldn't remember the numbers exactly, but I'd sworn that it was Joanna's. Apparently, she'd financed her degree by working for a discreet call-service catering to gentlemen who liked it rough and definitely tumble. I shoved the card in with the others, closed the envelope, feeling vaguely queasy, as if I'd peered down a gutter. Not because I'd found out what Joanna had done for the rent, but because I had no right to know. Joanna would be shocked to know I'd found out. I was shocked.

I pushed the envelope away. Brian got it, put it inside his jacket, zipped his jacket again.

I attacked the grits with a vengeance, trying to think away from that lurid stuff. I could understand Chris's knowing too much, if he'd raided his father's files for information. But how the hell had he gotten pictures? The mind boggled.

"I didn't look at all of them," Brian said. "I don't have the little black book any longer, but I can see what this means. Anyone could see what this means." He speared a shapeless hunk of fish over and over again with his fork, until he had reduced it to little white shreds. "Chris was a blackmailer. And, when he felt threatened, he hid his files in my stuff. Can you believe it?"

"No," I said honestly. "I'd never expect him to be that mentally alert."

But Brian didn't look like he'd laugh at anything. "What I want to know is what should I do? Can you help me?"

"What you should do is turn the stuff over to your friend Tony."

I nibbled on a piece of bacon, starting at one end and methodically making my way to the other end. Crispy but not burned. I'd forgotten what bacon tasted like outside Hangman's. Of course, Hangman's had a sparser clientele.

I looked around at the waves of swirling, scantily clad student bodies. The clientele Hangman's did have didn't make me feel like an old fossil.

"Much as I hate to tell you that, this is a job for the police." He should turn the stuff in to Tony, and then I'd be home free, and then . . . and then I could pursue the subject of Brian at my leisure.

He picked up another fry and ate it.

"Yeah," he said. "But I can't do *that.*"

He picked a picture out of the mass of others, pushed it at me, flipped through the notes for a page, set it on the table where I could read it.

The notations weren't even assigned a number, just my name. It said I was gay and promiscuous and that he expected to extract a passing grade from me, based on this information. The picture boggled the mind. Paul wasn't in it, and it showed a lot more than just my back. One of those times my mind had lost the battle with my body. But the place had been dark. How had Chris got this? Had the good-looking stranger been wired?

I looked up. I felt my cheeks heat. So, the gaffe about

the grits had just confirmed Brian's suspicions. Had he known this all along? No. He'd just found the pictures.

I took a deep breath. "Brian, my boss knows I'm gay. Most people probably know. I just don't make a big deal out of it. It's my private life. No one can blackmail me based on that. I'd have told Chris to publish and be damned."

Brian nodded. "I figured," he said. "But, don't you see, now that Chris is dead, Tony might not see it that way. He already has a bee in his bonnet about your alibi. This morning he called and asked me how well I knew you, and if I thought you might have killed Chris in a jealous fit. So . . ."

So I could read the policeman's mind. Great, just great.

"Besides there are the other victims," Brian said. "Tony is so officious. Wouldn't it disturb them to be interrogated by him? What if none of them had anything to do with Chris's death? Would it be fair to them?"

Fair wasn't the point. Fair wouldn't keep me out of jail.

I looked at Brian. He knew about me. And yet, he'd invited me to dinner and he was adamant about not turning me in.

Or was he protecting someone else? He was living with Joanna, wasn't he, these days? And Joanna . . . I thought of the picture. Well, she was head and shoulders above little frizzy-haired Tiff, who now bent over the table to fill our water glasses.

"Are you still staying with Dr. Zimmerman?" I asked.

Brian looked surprised, as though I'd just asked him what his favorite football team happened to be. "Yeah," he said. "I should be able to get my place back in a week or so, Tony says. But I'm not sure I should move back."

I nodded to Tiff, indicating that I'd also like a refill on

the beer and she sauntered off, to come back with a sweating glass of amber liquid.

"I understand," I said. "It can be dangerous, I mean, until you know who killed Chris."

Tiff put the glass in front of me and I took a sip.

"Oh, that's not it." Brian waved the suggestion that he might be prudent away with an impatient hand. "The problem is, Joa—Dr. Zimmerman seems to be afraid of something, and she wants me to be home all the time she is. It's strange. I think she must have seen another murder like this or something in the past, because she keeps talking about Chris getting murdered, and then she'll shudder all over, and she starts talking about car theft and borrowing people's cars . . . It doesn't make a heck of a lot of sense but—"

He gulped his water down, at a draught, and Tiff, who stood by the table, refilled it, politely. "I just don't feel I should leave her alone, although to be honest, I think she should get counseling."

She probably had, I thought. She probably knew that had been the beginning of her troubles. "Did you look at all the cards and pictures?" I asked Brian.

He shook his head, shrugged. "No. I sort of skimmed. It felt grimy enough. As though I should bathe immediately after. I wouldn't even have mentioned the picture, you know, to you, if it weren't for the fact that I knew we couldn't give them to Tony, and I had to get you to understand. But I just chanced to see it. I didn't like stare at each of them, or anything. I know we could remove yours and give the others to Tony but . . . you know, there might be other copies and that would get us in more trouble."

Well, yes. But if he hadn't looked at them all, there were good odds he hadn't seen Dr. Zimmerman's file. If he hadn't, he wouldn't have any idea what was affecting her. "So, what do you plan on doing?" I asked. "If you don't take this to the police?"

"I don't know," he said. He took another fry and ate it with determination. "I thought maybe if you'd help me, we could investigate them . . . some of them, find out what they're all about, and then maybe, maybe, we'd have an idea of who . . . who might have done it and you could . . . you could be free. *We* could be free of this whole nightmare."

The man lived just like he rode a motorcycle. Dangerously. Didn't he even consider I might be in league with a mass murderer? However unlikely, didn't he think it possible? Didn't he realize the dangers? I smiled at him. "In real life amateur detectives are called the next victim."

"Oh, I didn't mean to be blatant about checking these people," he said. "Just some discreet enquiries about where they were on the night of the murder."

"Brian, you'd need their names. I don't know about you, but most people in those pictures are total unknowns to me."

He nodded. "Yeah, I know. First we need to find the black book."

"You mean, the book taken by the person who searched your house and who is, presumably, a murderer? Do you have any other adventures planned for us? Perhaps we could scale Olympus and steal the fire of the gods?"

His smile twisted. "We could. But let's wait till next week. My calendar is full right now." He grinned. "Aw, come on, live a little."

I sighed. This was insane. I knew it was insane. Still . . . walking into Tony's office and handing myself in, bound hand and foot, struck me as even crazier. "All right. Let's look at this rationally. Any idea where this little book might be?"

"None." He smiled. "So, can I come by your office tomorrow, during office hours, and we can discuss where to start?"

My office was a spectacularly bad place to *start* anything. I wondered what Daphy would make of Brian.

I wondered if Brian planned to get me into a position where he could accuse me of impropriety. No. I really didn't think so.

Yet I'd feel safer in my own place. More risky as to how far the impropriety could go, maybe, but at least people would have to know he'd gone there of his own accord. It wouldn't be like in the office, where he could claim he had just come in to ask me a question and I'd pounced on him.

Tiff refilled Brian's glass. I'd never seen a more attentive drink server, and the sting of ridiculous jealousy made my voice more decisive as I said, "My house. Tomorrow. After your classes. When do you get out?"

He looked up, pensive. "Five o'clock, but—"

"I'll cook," I said.

"You *can* cook?" His eyes rounded, big and green and for a moment I thought he was going to add, under his breath *a man who dresses like you?*

"I used to do all the cooking while I was married." I waved my hand dismissively. "It was beneath Sherry. But I hate to cook for one person, so I don't."

He tilted his head to one side. "Won't Walter object?" he asked. "To my coming over?"

It took me a second to figure out what the hell he was talking about. I thought I'd made it clear enough Walter was history and that I lived alone. Maybe the man *was* careful about *some* things. Too careful.

"I haven't heard of him for over twelve years," I told Brian. To his sly expression, I added, "It wasn't the stuff dreams are made of. We parted in an emergency room. Don't go assuming anything, all right?"

He looked properly chastised. At least if one ignored the little smile.

I ignored the little smile. "Tomorrow at five."

"There's some names we know," he said. "From the black book. John and Paul Hogg." He looked up at me, calmly evaluating.

I wondered what game he was playing. Seeing if I'd defend Paul? Had he recognized the picture?

So I held my face impassive. "That's true. Do you have any idea how to investigate them?"

Brian shrugged. "I've met Paul, but not John. I think John lives in Denver. I could try to talk to Paul . . ."

Was this where I told him that, thank you so much, I could talk to Paul myself? Was that what he was waiting for? Which one would be better? To talk or to keep quiet?

I kept quiet. It came naturally.

Tiff refilled our glasses.

Brian's Mona Lisa smile enlarged, and he nodded to himself, as though in response to something.

We finished our dinner/breakfast in companionable silence, while I tried to figure out what to do. I couldn't take the pictures to the police. Not without getting arrested. But I needed to do something. That, for sure. Something other than attempting to investigate a crime I obviously was not qualified to investigate, and risking very gruesome death befalling me. And Brian.

Tiff waved at us as we left the restaurant and smiled—a smile probably helped along by the generous tip I'd left her.

Outside, snow had stopped again. In the cool, clear

moonlight, I paused by my car, to say, "Five o'clock."

To my shock, I found myself with an armful of blond, his lips pressed against mine.

There had to be a local obsession with my tonsils, I thought before I stopped thinking at all.

"Brian?"

We sprang apart.

Somehow—and to this day I can't understand it—a car had driven into the parking lot and stopped right beside us.

Joanna Zimmerman's worried face peeked at us, out the window. "It is you," she said. "I'm glad you're all right. I was so worried, sitting alone in the house." Her voice shook.

"Hi, Joanna," I said.

"Oh." She smiled at me. "Hi, Bill." As though she hadn't noticed me before.

Now, granted, Brian was taller than I by almost a head but, damn it, we'd been *wrapped* in each other. She had to have noticed the extra arms and legs, right?

I glanced at the windows of the Saloon, to make sure no faces were pressed against the glass, that no one had watched our performance. But since the windows on that side were equipped with mini-blinds, I didn't see anyone. Which was good.

Brian had bent to speak into the rolled-down window of Joanna's battered VW Beetle.

"Don't forget," I told him, and got into my own car. "Tomorrow."

What had I thought I was doing? I asked myself, as I started off. What on Earth did I think? That I could carry on with Brian right there in the parking lot? What would Joanna think? What would she tell? To whom? Elderman would hear about this, for sure. After all, Joanna slept with him.

Feeling like a complete idiot, but a complete idiot still buzzing with electricity from Brian's kiss, I drove home to Lockmaster.

XII

You Have a Certain Way of Flirting

At home, standing in front of my bathroom mirror, I wondered whether I should brush my teeth or leave them as they were.

Then I wondered what was wrong with me.

I *had* been kissed before, brushed my teeth afterwards, lived to tell the tale.

In my green pajamas, looking like middle-aged death warmed over, I appeared adult enough to be able to think about relationships rationally.

So, Brian had kissed me. Brian, whose roommate had been murdered. Brian, whom persons unknown had accused me of killing. Why couldn't I just brush my teeth and be done with it?

Because, Brian had kissed me, and I imagined that I could still taste his mouth on mine.

So why would deep-fried cod be any better secondhand?

At long last, feeling ridiculous and old, I brushed my teeth like a good little boy, combed my hair and got in bed.

To no avail.

The mattress on which I'd slept for much too long had been chosen by my father, according to his ideas of healthy living. If felt like a rock, only not as soft. My sheets, shroud-like, encircled me with my every movement. My blankets made me too hot, but without them I shivered in the cold.

I had a class to teach in the morning and should long ago have fallen asleep.

My mind dredged up the picture of me and Paul, the one that showed only my shoulders. And then the other picture, the one that would be easily identified. From the dark caverns of my psyche came the fear that the police would find out about them before they found Chris Hogg's real killer.

I should never have allowed my lifestyle to be kept so painfully secret. Although Chris would never have been able to blackmail me on this, who would believe it?

I'd kept my Bad Boys forays secret. I'd been married. I had, just the afternoon past, taken a woman out for coffee. Who would believe I wasn't in the closet? Who would believe I wouldn't kill to stay in there?

How come Brian didn't believe it? What did Brian know? Did he know who'd done it? But if he did, if he were an accomplice in Chris's murder, then why show me the pictures, why tell me he'd found them? To buy my silence? To threaten me into keeping to myself what I knew about Chris and blackmail?

My mind worried over the binds that my desire for privacy had wrought.

My heart searched the convoluted path of my feelings for Brian. I couldn't believe him guilty of murder, or of complicity, no matter how much I thought it over. There was always the fact that no one in his right mind would get himself thrown in the Nugget during a flood on a freezing night, while wearing nothing but his underwear. Besides, he'd kissed me. He'd kissed me. I mulled over that one fact, impossible yet undeniable.

I got up, made myself some strong coffee, on the principle that if homeopathy worked and I just had strong enough coffee, my body would counteract it by making me fall asleep. Though this method always worked before finals in college, now it only wound me up further. Great time to acquire a normal metabolism.

I paced the living room, took a second shower.

With my hair still dripping wet and a towel around my waist, I went to the phone, looked up Joanna's phone number.

Noticing what I was doing, I slammed the phone-off button.

I was not going to call Brian. Even that kiss should never have happened.

Troglodyte Bill emerged from the primeval muck of my back brain, looked at me out of red pinpoint eyes and asked why, if I could get the blond, I'd give him up?

Because he was my student.

Oh, so, I could get myself fired and have to live off my father's legacy. All right. My pride might be hurt with having to live off my father's inheritance, but exactly how bad was that, anyway? No more early morning classes, no more stupid students, no more Elderman.

Yet I liked teaching and the classes. Even the early morning ones had given me a role in life and a reason to go on all these years.

What if I chose Brian over the job and Brian didn't want me? What would I have then?

What if Brian, against all reason, really was involved in this murder? In my experience, people had done considerably weirder things than arrange to be thrown into a river in their underwear in the middle of the winter. Usually on some sort of sexual kick.

What if he wasn't involved but the Chief of Police

thought *I* was? What if I was headed straight for jail? Would this be a time to get involved with a young student? What could I do for him if I landed in jail? Give him the joy of corresponding with a death-row convict?

At the risk of wearing a circular rut in the carpet, I paced, until I threw myself on the huge leather sofa and tried to divert my thoughts to more rational channels.

There were plenty of them. The blackmail, for one.

The victims I could identify were odd enough. Mrs. Murphy, I remembered, and doctor Fielding, and the mayor, and Joanna, and Paul? And John? Whatever information compromised Paul and John, it had to be the result of Chris's own investigation efforts. Surely they wouldn't have gone to their own father for psychiatric counseling, would they? Then again, neither had I. Had getting my pictures been a side-benefit of following Paul around?

Did Chris have anything on his own father? That would explain old Byrnum's state of denial. It would also provide an additional motive for him to dispose of his deranged son.

But, how could I find the truth and what could I do about it? Even if all these people were guilty, or all innocent, how would I find out? Brian had said he would help. But how could Brian help, except by muddling my brain with a hormone rush?

I shook my head.

I could think. I could. I could think about things other than Brian, too. Joanna, for instance. Joanna of the dark-red hair, the long shapely legs, the perfect figure. Joanna who'd never seemed happy with anyone.

In her brief, sporadic outings with Sherry and I, she had seemed light-hearted, almost childishly so. For those times, before my marriage fell apart and I'd started avoiding hanging out with Joanna lest I give her ideas, she'd been the sister I'd never had, the childhood playmate, the girl next door, all rolled into one. We'd gone to picnics and movies together, and taken long hikes through the wilderness of Colorado.

She had seemed full of fun and spirit then.

Not now. I remembered how pale she looked, how tired. What was wrong with her? Why didn't she want to be left alone in her own house?

Chris had been blackmailing her. She drove a Beetle.

Into my mind, unbidden, came an image of Joanna dragging Brian out of her car, dropping him into the Nugget. She had talked about car theft . . . But wouldn't she if she'd used her car for a crime? Wouldn't she claim her car had been stolen? And she'd been afraid all the time. A guilty conscience would do that.

I closed my eyes tight, tried to see no evil. But my mind still showed me the image, with unforgiving clarity.

It was possible. She was a tall woman and from what I remembered, from playful bouts of arm-wrestling, a strong one too.

I sat up on the sofa, shaking.

Brian was living with her. What if she took a fancy, hit him over the head and dropped him into the Nugget in the middle of the night?

She must be a persistent woman full of willpower to have managed to make it through school on a night job of the personal, up-close kind.

But would Joanna have hurt Brian? I remembered the way she talked to him, the way she looked at him. As if he were her protector, and at the same time as though she had been worried *for* him. Joanna wouldn't have dropped him from that bridge.

Besides, if I remembered the figure I'd seen; if I hadn't

been dreaming or too drunk to see things properly, then the person who'd dropped Brian over the edge had long *pale* hair.

Joanna's hair couldn't have looked pale. It was dark red.

On the other hand, it was shiny. Light reflecting on it could make it look pale. What if Joanna's current neurosis was no more than a symptom of remorse? If she had attacked Brian while in a panic, she might regret it, try to make it up to him by keeping him safe and with her at all times.

I lay back down on the sofa.

But then, who the hell could it be? How could we find out who it was? The two of us, Brian and I, with no resources and no training? How could I keep the blond safe if he wouldn't call the authorities? I'd have to call the authorities, I realized. I'd have to call Police-Napoleon-Chief-Tony-Apollo-Marssano and tell him what Brian had found and why it was important. First thing in the morning.

Surely, if I called him, he wouldn't believe that I'd killed Chris. If I handed the picture to him myself, surely he wouldn't think that I'd been blackmailed over it.

I fell asleep and dreamed about an endless stream of people coming through the door of the purple house, each carrying his/her own ax and taking yet one more whack at Chris, *Murder on the Orient Express* style.

I woke up with my neck bent at an odd angle, my feet freezing cold, and with the distinct impression that I'd seen or heard something in my dream that would solve the whole puzzle, if only I could remember it.

What I remembered was annoying enough.

Furious as I was about the crick in my neck, less than pleased with my performance the night before, full of doubts about the future, what pissed me off the most was: if

Chris Hogg's murder had been a potluck, why hadn't I been invited? True, torture by essay did not compare to blackmail, but still, I had reason enough for revenge and I would have liked to have a whack. A little toe, perhaps. Maybe an eyebrow.

I realized all too well that this thirst for blood covered up my trembling inside and that I couldn't really hurt anyone, not even Chris.

In the bright light of morn, I wasn't all that hearty about taking the picture to the police, either. Tony would still suspect me. He would think I'd brought the picture in just to impress him with my honesty. It would, paradoxically, make him think me more likely to be guilty.

What had he been doing these twenty-four hours? He hadn't called on me to depose or to be interrogated. That was good, right? Or had he just been trying to tighten the noose fully around my neck before he alarmed me?

On the other hand, what might befall Brian if this thing weren't seen through to the end? Someone had already tried to kill him once.

I showered for the third time in less than eight hours, got dressed in my gray slacks, white shirt and the wine red pullover that made me look distinguished in a slightly decadent way.

I grimaced at the dark rings around my eyes, the pale peaked expression of the insomniac that stared at me out of the mirror.

In the middle of all this, I'd invited Brian over. From the top, again: What kind of an idiot was I? I hadn't asked anyone over, hadn't had a real date in ten years. I'd do it now?

Did I have any real dishes? A look in the cupboard reassured me that, yes, either Sherry had overlooked the

Limoges dishware I'd inherited from my father, or she'd been happy enough with our own set. I also found glasses: good crystal goblets and a set of beer steins.

Dusting my hands on my pants, I grabbed my briefcase and headed for the door.

Mrs. Murphy opened her door a crack, just as I stepped out. An unearthly blue-eye stared at me. With a delicate yelp she shoved the door shut.

I sighed. Couldn't make the damn woman happy. Didn't like me in tights, didn't like me in casual-conservative attire . . . What did she like anyway? Just like a woman. Couldn't live with them and why bother trying?

Something about Mrs. Murphy and Mrs. Murphy's attitude toward me nettled me, like an itch I couldn't scratch, but, like a raveled bit of string, it presented no end I could grab hold of and pursue.

I pushed the button on the elevator with more force than necessary; drove out of Lockmaster's garage in a way that made Brian's motorcycle riding seem tame; fumed into the University's parking lot; stomped out of the car and stormed through the door of the amphitheater barely in time to wake up my Lives II students.

In a nasty mood, furious at everything I couldn't control, I proceeded to interrogate bewildered, half-asleep students about the material we'd covered since the beginning of the year. A strict violation of the SOP that dictated they only cram before tests. They acted appropriately injured and brainless in equal parts.

Brian Quick sneaked in, ten minutes late, keeping close knit to the wall and then bending low as he walked between rows of seats, attempting to reach his normal front-and-center seat sight unseen.

Feeling an odd mix of relief at his being still alive and

visibly whole, and annoyance at his lateness, I glared at him.

Kiss a professor and you can come to class late the next day, right? He thought he could manipulate my feelings and stop my thoughts, did he? He thought it would be easy to befuddle this old fogy. I'd show him. "Mr. Quick?"

He'd been trying to slink half-bent behind the front row. At my words he straightened to his full height. "Doctor Yates?"

"May we know why you are so late this morning?"

He opened his mouth, closed it. His eyebrows knit in puzzled wonder.

Several students tried to mouth warnings at him. I saw a few fingers whirling helpfully near temples, before being pointed at me.

I don't think Brian noticed them. He stood there, staring at me. First he looked mad. Then he blushed. Then that damn Mona Lisa smile crept across his lips. His eyes sparkled with repressed mischief, which eyes were not supposed to do.

"I'm sorry, Professor Yates," he said, all prim and proper if one disregarded the mirth dancing in his gaze. "I had trouble sleeping. Kept dreaming about Shakespeare."

By the time I'd managed to close my mouth, and get my breath back, he'd taken his normal seat, front and center, and looked as though butter wouldn't melt in his mouth.

Innocent, was he? Played me like a fiddle was more like it. He could, too, mess up this old fogy and without physical contact at that.

I recited the lecture by rote, thinking that Brian was coming over in the evening and that no one could hold me to outmoded forms of behavior with a nineteen-year-old whose IQ quite obviously outstripped mine by a few points.

Except Elderman. Elderman could always claim to hold me to anything, outmoded or not. I dismissed the class at the end of the hour, waving them away happily. So, Elderman would fire me. So? Big deal. All right, I'd enjoyed teaching at the college, and it had provided a reason to get up in the morning. But there were other things in life. Oh, yes siree, I thought as, with a smile and an inclination of the head, Brian passed me on the way out.

Hormones solidly in control, the murder had become an insignificant detail in my mind. The danger of my ending up dead or in jail seemed well worth the possible reward.

I closed my briefcase, headed for the door, whistling. Tony *would* find the real murderer, somehow. I'd end up with the blond. We'd live happily for at least a few hours.

Halfway out the door, I found a Viking in my path. "Yates," Elderman said. "We need to talk."

We didn't need to do anything of the kind. But I knew semantics would be fruitless with him. Obediently, like a well-trained puppy, I followed him into his vanilla-and-leather office.

"Sit down, Yates," he barked, while he lowered himself into the armchair behind his desk.

I sat down in one of the cross-strap instruments of torture across from his desk and tried to look impassive.

Part of me felt like singing, *wow, he's going to fire me,* while the other part cringed whimpering, *he's going to fire me, oh no, oh no, oh no.*

In this schizophrenic frame of mind I waited while Elderman fiddled with his white, cylindrical pencil holder, pulled out a slick, aerodynamic pen, worried at it.

"Yates?" he said, again.

"Yes?" I encouraged.

He doodled on a large blotting pad in front of him.

Question for all the bright boys and girls in the class: why have a blotting pad in an age when ballpoint pens were the writing instrument of choice?

Answer: because it established you as a stuffy pedant and Elderman wanted to be perceived as a stuffy pedant. Coming from some insalubrious, undistinguished middle class background, he feared anyone would even suspect his bourgeois origins.

He cleared his throat. "It . . . Someone told me that you and Brian Quick have been seeing each other."

Oh Joanna, why did you tattle on me? Well, I did once think of her as a little sister. Little sisters tattled.

I stared and prompted, "Yes?" waiting for the announcement that Bile would have to, regretfully, part company with my stellar services.

"I'm wondering if perhaps, and this isn't an easy thing for me to admit—" He paused and stared at me, his gray-blue eyes devoid of expression.

Why he took so long to say it, I didn't know. Hadn't he always dreamed of firing me? He'd dressed extra nice for the occasion too. His long straggling gray-blond hair had been tied behind his back in a ponytail, and he wore a yellow-green suit, with a purple tie.

He took a deep breath, filling his huge bulk of chest. "I've been wondering, Bill, if perhaps I'm sensitive enough to minorities." He looked up.

I looked back. Yes? Minorities? Let me see, I thought Bile had, all told, through the years, maybe twenty black alumni, a couple dozen Asians and, being in Colorado, maybe double that in Hispanics.

We did have women, though. God, did we have women. Daddy's daughters sent here mostly because we *weren't* a party college.

But what exactly did that mean for Elderman? Was he intending on instituting an affirmative action admission program? Or was this just some vagary of pseudo-morals before he fired me?

Something along the lines, of, *I know I haven't been perfect, but still, we can't have you seducing undergrads.* It seemed as if the code of the Modern Sensitive Male required that sort of phony empathy.

Only I demanded a recount. If I was going to be kicked out on my ass, I'd want to have done something to deserve it. Something, damn it.

Elderman had held his breath so long, I expected him to turn blue. He pointed his pen at me, gun style, and blurted, "Sexual minorities and all."

Oh, was I that? Oh, goody, white-bread Boston Bill was a minority. Goody, goody, goody. I bit my lip, kept my mouth shut.

"Perhaps, in a small town like Bile, where there can't be many . . . huh . . . alternately gendered people, I can't be too strict about that rule on students not dating professors. I mean, I looked into Brian's file and he's of age and all, and I just wanted to tell you that we've decided to turn a blind eye."

We? Well, with Elderman it was probably the royal we. I cringed at the thought that he might have taken this to the trustees. Would he have?

I wanted to laugh, scream, tell him I was so glad I had his permission to seduce students. I did none of those. I just sat there, and my smile was probably more arch and bizarre than the one Brian had bestowed on me.

"There have been incidents at other colleges," Elderman said. "Suicides and so on, and if Brian should kill himself because he feels isolated, it would be much worse than anything his parents might assume about our school."

I didn't remember any incidents of suicide that could provably be traced to homosexuality but, like everything else, it was no use disputing. I nodded, and endured another half hour of strange Eldermanesque pronouncements.

At his paternal dismissal, I made it through the door, still in time to teach my writing class.

I felt as though I'd walked through a land-mine field and might unwittingly have got one caught on my shoe that could detonate at any minute.

What did Elderman mean by the bizarre lecture? I knew damn well, and he probably knew it just as well, if not better, that his story about exception in fraternization rules for sexual minorities wouldn't fly for a minute.

Not if it ever came down to someone accusing me of an abuse of authority. So, why would he tell me this? Did he intend to engineer my fall? Or was it because Joanna had asked him to go easy on me? Joanna was involved with him.

Or was Brian somehow involved in this? No. I couldn't contemplate that Brian might be in on the plan. True, I had known him, personally, for a very short time. Also true, my taste in men, for any sort of permanent relationship, bordered on the suicidal.

But still—No.

As Brian himself had said, there were people you couldn't suspect. Even if you should.

Afterwards, on my way to lunch, I stopped by my office, to grab a notebook and make a grocery list.

Torn between the need to find Chris's murderer, the wish to impress Brian and the vague, whimpering moral dictate that I not touch a student, I was in a fine mental mess.

To make things more interesting, another blond waited in my office.

He lounged on the hard plastic chair across from my desk, managing to make orange plastic look fashionable.

But despite the languorous pose, with his legs stretched out in front of him, his arm dangling to the floor on one side, when he looked at me, Paul Hogg appeared worried sick.

"Your secretary let me in," he said. "She said you'd be an hour or so." Before I could even think of a reply, he added, "Come have lunch with me. I need to talk to someone."

Jeez. Blonds to the left of me, blonds to the right of me. And here I was, father confessor to the multitudes.

XIII

You Put Me on a Pinnacle and Then You Let Me Down

I won't discuss the conversation that followed, nor how Paul tried to convince me to go to his house for lunch.

I ended up agreeing because what he said was so devoid of the sexual come-on I'd come to associate with Mr. Hogg, internationally famous artist and blond extraordinaire, that I assumed something had to be wrong.

He held his face too taut. His eyes had a haunted look, and dark circles around them spoke of a sleepless night not pleasantly spent. His hands shook when he attempted to gesture daintily.

Maybe he was about to confess to murdering Chris.

Chris had blackmailed him, after all.

I insisted on driving my own car, and he made sure to keep me in sight, as though I didn't know the way, as though I'd never been to his house before.

I parked behind him in the driveway, already having second thoughts. After all, last time I'd been here, he'd gone after my tonsils. What if he used an ax, this time? Worse, what if the Chief of Police saw those pictures at some point and decided that Paul and I had always been in cahoots?

Like a Victorian maiden fearing for my honor, I appraised my potential attacker's strength as he got out of the car, cool and slim in his pale linen suit and half unbuttoned white shirt.

But Paul came only to my shoulder and he was so . . . dainty. I could hardly see myself pinned against a wall, taken advantage of, having a fate worse than or even death itself thrust upon me.

We walked up to the door, with me keeping consciously a few steps back, to avoid the impression that we were together, that we were, in any way a couple.

Faustus barked from inside, and when Paul opened the door, Faustus darted at him, put his paws on his chest, licked him, ran to me, gave me the same treatment.

I remembered how moved I'd been upon first reading the Odyssey, at eight or so, by how—of all of Ulysses' retainers and servants—only his old faithful dog had recognized him when he came back home dressed in rags.

But, did the dog also recognize Ulysses' new friend? Did he receive him with just as much joy? Kind of put a wrinkle in the old tale of canine fidelity.

I patted Faustus on the head, standing as tall as I could to minimize the amount of doggie slobber deposited on my face.

Paul watched us, beaming like a father introducing a favorite son to a new lover and seeing the two get on like gangbusters.

We would have none of that.

Calmer, or at least back on all fours, Faustus followed Paul into the house, past the all-white kitchen, where Paul paused to remove two plates and a bottle of beer from the fridge. I followed Faustus.

"Help yourself to a drink," Paul said casually. He'd divested himself of shoes and jacket at the door, a tradition that I know is respected in many countries, but that I'd chosen not to imitate.

If I should have to beat a hasty retreat, I'd rather do it with shoes and jacket on, thank you so much.

The fridge, white and spotless like everything else in the house, contained a variety of cans of soft drinks, as well as a respectable selection of bottled beer. Did he always keep this wide a selection around? And if he did, what for? So his unexpected dates might find their favorite drink?

Speaking of dates, I mentally made a note to buy soft drinks before tonight, remembering that a bottle of my favorite wine would not be appropriate for Brian.

I grabbed a can of soda. Sometimes it helps not to have a buzz.

Paul hadn't sat at the little table where we'd shared coffee last time. Instead, he stood by a door on the far end of the kitchen, between a white armoire and a set of white shelves.

"Come this way," he said. "I usually have lunch in the studio. If you don't mind . . . I don't like breaking my routine."

He sounded like a pleading little boy.

I followed him into a large room with windows all around it. Five or six canvases in different stages of completion sat on easels and a huge hunk of gray rock took up the middle of the room. Someone had obviously taken a chisel and a hammer to it. Both tools lay nearby. Chips of rock and rock dust covered everything. From the rock, still roughly hewn, a male torso and a vague outline of a head emerged, like a colossus pushing out of a seaside cliff. Not a bad effect, though I assumed it was not final.

"You like it?" Paul asked.

"Looks interesting," I said. "What will it be when you're done?"

He grinned. "Hopefully a masterpiece." Looking at his

work, his eyes lost their normal blasé expression. Like a curtain, it lifted to leave his gaze naked, vulnerable, tense.

If he looked at me with half that intensity, I'd fall headlong into his arms.

But the taut expression disappeared as he turned to me. A wary, startled look replaced it. It resembled the oddly naked look on the face of someone who always wears glasses and is suddenly caught without them. "It's the first time I've worked in stone," he said. He turned his palms to me, displaying an expanse of raw, blistered flesh. "But I needed to. I mean, the idea—" He glanced at the statue and his expression softened again.

I was having trouble not liking him.

Why is it that people always seem sympathetic once you see what was at the core of their existence?

Then I thought that perhaps, having realized I'd noticed his blistered hands at our last meeting, he had started this project to have an excuse for the wounds. "Why don't you wear gloves?" I asked.

He looked shocked, like a worshiper when an infidel speaks in church. "I couldn't *feel* it," he said. "The stone. I needed to feel it, so I could know what I was doing."

"It seems to me you won't feel it too well through wounds, either," I said.

He giggled. "Oh, I feel it. Trust me. Hurts like hell."

He turned his back on the sculpture. "Pardon me, Doctor Yates. You said you had some errands to run during lunch. Let me not keep you. Let's eat."

All right. So, I was Doctor Yates, was I? After being Bill when he'd first met me, and Bill ever since? What exactly did that mean? In the office, I'd assumed he was keeping up a front, but what now?

I sat on a canvas director's chair, at the folding table

where he'd set the sandwiches and the drinks.

The sandwich, unwrapped from its linen napkin, revealed a pita bread, stuffed with salad greens and shrimp.

Paul sat across from me, took a bite of his own sandwich, a sip of his beer. He looked at me, eyebrows raised, lips drawn up at the corners, visibly amused. "You can eat. I'm fresh out of arsenic. At most you'll get some rock chips with your food. Good for digestion."

I tasted the food cautiously, not because I expected him to have poisoned the sandwich, but because it looked so green and leafy that it might have been concocted by my father.

It tasted all right. A little on the bland side. But his joke preoccupied me. Why would the thought of poisoning me cross his mind, even as a joke? "Why would you poison me?"

"I . . . I've been wondering about you, Doctor Yates." His moss green eyes gazed at me with an expression that looked much too familiar.

It took me two seconds to identify it as my father's *you-know-very-well-what-you've-done. Don't-hurt-me-any-further-by-making-me-explain-it-to-you* look. Just like in my childhood, when my father graced me with this glance, I had no earthly idea what I'd done to deserve it.

I wasn't about to endure it from a blond younger than myself. A blond who *giggled.*

"I have absolutely no idea why you're looking at me that way." I bit into the sandwich, ate a mouthful. "So it's no use your doing it."

He sighed, a staged sigh of exasperation at my obtuse behavior. "How long have you been involved with Brian Quick?" he asked. "What exactly did you want from me? At Bad Boys? Where do I fit in?"

Um. Um, Um, Um. What the hell did one make of those questions? In inverse order, I didn't want anything from him, and I had never been involved with Brian Quick, not in the way I was sure he meant. But I knew neither of those answers would satisfy Paul.

"Who told you I was involved with Brian?" I asked. "Whatever you mean by that."

He made a face. "A friend. She said you went out to dinner with him yesterday, and have a date with him tonight."

Ah, Joanna struck again.

Well, at least this time Paul had used the masculine pronoun when talking about Brian. We were making progress.

"Brian is in my classes, in college, and recently I've been helping him with some problems . . . having to do with what his family expects of him."

The lie came much more naturally the second time around. If I said it often enough, maybe I'd convince myself. "As for you . . . What I wanted from you? Would you settle for friendship?" I waved around at the statue and his canvas. "It's obvious that your passion lies elsewhere."

His face contracted. For just a second it looked like he'd either spit or shout out a string of curses. He did neither.

His face smoothed, unnaturally. He took a deep breath, nothing histrionic about this one, and grimaced. "Is it time for the *let's be friends* already?" he asked. "I usually get at least one good lay before that."

His voice had been unguarded on that one, all accents of affected cultivation absent, leaving only raw, diamantine cynicism. He stared at me, with intense concentration, though not nearly the concentration he'd devoted to his statue. There was pain in his eyes, but also an expectant hope, as if waiting for me to prove him wrong in his opinion of where our relationship was headed.

I felt as if I'd glanced over a vast panorama of countless men who'd deceived Paul Hogg and deserted him. I opened my mouth, tried to think of something I could say that would ease the wound without making me the next one to deceive him.

Because even with all his talent, with all his artistic fire, I knew Paul couldn't mean anything more to me than a nice body, quickly enjoyed and just as quickly forgotten.

Though I'd done it that way, countless times, with lots of people, what he'd said and the way he said it would never allow me to do that with him. Not now.

Another part of me wanted to tell him one doesn't love where one chooses. If one did, I would have chosen to love Sherry and never have killed her illusions and mine. If one did, I wouldn't be falling fast for dangerously enigmatic Brian.

I wanted to tell him that I did admire his talent, and that I thought he'd never fully devote himself to any human being. I wanted to tell him he was too good for me. But I also knew he'd heard all those things, too many times.

I thought of the ax, and of his bruised hands and instead of the nice, soothing talk, I heard myself say, in a harsh, grating voice, "You wouldn't happen to know where Chris's little black book is, would you?"

His eyes widened and his head recoiled, as if I'd slapped him. His face lost all color. His lips shook. He opened his mouth, tried to speak, but all that came out was an inarticulate sound.

He stood up. I stood up, too, because he looked like he was about to pitch forward in some kind of paroxysm. I wanted to be ready to catch him when he fell or, alternately, to run to the phone and call 911.

Faustus came forward, sat in front of Paul, made inarticulate whimpering noises that sounded like his master's.

Paul looked at me, his expression devoid of all rationality, like a hunted animal. "How much?" he asked.

"What?"

He took deliberate, measured breaths, "How much do you want?" he asked harshly. "You and Brian . . . I assume?"

How much *what* did we want? I wanted a lot of things very much and, judging from his kiss, Brian might too.

For all the good it would do us with the Dean of literature, the Chief of Police, the ax-murderer and, probably, the butcher, the baker and the candlestick-maker all breathing down our necks, trying to shape our destinies for their own benefit.

To separate us, the whole world conspired. Or so it seemed.

But why would Paul care about that? Well, besides jealousy, of course?

No. He had to be talking about something else.

The black book. He knew we wanted the black book. He wanted to know how much we wanted it?

I frowned at him. "The black book? We want it an awful lot. We think someone in that book killed your brother, so you have to see how important it is." Particularly for me. I'd look awful in day-glow prison uniforms. Not the thing for my complexion at all.

He did fall, but not forward. He fell to sitting on his chair, rocking it on its unsteady legs. Setting his elbows on the table, he put his head in his hands. For a long time, he remained quiet.

When he spoke, his voice came out tiny, indecisive, young. "Why are you doing this to me? I liked you. I really did. Why? So I might have been catty about Brian, but I didn't know that you two were involved. Not really. I thought you might be interested in him, but I thought you liked me better."

He looked up. He looked miserable and lost. "Now you threaten me with accusing me of murder. I didn't murder Chris, but I can't prove it, for the same reason I didn't keep our date on Halloween. My car battery went missing. I had to take a taxi the next day to go get a battery at the parts store. But I don't suppose that will do for an alibi. I could have bought a battery without needing it. If you tell my father about John and I . . . or even if you just tell him I was being blackmailed by Chris . . . Well, as busy as he is posthumously canonizing the bastard, he'll just turn me over to the police as a possible murderer."

He looked at me, for a while, in unrelieved misery. "I thought I was safe, now that Chris is dead."

Suddenly, his lips hardened. His eyes, still full of tears, grew cold. "That's just fine. If you're going to tell my dad, or the press, or John's boss, go ahead. Tell them. I couldn't care less. I'm tired of paying. Even if they think I killed Chris. Even prison has to be better than this."

"I don't want you to—" I started.

Appalled, I realized he thought I was blackmailing him. What do you do in a situation like that? Did Emily Post cover *how to gracefully disabuse someone who thinks you're blackmailing him?* I couldn't remember.

He shook his head. "No. You don't want to destroy me. You just want me to pay and pay and pay, till I have to turn out pictures on demand and by the book just to pay the bills, till I never have time to experiment with other forms, or study different means of expression, or live, or breathe, or own my own soul. My brother amassed a million dollars that way, from me and others, all to leave a tidy sum to his little strumpet of a newlywed wife. But I thought you were better than that, Dr. Yates. I thought you were human."

He shook his head again. "I'm done with it. Leave, please."

"I'm not blackmailing you, damn it," I said.

"Oh, no, I suppose you call it something else. Public relations fee, or something. But I'm not paying." He cried openly now. His lips trembled and tears dripped from his chin.

Perhaps it was my being brought up by my father, but I never felt comfortable when men cried.

"I don't want money," I told him. "I have no intention of telling your father anything. I don't want to cause you any pain. I just want to find out who killed your brother."

He shook his head. "Just go. Please go. You're like all the rest of them."

I wondered if he was drunk. I felt embarrassed for his lack of composure. I could get no sense out of him. Perhaps later. "Please remember I don't mean to harm you. I meant what I said about being a friend."

He didn't quite deny it, but his head shook a quarter turn anyway. His lips remained tight. Tears still rolled down his high cheekbones, to drip from his chin.

That time, no one escorted me to the door.

Faustus trailed me but only to the kitchen, his tail wagging but held down. I patted him on the head and he returned to the study, to put his head on Paul's lap and whimper.

I made it to my car, glad I had brought it and feeling that somehow, in a way I couldn't understand, I was the lowest life form in creation.

It wasn't until I got there that it occurred to me to think that Paul sounded awfully guilty, didn't he? His rationality had gone out the window when I mentioned the murder and asked him about his alibi.

Why?

XIV

You Go to My Head

I made it to college barely in time to teach my first-year writing class.

It went unexceptionally, and I don't remember anything about it. Not that I usually did.

While the students straggled out, leaving their assignments on my desk, Brian appeared in the doorway. His face was flushed, and he looked as though not absolutely sure whether to be furious or embarrassed. Delayed reaction to my questioning this morning?

Apprehensive, quaking inside at the thought that I would get from Brian a repeat performance of my scene with Paul, I looked up.

I tried to put on a performance of professorial concern for the sake of my remaining two students. All I needed, if someone was ready to call the police and tell them I wanted to kill Brian, was to look openly hostile to him. Or afraid of him.

"Yes, Mr. Quick? May I help you?"

He nodded, then shrugged. With a glance at the two people in the room, he too composed himself into a semblance of ordinary behavior.

"Yes," he said. His voice only shook a little bit. He didn't sound angry. *What* did he sound?

"Yes. I was wondering if you could . . . uh . . . clarify a

point or two of today's Lives lecture?"

My eyes widened, while the two students—a boy and a girl of remarkably pimply and scruffy appearance—turned on Brian expressions of round-eyed disbelief. I controlled my own amazement with an effort.

It was only an excuse. But, couldn't he think of a more plausible excuse than not having understood something in Lives? For crying out loud, there was nothing to understand in the whole damn course. Only stuff to memorize.

"Ah . . . certainly," I said. "If you wait a minute or two I'll be at your command and—" I stuffed papers willy-nilly in my briefcase.

Brian shook his head. "I believe it might be best if we go to your office, Professor. This might be lengthy. It deals with the question of the identity of the fair youth." He raised his eyebrows at me, his mouth taut as a fishing line with a twenty-pound catch at the end.

Oh shit, oh shit, oh shit, oh shit. The fair youth. He had got something out of Paul. Something that made him think I was the murderer? Mayday, mayday, mayday.

I demanded a recount. I'd never murdered anyone. Not outside my mind.

I don't know what my face looked like, but it must have been a veritable kaleidoscope of emotions. The two students scurried past, dropping their papers on my desk with all the aplomb of someone feeding a not-so-sane lion. They also gave Brian a wide and cautious berth.

I walked to my office on shaking legs.

Daphne Mallard sat at my desk, which had, of course, become covered in tiny little lavender-colored notes—the supernatural manifestation of the Mallard presence.

"Dr. Yates?" she asked, blinking myopically at me. "Dr.

Zimmerman called. She'd like to talk to you as soon as you have a minute."

I meant to reply calmly and rationally that I'd call Joanna soon, or some such thing. But I couldn't speak rationally. Not while on the verge of being turned over to the police, by Brian of all people. I growled. Which was not what I meant to do.

Daphy jumped up from my chair, and backed away. "Dr. Yates," she said.

I managed to say, "Please leave, Daphy. Please." I grabbed her by the elbow, pushed her to the door.

She disentangled herself from me with a fierce pull and snatched her soft leather briefcase from the desk before scurrying through the open door. I slammed it shut behind her and I turned.

Brian stood by my desk. He hadn't even sat down. He was that mad.

"Look, I don't know what Paul told you about me, but you have to take the source into account," I said. "He was disappointed in his . . . hopes of me."

I fumbled with the plethora of notes trying to get them under control. "I never meant anything by it, but apparently he did. I was so lonely. You see, sometimes, I get lonely enough, all I need is physical contact, not anything more, or at least I'll settle for physical contact and as far as physical contact went, he was fine. We met in a bar and I asked him out, once, but we never even went out. He didn't show up, and nothing ever really happened between us, except we danced and groped . . . But then there was no time for more and then when I went to his house he forcibly kissed me. But I wasn't counting on it and I didn't even cooperate, and I guess he was upset."

I stopped.

Brian was looking at me—open-mouthed, eyes agog.

Silence lasted for a couple of seconds, while I realized he hadn't meant what I thought by mentioning the fair youth. Desperately, I sought for a way to unsay what I'd just said.

"Sit," Brian told me.

I sat. And stared.

He pulled off his jacket and, from its ubiquitous inner reaches protected by increasingly less adhesive duct tape, extracted a bundle wrapped in a familiar linen napkin.

Frozen with terror, I thought he was the one who'd chopped up Chris and now he'd done likewise to Paul and had brought me the pound of flesh nearest Paul's heart to show me that the victim was well and truly dead.

But the contents of Brian's bundle were green, and made of paper. Tightly bound together. Many, many of them.

"There's five thousand dollars in there. Thousands, five-hundreds, a few hundreds," Brian said.

"And Paul Hogg said he'd get another fifty thousand to us as soon as he can raise them, and he's sorry for what he told you, and would we be nice and not tell anything to anyone because John has a family?" Brian's eyebrows arched. He sat on the left corner of my desk and looked at me. "Give."

Still shaking, unsure of how much he'd understood of what I'd said, of how much he might or might not know of Paul, I told him of my two visits to Paul's house, in complete and awful detail.

I told him of my curiosity about Paul's name in the black book and gave him a verbatim version of my conversation with Paul.

I did let him know of Paul's comments about Brian, because I wanted Brian to be on his guard should he ever visit Paul again. Brian's cheeks took on a high color, but he gave no sign of discomfort.

When I mentioned Paul's suspicions of Joanna Zimmerman, he shook his head.

"No," he said. "Not Doctor Zimmerman. Even if Chris was blackmailing her, she wouldn't do anything like that."

I remembered the picture of Joanna in leather, holding a whip, and kept my own counsel. Then I told Brian how Paul had acted when I asked him about the night of Chris's murder.

Brian sighed. "So, he thought we were blackmailing him, is that it?"

I nodded. "I think so."

"Do you think he killed Chris?" Brian asked.

I shrugged. "I don't know. We wouldn't have proof, anyway."

He took a deep breath. "What are we going to do with this?" He set a finger atop the pile of cash, as though afraid it would bite him.

"I don't know what we can do, short of driving by and throwing the packet of cash through his window."

Brian smiled, amused. "Huh . . . would you keep this until we can do the drive-by cashing? I've never seen that much money together in one place and it's making me downright nervous."

For just a second, I thought maybe he was trying to plant the cash on me, so he could turn me in to the police. Then I looked up into his eyes. He didn't look like he was trying to set up anything. As it was, should he be asked, Paul would tell the police that Brian and I were a criminal team. I nodded, cleared my throat and managed to say, "You haven't forgotten dinner, right?"

Mendacious. Very mendacious, but anything for the blond.

"No, in—" He looked at his watch. "Two hours. You sure you're cooking?"

"Ah . . . yes." I grabbed my briefcase, stuffed the cash in it. "I have to go."

"Yes," he drawled. "So do I. I need to go back home . . . well, to Professor Zimmerman's house, to drop off my books and stuff." He started out ahead of me, then turned back. "You drink?"

God, did he need to ask all the tough questions in one day? This time, I wasn't about to give myself away with no need, so I stalled. "A little. Occasionally."

He seemed amused by the reply. "Does the occasion cover at meals?"

"Huh . . . sometimes."

"Good," he said, and smiled.

"You're underage," I protested. "To drink."

He grinned. "Admittedly." He started to turn toward the door, his hand on the knob, ready to leave, then turned around again. "Just one more question."

Oh, what the heck. If you're in the frying pan, let the heat come on. "Shoot."

"Do people often kiss you against your will?"

I stared, then realized the corners of his lips were twitching up and down with repressed laughter.

"Only recently. And only blonds. It must be some epidemic around Lythia." Damn the man. "Something in the water." I gave a mock sigh. "I, personally, blame the large corporations who pollute the waterways. Why?"

He chuckled, smiled and said, "Yes, I understand, Professor Yates. I understand why you approached Paul and the rest . . . the picture that Chris got. I've never been quite to that point, but I've been close."

With that, the bewildering man was gone, leaving me open-mouthed with shock. Did that rule about sleeping with someone crazier than yourself apply to someone cleverer than yourself? If it did, then Brian was out.

I zoomed to the grocery store, and bought a mess o' soft drinks, two steaks, a package of frozen fries and one of those salad kits where everything is all chopped up and ready to eat.

I had a feeling Brian would disapprove of pre-prepared food, but there wasn't much else I could do and still have dinner ready on time. On a lark, I grabbed a bag of good coffee, a chocolate cake and two bottles of sparkling apple cider because Brian couldn't drink champagne and because hope sprang eternal.

Maybe when I got home, Tony would have left a message saying he'd caught the murderer. And maybe Brian wasn't smart enough to stay away from me. Maybe, just maybe, there would be something to celebrate.

Coming out of the grocery store, my arms laden with plastic bags, I bumped into Joanna herself.

She looked like nothing on Earth, her hair tied back, looking greasy, her normally impeccably attired body stuffed into a shapeless gray jogging suit.

"Bill," she said. Her hand clutched my arm. "Bill. You didn't call."

I remembered dimly what Daphy had said. "No, I'm sorry," I said. "I was in a hurry. Brian—"

She nodded. "You like him," she said.

Well. I shrugged. "I don't see how anyone can help liking him. He's a very nice kid."

She smiled, a smile that told me she knew quite a bit more of my intimate thoughts than I'd like anyone to know. For a moment I was afraid I would face another of those terrible, soul-baring moments I'd had today.

But all she said was, "Yes, he is. But listen, I need to talk to you. About my car."

I felt my jaw drop. "What?" My knowledge of mechanics consisted of the vague suspicion that all cars had a motor about them, somewhere.

Although I wouldn't have been particularly surprised had I found out that some of them moved by magic or perhaps had little captive gremlins that ran on treadmills inside them.

"Someone borrowed it." She stared intently at me, her eyes seemingly boring holes into my mind. "He stained the upholstery. I think it's blood." She blinked. Her eyelids looked red and swollen. "How do you get it out?"

"How did anyone get *blood* on your car?" I asked. "Who would do it?" Joanna was friends with a coven of vampires?

She shook her head. "Doesn't matter. Just a friend. I think . . . he might have gone shopping and transported some meat or something. How do I get it out?"

Father confessor to blonds, blackmailer, gender minority and now Aunty Bill, the laundry counselor and dispenser of household hints.

How many hats could one man wear? "Joanna. You know how I grew up. We had servants. I take my clothes to the laundry. They do them for me. Why would I know how to remove blood from anything?"

Then because the murder was on my mind, I added, "Do you think perhaps that I go about chopping up people on my sofas and then scrubbing the stains away?"

She whimpered and pressed a fist to her mouth. "Oh, Bill," she said. Tears sprang from her eyes.

Great, just great. It embarrassed me less than watching a man cry, but watching a woman cry didn't exactly make me feel comfortable, either. I put the plastic bag on the floor, fished in my pocket for my handy bundle of tissue, took one, pressed it into her hand.

"Joanna, you really, really should see someone about the way you feel. I don't mean a psychiatrist," I said, speaking as softly as I could. "You know, someone who would understand you."

She looked up. "It's just . . . I'm so scared because Brian is going out tonight. I know I shouldn't be, but it doesn't alter the fact that I feel this soul-crushing terror of being alone in the house."

"Then maybe you could go and stay with a friend," I said. Though sure that Brian would be upset and that it would completely put an end to all our chances of talking about the crime, all our chances of doing anything else, too, I added, "You could come and have dinner at my house. You know Brian is having dinner at my house, don't you? You could join us."

She giggled through her tears. "Hardly," she said. She looked up, violet-blue eyes moist. "You're a really nice guy, Bill, you know. Really nice. I told that to Sherry all the time. If only you'd been—Ah, well. Take care of Brian, all right? Be nice to him. Keep him safe. He's really innocent and there are some true bastards out there."

Flattered that she didn't consider me one of them, even more flattered that she thought I could *protect* Brian, I patted her on the shoulder awkwardly. "Look, I have to go, but I don't like the way you look, nor about the way you sound. Are you sure you'll be all right?"

She smiled. "I'll survive. I usually do, one way or another."

"You know my number, right?" I asked. I was in *big brother* mode. "Call me if you need anything."

She nodded, and ambled into the grocery store. I wondered what she was going to buy. Upholstery stain remover? Blood-away? Murderer-be-gone?

I picked up my bags, got to the parking lot, drove home.

With a bag on each arm, I stopped in my corridor, trying to extract the keys from my pocket by dint of wiggling my hips and fishing in my pocket with two fingers.

Which is when I noticed Mrs. Murphy.

She stood by her door, impeccable in a dark-gray dress and a pearl necklace. Her door stood ajar, showing a strip of light from inside. She was probably waiting for her husband. Perhaps they were going out for a romantic dinner.

I flared her a sympathetic smile.

She glared at me.

I was getting sorely tired of this. I'd already spooked one person and had lived to tell the story. So, I decided to dive right in, "Mrs. Murphy, we're investigating where the victims of Chris Hogg were on the night he was murdered. Do you have an alibi?"

Her china-doll eyes narrowed and her mouth puckered. She wanted to tell me she had no idea what I was talking about.

But her blue eyes darted this way and that, like the eyes of a cornered rat looking for an escape hatch. She cleared her throat, gave a little yelp and said, "Oh dear, oh dear, oh dear. Joanna said she'd taken care—"

She covered her mouth with her hand. When she uncovered it, her lips shook. She opened the door and called into the house. "John, this . . . this man is bothering me."

Not wishing to square it out with ninety-year-old John Murphy, I mumbled something, turned my back and hastened to open my door and get inside.

Which left me just the time to clean the cobwebs off several utensils, throw the steaks on the stove's built-in grill and the fries in the oven, find one of my mother's old tablecloths and put it over the eating-bar portion of the counter.

I'd finished setting this improvised table and was contemplating whether or not to bring out the Waterford crystal candleholders, when the doorbell rang.

Brian, dressed for the occasion—sort of—in brand-new jeans and a white sweatshirt with no sayings on it held his jacket over one arm, the helmet dangling from his hand, and a brown paper bag in the other hand.

He smiled at me.

I smiled back.

After a few seconds his smile faltered. "Are you going to let me in?" He asked. His smile expanded. "Look. I brought you a gift." He pushed the brown bag at me.

I stepped out of the way to allow him into the house. He came in, hung up his jacket and the helmet from my hat tree. I closed the door behind him, and looked inside the bag. A wine bottle shone back at me. I pulled it out, perused the label. Italian wine. I looked up at Brian.

He smiled. "Flowers seemed really stupid, and Mama Quick didn't bring me up to go out to dinner at someone's house without bringing my host a gift."

He winked, put his hands in his back pockets. "No crimes were committed. My sister Lou gave me four bottles when I came away to college. She said sooner or later I would feel an overwhelming need to get drunk and I might as well do it on the good stuff. Only I haven't felt any such need yet. I mean to get drunk. So, you can have it. The bottle, not the need." He glanced around the room and his brow furrowed.

"It's just the furniture I inherited from my father," I said, shying away from his expression. "Sherry never bothered changing the carpet and neither did I."

I realized I was apologizing to a student for the way my house looked. I remembered the way his house looked. Why was I apologizing? Well, because his place merited at least an "A" for effort.

"I'll send for some furniture catalogues first thing in the morning." I resisted an urge to ask him to choose the carpet.

He patted me on the arm, awkwardly. "It's all right. Really. Can I help with anything?"

"Huh . . . no. Everything is underway."

He walked past me and into the kitchen, looked in the oven, adjusted the temperature, turned the steaks over on the grill. "I've always wanted one of these indoor grills," he said.

"I had it installed the year before Sherry left. I used to cook a lot," I said.

"You've told me." He appeared so at home, so relaxed.

Why was I tense and scared and half-ashamed of my house and my cooking?

Because he looked like a walking dream and I looked like someone's wide-awake speculation. Because I hadn't had a date, not a real one, in ten years. Because, despite Sherry's encouragements, I'd never invited anyone over while I was married, and certainly not afterward.

How did I dare still think that Brian might somehow be involved in something as murky as an ax murder?

Because that was what had brought us to personal acquaintance. Because it would hang over us until it was solved. Because this wasn't a grope in the dark, or a one-night-stand.

Because, God help me, this mattered, it mattered like nothing had mattered since my own college days.

Oh, boy. So far from falling for him, I was already down and getting buried deeper and deeper.

I followed him into the kitchen, watched him poke at the steak with a fork.

"Good cut." He looked at the set-up on the counter and shock set his features into rigid disbelief. "And good china?" He turned to me, his cheeks dark pink. "Professor Yates—"

"Bill." My voice had got unaccountably hoarse again. It had the effect of making me sound like a dirty old man. *Want some candy, little boy?* "Call me Bill." Was he about to tell me this wasn't a date and I had no business pulling out the red rug? My heart thumped much too fast. I should know better. I should know much better. What kind of an idiot was I?

He raised his eyebrows, put the fork down, turned to face me fully. "Bill," he said it tentatively. "You don't have to. I mean, the good china and steaks and all. I'd have been happy with fast-food hamburgers and paper plates. I'd have been happy with nothing." He looked down at me. I'd heard about *if eyes could talk*. Well, his eyes held whole speeches. But I didn't know about what. As far as I could tell, they spoke Martian.

Yet, I felt myself blush. "Well, I did invite you over for—"

"I just want to talk and to be with—" He looked away. "We must discuss the crime. We must make a plan for how to get the black book back and we must figure it out, because I can't go on living with Doctor Zimmerman."

You could live here. I never said it. I couldn't say it. He turned around, started poking at the steaks again. The unbearable tension that had built between us sagged.

Paul's words echoed through my mind. *Is it time to be friends, already?* I'd been hoping for at least another kiss. I'd take what I could get.

"There's soda in the fridge," I told him, as I worked my way around him to rummage in the silverware drawer for a corkscrew. It was going to take wine, if we were going to be just friends. It was going to take lots and lots of wine. Because the tasks he'd set were impossible. We could no more find out who had the black book than we could fly to the sun. Meanwhile, if Tony remained convinced that I was it, this might be my one and only time alone with Brian.

Could very well be.

Out came the cork. The wine smelled divine. Hints of berry and citrus. I poured it into one of the crystal goblets. Brian rummaged in the fridge and grabbed a soda that he poured into the matching one.

He raised it to mine, invitingly.

I looked up, met his gaze and, not sure what the challenge was that I read in it, looked away. "To the solving of the crime," I said.

He laughed. "Not for our first toast, you don't."

Our first toast. Implying there would be others? My heart pounded its way up my throat. I felt dizzy. My mouth went dry. Was I dreaming, or did he imply there would be an *us* and an *ours* and *firsts* and *anniversaries* of those firsts?

Whatever inkling of rational thought had started in my mind stopped completely. I took the glass to my lips and drained it.

Brian's eyes widened, his brows went up. "On the other hand, I suppose we can have a first toast later," he mumbled.

His voice choked with something I was half-afraid would be laughter. He turned to the stove. "I think these steaks are done and the timer has gone on the fries. How about I pull them out and you hand me the plates to fill?"

I did just that, because my mind remained much too clouded for independent thought. We sat, each at one of the bar stools that had been purchased one for Sherry and one for me. Sherry had never used hers, though in the early days of our marriage I'd eaten breakfast at the counter every morning.

"So, what else have you been hiding from me?" Brian asked, halfway through the steak and my second glass of wine. "I mean, things relating to the crime. Besides your conversations with Paul?"

I told him about the other names I'd recognized in the black book. When I mentioned Joanna, he frowned. "Her name keeps coming up, but somehow I can't believe she would kill someone with an ax." He shook his head. "Not even Chris."

"I can't either," I said. "I used to know her pretty well and all." To Brian's inquisitive look, I added, "She was Sherry's best friend."

"Of course, she's a friend of sorts." Brian took a sip of his soda. "I mean, she had talked to me sometimes, when she visited Chris. On the other hand, I found it a little weird that she invited me to the Green Rapture party the night Chris was killed. I wasn't a member of the group. At the time I thought she just felt sorry for my pathetic lack of social life. But now I don't know."

I heard myself chuckle and realized I'd had too much wine. I looked at the glass. No. Still half-full. Maybe it was just Brian's presence.

But how could I have more than the legal dosage of Brian? I hadn't even touched him.

I mumbled, "I was puzzled about you eating rain forests and all—" I realized it hadn't come out right because he looked *really* confused. "I mean, cattle, that destroy rain forests, I mean the ranchers that do, for the cattle."

He looked at my glass, picked up the bottle, held it against the light. "When you said you drank occasionally, how occasionally did you mean?"

"No more than once a day," I answered, virtuously. Not a lie. Some of the *onces* were just prolonged over days and days.

He frowned. "Near beer?"

What, was he doubting my masculinity? "Bourbon."

His frown intensified but his lips shaped a smile. He set the bottle down. "We could find out if Dr. Zimmerman showed up at the party, you know," he said. "If she did, then she has an alibi."

Alibis. Clues, alibis, suspects. The man thought we had a chance, amateurs that we were, of solving this puzzle. He wanted to play at mysteries, while I wanted to play house, or a reasonable variation thereof. He expected me to be rational for his game, too.

"There's Mrs. Murphy," I said. I told him of my conversation with her.

He looked puzzled. "How old is she?"

"I don't know. Her husband is ninety. He still gets invited for faculty dinners sometimes, that's how I know."

"A ninety-year-old chopping someone up with an ax?" He shook his head. "Possible, I suppose."

"Well, there's always Paul," I suggested.

He shrugged. "Maybe, but . . . I don't know. I doubt it, somehow. He's really talented. You know that? Though I suppose that artists can kill, I can't imagine he would do it just to keep Chris quiet. Do you have any idea what Chris had on him?"

I shook my head. I had some ideas, but those probably owed more to my own perverse imagination than to anything Paul could have meant to say.

Brian went on, "Well . . . whatever it was, he paid, of course, but I don't think he'd murder to keep it secret. There's a difference, you know?"

I knew.

We finished the steaks in silence.

I slid quietly to the refrigerator, pulled out the chocolate cake. If I was going to live through this night, it would take wine and chocolate . . . and probably a full shot of morphine, but I didn't know where to get that. I looked at Brian as he stared at the fifteen-inch, chocolate-frosting-covered cake, his eyes immense.

I would eat myself silly, drink myself silly, coast through my last time alone with Brian in blissful dizziness. Tomorrow morning I could call the Chief of Police and tell him about the pictures, and tell him that Brian needed some protection.

On the other hand, back-brain Bill said, I could try for Brian. Just once. Something to remember in those awful days in the slammer, as the pet of some guy named Slasher.

I could. Supposedly. Technically. I told myself I would behave because I didn't want Brian to get involved with me, only to see me be dragged away in cuffs. I'd behave for Brian's sake. But I knew I would behave for fear that Brian would reject me. Because if he turned me down, where would I be then? I wouldn't even be able to dream.

Still staring at the cake in disbelief, he cleared his throat. "Can we have that later, maybe? I mean . . . don't you think it's a little much for just now?"

Later. He wasn't intending on running out, just yet.

"Oh," I said, and stopped, setting the cake on the counter. "You don't want it? Then what do you want to do?" I realized that at a subconscious level, my plans for this visit had consisted of feeding him continuously so he didn't get a chance to go away.

He stared at me. His cheeks turned bright red. He looked away. "We could do dishes," he said.

I waved my hand. "No need. The coat hangers—I mean,

the cleaning lady will do them. I have one. Comes by every afternoon." His eyes got big again.

My mouth continued, on automatic, "Cleaning lady, not coat hanger. Every day, I mean. My father left me a fortune in coat hangers."

His eyes got even bigger.

I cleared my throat. My cheeks burned. "I mean, my great-grandfather made a fortune in coat hangers and the family has done pretty well ever since, and my father left me a trust fund. I got myself a cleaning woman." I cleared my throat again. "Among other things."

His eyes resumed normal proportions, but he arched his eyebrows.

"I told Father that I had a soul beyond coat hangers. He said I had a mind below high finance." I looked at his worried expression. "It isn't true. The part about high finance. My mind is okay, and if I gave a damn about high finance I'm sure I could—"

He made a sound like a growl and I stopped.

He still sat at the counter, in front of our empty plates. I stood at the end of the counter, where I'd just set the cake. I'd talked to him with the earnestness of a little boy reciting his multiplication tables.

He took a deep breath, set his hand over mine, looked up—probably one of the few occasions he'd have to look up at me—and said, clearly, distinctly, "It's not your *mind* that's giving me problems right now."

Teleportation—instant transportation from one place to another—is possible. I know. One moment we were by the counter, talking, about three feet away from each other. In the next moment, without transition, we were on the sofa.

I don't know what other laws of physics we would have broken that night, if the phone hadn't rang.

As it was, it took five or six breaths before Brian said, "Noise?"

He wore only his underwear, just as I'd first seen him when I'd got him out of the river, though this pair was green and dryer. His eyes were only half-open and his hair had been messed up for good and all.

For once the more rational one, I said, "Phone." Tearing myself away from Brian, I put a leg on the floor. I managed to make my shaky way to the phone in the kitchen.

I was going to turn off the phone, so I could go back to the sofa. But some remains of sanity said it might be Joanna. Which was why I picked up the phone and croaked into it, "Joanna?"

"Oh, Bill, thank God you're there. Please help me. He says he's coming over to talk but I know he's going to kill me. Come over, come over right away."

Joanna's voice.

"Who's coming over?" I shouted into the phone.

The line had gone dead.

XV

A Fine Romance, My Friend, This Is

"Joanna?" Brian sat up. "Was that Dr. Zimmerman? Is something wrong?"

"Yeah." Slowly, the idea that it would be impossible to go back to the sofa and to our former entertainment formed in my mind, like a blotch on a new shirt. "Yeah. It was. She sounded scared."

I flipped frantically through my address book, looking for Joanna's phone number. Dialing it, I thought this would teach me to not get the call-back feature. I'd assumed that since no one ever called me that I wanted to talk to, I had as much use for it as a fish has for an oxygen tank. The ringing stretched, endless.

Just as I was about to hang up, she answered. "Hello?"

"Joanna, this is Bill. What's wrong?"

"Nothing." She sounded puzzled. "I'm afraid I don't understand."

Her voice was cool and collected. Much too collected. I remembered the woman I had seen in the grocery store and couldn't connect her to this crystal-clear voice.

"Listen, Joanna, the grocery store. Remember what we talked about?"

"Yes, I remember, and no, I don't mind if Brian stays the night. Why should I mind? I'm not his mother."

Chill sweat crept down my back. Even I was not that

stupid, nor that addled by hormones and wine not to know that someone was listening in. Because we had said nothing about Brian staying the night.

"Just go ahead. Have fun," she said.

She hung up.

I stood there, holding on to the phone, wishing it had a camera attached. More, wishing that it had a thoughts-reader attached, that would allow me to know just how real Joanna's peril was. Part of me had entered its *this better be good* mode.

Brian had got up from the sofa and knelt in the middle of the living room, disentangling his clothes from mine.

This was another mystery because I hadn't taken off any clothing, mine or Brian's, and I don't think he had, either.

How my sweater and shirt ended up five feet away is a mystery. How Brian's sweatshirt and pants ended up knotted in my clothing is still more mysterious.

I think the UFO tracking people should look into it.

He frowned.

Oh, this better be *very* good.

"I think we'd better go over there," I said, as I joined him at his task.

He nodded, managed to pull his jeans free, started slipping them on. "I figured."

"How did these ever get tied together?" I pulled my pullover free, got it on.

Brian's eyelids twitched and he smiled, but he didn't answer.

Minutes later, fully dressed and in our jackets, we rode the elevator down. In the elevator, Brian required and got a full explanation of my conversation with Joanna, including how much I might have said about him in the grocery store.

When the elevator stopped and the door opened, Brian

looked puzzled. "This is not the lobby I came in through," he told me.

"Underground garage," I said. "You didn't see the entrance?"

He shook his head. "No. I parked Bucephallus in the outside parking lot."

"Oh, that will be good for it," I said ironically, as I walked to my car, unlocked the passenger door, then my own, sat down, turned the engine on. It made no clicking sound, no answering motor roar.

"It can't hurt it," Brian said. "Very few things can hurt rust." He seemed to notice the lack of response from my car. "Problem?" he asked.

"Yeah," I said. "Won't start."

I got out of the car and, with macho bravado, popped the hood. Considering how much I knew about cars, I'd only have noticed if, say, the whole engine had been replaced with vanilla ice cream. But I thought maybe the car gremlin had indigestion. Maybe it could use a pat in the back. I mean, I'd never even told it that it did a good job, had I?

It didn't help that Brian, crowding in close and looking over my shoulder, said under his breath, "What the hell?"

What the hell, indeed. I stared at the engine. Was some part obviously fused? Was I missing a big note that read, *gone fishing, back soon, the car gremlin?*

I blinked at it.

"Well, Dr. Yates," Brian said. "If we really want to check up on Dr. Zimmerman, I think you'll have to have your first motorcycle ride."

I stared at him. "Stop calling me Dr. Yates. And why should I ride a motorcycle?"

He stared at me, expectantly, as though waiting for the

punch line, then sighed. "You do know your battery is missing, don't you?"

I continued to stare.

He sighed, put his hands on my shoulders and physically guided me into turning around. He pointed at some wires and said, "Those are your battery leads. They don't do a whole lot of good when you don't have a battery. Did you take the battery out for some reason?"

"No," I said, indignantly. "Why would I take it out?" I shook my head.

Oh, so now he thought I was an idiot. Make that, now he *knew* I was an idiot. "I don't even know what the battery is. I don't *do* mechanics. I don't *do* manual labor. I . . ."

I looked up at his expression and decided it was time for some serious groveling if I ever wanted for there to be a sofa in my future again. Distant future, as things looked. "I'll learn, all right? I just never had to do it. The . . . the coat hangers, you know."

"Right," he said. "The coat hangers." He nodded knowledgeably. "Come on. We'll take Bucephallus."

He turned, took a step, came back, punched my upper right arm, lightly. "Come on, *Bill.* You don't have to be a mechanic to make me happy. Really. You know other things. Shakespearean biography and all."

Oh, right, mock me, I thought, as we hurried up the cement steps out of the garage and onto the snow-dusted parking lot, swept by a bitterly cold wind.

Brian had parked away from all the lights because, as he solemnly explained to me, while dusting the snow from his motorcycle, no one but a would-be joy-rider would steal Bucephallus, and a would-be joy-rider wouldn't even notice it in the dark.

In a college town, where even bicycles got stolen and

where apparently there was a burgeoning midnight-auto-parts market for batteries, this seemed like specious reasoning.

He hesitated for a moment, then mumbled. "I only have one helmet. You can have it."

I shook my head. "No. It's yours." He would be up front, more exposed. Besides, I was the elder here. I was supposed to protect him. I was super professor. I was Boozeman Invictus.

"You sure?" he asked.

I nodded.

"But I don't like—" The jade-green eyes searched mine. "Is it all right? With you, I mean?"

I thought of Joanna and her double-talk on the phone. This better be very, very good. "Yeah, it's fine." You too can lie easily in a very few lessons.

We got on the bike, with me behind Brian, my arms around his waist for safety. The position compensated for a lot of things. He smelled of after-shave and sweat and the way I had to hold onto him, I could feel the movements of his every muscle.

I'm struck, I thought with a mental sneer at my pitiable condition. Struck like a schoolboy with a crush on a classmate. Here, we're about to go look up Joanna who's got herself in God alone knows what harrowing trouble, and I'm thinking about how Brian feels and, for crying out loud, how he smells.

But there was nothing for it. Besides, thinking about how Brian felt kept me from thinking about the way he rode the damn bike over every hump on the road at top speed, coming down on the other side airborne and landing with a thud; taking corners recklessly, race-car-driver style.

My head was freezing. Unlike Brian, I wasn't in the habit of wearing gloves, so my hands froze too, which probably provided the excuse for how they attempted to burrow into Brian's jacket.

The turns were a problem, too. Brian seemed to think we should lean inwards, into the curve and toward the ground.

After my instinct of self-preservation pulled me the other way through a few turns and we wavered all over the lane, he growled orders at me.

The gist of it seemed to be that I should do what he did and keep my thoughts to myself.

It made no sense whatsoever, but he didn't seem to be in the mood to discuss it rationally. So, on the turns, I closed my eyes and leaned the way he did.

Scared the crap out of me, but it seemed to keep him happy.

Anything for the blond.

We drove past the area of town where Brian lived, and out through the warehouse district, on the road I'd driven when bringing him back from the river. A sharp turn left took us into the country, to Briar Oat. This development had been started ten years ago when a subsidiary of a big computer company had first considered, then withdrawn, plans to build a plant in the outskirts of Lythia.

The entrance we zoomed past, at slightly below the speed of light, looked all right—a large brick wall with huge metallic letters spelling out Briar Oat. But on the road right after, shabby decay set in. Most lots had never been built on. The knee-high stalks of weeds waved in the wind, above the snow. Some houses were left unfinished and had become mournful skeletons of buildings through which the wind whistled.

As for the houses that were finished, they were fine two-story houses that might one day have suffered no greater blemish than being unimaginative. Now, with peeling paint and plastic over the windows, they looked slummy and scary.

Amid them nestled small, pre-fab squarish buildings. Both types had seen better days. Weeds and broken toys lay deep on front yards.

I'd never actually been in Briar Oat. I'd passed it by on the road, but I'd never turned into it. I hadn't realized it was this bad.

My memory of where Joanna had lived, back in the time when we'd seen her regularly, I called to mind a tidy townhouse with a handkerchief lawn and sparse but good furniture. What had happened? Had it been just the blackmail? Could Chris have been taking that much?

Brian took a sharp turn left, shoved the bike up a steep driveway and almost to the garage door of an undistinguished brown house. He parked at an angle, kicked the stand down, dismounted. I jumped off before I pulled the bike down with me.

The two windows that faced the street were dark. No sound came from the house. How long had it been since I'd heard from Joanna? The ten minutes to get dressed and out of the house.

Easily ten minutes, since UFO aliens had played cat's cradle with Brian's pants. Another ten minutes to fool with my car and work our way out of the garage and onto Bucephallus, and twenty minutes to ride out here, in the freezing cold, on the motorcycle.

Too long.

Brian, his helmet in one hand, pounded on the door, pushed the doorbell with the other. When no one answered, he called out, "Dr. Zimmerman. Joanna?"

He turned a wild, pale face to me. "No answer."

"Perhaps no one is in." It was just possible she might have gone out with her boyfriend. Or alone. It was possible she'd run screaming out the back door.

He shook his head. "No. No."

"Don't you have a key?" I asked.

"Only a back door key."

"Then we'll go to the back door," I said. "Can we try the back door?"

He nodded. "Oh."

He opened the gate on a low wire fence, walked around the house, past two dark windows, to a broad patio door overlooking a meager square of concrete and an expanse of seeding, snow dusted lawn.

"If she's in—" He let the thought drop, knocked at the patio door to no avail, tried it. Nothing.

"Maybe she went out," I said. The dark house felt empty and it felt wrong to be here. What if police came and thought we were vandals? This region must suffer a lot from vandals. Well, technically Brian was a guest here, but who would believe that? I looked up at Brian.

His pale drawn face was tilted up, as he sniffed intently.

"Brian, maybe we should go and call from a phone booth."

He looked down at me and said, "Gas."

A rude response at best. I felt duly offended.

Until shock replaced offense when Brian fished a key from his pants pocket, fumbled with the lock, and flung the door wide.

Then I understood.

The pungent smell of the chemical additive to natural gas came pouring out at me.

Definitely gas.

The smell made me gag. My eyes watered. My head swam.

Brian ran headlong into the house.

I couldn't allow him to go on like that, and play the hero all alone, could I? Not if there was to be a sofa anytime for us again.

I turned away from the stream of gas smell, took a deep breath, held it in and followed.

"Open the windows," Brian shouted from somewhere deep in the entrails of the house.

I obeyed, pulling up the thin aluminum-frame windows one by one. For the next few minutes, my mind was taken up with holding my breath until I got the window open, leaning my face into the screen, breathing, running to the next window. This way, I took a tour of a bookshelf-cluttered living room, a sparse guestroom where Brian's clothes rested on top of a ratty armchair, a messy kitchen with dirty dishes in the sink and empty pill boxes on the counter, and finally a bedroom where Joanna lay in the middle of the unmade bed.

Brian knelt on the bed, beside her. She wore the same gray sweat suit I'd seen in the afternoon. Only now, she didn't look distressed. Her pale, fine-featured face had been washed clean of expression. Her blue eyes stared ahead, sightlessly. She looked dead.

Brian pushed on her ribs, and breathed into her mouth.

I opened the window. As fresh air rushed in, I said, "She should be all right." Frankly she looked anything but all right. Did Brian expect me to help? She looked gray and dead. She had become something nonhuman. I didn't want to touch her.

"Natural gas isn't poisonous. When Sherry and I bought the condo the gas company told us they had changed the formula and it was no longer poisonous." Though the smell around me, the feel of gas in the air seemed to be stinging my throat, I didn't want Brian to think I was weak. And I couldn't understand how it would have made Joanna that sick. Or . . . killed her.

Brian glanced up at me, but didn't answer. He went back to his resuscitation efforts.

"But it isn't poisonous. They changed the formula in the seventies."

He glared at me, let his arms droop. "Just call Tony. Would you?"

I decided this was not a good time for a chemical lecture. Leaning on the bedside table, near an empty coffee cup that matched the one on the other bedside table, I looked at Brian. He'd stopped attempting to revive Joanna and just sat there, on his heels, his face drained of color, looking more tired and washed-out than he had when I'd pulled him out of the river.

The gas must have been affecting me, poisonous or not, because I got a headache behind the eyes that felt like it throbbed with my every attempt at thinking. "I don't know Tony's number."

Brian looked up. "The police station. It would be listed in the beginning of the book." But before I could take a step, he said, "No, on second thought, don't touch anything."

I followed Brian as he wavered out of the bedroom, ambled down the hallway to the living room. There, he flipped through the phone book, touching only the inner pages, and scrupulously avoiding the cover. He dialed the phone using his pen, and he held the receiver in an odd way, between thumb and forefinger, as though it were hot. With the phone to his ear, he turned to me, "Put you hands in your pockets."

"What?"

"Put your hands in your pockets," he said. "So you don't leave pri—Tony? This is Brian. Ah . . . Yes, it's an emergency. I'm at the house of Professor Zimmerman, where I've been staying? Ten twenty five, Appledorn lane, in Briar Oat development. I'm afraid she's dead."

A short silence and then, "She isn't breathing, her pupils don't respond to light and I couldn't feel a heartbeat, but rigor mortis hasn't set in. The house was full of natural gas. I turned the stove and oven off on my way in."

Another short silence. "Fine, it might not be poisonous. She sure as hell is still dead. Right. Fine. Right. We'll wait. Outside? Fine. We'll wait outside. Who? Oh. Professor Yates is with me."

Another short silence. "Stow it, Tony. You're not Iggy. Easy on the sermon. Right. Tony, I'm not an idiot. There's a dead body here. Are you coming or not, Mr. Police Chief, sir?"

He slammed the phone down, glared at me. Then, as though realizing I wasn't Tony, his eyes softened. "Tony," he said under his breath.

Like a good little boy, I kept my hands shoved deep in my pockets, hoping he'd notice. As upset as he looked, the last thing I wanted to do was piss him off further.

He didn't put his hands in his pockets, though. Or not both of them. He threw his left arm over my shoulder and said, "Tony said to wait for them outside."

XVI

Not that I Consider It a Sin

I don't know how long we waited outside Joanna's house. We couldn't exactly hug, not out there, in full view of her neighbors. God only knew what people in this neighborhood thought of that sort of thing.

So, even though I needed human touch like never before, we stood, side-by-side, with about a two inch breezeway between us, while the wind whistled around us, and snow started falling again.

The memory of Joanna's corpse inside, that husk that life had abandoned, made me feel colder inside than anything the weather could do to my outside.

After a while, Brian said, "I'm sorry we don't have helmets on."

I nodded, breaking off a few icicles.

Then Tony arrived, roaring through the neighborhood and up the driveway in a late-model Porsche. I thought, at a distance, through a snowstorm, that could look like a Beetle. With Brian being his childhood friend and all, he'd spare him, or course. But I couldn't imagine Tony with a long blond wig.

Tony got out of the car, carrying two large bags and a variety of cameras. He stormed up to us, stared at Brian. "Why is it that there were no murders in this town before you moved in?"

Brian, looking half-dead, answered with remarkable aplomb, "I've lived here for two years."

Tony glared at me. "What about you, Dr. Yates? How long have you lived here?"

"Ten years," I said, not even bothering to deflect the implied accusation.

He walked past us and into the house. We followed. Or rather, Brian followed and I followed Brian back in through the bookshelf-filled living room.

Tony must have heard our steps behind him, because he turned back and barked, "Keep your hands behind your backs. Don't touch anything."

Bacchus told me to put my hands in my pockets. Now Apollo wanted my hands behind my back. I compromised by putting my hands in my back pockets. Brian did, too.

Through the living room, we came to the hallway and through that to the bedroom. There Tony took a look and a quick feel of Joanna, muttered, "Shit," pulled out his cell phone and started dialing. "Did you move her?" he asked. "Or was she like this?"

"I tried to revive her," Brian said. His Adam's apple worked. "I couldn't leave her like that, without trying—" He stopped, looked green.

Tony looked up. "Why didn't you two stay outside?" he asked, in an exasperated tone. "Go to the living room. Sit down and stay out of my way."

We trundled down the hallway, Brian once more in the lead. At the doorway to the kitchen I smelled something hot and stopped.

Brian looked back. "What—?"

"Something smells hot," I said, and pointed inside.

He sniffed the air, entered the kitchen. On the kitchen counter, amid the plethora of dirty dishes, sat a crock grill, one of those contraptions that consist of a crockery bowl with an incandescent coil inside and a metal rack on top.

Brian reached for the plug, pulled it. It had been inserted into one of those timer thingies and that in turn into the wall plug. Brian stared at it. "Tony. Tony?"

"What?" the Chief of Police came out of the bedroom, a camera strap hanging around his neck, camera dangling down.

Brian showed him the grill, pointed out how it had been plugged in.

Tony felt the top of the grill, scowled at Brian. "You shouldn't have turned it off before you called me. Are you stupid? You turn off the gas, you turn off the grill, you open windows. Who are you? Mr. Safety Person?"

Brian looked surprised, then angry. "If I hadn't turned off the gas and the grill, we would all have blown up," he yelled back.

"So you say," Tony said. "So you say, but you're the man who persists in being emotionally involved with someone that someone else said killed you."

"I didn't kill him," I said, trying to find my way through his strange sentence. Didn't they teach Police Chiefs to parse anymore? What was this country coming to? "How could I have killed him? He's alive, isn't he?"

"Yeah," Tony looked at me. "But perhaps what the caller meant was that he'd seen you carry a corpse out and he thought it was Brian. Your boss says you have an unhealthy relationship with Brian and that you often go strange over students of yours. He says you had several years of psychiatric care and then stopped it of your own volition and without the doctor's concurrence. Is that true, Dr. Yates?"

I stared. So, Elderman had blackened my name. What

else was new? "I've never had a relationship with a student of Bile. Ever. My psychiatrist divorced me, so I assume she thought I was cured."

He frowned, as though thinking I was trying to make a joke. Then he sneered, "How long have you been involved with Brian, Doctor Yates?"

"I'm not *involved—*" I started and stopped.

Brian had started speaking at the same time and said, "Since this evening."

We looked at each other. His lips made an effort to twitch upwards at the corners.

Tony looked from one to the other of us. "Just go," he said. "To the sofa. Sit down. Stay there."

He escorted us to the sofa and saw us seated, side-by-side.

I wanted to hold Brian's hand. After his statement that we were involved with each other, I wanted to talk. Were we involved? What did he think of my denying it? Was he mad at me?

I didn't look at him and I didn't move. I sat with my hands in my lap. I couldn't talk about *us* now, and I couldn't do anything either. Not with Joanna dead in the other room, not with Tony waiting to nail me for murder. Not when Brian might be mad about my response, or thinking about what Tony had said. Not when he might have thought better sofa-wise and might withdraw his hand if I reached for it.

Tony picked up and dropped bags and cameras in the living room. As we watched from our ringside seat in front of the hallway, he went in and out of the bedroom, carrying different implements: measuring tapes and cameras, mysterious vials.

Flash bulbs erupted, shining through the doorway.

Brian shifted his legs one way and then the other, sighed. He changed his position on the sofa. Finally, he got up, went down the hallway, peered in the doorway to the bedroom. "Tony? Can I help?"

"No."

"But I know all this stuff, from research, you know? For writing?"

Tony made some sort of explosive sound, between a sigh and a hiss. "No, damn it. Brian, you're a suspect. Since when do suspects help with the investigation? And damn it, stop touching that doorway."

"Oh. Sorry." Brian dutifully put his hands in his back pockets and returned to the sofa.

Moments later, Teutonius Ram came in through the door, gave us a toothy grin and said, "You two certainly get around."

We nodded our acknowledgment.

Ram's addition made the scene much more entertaining, as he played low comedy to Tony's high drama, dropping vials of fingerprint powder and putting his own fingerprints on just about any flat surface.

After about an hour, Tony came out and handed us a ruled yellow notepad apiece, asking us to write our accounts of the evening and sign them.

We wrote busily for a while, and then I noticed Brian had stopped and stared at me, his color high. I looked down at the pad in his hand. He claimed we'd been sitting on the sofa talking when the phone rang.

No policeman being in sight, I nodded at Brian. I couldn't see what the big difference would be if the police didn't know that Brian had been conducting an exam of my tonsils. All things considered and Tony's incipient homophobia taken into account, it was probably best if he didn't know.

I made sure to duplicate Brian's effort. Tony hadn't taken care to separate us while we wrote the accounts, though he did now and then come out of the bedroom and look sternly at us.

He came to collect our reports. "Now, you wrote down anything that might be related?" he asked.

We both nodded dutifully.

"I should question you verbally, but I'm short on manpower right now," he said. "Womanpower, too. If you promise not to discuss it with each other and can come by the station tomorrow at around two in the afternoon . . . I think these will do. You know any facts you omit might give us a clue against you." He looked from one of us to the other, collecting nods. "I would then be able to fill in the holes in your statements. Right now, you two should go home and to bed."

We glared in unison.

Realizing what he had said, he glared too, and his cheeks colored a dark red, while his lips pulled downward in a scowl. "I mean, you two should go home and get some rest."

"Tony," Brian said. "I don't have a home to go to. I've been living here."

Tony visibly had about enough. He threw the two pads on the scratched-up coffee table, turned to Brian, hands expressively raised, palms upward, "What? You want to sleep here? At the scene of the crime, before we finish the work up? This guy is your *friend,* isn't he? You said you're involved with him. So, why don't you stay with him for the night, which I'm sure you were about to do, anyway? Maybe he'll be the next one to show up dead. Rooming with you is obviously hazardous."

"I'm not his *friend.* Not that—" I started, running

through his insinuations one stop at a time.

Brian took a step backwards. "Can I at least take my clothes with me?" he asked.

"No. Nothing leaves the crime scene." Tony crossed his arms on his chest, defying challenge.

Brian stared and looked like he was trying to come up with a really good reply, but before he could, Ram ambled into the room, carrying a typewritten page, "Here, boss, look here. This was out on the corner of the back patio."

He pushed it at Tony and Brian and I edged to read over his shoulder. The page read,

To whom it may concern,

I, Joanna Helena Zimmerman, being of as sane a mind as I'm likely to be, have decided to put an end to my own life. It is an easier means than undergoing trial and punishment for my crime, but I want to leave it clearly stated that I alone am responsible for the death of Christian Armand Hogg. He had been blackmailing me for several years, and I could not live with it anymore, so on Halloween night I took an ax and attacked and dismembered C. A. Hogg, dumping his body in the Nugget River. You will find the ax in my woodpile. You will find stains from his blood in the luggage compartment of my car.

Sincerely,
Joanna Zimmerman.

"She'd never do that," Brian said. "Who'd leave a suicide note on the patio?"

Tony started to open his mouth.

Just then a black man that made both Brian and Tony look small and average as to looks, came through the door, carrying a large black bag. "The body?" he asked Tony.

"In the kitchen, Doctor White. If I may—" He turned around, looked at us. "You two get out of here. You have no place in the scene of the crime. Don't take anything with you."

Brian looked as if he'd dispute the point, but I pulled at his sleeve and must have looked my embarrassed confusion. He frowned at me, then shrugged. "Can you lend me a razor, Dr. Yates?" he asked. "And pajamas?"

I nodded. I'd lend him or give him anything at all he wanted, even if he called me Dr. Yates.

It wasn't until we were back in my condo that Brian pulled a small black book from inside his jacket and threw it on my coffee table.

"What is that?" I asked. But I knew what it was. "Where did you—?"

"It was sitting on the bedside table," he said.

XVII

And I Find You Spinning Round in My Brain

I stared agog at the small black book.

Joanna had it. That meant Joanna had taken it from Brian's house. So, Joanna had broken into Brian's house sometime over twenty-four hours ago, when everything had been overturned. It made sense. She had seen us at the restaurant, left before anyone noticed Chris's head on the TV. She'd probably thought she was safe for a couple of hours.

Everything had also been overturned on the night of the murder. So . . .

Joanna.

Cobwebs danced in my mind, obscuring my thoughts. A glance at the wall clock told me it was three a.m. How did that quotation go? In the dark night of the brain, it's always three o'clock? I was fairly sure that wasn't it, and yet it applied. I stared back down at the notebook and up at Brian's defensive scowl. "Why?" I said. "I mean, why—the notebook?"

He must have been expecting censure or at least annoyance.

My bafflement made him ease on the scowl, look embarrassed, shrug.

"I don't know. I mean why she took it," he said. "I probably would have given it to Tony without much thought. I checked and your name isn't in it. But I'm very tired and Tony told me not to take anything and I—"

He shrugged again. He looked up. "But maybe it can help us find out who killed Dr. Zimmerman, all the same."

"Who killed her?" I repeated. "*Who* killed her? Brian, you read that note as well as I did. You're not stupid. You know the signs. She had the book. That meant she searched your house. Your house was also turned upside down on the day of the murder. I told you that she asked me how to remove bloodstains from her upholstery. She killed Chris and she killed herself."

He poked his lips outward.

"Women don't type their suicide notes," he said. "No one would leave a suicide note on an outside patio."

"How many women do you know who've committed suicide?" I asked, trying to keep rational against all odds. "If she was intending to blow herself and the house up, which is the only use I can imagine for the grill being timed and the gas on, then the outside was the most logical place for a suicide note."

His lips hardened into a straight line that had the advantage of disturbing me less. "Why would she want to blow up the house?" he asked. "You have to ask yourself that. Why?"

"Why would anyone want to blow up her house? Even a murderer if there was one?" I countered. "Your place wasn't blown up, was it?"

He glared at me. "I knew Doctor Zimmermann," he said. "She would not, under any circumstances, commit suicide. Now, if I could borrow pajamas and maybe a razor for tomorrow, I'll make free use of your sofa."

"I . . . uh . . ." I said inanely, thinking of anything, anything at all to make him stop being all cold at me. "I have a guest room. But . . . but it's full of boxes. My father's boxes. I haven't unpacked."

"The sofa will be quite good enough." He looked up, pleadingly. "I think we're both very tired and could both use our rest."

Rest. I was not invited to the sofa. That's what I got for not controlling my tongue. What kind of an idiot was I, again? Why did I do these things to myself?

So Joanna had committed suicide. She had killed Chris. It fit. It explained the VW, and someone with long hair dropping Brian from the bridge. It explained her not killing Brian, giving him a chance to survive, although she'd have to be spooked and confused enough by that time to think it necessary that she should drop Brian from the bridge with Chris.

But then, if Joanna had just been impelled by blackmail to kill someone in cold blood, she would have to be feeling out of her mind and half insane.

The only thing that didn't fit fully was the color of the hair, but then maybe the light had caught it just right. Joanna's hair had always been shiny.

It also explained her nervous breakdown after the murder. Remorse and fatigue and a bizarre need to keep Brian safe. To make up to him for having almost killed him?

I stared up at Brian and said none of this. Brian wanted to believe her innocent. Why shouldn't I let him believe it? What did it matter to me? As long as he didn't believe me guilty. And he obviously didn't.

I could have kept quiet. Now I'd be sofa-less for the night, maybe forever. Foot in mouth disease. Probably incurable.

I went to my room, retrieved pajamas from one of the drawers, stopped by my bathroom and found one of the small disposable razors I'd bought a few years back for when I stayed overnight with someone. This had happened so often that I had almost the entire bag.

In the living room, I handed the bundle to Brian and said, "The guest bathroom is the first door to your left."

He nodded, looking slightly dazed at my business-like manner.

If he thought he was the only one who could act cold and dignified, he needed to be taught a lesson, the sooner the better. So there.

My cool dignity lasted all the way into my bedroom, where I leaned against the closed door and again started wondering what kind of a moron I was.

I had Brian there. In my own house. Bacchus himself. And here, I was going to sleep alone and virtuous in my single bed.

I made it to the bathroom, eventually, and took a shower in what I meant to be soothing warm water. This purpose was somewhat hindered by the fact that Brian must have had the same idea at the same time.

The water alternated between freezing jets and exfoliating heat. I emerged from this bi-polar treatment pink, scalded and frozen.

Dressed in my own pajamas, I headed for bed. You'd think as tired as I felt, sleep would be the least of my problems.

You'd be wrong. Closing my eyes, I'd drift into a semblance of sleep, only to find the image of Joanna, blue and dead-looking, there in my mind.

"Natural gas isn't poisonous," I muttered, and punched the pillow and lay my head back on it. But then she had to have died of something else. Besides, Brian was right: why the gas? Why the grill turned up to cause it to explode, presumably when it had filled the house enough to induce total destruction?

Out there, Brian's footsteps left the bathroom, walked to the front door. I heard the door lock click into place.

Securing the castle. Oh, was I supposed to be the maiden cowering from the dragon?

Brian's footsteps went to the kitchen.

I heard the sound of running water filling a glass.

I visualized Brian in my kitchen, drinking a glass of water, getting ready for bed.

I thought of my conversation with Joanna in the supermarket.

The funny thing is that, no matter how I ran it through my mind, it didn't sound like the conversation of someone who'd intended to kill herself.

Oh, yes, she'd mentioned that a friend had stained her car's upholstery with blood, and that was probably the oldest dodge in the world for confessing without confessing, but it also wasn't like Joanna. Damn it, I'd known Joanna pretty well. Joanna had known me well enough that she would just have told me outright that she'd killed Chris and would I help her.

And she knew I would. Because Joanna knew I had no great love for Chris and she would have known I was a trustworthy friend.

Or would she? She also knew I liked Brian and, if she'd hit him over the head and dumped him in a river . . . She had asked me if I liked Brian.

I heard the sofa in the living room creak. Brian turning, I thought.

I wondered if the memory of having me there, with him, on that same sofa, haunted him any, and then I wondered in what way.

Perhaps he realized what he'd done and with whom and got an attack of the creepy-crawlies. Curiosity and hormones can rule you at nineteen. But, eventually, you do come to your senses.

Why was Brian so interested in defending Joanna?

The sofa creaked again and I turned in bed, as if moved by invisible strings, coordinating our movements.

Was it because he didn't believe she had killed herself? But why? How would he know? It didn't make any sense.

Exactly how had Joanna died?

Natural gas wasn't poisonous. Granted, she might have had a compromised respiratory system . . . somehow. But . . . no. I'd have heard.

I thought of the pillboxes on the counter. They'd looked empty, lying on their sides.

I wished I'd read the labels on them.

Brian got up from the sofa, his feet hitting the floor with a loud thud. I heard him thump his way to the kitchen, and then the noise of crockery, the sound of running water. *What* was he doing?

I tossed and turned a couple more minutes, listening to Brian move around. My bedside clock showed four thirty.

If Brian could be up, why couldn't I? Lying in bed didn't seem restful at all. My body hurt from all the tossing and turning. The sheet had become damp with sweat and wrapped around my legs in tight coils.

I got up, found a decent-looking red and black plaid robe, as opposed to the blue paisleys I'd inflicted on Tony, and proceeded to walk out the door and to the kitchen.

And stopped. Brian stood by the sink in my pajamas. Most of his forearms, a good portion of his ankles, and his flat-and-tight midriff were exposed. As I watched, he rinsed a dish and dropped it with some clatter in the dishwasher.

Looking up, he saw me. "I'm sorry," he said. "Did I wake you?"

Wake me? Why should he, when he was only making as much noise as your average volcanic eruption? I mumbled something.

He nodded. "I couldn't sleep either. I kept thinking. You see, you seemed to believe that Dr. Zimmerman committed suicide, but I couldn't believe it. I couldn't believe that Dr. Zimmerman had hit me over the head. But I didn't know why."

Those jade-green eyes gave the benefit of their full focus. "Then I figured it out. Smell."

Smell? I stared at him. Let me guess. Murderers smelled of murder? Nah. He didn't look insane, or stupid.

"Smell," he repeated and, staring at my stubbornly unenlightened face, dropped another plate in the dishwasher, sighed, and consented to explain. "Just before I went down, I smelled a pretty strong scent. Perfume or cologne. I'm not sure which. But it wasn't a female scent."

He wrinkled his forehead. "It smelled like the cologne you were wearing when . . . When you came over to my place and fell asleep on the table."

It took a few minutes for this one to percolate through the fog in my brain, but when it did, I found my muscles tightening.

Just because I disagreed with him on one little detail of crime solving, he'd decided I was the villain. Oh, no sofa at all. Ever. My stomach tightened, too, at the prospect.

"Now, listen here," I said. "I'll take this bullshit from your friend, Tony, but not from you. The bartender at Bad Boys lied. He would, since he couldn't admit to the police that he let me out while thoroughly wasted. But I was, and it took me about two-and-a-half hours just to drive to

Lythia. I took back roads and drove an average of twenty miles per hour."

Brian frowned. "What exactly *is* Bad Boys?"

"The place where Chris got that picture of me. You probably would have heard of it, if you weren't so isolated. It's a gay bar—"

I remembered my Elderman-bestowed minority status, cleared my throat and amended. "Pardon me, an alternate lifestyles nightclub down in Cowpatty. It caters to all the gays and half a dozen free spirits who just enjoy the craziness, from all the little towns this side of the mountains. I was there the night Chris died, that's why, the costume . . ."

My explanation lost impetus.

Brian shook his head violently. "Oh, no. You can't think I suspect you of trying to kill me. I've never suspected you. You wouldn't do something as stupid as drop me in the water and get me back out again. What purpose would it serve?"

Well, yeah. But then what purpose would it serve any murderer dropping him in the water without making sure he was dead first?

Throwing a cut-up body and a not even dead one into the river together?

Presumably killing a woman by some means and then setting it up so her house would explode at some point in the not-so-distant future?

Wouldn't it have been easier to sit in a car around the corner for an hour and then fire a bullet into the house? It would ignite a fire, and they probably wouldn't find the bullet after the explosion. Not and identify it as a bullet. At least not with the resources of Lythia Springs police force. Not even with the help of the Colorado Bureau of Investigations. Who, at any rate, wouldn't care that much about a murder in a tiny place like Lythia?

So, the killer had made this far more complex than need be. Face it. We weren't dealing with rationality here. Which, of course, sounded just like my modus operandi and if I didn't know better I would suspect myself. But I didn't say anything.

One thing was putting my foot in my mouth. Another was holding my mouth open with pliers and carefully inserting both feet.

"No," he said. "What I meant is that someone else, who wore the same cologne you wear, must have been in my house at the time. What is the cologne? That you were wearing, I mean?"

"Athos, the scent for the brooding man." I sat on one of the bar stools, set my elbows on the counter, dropped my face onto my hands.

Brian looked at me a second too long, as though doubting my word on colognes, then nodded. "Right. Someone else in Lythia wears it."

I groaned. "Probably half the faculty and some of the students," I said. "It's expensive but not prohibitive. Sherry sends it to me."

Brian nodded. "Yes, fine. So maybe half of the *males* on the faculty wear it. It's not a woman's scent. It couldn't be worn by Professor Zimmerman. Therefore it wasn't her I smelled that night. Either she didn't do it, or she had a male accomplice. What if she had a male accomplice; did he kill her? Maybe he wasn't her accomplice at all . . . Maybe he was the principal."

This seemed pretty gender-bound reasoning coming from a gay man, but I didn't want to tweak him, so I didn't point out to him that male professors don't usually go around in tights. But I had.

Still, I couldn't think of any good reason for Joanna to cross-perfume, after all. Only that she might have got the cologne as a Christmas gift from Sherry, as I had. But in that case why would she use it, instead of passing it on to a male friend?

"How well can you remember the scent?" I asked Brian. "How accurate can your memory possibly be? You got concussion or a close relative of it shortly afterwards."

Brian set his lips in a straight line.

The sofa became a tiny speck in the panorama of my future prospects.

"I know smells," he said. "I always remember smells better than anything else." He cleaned the top of the grill with the dish sponge, looked up. "At any rate, you know, we probably can check and find out if she was at the Green Rapture Party all night. If she was . . ."

"The police will think of that." I had a sudden sneaky suspicion. "In your little written report, you did tell Tony about Green Rapture, right?"

Brian shrugged. "Yeah. I didn't want to, but he is the Police Chief."

Well, yes. Throwing a tiff at the police didn't exactly qualify as self-preserving behavior. Nor did stealing things from the scene of the crime, for that matter. I thought of the black book.

I watched Brian pull the large chocolate cake out of the fridge, and open the pantry door, and pull out the coffee packet I'd bought the day before. "Do you have a grinder?" he asked.

I went behind the counter with him, and we looked through the cabinets, till we got hold of the small, cylindrical gadget.

I took charge of grinding the coffee while he got out the

dessert plates and set a slice of chocolate cake on each of them.

In the middle of the night, foggy with sleep, I had to wonder what exactly I'd thought when I'd bought that enormous, gooey cake.

And why would Brian want it right now? I watched him lick frosting off his fingertips.

Brian took a tentative stab at his cake with a dessert fork.

He was nineteen. He hadn't eaten anything in . . . Oh, ten hours. Of course, he'd be starved.

I finished grinding the coffee. After a moment of panic that Sherry might have taken it, I found my percolator and started it.

"All right," I said, looking at Brian as he methodically and, seemingly not consciously, disposed of the huge slice of cake. "Suppose Joanna didn't kill herself. Who could have done it?" He should have come over to discuss the crime, the evening past. That's what he said he would be doing. He should have come over to have a rational discussion. Why had we ended up on the sofa? Why had I allowed it?

As tired as I was, I felt that if only Brian and I had kept our conversation on track, then Joanna wouldn't have got murdered. If only we'd talked about it, discussed it rationally, we'd have found the real murderer in no time at all, wouldn't we? No time at all.

The coffee was done and I pulled down two cups. I poured coffee, asked, "Sugar?"

Brian nodded.

I found some of the fructose that Sherry had bought while on her macrobiotic kick and handed it to him with a spoon and his coffee cup, the pink one that read, *Aerobics keep you lite on your feet.*

He stared at it.

"My wife. I mean my ex-wife. I mean, Sherry got it. When she was doing—" I took my own cup to my lips, to stop the monologue about Sherry.

What did I think? That I was going to impress him with my heterosexuality this late in the day?

Then I saw his eyes staring at my own cup, and brought it down enough to glance at what it said and groan. It was the other Bad Boys cup, with the logo on one side and *You Make Me Feel So Good,* on the back. Well, so much for heterosexuality this late in the day. I felt myself blush.

Brian smiled. Mona Lisa again.

I had to get new dishware. Instead, I made it to the counter, got hold of a pad of paper that I kept by the phone to write the unlikely important message and said, "All right. Whom do we suspect?"

My hand shaking from lack of sleep, I wrote down *Suspects, Motives* and *Opportunity.*

"Off the top of my head," Brian said. "Everyone in the black book."

I got the book, wrote down those names I recognized, figuring those were the ones I had access to: Paul, John, Mrs. Murphy and. . . . But Joanna was dead. Motives. Blackmail. Alibis. Paul said his battery had been stolen. Paul said.

I remembered that my own battery had turned up missing from my car. Did the murderer have any reason to suspect Paul would go to Chris's house that evening?

I had to talk to Paul again. I had to talk sense into him. I suspected he knew something, buried in the mountain of useless information in his mind, and his preoccupation with what lay in a more southerly location. "I need to go talk to Paul tomorrow," I told Brian.

He looked up. He'd cut a new slice of cake and was

making fast work of demolishing it. "Want me to come along?"

I shrugged. "If you wish." Paul might be tempted to greater lunacy confronted with both of us together. But at least Brian would be there. I would have a witness. Just in case Tony decided that Joanna really hadn't killed herself and developed a fascination with me. In which case, I'd rather have backup for my every conversation with another suspect.

Brian looked over my shoulder at what I'd written. "Do you want to look at the pictures?" he asked. "See if we recognize anyone else? I mean, it seems so dirty, but . . . We must look through them."

"Yes," I said. "Tomorrow."

"Looks like a full day," Brian said and smiled.

"Yes," I said. My vocabulary was becoming constricted by sleep. "I think I need to go to bed."

"You haven't even had your cake," Brian protested.

I looked at him, dolefully. "You have it."

When I left, he was halfway through demolishing it.

In bed, I thought that the missing battery was the key to it all. It seemed like too much of a coincidence for both my battery and Paul's to have been stolen the night someone we knew died. There had to be a reason and the reason had to be to keep me at home. Of course, whoever it was hadn't realized that I had alternate transportation available.

Out of nowhere, I thought of Elderman giving me permission to go after Brian and wondered if perhaps, just perhaps, the reason he'd done it was to ensure I'd be too busy all night to think of Joanna?

Still, why should he think I would come to Joanna's succor, anyway? Why would anyone? We were friends, but not lovers.

Someone had to know us pretty well to know the link of protection and mutual reliance that had been built between us, a decade ago. And to guess it could be re-activated by need.

Sherry knew that. Sherry was in California. There were airplanes.

I wanted to dial her up, but I couldn't even summon enough awareness to open my eyes.

First thing tomorrow morning I'd call her. First thing after that I'd look for her picture amid Chris's collection. And Elderman's picture, too, while I was at it.

XVIII

Like the Kick in a Julep or Two

I woke up pounding on the alarm clock, trying to stop it. I'd slept a couple of hours. Good enough for university work.

Deciding to bypass a shower, I got myself dressed. Didn't want to shock the blond by wandering around in the morning in next to no clothes.

While shaving in front of the mirror in the bathroom, I marked each of the creases in my less than elastic skin and the dark, dark circles around my eyes. A paragon of masculine beauty I was not.

So, why would Brian want to sofa with me? Was he insane? Or did he want to influence my thinking, to deceive me, to . . . incriminate me? Was that why he wasn't happy with the idea of Joanna having committed suicide? Did he mean for me to get killed? Arrested?

I shook my head at the narrowed eyes, the sharp suspicious expression of the Bill in the mirror. Brian was not Lupi. Couldn't even begin to be like him. There couldn't be two people like that.

Thank God.

Out in the living room, Brian still slept.

I'd never given him a blanket, not that it was needed, as I kept my heating up on sweltering. So he lay uncovered, with a leg off the sofa, his foot resting on the floor and the other leg on the sofa, stretched out. His white elongated foot rested on top of the sofa arm.

Sixteen triple-A, if I didn't miss my guess. One of his arms crossed over his face, hiding his eyes, the other arm supported his head from behind.

Tearing myself away, I went to the kitchen, drained the coffee pot into my dirty coffee cup and drank the bitter, acid liquid. Chocolate cake would have to do for breakfast. You know the routine: eggs, cereal, milk, everything you should be having for breakfast is in fact contained in chocolate cake. With a whacking dosage of fat and some nice, nice artificial serotonin, a.k.a. chocolate. Considering how little I'd slept and the shock I'd endured the night before, I needed all of it, the extra sugar included, just to stay awake through the day ahead.

But when I opened the refrigerator, I realized my breakfast would be meager. Brian hadn't done something so crass as finish off the chocolate cake. He wouldn't. Instead, he had left a single slice, so thin that it wouldn't stand up on its own.

I brought the whole container out on to the counter. Breaking pieces off the cake, one by one, I started eating while casting an appreciative eye over Brian's lean and muscular frame and wondering where he put it. Looking at him, you'd think he'd never eaten an ounce of surplus fat, ever, in his whole life.

As soon as breakfast was improvised, I got back to the bedroom. Remembering my suspicions of the previous night, I dialed Sherry's number.

Her answering machine responded, cool and collected, "Hello, you've reached Sherry's and Henry's home. Your message is precious to us. Please leave it at the tone."

So . . . she wasn't home. I waited while her machine slowly paged forward through all the comments. She had been away for a while. She could have been in Lythia Springs last night, killing Joanna, and she wouldn't have gotten home yet. I thought about it for a moment, then started the only message that guaranteed that Sherry would pick up the phone, if she chanced to hear it, "Hi Sherry. I wondered if you'd got my check." I waited. "Check. Money, money, money, money." Nothing. "Well, um, call me back, okay?"

Had I just locked myself into sending Sherry a whole bunch of money for nothing?

Ah, well. What else was the dirty green stuff for? I started toward the door, briefcase in hand. Then stopped. I retraced my steps to the phone and called a cab.

My car still lacked a battery, which I took to mean that the little car gnome wouldn't make it run. I still couldn't understand why the lack of one little part should cause the motor to stop, but I also wasn't about to wake up Brian and ask for an explanation.

My seven thirty a.m. class on Tudor literature, another of Elderman's little jokes, was a rousing success. Most students remained awake till the end.

Afterward, I drifted to my office. I'd actually asked Daphy to take over teaching Lives II. I had to let her teach something, sometimes, to give her a sense of purpose in life and prevent her pigtails from drooping too desolately.

Daphy sat at my desk, lavender notes to the wind. "Professor Yates?" she asked, and stared at me, eyes wide, and blushed a little.

Had she heard about Joanna? No. Or at least unlikely. No tears marred her heavy black make-up and I couldn't imagine someone shedding tears for Chris and not for Joanna.

"Yes?" I asked, cautiously, hoping she wasn't about to

tell me that I had to teach the class after all, because she'd had a galloping attack of true love or some other such nonsense. Only one of us could have an attack of nonsense at one time.

I wanted to go home and get some lunch, call the mobile mechanic and get a new battery so I could get to the police station under my own power.

She beamed. "About . . . huh . . . Lives. I thought I would expound on the Drake theory and perhaps suggest, you know, just a touch, the royal bastard idea. I know most serious scholars despise it, but—"

She went on and on, riffling through lavender notes as she spoke. I finally managed to tell her that yes, everything sounded fine, and make a clean getaway.

The idea of Shakespeare's having been a bastard of Elizabeth the First was, at best, sheer lunacy, but then none of the students in Lives would hear it. Daydreaming, sleeping and necking took up all of their brain cells. One advantage of letting Daphy take over Lives was that any damage caused remained limited.

I took a taxi home, took the elevator up from the front lobby. For once I didn't see Mrs. Murphy.

Mrs. Murphy.

She'd been in Chris's black book.

I tried to picture her attacking Joanna, setting up the gas and the grill to make it all explode. How? Unless, of course, she was being blackmailed for pyromania. We'd need to look over those two records, correlate them.

Neither Brian nor I seemed able to bring ourselves to look at the things.

I wondered if Chris had suffered from the same reluctance, if that was what had caused him to keep two separate records.

Nah. Security, most likely. A victim could get hold of one but not the other. Knowing Chris and how his mind worked, I was surprised he didn't have other copies.

On the other hand, perhaps he did.

My reflection on the mirrored inside of the elevator looked like nothing on Earth. I wondered what Brian would think of me.

What had he found to wear? He hadn't brought any of his own clothes and mine were bound to look funny on him. How much Brian did they leave exposed?

Feeling like a dirty old man, I opened my door.

The place smelled of baking bread.

I stopped. "Brian?" I called, into the homey-scented recesses of the place I'd slept in for ten years.

He got up, appearing from behind the kitchenette counter like a jack-in-the-box. "Oh," he said. "You're home. I thought you'd be at work till twelve thirty." He grimaced. "Lives Two."

He'd memorized my schedule? Why on earth? "Yes, I should have been gone till twelve thirty. However, Daphy is teaching Lives."

"Daphy?" He wore my gray jogging suit just slightly short on his mid riff, but that only reached to the middle of his arms. I noticed, as he came out from behind the counter, that it came up about ten inches on the ankle.

"Daphne Mallard. She wants to be called Daphy." I took my shoes off, set my briefcase down.

"Your wife called," he said.

"My what?" I turned around to face him.

"She *said* she was your wife." He blushed and wiped his hands on a kitchen towel in what looked like an exculpatory gesture.

"Sherry?" I asked. My God, the woman had married

three times—count them three—in the years since leaving me. Couldn't she stop considering herself Mrs. William S. Yates? Was I that unforgettable? *No, just that lucrative.*

He nodded. "She said you called her. Wanted to know what check you were talking about and how much you'd sent." He wiped the already clean counter with the hand towel, looked at me out the corner of his eye.

"Sherry." I walked toward the kitchen.

He had brought out pots and pans and scrubbed them. From the look of it he had also washed down the counters of all visible dust. He stood, organizing my silverware into a compartmented tray I'd never seen in my drawer before. Purchases and innovations.

He looked so homey that I barely resisted an impulse to kiss him and say, *Honey, I'm home.*

"You called her?" He looked anxious. "Your . . . Sherry?"

Why did he look anxious? "She's not my Sherry and yes, I called her," I said. "Last night I thought of the best proof we had that Joanna's death might be foul play." I looked up, hoping he'd notice me conceding the point.

He polished silverware.

I sighed. "It was that someone stole my battery. However, if someone stole my battery to keep me from going to Joanna's rescue, he had to know that she trusted me. He had to know that I might deserve the trust . . . or she did. The only person who even suspected how close Joanna and I had got—as friends, mind you—was Sherry. Also, that someone would need to know what I drove and where the car was likely to be."

He frowned.

I explained my theory that someone had stolen Paul's battery because he'd said or done something that indicated he might go see Chris. Then I counted on my fingers the people who might know I would come to Joanna's rescue: Joanna herself, Sherry and maybe Paul, judging from his misguided jealousy.

Brian frowned still.

I told him that I thought this made it urgent for us to go to Paul's house and talk to him. Not just like any other of Chris's victims, but as an important witness. The whole theory hinged on the fact that he might have said something that had been interpreted as a burning desire to visit Chris.

"We?" Brian asked, hopefully, reminding me.

"We," I said. "But not right away. First I have to get a mobile mechanic out here and get a battery for my car. I'm not riding that contraption you call a bike again." At least not with him doing the driving.

"Not needed," Brian said. "Already got a battery this morning. So we can go to Paul first, and then go see Tony. You remember the appointment with Tony, right?" He opened the fridge, looked at the seeming cornucopia of offerings inside. The fridge had never been that full. Ever. "What do you want for lunch, before we go see the oh-so-sensitive artist?"

Interesting. Was *Brian* being catty now? Something akin to smugness warmed my soul.

"Anything. You went shopping. You seem to have bought an awful lot . . . I mean . . . How much do I owe you?" If he was going to take control of the seduction bit, the least I could do was pay for the food. And if seduction was gone for good, then even more so I should pay for the food.

"You don't owe me anything," he said. "Except for the battery. I'm afraid I can't cover that, but if you let me stay here, at least for a few days, I'll cover the food and stuff like that. It's the least I can do."

I bit my tongue. He would still be paying rent for his old police-impounded place. If so, then he would be very tight on money. However, if I offered him money, chances were it would offend him mortally.

I had to find a way to get around this, somehow.

"I think," Brian said, contemplating the inside of the fridge. "That the lunch *de rigueur* before interrogating refined artists and being interrogated by the police consists of sandwiches and . . . what's your preference? Coffee? Milk?"

"Coffee," I said, still half asleep.

He declined my help and pulled cold cuts and cheese out of the fridge, pulled a loaf of bread from the oven and contemplated it critically. "It's going to be too hot to cut."

Despite these and other doom-saying pronouncements, the bread tasted wonderful, as did the coffee and everything else.

"I left the bread rising while I went to get your battery," Brian said, as he sat beside me and ate his own sandwich with a tall glass of milk. Whole from the looks of it.

I could get used to this.

If I lived long enough and no one arrested me.

Both of which seemed doubtful. This kid's roommates had an eerie way of showing up dead. Calamity Brian? Was I next?

As for being arrested, if Joanna truly hadn't killed herself, the Chief of Police was bound to figure it out. Tony boy might be inexperienced but he didn't look that dumb.

I looked at Brian's hands, as he put the dishes away. Large, capable hands. Good with an ax and probably very good at overpowering a slim woman, killing her, and turning on the gas.

Brian had a good alibi for both nights. Except, he could have killed her before coming over, couldn't he? Had he made a recording that would call me?

No. If he had, Tony would find evidence, right?

I stared sideways at Brian. Was that why the house had been set up to explode?

Brian looked at me, raised his eyebrows. "What?"

No. Then, why would he prevent it exploding? If he had timed all that, he'd have made sure the call came late enough that when we got there the house had already blown up.

And I'd called her back, and that was certainly no recording. On the other hand, she didn't appear to remember calling me before. If there was someone there . . . someone she couldn't mention . . .

No, I was being paranoid. Same as imagining Brian rigging up machines to call me back.

"What?" he repeated.

I smiled at Brian. "Nothing. Just looking at you."

His eyebrows rose further. He smiled and shrugged, resumed eating his sandwich.

Besides I liked him. I wouldn't like a murderer.

Oh, sure, my first lover had tried to kill me by drug OD and bizarre cult-like means, but now I was older and I knew better, didn't I?

XIX

He's Funny That Way

Paul didn't open his oak-paneled door at the first ring, or the second. I had just turned to Brian to say that maybe, just maybe, we should try to find a half-open window to fling the money through and leave well enough alone, when the door opened a crack.

A moss-green eye, about as rational and human looking as a trapped mouse's, peered out at me.

Paul yelped. The door slammed shut. Faustus barked.

I knocked at the door and called as loudly as I could without making an announcement to the whole neighborhood. "Paul, please open the door. We've brought your money back."

It took a while and the sounds coming from the other side of the door could either be deadbolts sliding shut, or deadbolts sliding open. On the other hand, they could very well be deadbolts being shut and then opened, very quickly.

This time, the door flung open enough to reveal Paul's face, a haggard, pale expanse of flesh within which colorless lips writhed aimlessly and out of which glazed eyes stared. Or at least, one glazed right eye. The other eye hid beneath an untidy mass of hair. He wore long boxer shorts in what looked like silk and must have once been white but had gone the grayish tinge of underwear worn on its own for a while.

He smelled like a distillery.

Had he been drinking since I'd left?

Brian took a step back, extended Paul his money, tentatively, at the end of his arm, giving the impression he would have wished for the proverbial ten-foot pole.

Paul stared at the packet of green stuff a long while, frowning, as if not having any idea of a possible use for green rectangular papers with pictures of dead presidents on them.

He put a finger forward, poked at the bundle, looked up at Brian, gave the strangest, most lopsided grin I'd ever seen and lisped, "That's so sweet of you."

Fat lot of good it would do us to ask him anything. He was drunk past any rationality he might ever have had.

He stumbled forward and tried—I think—to hug Brian. Brian supported him on one arm, preventing him from falling, but keeping him at bay.

"Let's take him to the kitchen," I told Brian. "He needs some coffee." Probably a stomach pump, too. What was a lethal dose of alcohol? I opened the door. Faustus stood back, looking indecisive. He half-growled in his throat, looking at Brian.

"Good doggy," I muttered, closing the door behind me and taking Paul's other arm, to help Brian support him.

Faustus' tail wagged.

We walked toward him. He leaped forward, joyously, hindquarters a-wag, the very picture of a doggie in heaven.

I managed to avoid falling on him and patted him with my free hand while we carried Paul in.

"He likes you," Paul said. "He really likes you. That's why I can't understand why you're a crook, because Faustus doesn't like crooks, does he, Faustus? No, nice doggie Faustus doesn't like people who hate his Paul. He didn't like Chris. Not one bit. He liked chasing Chris."

There was a lot more like it, all of it so slurred and muttered that I only half-guessed at the words.

Paul turned baleful eyes to me, then looked at Brian. "You shouldn't believe in him, see. He'll promise all sorts of things, but really, he's just like all the rest of them, out for a good time and nothing else."

How Brian bore up, I didn't know. I tried not to look at him, afraid I'd find him agreeing with Paul.

The living room smelled acidly of vomit, but I wasn't in charge of finding and cleaning stained upholstery. Auntie Bill of the household hints and management had retired before ever going into business.

We maneuvered Paul into the kitchen, sat him at the breakfast table.

A look in the studio told me that Paul had been working. If you could call it that. The lovingly sculpted stone colossus had been given a head that exactly reproduced Chris's cut-off head. As seen on TV. I looked away from it.

Paul had put his face down in his arms and cried softly, while muttering to himself. A sheet with scribbles on it sat by his elbow.

Brian, apparently the god of kitchens and at home in all of them, had found coffee and the coffee making apparatus and started the whole thing going. The smell of coffee erased some of the pungent, acrid odor of vomit and alcohol.

I looked at Paul.

Had I ever got this stinking drunk? Literally stinking? Had anyone else ever seen me like this?

I thought about it. Oh, yes, sure. Sherry. Joanna. Elderman, when he'd been sleeping with Sherry. Probably Mrs. Murphy, too, and the other neighbors.

Why hadn't anyone ever told me how awful it looked?

Then I remembered how awful it felt and the dark pit of despair and self-loathing that fueled my drinking binges.

I looked at the list at Paul's elbow. It said things like breakfast table; dining table; three leather sofas; bed; stove; refrigerator. In front of each of them were two prices, one marked "Garage Sale" the other "Optimum." The optimum column had been totaled at the bottom at twenty-five thousand and then circled viciously with the pencil, over and over. The pencil had broken, both pencil and tip lying beside the sheet.

I touched Paul's arm, as gently as I could.

He looked up, his expression vague.

"Paul? These prices . . . Why do you want to sell your furniture?"

He made a sound, halfway between a hiccup and a sob. "I don't. You see, I don't have any money. What I gave you was all I had in my bank account." He hiccup-sobbed again. "Chris thought I was good for fifty thousand. I don't have fifty thousand. Haven't finished anything." He raised a hand and counted on his fingers. "In one, two, three . . . oh, six months. Don't have cash. Hard pressed to make payments . . . house and car." Hiccup-sob. "Couldn't make them without—"

He tapped the bundle of cash he'd carried pressed to his chest and set on the table in front of him.

Brian approached with a tall, smoking cup of coffee.

"You're just so sweet." Paul reached over, grabbing Brian's wrist and slopping some of the coffee onto the table and floor, apparently without noticing it. "Why don't you forget the loser and stay with me? I'll make you happy."

Oh sure. Did I come across this pathetic when I made drunken passes at someone?

Brian held his face in stony impassivity. He set the cup down on the table, managing not to upset it any more, and put his hand on Paul's shoulder. "Drink," he said. "It will make you feel better."

Fine. I'd find the one man in the world on whom drunken passes *would* work, and Paul was the one who was drunk, not me.

Brian stood up, went to the corner, where the dog dish stood empty, and where Faustus had been whining.

So, it was up to me to get some coffee into Paul. I did manage to get most of the contents of the cup into his mouth, with a lot of cajoling from me and teary protests on his part.

Two minutes later, almost to the second, Paul's eyes lost their glazed look and his face its soft, droopy expression, the first replaced with a gaze of utter despair and the second with an intent frown. He looked from me to Brian, yelped, stood up.

Not again.

"Brian, how strong was that coffee?"

Brian threw the empty dog food can in the trash, turned around. "If it had been any stronger, it would have led revolutions down in South America. Why?" Then he noticed Paul's upright position and stepped over to stand by my side.

Which was probably the wrong thing to do.

Seeing us present a united front, Paul stepped backwards, toppling the chair with a loud crash.

Faustus looked up from his food and barked.

"Stay away from me," Paul said. "How did you get in?"

"You opened the door," I said.

"When we gave you your money back," Brian put in, pointing at the cash.

Paul's frown grew even more intent. He looked at the cash, then up at me, then at Brian.

I cleared my throat. "I find that cold showers often help." And clarified. "I mean, to get over a really good drunk."

"Was I drunk?" Paul asked. He looked at his coffee cup. "Am I drunk?"

"Yes, you probably still are," I said, and cleared my throat again. "I find cold showers—"

He waved me into silence with a slapping motion of the hand, up and down. "Why did you give me this money?" he asked, frowning upwards.

"We never wanted it," Brian said.

We. Good. Let's keep it we. Even with the irresistible distraction of another drunkard on the premises.

"No?" Paul's face twisted with the effort to think through the remaining alcohol fumes. "Why not?" He pointed at me. "You said you had seen Chris's black book." His shaky finger pointed at Brian. "And he said he had the pictures."

Brian nodded.

"You wanted to ask me questions about Chris's death. I thought—I thought—"

"No," I told him. "No." To have finished that sculpture he would need to have worked through the night, wouldn't he? He would need to have been pretty drunk by then, because who would do that while aware? So he couldn't have killed Joanna. And that meant he probably hadn't killed Chris.

Besides if it hadn't been him stealing my battery and lending credence to the theory that his, too, had been stolen, then my battery really must have been stolen by someone else and—

My head reeled. I wondered if drunkenness could be contagious.

"We never thought you committed the murder." A lie here, a lie there, and soon you too will be an expert. "We just need your help to figure out who did."

He looked at me, suspiciously. "Why? Killing Chris . . . public service. Should give the bastard a medal, maybe a marching band. Preventing pain . . . healing society. Good stuff." He nodded, grinning.

Brian made an odd choking sound and said, "Dr. Zimmerman was killed too. I was almost killed."

"What?" Paul asked. He looked from one to the other of us. "Who would kill—" He stared at Brian.

"I find a cold shower often helps—"

"Awright. I heard you already." Paul looked at me, sighed. "Cold? How cold? Oh, fine."

Turning on his heel, he went up the stairs. Thump, thump, thumping, step-by-step, with a dragging cadence.

I looked at Brian, who had knelt on the floor and was fast becoming Faustus' best friend.

So that when he next visited the dog wouldn't give him problems?

I didn't want to go to the studio and face the posthumous portrait of Chris Hogg. I didn't want to go into the living room and maybe run into a puddle of vomit. I also didn't want to stay here and stare forlornly at Paul's list of worldly possessions. If I did, I might very well dip into my father's inheritance to give Paul a hundred thousand or two, and I'd already arranged—more or less—to send money to Sherry and all I needed was another dependent. I could not support a despondent artist in addition to one deranged psychiatrist. There were laws about how many pets a man could have.

So I looked at Brian, who petted the dog.

From upstairs came the sound of a shower running.

"What did he drink?" I asked, more to pass the time than because I expected an answer. I suspected he'd gone through the international selection of beers in his fridge.

Brian gave Faustus a final pat, stood up and opened the trash can. It contained three empty bottles of brandy. Oh. Intent *and* malice. Paul had wanted to do damage.

How much was the lethal dose of alcohol again? For someone with the body mass of an undernourished flea?

No heavy thud came from upstairs.

Brian wandered over to the table, looked at the meager list of Paul's furniture and accouterments. Including, I noticed, a set of chisels. Selling his art materials. Then I thought of what he'd lately done with them. Maybe he should sell them.

"Poor guy is at the end of his rope, isn't he?" Brian asked. He frowned at the sheet, tapping it with the end of the broken pencil. "If Chris was demanding fifty thousand . . ." He let the thought trail like the frayed end of a noose.

The shower stopped.

Brian and I stood, listening.

Thumps, heavier than they'd been when going up, came down the stairs.

Paul emerged into the kitchen via the dining room. His hair dripped, and he'd wrapped himself in his clean white terry robe, which made him look even paler, his complexion even more dishwater-dingy.

He looked at us and frowned and for a moment I thought we'd have to go through the whole explanation routine. But no. He slid toward the cupboard, got a large bottle of aspirin, shook two or three onto his palm, swallowed them dry, made a face.

He turned back, leaned against his sink. “Did you two really bring me my money back?” he asked.

We nodded.

“Oh,” Paul said. “So I didn’t hallucinate that.” He spread his palm over his eyes. “God. My head hurts. I’ve never drunk that much at one sitting in my life.”

“I’m afraid,” I said, and cleared my throat, “I don’t know what the lethal dose—”

Paul lowered his hand and looked resentfully at me. Or maybe the resentful squint was part of his headache because he attempted a smile.

“I don’t think I’m poisoned,” he said. “Or I would have died by now. I did most of the drinking before seven last night.” He wrinkled his nose. “And most of the throwing up. God. I can’t afford a cleaning service anymore. How in hell am I going to clean leather sofas of all things?”

He let his hands hang at his side, looked at both of us. He essayed the smile again, and came closer to a real one this time. His lips actually curved upwards. “All right. So I misjudged both of you. Or at least I did on second take.” He looked from Brian to me, then back again. “You don’t want my money?”

I shook my head and barely resisted offering him some. I did however mutter something about being on the market for some paintings, since I wanted to get rid of the hunting prints I’d got from my father.

“You don’t have to,” Paul said. “If I can pull myself together and finish . . . something, I can get the money. What I finish sells. I just haven’t been able to do anything with Chris hanging over me . . .” He gave a chuckle that sounded almost like a bark. “Yes, I realize that gives me a great motive to get rid of him.” The laughter returned, repeated, spasmodic, losing itself in a fit of coughing. “You know, the worst part is that I resent not having done it. I'd feel so much better if I had at least taken a whack at him."

I found myself nodding in empathy. "I know," I said. "An eyebrow. Maybe a toe."

Brian sighed, a chest-shaking sigh. "I figured I deserved at least an elbow, perhaps a knee." He looked up. "For the time he cleaned the dishes with a blowtorch." He shook his head. "I've been feeling awful about wanting to kill him and regretting not having had a hand in it ever since he was found."

"*You've* been feeling awful?" Paul asked. "My father has arranged for a memorial service and I'll have to pretend . . ." He shook his head in turn, looked back up at Brian. "You're all right," he said.

He looked at me. "As for you, I always thought you were more than all right. I'm sorry. For what I said—About Brian—I saw the way you looked when I mentioned him and I was so jealous. I was right, of course." He opened his eyes wide, squared his shoulders. "I'm glad I still have a headache to distract me, otherwise I'd be crying and carrying on." He looked at me again, his eyes softened. "I've always wanted what you have."

He'd always wanted a half-dead career, or perhaps black curls fast going gray . . . Or was it the round, unexceptional features he really had a hankering to possess?

"I mean the two of you." He looked at Brian, shook his head.

What we had? A really bad case of unfinished business? Suspicion and nagging misgivings? Oh, yeah, didn't everyone want some of that?

Never mind. "What we wanted to know," I said, changing to the role of mystery solving super-professor-sleuth again, though I suspected Paul had stolen the Boozeman barrel from me. "What we must know is if anyone had a reason to suspect that you might come and see Chris the night he was killed?"

Paul frowned. "Why?"

"Because someone stole your battery. Someone stole my battery, because they thought I might come to help Joanna . . . Dr. Zimmerman." I explained the whole theory, which involved explaining how Brian and I had found Joanna and why we thought she had not killed herself.

Halfway through, Paul asked Brian for another cup of his special paint-removing coffee. "It might strip my stomach lining," he said. "But it seems to do wonders for my thoughts."

Brian had obliged and I'd repeated my explanation.

At the end, Paul frowned at me. He shook his head. "But you see, I only told Chris. I only told Chris himself. That I'd drop by, to bring him a partial payment." He pointed to the packet on the table. "That."

"No one else?" I asked.

"No one else. I was going to drop by on the way to Bad Boys and then I was going to meet you and spend the night with you and then I was going to—" Something fiery and determined came to his eyes.

I knew, without his saying it, that he'd been intending on one wild fling before committing suicide.

I felt a chill, as if I'd touched a chord of despair within him, a chord of abandon higher and louder than I myself had ever experienced. Even after Lupi tried to kill me.

I wondered if Chris had seen that look and misread it, and if that was why he'd hid all his notes and his pictures in Brian's possessions, lest Paul would steal them.

Drinking his coffee, Paul had wandered over to where he had a direct line-of-sight to the studio.

He shook and made a gagging sound and if Brian hadn't rushed to the rescue, the cup of coffee would have ended up broken on the floor.

Paul turned to me, mouth agape. "Did you—Did you? Did you do that?"

I shook my head. "Look," I said. "I have many talents, and I've been known to sketch a bit. But I don't sculpt and not in stone. That required a bigger drunk than I've ever indulged. No."

"Gahhh," Paul said. He refused the cup of coffee that Brian tried to hand back to him. He went into the studio, approached the large stone thing, ran his hand over the features, as though wanting to make sure of their solidity.

"Gahhh," he repeated. "Revolting. That's not . . . not what I had planned at all." He stood immobile for a moment, contemplating the thing.

"You know, if I call it something like Memorial, I probably can sell it." He grinned. "The newspapers are all full of stories about the tragedy that befell my family. I can exploit that. Isn't that just what Chris deserves?"

He turned around and smiled, a naughty twinkle in his eye that for once didn't seem to relate to sex. "You know none of my family is getting any of Chris's money? Not even poor Dad, who could use it? Apparently Chris married Tiff and the money is in both their names. Yeah, the little so-and-so stands to inherit all his ill-gotten gains."

"You could sue," Brian said. "I mean for—"

"Blackmail?" Paul asked. "Get it all out on the street that I was being blackmailed and why." He made a face. "Even if I could stand it, I don't think John could."

He must have read bafflement in my expression, because he blushed and said, "Come on, you've seen the pictures."

"No," I said.

"Not all of them," Brian put in. "We . . . we keep saying we will, but we haven't. It's . . ." He made a face.

"You're sweet. You really are." Paul smiled at Brian. Then he bit his lower lip.

"Can I have them? I mean, mine? Can I have them and burn them so that—" He stopped, blushed again.

"As soon as this is over with," Brian said. "Yes."

"Oh, good," Paul said. "I was so afraid you'd turn them over to the police and they'd end up in some file and eventually fall in someone's hands again." He shook his head. "Maybe I could take it. The artistic community is very forgiving. But John is in this investment firm. He's married." He shook his head again. "We were awfully young. We didn't know . . ."

I wondered if Brian was getting the drift. I was getting a fairly good idea of why Paul had paid and paid and paid.

Yet, he seemed so likeable, so . . . damn wholesome. And he said he'd been young . . .

I refused to think about it. That was the problem of blackmail, I thought. Like those horrendous pictures Victorians hung in their children's rooms, they kept the sin ever before the sinner. Maybe Paul, too, should have a chance to grow up. To forget.

Oblivious to my moral dilemma, Paul smiled at the disgusting statue. "I'll sell it and make money off Chris, that's what." He turned back to us. "I'm sorry I couldn't help you anymore. I need to polish this thing and see if I can get it to the gallery in Denver that asked me for a piece for their show." He turned his back on us. He got some gray powder from a pack, and some liquid from a bottle, and a thick cloth.

I looked at Brian. "I think that's the bum's rush."

To my surprise Brian didn't look the least offended. He nodded, smiling at Paul's back.

If I'd known he fell for drunken slobs with a hidden past of perverse sexual peccadilloes . . . Damn it, my boat had come in and someone else was rowing it away.

Faustus followed us to the door, wagging his tail.

Paul hadn't exactly put paid to the theory of murder and battery theft.

So, only Chris had known of his planned visit. Chris might have talked. To his . . . wife? To someone else? Had he bragged about his ability to bring Paul to despair? He might have. I remembered the essays he'd written. It was the sort of bastard Chris Hogg had been.

I'd tell my theory to the Chief of Police, I thought, on the way downtown.

If I could manage it without mentioning the blackmail business.

The question was, if I convinced Tony that Joanna hadn't killed herself, would I be putting the noose around my own neck?

XX

What Can I Hope For? I Wish I Knew.

A brunette who had seen better days sat at the front desk in the Chief of Police's office, doing something with mysterious index cards and a cheap cardboard file holder. Around her stretched what I supposed was the reception area but might once have been everything from a meeting hall to a jail. Gloomy and dark, it extended back a good twenty feet and upward a good ten, to naked rafters from which one expected to see a cow rustler or two hanging.

At the back, I thought I discerned a series of doors. It was hard to tell, as the only light in the entrance came from a small window behind me, and the glass had long ceased being transparent, having given out under a coat of dirt and cobwebs.

We stood there, while the woman sorted her index cards.

I smelled mildew and dust.

Brian cleared his throat.

The receptionist looked up at us, over her reading glasses, as though sure we'd come to steal the national treasury and had just got this building by accident. "May I help you, gentlemen?"

Duels had been fought on Main Street at high noon for lesser insults than the tone she used to pronounce *gentlemen.*

"We have an appointment to see Tony," Brian said

firmly. He looked tired, or perhaps he was still thinking about Paul.

I wondered if I could buy a bottle somewhere and get drunk within the next hour, to prevent him from going and throwing himself at the artist. Anything for the blond.

"Police Chief Marssano," Brian said to the woman's blank stare.

The look of disbelief intensified.

She pushed her glasses back and told us, firmly, "We'll see."

Meaning, it seemed, that we were naughty lying boys and would be held after class until we repented.

She got her ponderous self out from behind the desk and walked to the back of the room and down a long hallway, until her shapeless gray dress merged with the dingy gloom.

We heard her voice, then a male voice. She sounded incredulous.

Coming back out, she said, "Police Chief Marssano would like to see Mr. Quick. And then you."

The admission visibly hurt her. She didn't even show Brian how to find the legendary Chief of Police of Lythia. Instead, she parked her bulk behind the desk and went back to her index cards.

He walked the same route she had until his blond hair vanished in the dark hallway.

I heard the echoes of two male voices, too distant to identify, much less discern the words they pronounced. They remained even for a long time, in a pleasant conversational pace.

Looking around, I found a row of metal chairs to the right of the receptionist, against the wall.

The secretary/receptionist shuffled her index cards, wrote this on one and then that on the other, all the while staring at me over the top of her glasses.

I bit my tongue, to keep from asking her if she knew the way to Fort Knox.

I ignored her glare by stretching my legs in front of me, reclining as much as the hard metal chair would allow and closing my eyes.

"Professor—Bill?"

I felt a hand on my shoulder, opened my eyes. Brian withdrew his hand, smiled at me. "You snore."

Well, yes. Why did this make him sound like he'd just made the most wonderful discovery?

If it weren't for the receptionist at her desk, her gimlet eye intent upon our every movement, I would have told Brian that he had really odd tastes in men: drunken slobs, guys who snored. I'd just bet if he met a good belcher he'd be gone.

I brought myself to sitting upright with some effort, my bones having got used to the confines of the chair and being loath to change their habits.

"Tony would like to see you now." Brian's smile had vanished. He looked upset. I wondered why.

I could go back to snoring. Any minute. Again, the glare of the receptionist restrained any such verbal reassurance.

I stood up. My joints creaked their protest.

I had been right about the doors at the end of the room. There were five of them. Four were closed. The open one revealed a room that didn't look like part and parcel of the same building that housed the entrance room. Clean, spacious, freshly painted white, Police Chief Marssano's office contained a white desk with a glass top, two leather chairs facing the desk, another one behind it, wooden bookcases around the walls. The walls were adorned with pictures in bold red frames. One of the pictures showed a red Porsche, another a cliff-top house on a seaside village. The third, bigger than the other two, drew my eyes and held them in fascination as I walked into the room.

It showed a young, dark-haired woman in a tight red wool dress. Though it looked like the enlargement of a snapshot taken in a casual situation, the woman had to be computer-enhanced. They just didn't make them like that. Not since the last inspired artist of antiquity had sculpted the perfect Aphrodite.

Someone cleared his throat, loudly. "You know my fiancée, by any chance, Dr. Yates?"

I turned to see the Chief of Police standing up behind his desk, staring at me with an expression halfway between baffled and amused.

"Your fiancée?" I asked.

He waved toward the picture. "Regina Angelica? Gina to her friends?"

I shook my head.

Tony cocked his head sideways. "You seemed very . . . interested."

"She's beautiful," I said, feeling my cheeks color as I sat down on the chair across from his desk. "Ahem. Congratulations."

He sat down, too, and stared at me, eyebrows low over his eyes. "So," he said. "Tell me verbatim what happened yesterday night."

Yesterday night. The sofa. It felt like years ago. Now I knew that it must have been a fluke. The man's true interest lay in belching drunkards.

For the first time in my life I was disqualified by reason of sobriety.

Skirting around that piece of furniture that had come to embody my dearest memories and my most forlorn hopes, I went on to tell about everything else. Everything else, except the pictures and the black book and everything I knew about blackmail, which I'd also left out of my written account because I really didn't want to put a noose around my neck.

I wondered if Brian had talked, but I didn't think so. Brian, being Brian, and apparently possessed by the spirit of Poirot, Lord Wimsey and Nero Wolfe all rolled into one—though in a much nicer package than any of those fictional sleuths—would want to keep it all to himself. So that he could go poking around dark corners and interrogating perfect strangers, who, of course, would fall all over themselves to give themselves away to him.

Tony listened to my little speech with eyebrows raised, reclining on his chair, his feet on his desk and his hands behind his head. He didn't bother to make notes, nor should he, since I had written all this in the report last night.

At the end, he took his feet from his desk, sat upright. "Incredible. Word for word what you wrote," he said.

Oh, yeah. Well, I'd had practice memorizing and reciting my own drivel. All those years of teaching Lives.

Tony set his elbows on the desk, leaned forward, looked at me, his black eyes piercing. "So, you don't want to change anything about it, do you?"

I stared. Had Brian . . . ? Or was Tony playing the *your accomplice confessed* game? I shook my head.

Tony glowered. "Dr. Yates, who are your enemies?"

I stared, opened my mouth. Really stupid students, I thought. Like the dumbbells that didn't know any grammar but wanted to be great writers. And the daddies who financed their dreams. I closed my mouth.

"How do you feel about Doctor Carl Jung Elderman?"

I frowned. "That he's annoying?" I shrugged. "I don't know. I avoid him when I can."

Tony frowned. "University gossip has it that he was your wife's lover."

I sighed. "Yes. Still, you see, Sherry and I had an arrangement. My father chose her, arranged for her to marry me. Not that I put up too much resistance. I was only sixteen. All the same, it wasn't my idea."

Tony stared. "Sixteen."

"Huh . . . yeah. I . . . got into some trouble and my father thought I needed settling down, so he offered to pay for Sherry to get her specialty training. She was one of his doctors. She was—She is considerably older than I am."

Tony stared. I could see his mind working, see him approach the thought then back away from it. He shook his head, as if to rid himself of the intricacies of my life story. "So, you didn't mind Dr. Elderman being your wife's lover?"

I shook my head, smiled. "Better her than me."

Tony's eyes rounded and his lips almost formed a smile before he got control of them. He nodded. "When I questioned him he told me how unstable you were and how you had been under psychiatric care. He told me all of this unprompted, unasked."

I sighed. "Elderman has always been jealous of my money. I don't know why. My father left me a fortune and he . . . well, he more or less bought me my position in Bile. I think Elderman thought I would never have got it otherwise. I could have. I had offers from colleges in California. My father just thought that California would be bad for me . . . That's where I'd got in trouble before."

Tony tilted his head sideways. "Would Elderman hate you enough to spy on you? To make an anonymous call about you?"

I shrugged. "He's been strange lately," I admitted. "Stranger than usual." I thought of our recent talks. "He seems fixated on Brian."

"So, if he saw someone leave Brian's house dragging an unconscious Brian, he might assume it was you?"

"Yes, but he couldn't have mistaken Dr. Zimmerman for me," I said. "She was a woman."

Tony waved that away. "She was wearing a heavy, large, man's raincoat. At least, we found it in her home. Blood-stained."

Oh.

Tony shook his head. "Anyway . . . we're just trying to tie it up, trying to figure out who used the first phone booth on the way into Lythia. Even though it's the warehouse district, the phone is just outside the convenience store. We have a pretty good description of who used it."

"Oh." I said.

"Your wife . . . your ex-wife. She's a doctor. Does she still go under the name Yates?"

I stared. "Yes. Her degree is under that name, and she's kept it."

"Hmm," Tony said. "Elderman said she was close to Dr. Zimmerman, is that true?"

I nodded.

"Close enough that your wife might have called a prescription for her to a local pharmacy?"

I stared.

"The sleeping pills Dr. Zimmerman used in her coffee, to kill herself. They were prescribed for her by a Dr. S. Yates."

"Yes," I said. "Yes, they were close." Though I never knew Sherry still prescribed anything for Joanna. Then again, Joanna would hardly have asked Dr. Hogg, would she? "So, you really think Joanna killed Chris Hogg and then herself?"

Tony sighed. "Yes, much to Brian's chagrin. I suppose you too subscribe to the crazy notion that she was murdered?"

The crazy notion? I didn't want to touch that. Instead, I followed the thought that Tony no longer suspected me. Which was why he'd relaxed while talking to me.

There might be hope, yet.

I might get the blond without the police objecting, too.

And yet, Joanna was my friend, my adopted little sister. "There's something you have to know," I said. And I proceeded to tell him all about the stolen batteries, all the while maneuvering so as not to mention that Paul had been blackmailed.

Tony sighed. He looked pityingly at me.

"All right. I know Brian is a fool, but let's see how much of a fool you're willing to be for his sake. Let's admit someone might have planted the ax and, somehow, the blood. There's more. Will you explain to me how the mythical someone planted Dr. Zimmerman's fingerprints all over Brian's rifled and overturned furniture, books and possessions?"

XXI

Don't Take the Dreams to Which I Cling

By the time we left the police station, Brian looked even more tired and pale.

To make things more cheerful, a snowstorm had started outside. Big thick flakes obscured the car, the edges of the parking lot, the road.

Cars crept by, slowly, lights on.

When we'd come in, the weather had been cold but mild. Neither of us wore a jacket.

I got the ice scraper and went after the frost on the windshield, while I told Brian to get in. He insisted on staying out and using his bare hand to brush snow off the windows.

He didn't look well.

When we finally got in the car, he was shivering, and his hands had turned blue. Resisting a temptation to rub his fingers and make it all better, I turned the heat on full blast and hoped it would do the trick.

He held his hands to the vent, as though it were a fire, while I drove the car, in creeping steps out of the parking lot, guessing where the ramp was, guessing where the edge of the road might be, guessing . . .

Missing my guess, I scraped the underside of the car, then thumped the back hard as I pulled out onto the street.

"Now it's up to us," Brian said.

I tried to discern, through the hazy white curtain ahead, where the road might turn, and where it might go. The lights of the car did no more than add a hazy, spider-webby glow. I didn't ask what was up to us. I didn't want to know.

He told me, anyway, while he hunched forward on the seat, warming his hands. "If Tony believes that Dr. Zimmerman's death was a suicide and won't do anything about it, then it's up to us to investigate it further."

I leaned forward, too, trying to see through the windshield. Were those the lights of a car just ahead of us?

I pumped the brakes, slowing just enough that by the time I determined they were not car lights but the reflected light from a shop window, I could turn without going up on the sidewalk.

"He seemed to have some pretty convincing arguments," I said, because Brian seemed to expect a response, hunched as he was over the heat vent, and staring at me, expectantly. "For suicide. I mean, the fingerprints in your house and all."

Why did he want it to be murder? Did he want it to be me? Was he really trying to implicate me?

His chin went all square. "You can't mean that. Just because—I don't believe it."

He didn't believe it, and his not believing it, of course, settled the matter. Oh, God, had I ever been that young?

I kept my eyes off him, because if I looked at him I'd be quite willing to concede that the sky was bright pink, the sun a flashlight and the moon made of green cheese. I'd also be willing to confess to murdering Chris Hogg and Joanna, too, while I was at it.

Ahead, the snow fell ever thicker. The windshield wipers couldn't keep up. I stopped, or rather, slid the car until it slid no more, got out, swept the snow off the windshield.

It didn't improve things much. Even out there, all I could ascertain was that the snow was wet and clung to my face, intruded in my nostrils, filled my mouth when I opened it for a deep breath.

I thought I discerned, with my cold-stung eyes, the turn of the road just ahead, that, at a creeping pace, would lead us to Lockmasters.

Brian stared at me as I silently got in, sat down, closed the door and attempted to navigate us down the hill.

The gas tank was on a quarter full. I could very well run out. All the scary stories of people lost in a Colorado snowstorm who died buried in snow in the middle of inhabited areas, only to be discovered by the road-clearing crews a week later, came to mind.

"You can't believe that about Dr. Zimmerman," Brian said. "You couldn't. She'd never hit me on the head and drop me in the river."

Ah. *I* could, I supposed.

The car made it down the steep street that led to the Main Street of Lythia at a barely controlled slide, while I prayed I wouldn't get a red light or a car in my way at the bottom of the hill, because God knew I couldn't hope to brake.

He'd never seen Joanna in a dither. Even I had never seen Joanna after she made such a big mistake as kill someone. On the other hand, I'd seen her scared. I could very well imagine the panic she must have flown into when she realized what had happened, what she'd just done. Brian just had no experience of panic.

Through the haze of snow, I discerned a red light and the creeping white lights of other cars going the other way. Oh, God. I pumped the brakes frantically, sliding all the way.

At the last minute, when I was ready to twist the wheel sideways to prevent us crashing, the light changed to green. We slid through the intersection.

"She wouldn't have killed Chris with an ax," Brian said.

I was trying to think of a tactful way to tell him that he couldn't possibly know Joanna like I knew Joanna. But hot, nervous, filled with relief at having escaped the intersection and with nervousness about the rest of the way, what I said was, "Brian, you're painfully young. You don't know a heck of a lot about people. Please shut up."

The second after I heard the horrible words come out of my mouth, I wanted to call them back. The minute I heard them, I knew Brian couldn't possibly have suspected me. If he thought someone had killed Joanna, he knew it couldn't be me. I'd been with him. On the sofa. So, if Tony accepted Brian's version, he'd also have to exonerate me.

I wanted to rewind the last minute and record something different. I couldn't.

I saw Brian's head move back, saw him stare at me incredulously, watched his jaw turn all angles and his lips go stiff and straight.

Damn, damn, damn, I thought, as I drove, recklessly the rest of the way, into the underground garage of Lockmasters.

"If you don't mind, I'll come upstairs and pick up my things," Brian said, all formal.

I stared at the snow on the hood of my car, glaringly bright in the insufficient light of my condo's underground garage. "Where would you go?" I asked.

"Back home. Tony has released the site, since he's closed the investigation."

How he could speak while keeping his lips straight and rigid was a mystery of physics. How he managed to get out of the car without allowing his gaze to brush any part of me, not even once, constituted another mystery.

"You can't be serious," I said. "How could you go? On Bucephallus? In this weather?"

He didn't even notice that I'd called his bike by its given name.

He just said, voice colder than the storm outside, "I'll do fine, thank you. I've been through worse weather." He slammed the MG door shut.

The ride in the elevator had never been so long. I kept looking at Brian and at his reflection on the mirrored walls. Tall and lean and oh-so-offended.

Beside him, I looked small and dark and shell-shocked.

I had no reason to be shocked. I was an idiot.

In a daze, I followed him into my condo. He picked up his own dirty clothes from the living room sofa, and walked toward the guest bathroom.

I followed.

He shut the door in my face.

"You bought all this food," I said to the smooth, closed door. "You can't leave."

A cold fear at my heart, a dreadful feeling of lonely despondency told me that, yes, he could very well leave. But damn it, damn it, damn it, I didn't want him to.

He didn't answer for a long time. When he opened the door, he was fully dressed in his own clothing. I felt cheated that I wouldn't be able to at least glimpse his wrists and ankles. He held the gray bundle of my jogging suit on the crook of his elbow. "I'll take this and wash it and—"

"No." I found my voice, snatched the clothes from his elbow. Wash them? I didn't think so. It might be the only thing I had that reminded me of Brian. Ever. "Why don't you stay?" I pleaded, hearing despair and humiliating whining in my voice. "You could have dinner and then go."

He shook his head. "I don't believe so, Professor Yates. I have a Bile Writer's Club Meeting early tomorrow."

Good God, I'd been traded in for art.

I followed him to the door, as shameless and slavish as Faustus when he'd followed us. Only, if I had a tail, it wouldn't have been wagging. It would have been trailing behind me, lower than a worm's belly.

At the door, he actually had the nerve to stand and give this stiff-lipped little speech, about how grateful he was that I'd let him use my sofa for the night.

My sofa. I'd gladly have let him use anything.

Here, he was thanking me for the *sofa* of all things.

I watched him enter the elevator before I closed the door. Slowly, it was borne upon me that there wouldn't be a sofa in my future. Not with company. Or not with Brian for company. Never again.

I set my Brian-used jogging suit on the back of a chair with care appropriate to saint's relics.

In the kitchen, the cabinets under the counter were untouched, as was my cache of bourbon. Brian's organizing either hadn't extended here, or he'd left well enough alone.

I got a cup from the cabinet, a pink vessel cheerfully illustrated with a smiley face and the words, *I'm OK, You're Definitely Weird.*

The bourbon burned going down, but it warmed some cold, cold center within myself. I took the bottle to the sofa, dispensing with the nicety of the cup.

Closing my eyes, I tried to get used to the idea that Brian would never again call me *Bill.* He would never get any closer than just one more face in my classes, one more set of papers to correct.

I couldn't.

Though I'd never been sure on the matter of the sofa, at some level I'd counted on having Brian at least as a friend.

I'd thought I'd be able to talk to him, joke with him, as a friend, until he graduated. I'd hoped to watch him growing a little more mature, the possibilities of a relationship between us more palatable. I'd hoped that maybe, just maybe, he'd develop an unlikely fascination with fast-aging college professors who taught boring classes.

Now even that distant hope was gone.

I couldn't get used to the idea. I looked at the clock. Five p.m. on a Friday night. Come Monday, I'd be teaching Lives and Brian would sit on the front row, handsome and remote, unavoidable and unattainable.

My heart would break.

I drank and drank, till a warm haze enveloped my mind and I couldn't think clearly, couldn't clearly picture Brian sitting in class, a stranger, out of my reach.

Out of nowhere, the thought came that Tony still hadn't explained the missing battery, or for that matter the grill. Who the hell blew themselves up when they committed suicide? I shrugged. So, my battery had been stolen, as had Paul's. Maybe there was a gang of battery thieves operating in Lythia. Certainly, coincidences did happen.

Wait . . . hadn't Mrs. Murphy said something about Joanna taking care of Chris? If I proved to Brian that I had been right, would he forgive me my ham-handed phrasing?

I sat bolt upright, splashing the remaining half of the bottle all over myself. Mrs. Murphy.

She had been going down in the elevator, hadn't she, when I arrived on Halloween? What the hell had a respectable old lady like that been doing out at that unholy an hour? And fully dressed, too.

Bleary eyed, ignoring the fact that furniture, walls and

floor all appeared to sway and that I felt as though walking demanded sea legs, I made it to my door, opened it, stumbled across the hallway, laid my hand against the Murphy's doorbell.

I don't know how long it took for Mrs. Murphy to open the door.

When she did, she stared at me.

"No, please. Don't close the door," I said, before I realized she was making no effort to close it, just standing there, staring at me, eyes open wide, with the expression of a bird confronted with a snake. "I don't want to blackmail you," I said. "I don't want to upset you." I turned to her.

She still looked thunderstruck, but slowly her lips shaped something like a disapproving scowl. "You've been drinking."

"Undoubtedly." I lifted my left hand, where I still held the bottle, God alone knows for what reason. "The blond left. I insulted the blond. No more Bambi-Brian-Bacchus. So I drank. Still, I need to know . . . did Joanna kill Chris?"

Blankness faded from the china-blue eyes, replaced with sheer surprise. "Joanna?" she asked. "Zimmerman?"

I nodded. "Did she?" I asked. "The police say she did, but the blond says she didn't. I . . . I just want to know. I used to be her friend."

"Why should she kill him?" Mrs. Murphy asked. "All she wanted was the black book and the photos. Her friend said he'd be seeing Chris that night and could he borrow her car because he had some problem with his car. So she asked me to drive her there. I have this Viper that Mr. Murphy just bought and I don't mind driving at all, even in adverse weather. So we looked for the book. That's all we did. Neither of us could afford the blackmail anymore, and Joanna expects to get tenure and she really can't have this standing in the way."

I leaned against the doorframe. That's all they'd done. Mrs. Murphy had been there with Joanna, and she said they hadn't killed anyone. I tried to picture Mrs. Murphy witnessing an ax murder and lying about it. I couldn't.

Mrs. Murphy looked up at me, her eyes bright as a bird's. "Just ask Joanna. She'll tell you."

So, she hadn't heard of the latest death. Tony must have kept it out of the papers, for once. I didn't have the courage to tell her. "How did the place look when you got there?"

Mrs. Murphy wrinkled her nose. "Clean. Much cleaner than I expected that horrible boy to keep it. I'm afraid we left it in a big mess. It did smell a bit too much like bleach when I got there, but it was clean and neat."

I stared. Bleach. The murderer had already cleaned up. Brian had been in the car, headed for the river. I'd been leaving Bad Boys, depressed about Paul's standing me up, blissfully unaware that I would fall hard for someone in just a few hours. Then I would leave him with the Chief of Police, and go home and see Mrs. Murphy. "But . . . you were *leaving* when I got here."

She nodded. "Oh, that was afterwards. Dear Joanna found that she had stains on her upholstery and she wanted me to come over . . . I told her possibly her friend had spilled something. She thought it was blood, but at the time I thought that was unlikely. She was so upset. She got more upset when they found the dreadful creature all chopped up. Not that she'd believe her friend had done it, and really, I have trouble believing it too, though her friend is not what I'd call suitable."

I blinked myopically at her. "Why would Joanna call you?"

Mrs. Murphy looked surprised, then sighed. Her cheekbones colored a bright pink. "Joanna is my daughter. She . . . she married a dreadful man and then she did some rather horrid things, but she got divorced and now she's settled and her troubles are all behind her, and we're friends." She looked at me dubiously. "I hope you won't tell people. About her getting married, I mean, to an awful man. She said I could trust you, that you're a good man, despite . . . well . . . the clothes you wore the other night." She sniffed. "Though in my time no man would wear a mini-skirt." She sighed. "Joanna always says you'd be the man for her if you weren't . . . well . . . funny."

Yes, well. Very funny. Watch me laugh.

"Frankly . . . well, dear Joanna does have odd tastes."

I wondered how long it would take the authorities to figure out who Joanna's next of kin were and notify the bright, chattering Mrs. Murphy.

Then I wondered why Joanna had never told me who her parents were when they lived just next door. Perhaps she had. So many things I'd never paid attention to. She told her mother I'd be the one man for her . . . God help us.

Maybe it was best for all concerned I'd never noticed any inkling of that in Joanna. I might, just might have been tempted. To her regret and mine.

"Her friend, this man she's been seeing," Mrs. Murphy said. "He's not very good for her. I'm sure he beats her. He stained her car upholstery that night. Quite probably blood. She's thinking of moving to another town. She's been circulating her resume. Of course, if she gets tenure . . ."

I couldn't stand it anymore.

I don't know what I told Mrs. Murphy and I'm not absolutely sure how I drove across town amid the still blinding snowstorm, as drunk as I was.

Next thing I knew, I was standing on the blond's doorstep, half-filled bottle firmly under my left arm.

I had no clue at all how to get Brian to listen to me, and even less clue how to apologize, how to get his chin to soften, his lips to speak normally again.

While I stood there, thinking that Mrs. Murphy had as well as named Elderman, because he was Joanna's friend, the one who slept with her, and at the same time, a friend had borrowed her car.

Elderman had tried to implicate me in the crime.

Elderman.

I realized that because of our unspoken reluctance to touch the pictures, Brian and I had never searched the picture packet for Elderman's face.

XXII

Listen, My Heart

I had only the time to worry that perhaps Brian hadn't made it home, perhaps the motorcycle had crashed somewhere and I'd driven by his twisted corpse, snow-blind and unknowing.

The lavender door opened. Brian stood there, his body definitely not twisted. He wore thick jogging pants and a heavy pullover and stared at me, his jaw attempting to go to straight angles, but his eyes wide with shock.

Behind him, I saw the living room, halfway in a semblance of order. I'd slept on his table, back when the world was young and new, it seemed. Back when I had hope.

I looked up at him, miserably, trying to figure out how to say something, anything, that wouldn't make him shut the door in my face.

"We have to find a picture—"

The world spun twice and my stomach attempted to careen toward my mouth. I'd drunk on an empty stomach and then I'd run about, driven across town. Suddenly, verticality seemed more than my body could handle. I felt myself lean forward and tried to speak normally, but my voice fluttered from a whisper to a yell. "Picture of Elderman."

Brian's mouth opened. His eyes had an I-don't-believe-this expression. I thought he would yelp and close the door.

"Don't—" I tried to step forward and hold the door open. Instead, I fell straight down, while my stomach shot toward my mouth.

Next thing I knew, Brian was holding me upright, as I retched. All over him. I tried to stop it, but the stomach-tightening spasms just kept shaking me and I kept throwing up.

He didn't push me way. Perhaps he was too shocked. Or perhaps he thought—accurately—that if he pushed me the slightest bit, I'd bash my brain in on the doorframe.

All the while I tried to speak, to explain this was not what I had intended to do, that I had not meant to throw up on him.

"What have you done to yourself?" Brian asked. He didn't sound mad. More disgusted. He pulled me into his house, closed the door.

It was almost as cold inside the house as outside.

Disconnected, senseless like disjointed frames of a post-modern movie, I saw the stairs, as I was pulled up them, then glimpsed the inside of a bathroom with a claw tub and a standing sink.

Brian turned the shower on. I heard it. I tried to speak but couldn't. My mouth tasted foul and I felt dizzy.

He helped me over the side of the claw tub. I let him guide me.

Next thing I knew, I was standing, fully dressed, under freezing water.

One second, two, three. Sobriety or a reasonable surfeit thereof, hit me. I'd thrown up on Brian.

He'd stuck me, fully dressed, under freezing water.

A punishment?

I couldn't ask. He was nowhere in sight. Navigating the perilous edge of the tub, I got out, tiptoed to the door of the bathroom, closed it. The ambient temperature was so chilly that my teeth chattered. I adjusted the water to a more reasonable temperature, peeled my clothes off, got into the shower again.

After two minutes and some vigorous use of Brian's soap, I felt human enough and de-stunk enough to step out.

It was still freezing, out there.

Two towels awaited on the rack. The thought that one of them might be Chris's made me shiver, but nowhere as much as the temperature did. Both towels looked clean. I grabbed one, dried myself, stared at the mass of soggy, wet clothing at my feet. I couldn't put them back on.

I'd just struck a compromise and wrapped a towel around my waist and my arms around myself, meaning to go out and search for Brian, when he knocked at the door.

I opened it a crack. He handed me a cup of paint-peeling coffee, muttering, "Maybe I should patent the recipe. For the coffee."

I took the cup, opened the door fully.

Brian stared. Visibly stared at me. His cheeks colored. He looked away. "I'm sorry," he said.

Ah, yes, I bet he regretted that sofa now. I'd never exactly had a buff athlete body. Even while young and reasonably in shape, the best I could boast was a lean, wiry body.

I drank the coffee. It was so strong that I felt my eyeballs bulge as I drank it and fully expected a little chimney to appear on the top of my head and let out three sharp hoots, cartoon style. Brian had, mercifully, put in what tasted like five cups of sugar. So, maybe he didn't hate me.

He sidled past me, grabbed my dirty clothes from the floor. "I'm sorry," he repeated. "It's freezing cold in here because the heat failed and I haven't been able to make it work again. The landlord said he would have someone here in a couple of days. We'll get you some clothes."

His own clothes, I noticed, remained vomit-splattered. "Come," he said.

I followed him, across a narrow hallway to a bedroom just large enough to contain a double bed and dresser and a bedside table, of twenties vintage, an armchair and a small white desk.

He rummaged in the dresser drawer, brought out a pair of jeans and a white sweatshirt, threw them on the bed. "Put these on," he said. "Drink your coffee. I'll go shower and change." He picked up another bundle of clothing and left.

He didn't seem mad, I thought. Even though I'd thrown up on him, he looked considerably less aggrieved than he'd been when he'd left my place. Maybe he'd realized I hadn't meant to insult him. Or maybe he really *did* like drunken slobs. In nascent hope, I put the jeans on.

They were too large on the waist, so they looked like hip-huggers and gave me an awful lot of leg to roll up at the bottom. On the other hand, the sweatshirt, an XXL printed with *OUR LADY OF PERPETUAL PURGATORY* in fiery letters, and *The Fighting Jesuits,* in more discreet black type just beneath it, was long enough to cover my extra portion of exposed mid riff.

Having put the clothes on, I sat on the bed, drinking the coffee, thinking of what I'd tried to tell Brian, what I'd tried to ask him just before I got sick. Something about Elderman.

Oh, yes, the pictures. He'd probably brought them, inside his jacket. Could we look at them? Had Brian looked through them all at any time? Could we also look through the notebook, see if it mentioned Elderman?

Because I was still half-drunk and to think was to do, I

got up, marched across the hallway, opened the door to the bathroom and managed to get out, "Do you think we could get pictures of Elderman?" before the scene in front of my eyes made its way to my synapses.

Brian stood outside the bathtub, completely naked. He had a foot on the toilet lid, a towel in his hand and was drying his leg. He was even more naked than when I'd got him out of the river. By the light bulb on the ceiling of the bathroom, I could see each one of the very pale hairs that glimmered across his skin, descending from his chest and making a line down his flat belly, a line that bifurcated around his belly button and—

He made a sound like coughing. "I'll be out in just a second. If you'd wait," he said. "Please."

The *please* had such a tiny, embarrassed tone, that I felt like a peeping Tom—which I suppose I was—and closed the door with a bang and retreated to his bedroom.

God, oh God, oh God. I took a sip of the coffee. I really, really, really wanted to do myself out of any chance, didn't I? Now he'd think I was a dirty old man. Good Lord, *I* thought I was a dirty old man.

All I'd wanted to do was tell him about Elderman.

With the thought foremost in my mind, the first thing I told Brian, as he came sliding into his room, fully dressed but with his cheeks still red, was, "About Elderman. We must find pictures of him."

Brian stopped. He looked at me. A frown distorted his features. "You want pictures of Doctor Elderman?" he asked. He seemed to mull this over. "Why?"

Oh. After what had just happened, this might not be a good time to talk about pictures. He probably thought my interest in Elderman was of a completely different nature. He probably thought I went about looking in people's windows and collecting pictures of my colleagues in their under things. Or without.

I groaned because the thought of Elderman without under things revived my nausea. He'd once suggested to Sherry that we make a threesome of it. We hadn't, of course. I had my standards. They might be low, but they existed.

"I meant we need to know if there were pictures of Elderman in the envelope," I said. "If he was being blackmailed."

"Oh." Brian extricated my shoes from the mess of my clothes that he had deposited in a corner of his bedroom. "Um. They're wet but it can't be helped. I wear a seventeen. There's no way—"

No, there was no way. I wore a size twelve.

Brian sighed. "You'll have to wear them wet. Is it all right if I give you an extra pair of socks and a couple of newspaper holding plastic bags, to kind of insulate your feet?"

It was okay if he gave me anything at all, and—miracle—he was talking to me again. Fireworks going on in my brain, I managed to nod.

He disappeared, to come back with socks and two long, bright yellow bags. The Conspirator's packaging of choice. "Now, what was this about Doctor Elderman? Why do you think he might have been blackmailed?"

I started detailing my talk with Mrs. Murphy. Brian frowned and nodded.

"I don't suppose you looked through the pictures?" I said.

He shook his head. "No, but . . ." He sighed. "I'll get them."

"Come on," he said. He headed downstairs.

I followed at a slower pace, my head still feeling like it floated a good three feet above my neck. I would never, ever, drink that much again.

Downstairs, Brian pulled the picture packet from inside his jacket's secret compartment, and we moved to near the standing light to look.

It took us a half-hour, there were so many pictures. Although, all told, there probably were no more than twenty-five subjects. Chris had just made sure to get as much as possible on each person.

We glanced each at half the pictures, and then we exchanged our discard piles and looked through those.

The picture of Paul was what could be expected. Yes, John was also featured in it.

The pictures of Joanna boggled the mind since presumably Chris could not have come across them until long after Joanna had retired from the body trade. So, who'd got them? A client? How had Chris tracked them down?

Looking at Joanna, with her slim figure, her red hair, her fine, defiant features, I felt my heart tighten. All gone.

Try as we might, neither Brian nor I could find even a part of Elderman on any of the snapshots.

XXIII

As You Walk into My Arms

"It's all right," Brian said. "I'm sure Tony will figure it out."

"How?" I asked. "He thinks she committed suicide."

He shook his head. "Don't be so sure. Just before you arrived, he called to verify the story of the battery theft. He said he'd talked to Paul."

I wondered what Paul had told him. Had Tony questioned him in person? I'd have loved to watch Paul react to Apollo. This thought reminded me that I had some groveling to do. "I'm sorry, Brian. I really am. I didn't mean to imply you were too young to talk to. I was just tired and nervous and—"

He grabbed my upper arm and squeezed. "It's all right. I understand. I'd already figured that out, before you showed up. I was going to call you. I'm the youngest in my family. I . . . It's one of my hot buttons, to be told I'm too young for anything."

"Oh," I said.

We stood, shivering, at the bottom of his stairs, and I wondered if I might be allowed to hug him. For warmth, if nothing else. I remembered what he had said about his heating. "Why don't you come and stay with me?" I asked. "It's warmer in my place."

He hesitated, just a few seconds. Then he took a deep breath. "I'm not sure . . ."

Oh, God, he thought I would attack him. "I won't bother you, really."

He frowned, took another deep breath. "Look," he started. "About what happened, the other night, on your sofa—"

"It will never happen again, I promise," I said, and since this didn't seem to satisfy him, added, "Nothing will ever happen between us again, unless you specifically request it."

His eyes got very round. He sighed.

"Look, I understand you're embarrassed, but you don't have to be," I said. "Lots of people do things—You're very young—"

He hissed. An explosive sound. "If you mention my age again, I'm going to do something awful. Probably with an ax."

Oh.

"Please," he said. "Please, get in your car and drive home. I'm going to collect a few things and I'll be there, in a few minutes. Then we'll talk. I have to take Bucephallus. I need Bucephallus so I can go to my writers' meeting early tomorrow."

Oh.

Unable to do anything but obey—Brian was obviously in some sort of a mood—I left, got in my car and drove home like a good little boy. It's not that I didn't worry about Brian riding through that storm on the decaying Honda. It was that I didn't dare say anything about it. He'd probably be offended I didn't trust his driving.

I wondered what he wanted to talk about. Probably the limits to our relationship and what not.

It was all right. I could take it. Really. At least, it wouldn't be a completely Brian-less future. He obviously trusted me to some extent if he was willing to come and spend the night.

Perhaps after a few years he'd come to appreciate my intellectual qualities and my deep-seated emotional maturity, which I planned to acquire first thing in the morning. Then, when he was maybe forty or fifty, perhaps we could get together and grow old together.

Or, at least, I'd be old already when he was fifty, but maybe not *too* old. Maybe. There was hope. Of a sort.

Meanwhile, I would get to see him on the sofa in the morning.

Cold comfort, but comfort.

I parked my car, made it to my home.

The message light blinking on the machine signaled a call from Sherry. She wanted to know what the police wanted to know about the tablets that Carl Jung, a.k.a. Elderman to the rest of the world, had asked her to prescribe for Joanna.

Elderman again.

Then again, perhaps Joanna had felt more comfortable going through Elderman when getting a prescription from Sherry. After all, they hadn't been that close since Sherry had moved away.

No.

All right. It sounded fishy, but then Elderman had no motive. Why would he kill Chris?

He could have killed Chris for Joanna. After all they were lovers. But no. I grinned at the thought. Elderman would never do anything for anyone else. Chris wasn't blackmailing him. And Elderman wouldn't stop on his way to pick up something for the grocery for someone else, much less commit murder for someone else.

He never did anything for or to anyone without getting

something in return. Perhaps that wasn't such a bad idea, either, as an approach to life. Look where it had got him, while I didn't even have tenure.

I looked at the clock and ascertained that I'd come home ten minutes ago. Where was Brian?

To prove to him that I did have other things on my mind, besides his, admittedly distracting, body, I got stuff out, started making sandwiches. Neither of us had eaten dinner, after all.

I was halfway through putting mayonnaise on the bread when the doorbell rang. I left everything on the counter, went to open the door.

Brian didn't wait for an invitation, came in, closed the door behind himself, dropped his shoulder bag by the door, took his shoes off, took off his jacket and hung it with his eggplant-colored helmet on the coat tree.

"I was making sandwiches," I said, "since we haven't eaten."

He nodded. His lips were pressed tight, but not in a straight line like they'd been before. His eyebrows were low over his green eyes, but he didn't look mad. Or not exactly.

He followed me to the kitchenette, sat at the counter, pulling himself up by the strength of his arms and letting his legs dangle off the edge.

I resumed my work, layering slices of cold cuts and cheese on the bread.

"I'm going to drop Lives and Creative Writing," Brian said.

I almost dropped the pickle jar I'd got out of the fridge. "Why?" I asked. Maybe I was wrong. Maybe he didn't want to see me, ever, ever again. He was even willing to give up courses in which he'd been doing very well, just for the sake of avoiding me. "I mean, I won't bother you at all, I promise."

He looked up at me and his frown deepened. "That's what I'm afraid of," he said.

"Beg your pardon?" Now he had me.

"I'm afraid you won't bother me," Brian said. He reached over, got a slice of pickle I had just set down, started eating it. He took a deep breath. "Besides, Lives is so very boring."

"Well, yes. But you've already taken a year of it, and if you drop it now you'll lose credits for half a semester and why should the boredom only get to you now?"

Brian reached over, snatched another pickle slice. I resisted an impulse to smack his hand. He might smack back.

He looked up and frowned worse than ever. "Because now I can see you without it being in class. This way it will be easier on everyone. It will look less like favoritism if I should get a good grade, too."

"What?" Now he made no sense at all. I stared, mouth idiotically open.

Brian reached over, got a pickle slice, put it in my mouth.

Nothing for it but to close my mouth and chew.

While I was chewing, he said, "Bill . . . you said we wouldn't do anything I didn't specifically ask for. My mama taught me never to use four-letter words."

I swallowed hastily, ready to start with a torrent of apologies.

Brian reached over, put his hand over mine. "Why don't we adjourn to the sofa?"

There was definitely something wrong with the space-temporal properties of my living room. Again, through no effort of either of us, and without conscious movement, we were on the sofa.

On the sofa with Brian, I said, "You know, you don't

need to drop out of Lives. If you have exceptionally high grades, we can always say I'm giving you special tutoring."

I knew I'd made a mistake the moment I said it.

His eyes had been dreamy, half closed, but they bolted open and stared at me, in growing horror.

"I didn't mean that literally," I said in a hurry. "I wouldn't do anything dishonest. Of course you can drop out of Lives if you want to."

"No," he said. He wriggled out from underneath me, easing me onto the cold leather of the sofa.

"That's not it. It's—" He sat up straight. "I think I know what happened to Chris and who killed Professor Zimmerman. Why Chris was all chopped up and I wasn't, though the murderer, surely, must have thought I was dead too. I think I understand it."

"What? Now? You were thinking about that the whole time?"

He was slipping his pants and shirt on. "No." He grinned. "Of course not. Don't be an idiot. It's . . . what you just said. I need to talk to someone, and then call Tony and I think we can wrap this up."

I sat on the sofa, disbelieving, the cobwebs of quasi-dispelled drunkenness joining the shock of frustrated desire. "You can't leave me like this." Realizing what I'd said and the way it sounded, I added, "I mean, if you really have to you can, but—"

He kissed me. His technique was improving fast. Good student. Willing teacher. Why was he leaving?

"I'll be back in about an hour," he said. "Don't go anywhere."

With that he grabbed his jacket and the helmet that he'd hung on the hall tree and was gone.

XXIV

Just Seems to Be the End of Me

I sat there, trying to collect my impulses and vague frustration into something resembling thoughts. The result went something like this: *Oh, damn. Sofa cold. Brian left? Why left? What did I say? Oh, damn. Last thing I said. I said. What the hell did I say?*

Finally, after much effort, sitting on my sofa in my underwear, I realized that I'd said something about special tutoring. This sparked a long-lost memory. Something someone had told me. Someone related to the Hogg case.

Who had talked to me about tutoring? Who would talk to me about tutoring? Someone at school? Joanna? One of the students? Brian? Elderman?

Elderman? No. However, it did relate to Elderman. With whom had I talked about Elderman?

I chewed the inside of my lip, in deep thought, while I got up and went in search of clothing. My clothing, as opposed to Brian's hand me downs.

Squeezing into a pair of my very own sweat pants, I remembered the conversation had also included mentions of my clothing.

Trisha Hogg.

Suddenly, with sparkling clarity, I remembered what she had said about Elderman tutoring Tiffany. She had said it with a snickering, ironic tone, as though what she meant had nothing to do with any academic discipline. Had Brian known this? Did Brian suspect Elderman of being involved with Tiffany? If he did—If he did, that gave Elderman a hell of a motive, didn't it? Though what the hell it meant for chopping up some bodies and leaving others whole was beyond me.

Trisha Hogg. Did she live with her dad? I got the phone book out, searched through the pages for Dr. Hogg's home number. Fortunately Byrnum wasn't exactly a common given name.

I dialed the number, praying that I wouldn't hit the answering machine.

A cool, collected voice that I knew much too well answered the phone. "Hello?"

"Paul?" I asked, realizing belatedly that perhaps it was John. How alike did identical twins sound?

I was in luck.

The voice answered with, "Dr. Yates?"

So, it was Paul.

"Yes. Can I speak to Trisha?"

"Who?" Great incredulity marked every inflection.

"Trisha. Your sister?"

"Oh. Oh?"

"I need to ask her something. Relating to the crime. Just something relating to the crime. Is she there?"

An intake of breath. "Ah . . . she's here. We were preparing the details of the memorial service. I'll call her, but first . . . huh . . . I wanted to thank you. And Brian."

For what? Not blackmailing him? What exactly was the man's standard of behavior for his acquaintances? Never mind. "You're welcome." As a new thought occurred to me, I yelped, "Wait. Who told you that I had a date with Brian yesterday night?"

He was silent for a minute then spoke in a lower voice. "Tiff," he said. "I met her at the lawyers. We were talking about the estate. And she said—The little bitch knew I liked you. She said that she'd seen you with Brian. She'd heard you make a date. Why?"

"I'll explain later. Listen, one more thing, do you happen to know where Tiff was when Chris was killed?"

"Yes." No hesitation. "That's why he wanted me to come over that night. Brian would be out and Tiff was working at the Saloon till two in the morning. Is that all you need to know?"

"Yes," I said. Tiff at the Saloon. Tiff was pregnant. Tiff knew Brian. Tiff had heard me tell Brian to come over that night, and then Elderman had given me the little speech about gender minorities. Oh. Besides, Tiff had known that Joanna was afraid of being alone, that she might very well call, if not me, at least Brian, who would be at my house.

So, Tiff had been an information leak, but not an accomplice. She hadn't looked smart enough to be involved in a crime. Hell, no woman stupid enough to be involved with Chris *and* Elderman would be smart enough to do much of anything except maybe breathe through her mouth.

She would have told Elderman what she'd overheard. Hence the battery theft. Chris might have told her that Paul was coming over on the night he was killed. Probably bragged about how much money he would get out of his brother. Tiff would have told Elderman. Probably the only reason Brian's motorcycle had escaped a similar treatment the night Joanna had died had been that he'd parked it out of sight, outdoors, away from lights.

Did Tiff know that Elderman had killed Chris? Probably not.

I took a deep breath. "Paul? Could I please speak to Trisha, now?"

"Yes. You have to tell me what this is all about later," he said. I heard footsteps waltz off and his voice, noticeably higher and more inflected, sing out, "Oh, Trisha. Gentleman caller for you."

Trisha's voice said something unintelligible.

"He *says* he's Professor Yates," Paul drawled out. "I wouldn't trust him for a moment, deary. Smart men are dangerous. Particularly for little dumb blondes."

Well, Paul was back to his old self.

A hand was pushed over the phone and through it I heard the vaguest murmur which sounded like Trisha reminding Paul that he was blond also, and casting aspersions on his intelligence. From the sound of it, something low and vicious. Then she breathed into the phone, "Professor Yates?"

Oh, great. Chalk another one to expectations I'd never be able to fulfill. All this while, bets could be taken, Paul was around the corner guffawing into his still-wounded hand.

"Miss Hogg?" I answered, trying to keep things cool and distant.

"Call me Trisha."

Ah, yes. Sure. "Huh . . . Trisha . . . when you told me that Dr. Elderman was tutoring Tiffany, but probably not the way I tutored Brian, what exactly did you mean?"

There was a long silence. "Tiffany? You are interested in *Tiffany?*" She took breath in, noisily and added, completely unguarded, "Lord. I'd take Brian better."

I could hear Paul laughing.

Oh, God. "Um, no. I'm not. Interested in Tiffany, I mean. Brian is. He has a bad crush on her, and he was wondering if now that Chris is gone he might have a chance. He just suspected her of being involved with a professor and he thought another professor would be in a better position to investigate."

A shorter silence. "He has good reason to suspect," she said. "She works at the Saloon and a couple of times, when I was out there, I saw her kissing Elderman out in the parking lot. I never told Chris, because the little bastard didn't deserve to know anyway."

Um. Oh. Yes.

I stood at the phone, thinking. Had Brian gone to interrogate Tiffany? I remembered they seemed to be friends or at least close acquaintances. But, what could he ask her? Whether she'd slept with Elderman? What made him think she'd answer him? Could he have thought up something so stupid?

"Dr. Yates?"

"Um. Yes, Trisha. Yes. We must go out to dinner sometime. Soon. Somewhere nice." With that, I slammed the phone down.

So, I'd condemn Elderman on the basis of unsubstantiated rumors that he had played around with Chris's wife? And that he'd been Joanna's boyfriend and the most likely to use her car and get Chris's blood on it? And that—

I remembered what Brian had said about the man who'd hit him on the head wearing Athos.

Frankly, I'd never paid much attention to Elderman's smell. But knowing Sherry, I thought it very likely that she might have sent Elderman the same gift she sent me; probably the same gift she sent all her ex-husbands and ex-lovers.

I dialed the phone before I realized what I was doing.

"Hello?"

"Sherry?"

"Oh, William, dear. I've been waiting for you to call. What check did you mean? Why did the police—"

"I do not have time for this."

If Brian had gone to see Tiffany, would she call Elderman? Would Brian be found dead tomorrow, this time chopped up to pieces? The thought was unbearable. He wouldn't die. Not now. If I had to keep him alive and safe by the force of my will, I'd do it. He wouldn't die. Not mid-sofa. "Did you send Elderman a bottle of Athos for Christmas?"

"What?"

"Did-you-send-Elderman-a-bottle-of-Athos-for-Christmas?"

"William, are you jealous?" She sounded somewhere between gratified and shocked.

"No. Elderman. Athos. Christmas. Did you?"

"Why, yes. I always do, but—"

I slammed the phone down, looked frantically through the phone book for the number at the Saloon. I assumed Tiff didn't go under the name Hogg since she didn't actually even live with Chris. So what name did she go under? I called the Saloon, asked for Tiff.

The slow teenager on the other side asked, "Tiff Morden?"

"She works at dinner time," I prompted.

"Tiff Morden," he said. "She's not here right now. It's her day off."

The phone book came out again while I prayed under my breath that dear old Tiff had a phone line under her name. She did. I dialed with shaking fingers.

"Hello?" she called into the phone.

Behind her, I heard two male voices, both much too well known to me. Brian and Elderman. Neither sounded pleased.

I dropped the phone, ran out the door, grabbing my jacket on the way out and putting it on while I ran down the stairs, unwilling to wait for the elevator.

I tore out of the garage like a bat out of hell and skidded through the snow-covered streets in the little MG at well above safe speeds. Although I'd only glanced at it, I had memorized Tiff's address on sight. It was on Kit Carson way, a place that I, by now, could find blindfolded, since it was halfway to Brian's place.

Brian was at Tiff's. So was Elderman.

I don't think I'd have noticed if I'd run over someone, but I'm fairly sure I didn't because no one ever called me on it and there was no weird debris on my car the next day.

All I could think was that I didn't want Brian to die.

I drove by instinct, more than by sight, through the thick snowfall. All the way to Kit Carson.

In front of the unassuming pink house, number 35, where Tiff was listed, a motorcycle and a slinky sports car that looked just like the Murphy's car, shared the driveway. The motorcycle was achingly familiar.

I skidded to a stop against the sidewalk, and had just turned the lights off and put my hand on the doorknob, ready to go in there and tear Elderman into pieces so small that no forensic specialist could ever reconstruct him, when the door opened.

My heart stopped. I fully expected Elderman to come out carrying or dragging a dead Brian.

Instead, Brian came out, Elderman right behind him, his arm holding onto Brian's. He opened the door on the passenger's side of the slinky sports car and pushed Brian through, getting in after him.

From their relative positions and the fact that Brian

would be driving, I suspected that Elderman had a gun on Brian.

I waited. The lights on the car came on and it started, on its hesitating way out.

I gave it some distance. When I almost couldn't see the lights anymore, I turned my fog lights on and started after them.

Since I couldn't see the actual car, but only the lights, I hoped no one would get between us, and thanked whatever divinity had caused it, for the low traffic on this very snowy night.

Like a car chase in slow motion, we processed from Kit Carson out to the warehouse district and on the back roads out of Lythia.

Slowly, I realized where we were headed and cursed under my breath. "It's the criminal who's supposed to return to the scene of the crime, Brian. The criminal, not the victim."

The man had a definite lack of B-movie culture. What was he doing, bearding the tiger in his lair? What did he think he was doing?

"You don't confront the murderer, Brian, damn it. You tell the nice policeman, in this case your childhood friend Tony, and let him take care of the big nasty man. Confronting him is about as sensible as going down to the basement during a thunderstorm on Halloween."

If I ever got him back alive, I was going to shake him until his teeth fell out.

I was going to remind him of how young he was. And then I was going to buy a television and make him watch every cheap thriller ever made. On the sofa. Snugly by my side. We'd make popcorn. We'd be cozy and domestic and—

The sports car stopped by the bridge, and I stopped far enough behind it that I wouldn't be easily seen in the storm.

I got out, into the freezing air.

Ahead of me, Elderman talked. "Get out. Go to the bridge."

"Why?" Brian, sounding calm and collected, as though he were out for a walk with an old friend in a safe neighborhood. "Why not shoot me here? You're going to have to shoot me, you know? I'd have made you shoot me at Tiffany's, if I weren't sure you'd kill her, too, afterwards, just to hide it."

Elderman muttered something, from which, "goody-two-shoes" emerged. "You will go to the bridge and you will jump," he said.

Brian stood, his outline clearly visible through the snow. "I don't think so. I can't. I'm Catholic, you see, and suicide is a sin."

Elderman let lose some profanity on the subject of what other things Catholic boys weren't supposed to do.

I'd never heard Elderman that out of control.

"Well, yes," Brian said. I could hear a smile in his voice. "That too. However, if you had gone through catechism, you'd know the difference between a mortal sin and a cardinal one. Suicide is a cardinal sin and one that, by its very nature, does not provide for absolution, repentance or divine grace. As such—"

A scuffle.

I saw Elderman rush forward, and Brian step back.

"You don't want to punch me," Brian said. "Not if you want it to look like suicide. Forensic experts will notice bruises inflicted before death."

Elderman took two steps back, holding the gun with two

hands, in classic posture. "Go to the bridge, or I blow your goddamn brains out right here!"

I essayed a run, slipped on the ice at the river edge, struggled to my feet, holding on to sparse scrub oak and scratchy rocks.

Slipping and cursing under my breath, I hurried along the riverbank.

Brian. I must get to him. I was way too far away. To far away to reach them, though I could hear them clear as day through some acoustic trick of the Rocky River valley.

Elderman stood, ready to shoot.

I heard myself yell even as I ran, "Elderman, you sonofabitch, can you deal with someone your age, or just college boys?"

A blast echoed. A bullet hissed by me. By me. Not Brian. Thank God. Another bullet hissed by so close I felt the wind of its passage. Of the half-dozen damn things Elderman could do properly, shooting would be one of them.

I remembered some old yarn about the bullet you hear never being the one that kills you, and broke into a run on the river bank, scrambling forward as fast as I could, accounting for slippage on the snow.

Another bullet whistled past me, and another embedded itself into a trunk ahead of me.

Brian jumped. He grappled with Elderman. I had no idea who was winning.

The air was too cold, my lungs too small, my legs too out of muscle, my whole body too worn out. I was too old for this.

Brian lifted his leg to impossible heights, kicking the gun out of Elderman's hand. Both of them started to run for it, slipped, recovered.

I jumped. I landed literally on Elderman. Lucky, as I couldn't have calculated it.

Brian had the good sense of stepping back.

My hands closed on Elderman's neck.

"Yates," he yelled. "Yates, you goddamn sonofabitch. I should have known you'd be with your boyfriend. Damn little rich boy. Always gets the boyfriends and the girlfriends and the wives and all the money to splash around. Just couldn't let someone else have a piece of the pie, could you?" Elderman said through clenched teeth, while one of his hands tried to gouge my eyes and the other clawed at my right hand.

He writhed under me. "Have I ever told you how much you disgust me, Billy-boy?"

I grinned, despite the intense pain on my face. My hands felt frozen and I had trouble keeping a hold on Elderman, who twisted like an eel, but my anger overrode all. "Have I told you it's mutual?" I asked.

"Move away," I heard Brian growl. "Let go of him, Bill, damn it. I have the gun."

I got off Elderman and stepped back.

Brian held the gun steady, his face taut.

"You wouldn't shoot," Elderman said, not too assuredly.

"Like hell I wouldn't," Brian answered cockily. "What's another mortal sin I can't repent?"

"You'd have to explain why." Elderman stood up, straightened himself, dusted his clothes. "As it is, you'll have to explain assault and battery."

I heard Brian say, "I called the police before I went to Tiff's."

"Yes," a familiar voice said out of the darkness. "I think you're the one who will have to explain your conduct, Dr. Elderman. I'm a police officer. You're under arrest. You have the right—"

Elderman was running, running toward the bridge.

In the dark, with the whole thing muffled by snow and ice, he was a lone figure running in the whiteness, and neither Brian nor Tony fired.

He moved very fast. I stepped forward with some vague idea of grabbing him.

"Don't get in the way," Brian yelled. "I have him in my sigh—"

Elderman made for the low wall of the bridge and jumped.

There followed the most sickening of noises, a sound of breaking bone and tearing flesh.

It took me a while to move, but when I did look over the side of the bridge, I could see Elderman would never make good on his escape. In the last few days, in one of Colorado's turn of weather, water had frozen up in the mountains, and the flow of the river decreased precipitously. Elderman had hit icy rocks head on. As I looked, blood formed a Rorschach on the shining ice.

I stepped back, shaken by dry heaves, though there was nothing left in my stomach, after throwing up on Brian and then fasting.

Brian put the pistol down carefully and walked up to me uncertainly, as if not sure how he'd be received.

I opened my arms. He stepped into them.

"You triple idiot," I told him gently, ruffling his hair, considering every word, feeling his warmth, blessing his proximity. "Didn't you ever watch a single thriller? What did you think you were doing?"

He shivered against me and didn't speak. Shock?

Tony came up, stealthy, silent.

I kissed Brian's hair, held him tight. He felt frozen. He wasn't wearing his jacket. Or his helmet. He had to be frozen, standing out here in the cold. "It's over," I told him. "It's all over."

Tony walked to the bridge, looked down, walked back to us. "Go home," he said. He chuckled. "Go to bed. I mean that. There's laws against this type of behavior in public."

Brian looked up at his friend. "What about statements and—"

"Just go," Tony said. "I saw it all and I'll take care of everything. I'll see you in the morning." He added in a tone of great resignation, "Ram should be here any minute now."

I would swear the policeman was being benevolent.

XXV

If That Isn't Love, It Will Have to Do

I woke up staring at the ceiling and feeling like a kid *after* Christmas morning. A kid who'd got the proverbial red bike, the puppy and everything else his little heart could desire.

I lay on my bed, squeezed up against the wall. Keeping me in that tiny little spot was a naked, tall muscular man, whose face, in sleep, looked even younger than it was and who drooled on my pillow while snoring contentedly.

Ah, well, I supposed turnabout *was* fair play.

Bambi, Bacchus. In my bed. Alleluia.

I wanted to stay like that for the rest of my life, or at least until starvation set in. But hydraulic pressure mounted against my bladder. The side of my face, where Elderman had scratched me, throbbed with a dull heat, and my back, pressed up against the wall, was starting to cramp with arthritic ache. Some of us weren't nineteen anymore. While some of us—I grinned—blessedly were.

I stared at Brian's relaxed sleeping face, turned toward me, his features so innocent that he looked positively angelic.

As I tried to ease myself out of bed, clambering over Brian's sleeping body, I thought that if the man really was an angel, then his wings must be black and charred around the edges. Sulphur, anyone?

Out in the bathroom, I took care of the immediate need, then stood in front of the mirror, staring at my face. The scratches Elderman had inflicted and that I, for some reason, had forgotten to disinfect the night before, had turned into heavy red welts, pulling my skin tight around the left side of my face. I got the hydrogen peroxide out, started dabbing at my face with a cotton ball.

The rest of my face didn't bear looking at, and I tried not to. Rings around my eyes from a sleepless night, a heavy shadow of beard making me look like a bum, and the general sags, folds and creases of a middle-aged man who over-indulged.

Brian came pattering into the bathroom, eyes half closed.

"Hi, Bambi," I called out.

He turned his face in my general direction, did a sleepy double take. "Oh, please, no. Not in full light of day and not out of the bedroom."

I ignored his complaint. We were in the bathroom, which was right next to the bedroom and technically part of the bedroom suite. The light coming through the blinds could only charitably be called *full light of day*. So what was he bellyaching about?

"You weren't in bed," he said.

Guilty as charged. Part of the problem, I thought, as my spine protested against exertions and unnatural sleeping positions, was that my bed was so small. "We need to buy a new bed," I said.

He nodded. Then he looked intently down at me. "We?"

"Oh, I'll pay," I said. "But you have to help me pick it."

He blinked his confusion. "Right now?" He looked down at himself. "Naked?"

I looked him, up and down. "I guess it can wait a little."

"How little?"

We were in the middle of a kiss when the doorbell rang.

Brian pulled away. "Phone?"

I shook my head. "Doorbell."

"Oh," he said, and relaxed, then recoiled, looked at me with a panicked expression. "Doorbell?"

I vaguely remembered seeing the clock on the bedside table and it had been six. a.m., unless I'd slept the whole day away. "It's weird," I said. "This time of morning."

Brian was already in my bedroom, frantically looking around for the clothes that, if memory served me, we'd left strewn over most of the living room.

I went to the closet, got two of the endless supply of robes that constituted the debris of Sherry left behind in my life. Before she gave Athos, she gave robes. I wondered if a matching set of robes hung in Elderman's closet.

I handed Brian one, and, draping the other one around myself, I hurried to the door wondering who in hell would call at this time in the morning.

A peek through the bull's eye showed . . . Tony. Bright and fresh and fully dressed.

I yanked the door open and said, "You know, that thing about the law never sleeping is supposed to be a metaphor. Go home. Go to bed."

He chuckled and waltzed in past me. "When I go to bed I sleep," he said. "When I get up, I work. Unlike some people." He gave a jaundiced eye to Brian who, in a much too small blue and gold robe, had come to stand beside me.

Brian sighed. "I'll go make coffee," he said.

Turning around, he disappeared into the kitchen. I closed the door behind Tony and followed them into the house.

Tony sat on my stool, so there was nothing for it but to stand in the kitchen, leaning against the counter while

Brian made coffee. I wasn't about to sit beside The Law.

"I have a few dozen questions," Tony said. "Starting with what made you think that Elderman was having an affair with Chris's wife?"

"Was he?" I asked. I'd never known for sure, after all.

"Definitely. Tiff thinks the baby is his. She told him she was pregnant and she was afraid that Chris might notice that the baby didn't look like him. I think that's when Elderman started thinking he had to get rid of Chris. Besides, there was the money."

"A million dollars?" Brian asked, as he turned the percolator on.

"Actually a million and change," Tony said. "But how did you figure it out?"

"The money? Paul told us."

Tony shook his head. "Elderman. How did you find out?"

Brian turned around. "Well, Bill and I were—" He blushed violently, stopped.

So, he'd retained a semblance of modesty, had he?

"When he mentioned something about tutoring," Brian hurried on. "I remembered some snickered comment from a classmate about Elderman tutoring Tiff and I thought, of course, that's why Chris had been chopped up and I hadn't.

"I think Elderman thought I was dead, too and, anyway, he was in a hurry, because Joanna arrived at about that time to search out the house. I think he must have just run my mop with lots of bleach on the floor, thrown me into the back of the car and hoped."

Tony nodded. "The mop was in Dr. Zimmermann's closet. Why Dr. Zimmermann's obsession with searching your place?" Tony asked. "That's another question. I eventually figured out it didn't have anything to do with the crime, but why would she do it, anyway?"

Brian shrugged. "I don't know." He looked at me.

I looked back at him, sharing the private knowledge of the auto-da-fé in which we'd burned all the pictures and all of Chris's notes, last night, just before things got interesting. All, that is, except Paul's stuff. That we'd give him so he could destroy it himself. As cynical as he was, nothing else would do.

"She was close to Chris for a while," Brian said. "Maybe he got naked pictures of her."

I apologized silently to Joanna's memory. Close to the truth, but a smear to her memory all the same. Yet, sometimes one had to lie to protect the guilty.

Tony nodded, as though conceding the point. "So, she arrived to search the house while Elderman was butchering Hogg . . . How do you know that?"

"I don't know if she got there while he was—" I shrugged. "I think she arrived as he had finished. I know the time because her mother told me," I said.

"Her . . . mother?"

"Mrs. Murphy."

"We searched high and low for next of kin," he said. "You knew? All this time, you knew?"

I shook my head. "Not until last night."

Tony sighed, hit the counter hard with his palm and said something that sounded like, "Why nobody tells me anything."

I didn't tell him it was because he didn't get drunk enough.

Brian charged into the breach, "Anyway, I assume Elderman intended to chop me up, too, having got me unconscious, but then Dr. Zimmerman arrived. He wouldn't know who it was, so he just loaded me in the car whole.

You see, it didn't matter if someone thought I had been murdered, nor if I were identified. There were even chances that someone would know or suspect I was gay and with all the talk about gay students killing themselves out of lack of support, or what not, it would have passed as suicide. And if not, he'd never have been suspected." He made a face. "The sonofabitch would probably have managed to turn my death into a civic, politically correct occasion and show everyone how sensitive he was."

"But why did he bother to chop Chris into stew meat?" I asked.

Brian reached into the cupboard, brought out cups, started filling them. "Because he was hoping, as fast as the river ran just then, not enough of Chris would ever be recovered to be identified. Tiff would still have access to the money." He looked at Tony. "It was in both their names, wasn't it?"

Tony nodded a confirmation.

"Right," Brian said. "But then, you see, Tiff could get the money and Elderman could go through it, but he wouldn't need to marry her, in fact wouldn't be able to, with Chris just missing. In seven years, he'd have appropriated all of Tiff's money and could give her and the kid the cold shoulder." He handed Tony a cup of coffee in the cup that read, *Friends Are The Sunshine Of Life.*

Tony took a sip, then looked at me. "Pleasant people, you professors."

"Hey," Brian said.

But I ignored the stab and said, "Elderman always felt inferior, always felt different. That's part of why he had it in for me, the other part, of course, being that he probably recognized my car through the storm, when I stopped by the bridge. But he probably would have tried to implicate me, anyway. He slept with my wife while we were married, and she gave him money, but it was never enough. It was never enough to make him feel better. He still thought I was his superior just because my family was rich. And he hated me for it."

"Like Chris," Brian said. "He had a million in the bank, but he shared a two-fifty a month house with me. He was never satisfied."

"So, are you moving back? To your place?" Tony asked.

Brian looked at me. For a moment, we just stared at each other.

I shook my head, "No. I don't think he is. I think I need a roommate."

Brian smiled.

Tony made a sound at the back of his throat, but spoke civilly enough. "I hope you know what you're doing, Brian. I hope you won't . . . Well, you're theoretically an adult, but you're much too young."

I chuckled into the coffee cup that Brian had just handed me and looked up to see Brian stare at Tony, eyebrows raised.

"Ax?" I asked.

"Fresh out," Brian said. "Dang." He winked at me, sipped his coffee.

Tony, obviously puzzled by the exchange, looked from one to the other of us.

"So, are you going to stop talking to me again?" Brian asked. "Like when I told you I was gay, two years ago?"

"No." Tony shook his head, sighed. "No. I'm older now. It's your life. I don't think. . . . Well, it's not what I expected from you. But it's your life. I just want us to go on being friends."

I looked at him and suppressed a smile. What did you

know? The Chief of Police might yet become a real person.

"So, what do you do with the case, now?" I asked, looking at Tony. "Is it closed?"

Tony nodded. "Oh, yeah. Gave it to the papers. Only I still don't know how Chris got all that money. You wouldn't happen to know, would you, Brian?"

Brian shook his head. "Nah. Knowing Chris, though, I'll guarantee it was illegal."

Tony sighed. "That's what bothers me. I figure drugs, and I never saw any sign of a big drug trade. Ah, well, maybe he sold out in Cowpatty and not close to home. I don't know how the papers will dress it up."

"Trust the *Conspirator*," I said. "They'll probably make a crime of passion out of the whole thing."

Tony nodded, then took a deep breath and hissed it out in great relief. "One thing I have to tell you, I wasn't as blind as you two seemed to think. The reason I responded to Brian's call so quickly is that I'd already followed another trail to the same end. I had got Elderman identified as the man who'd made the anonymous phone call, and it had been him who picked up Dr. Zimmerman's sleeping pills from the pharmacy, and him who had asked your wife to prescribe them."

"My ex-wife," I said. "That was stupid of him."

Tony shook his head. "Not at all. If the house had blown up as he had arranged, then we might never even have figured out she'd died of an overdose. All the same, when Brian told me of the link between Elderman and Mrs. Chris Hogg, it all became crystal clear. I sat by the phone about two seconds, and then I realized that Elderman might very well be visiting Tiff, and then what would Brian do? So I got to Tiff's just in time to see you pull out." He grinned at me. "So I followed you, while you followed them." He stared into the blue with a wishful little smile. "It was interesting while it lasted, but I'm glad it's over. I don't get paid enough for this. Thank God, with Lythia's crime rate, there shouldn't be another murder in my tenure. Heck, not in my lifetime."

Brian chuckled, I wasn't sure why. He sipped his coffee from the cup that said *Are We Having Fun Yet?* Above it, his eyes shone devilishly in my general direction.

Elderman was gone. Which meant Dr. Fielding would become Department Head and, since we'd always been friendly acquaintances, probably give me tenure within the month. The crime was solved and there would be no more deaths. And, best of all, I'd got the blond. There would be no more white-knuckled drives to Bad Boys, no more being stood up, no more nights alone with the bottle of bourbon. Or at least not for a long while.

I found myself smiling like a loon and drowned my grin in coffee from the cup that read, *Damn I'm Good.*

About the Author

C. S. Laurel lives in Colorado Springs, in a home ruled by multiple cats kind enough to allow humans to share the accommodations. Laurel has made forays into the academic life in the form of teaching at a few colleges over the years. All other resemblance to Bill Yates is purely coincidental.